KISS THE GIRLS AND MAKE THEM SPY

AN ORIGINAL JANE BOND PARODY

KISS THE GIRLS AND MAKE THEM SPY

AN ORIGINAL JANE BOND PARODY

MABEL MANEY

HarperEntertainment

An Imprint of HarperCollins*Publishers*

HarperCollins books may be purchased for educational, business, or sales promotional use. For information please write: Special Markets Department, HarperCollins Publishers Inc., 10 East 53rd Street, New York, NY 10022.

FIRST EDITION

Designed by Rhea Braunstein

Library of Congress Cataloging-in-Publication Data

Maney, Mabel, 1958–
   Kiss the girls and make them spy : an original Jane Bond parody / by Mabel Maney.—1st ed.
      p. cm.
   ISBN 0-380-80310-0 (acid-free paper)
   1. Women spies—Fiction. 2. Lesbians—Fiction. 3. Twins—Fiction. I. Title.

PS3563.A466 K57 2001
813'.54—dc21

2001024162

01 02 03 04 05 RRD 10 9 8 7 6 5 4 3 2

3 JUNE 1965
FRANCE

The château of the Duke and Duchess of Windsor
The French Riviera

Hᴵɢʜ above the earth, where the atmosphere thins into nothingness, there is no weather. No clouds, no storms, no flashes of lightning. Here on the Riviera (for many, the closest thing to heaven on earth) the summer sky offered a show that could rival the opulence of the nightclubs and casinos, if anyone were to bother to look up. The month of June was high holy season on the Riviera, a time when the idle rich come to worship at the blackjack tables. They took little notice of the world outside. For that to happen, the sky would have to open up and rain cash.

A thin, sad-faced man in silk vermilion lounging pajamas stood on the balcony of a majestic villa overlooking the sea and stared at the heavens. The sun was setting through a patchy veil of pink clouds; its fiery red corona gave off sparks as it sank past the horizon. Soon the stars would shine like diamonds in the deep blue evening sky. The bright lights of the casinos and nightclubs would flick on, and the garish neon would wash out the sky, making the stars distant glimmers. The playhouses of the rich and bored were open all night, and the man on the balcony had spent much of his life, and a great deal of his fortune, in them. He was an old man now, and he had wasted most of his life in the pursuit of meaningless pleasures. It had been almost thirty years since he had done anything of consequence. His name still made the society columns on a regular basis, but for a man who had once ruled a kingdom, it was a sad second prize.

"Watercress or cucumber?" the Duchess of Windsor asked her husband.

"Watercress."

"How many?"

"Three."

The duke looked crestfallen when he saw his plate.

"Is something wrong, Pookie?" wondered the duchess.

"There are crusts on my sandwiches."

"Chef had a row with the chauffeur this morning and quit. The butler made these. You'll just have to be brave, dear, until our servant crisis is resolved."

The duke pushed aside his plate—he detested crusts—and turned his attention to the day's mail. He knew without looking that the thick cream-colored envelopes held the usual invitations to luncheons and dinner parties and fashion shows. Twenty-eight years had passed since he had abdicated his throne in order to marry his beloved Wallis Simpson. The scandal had long since died down, but the couple could still draw an audience, even if it was only one large enough to fill a dining table.

The duke sometimes felt like an ugly old curio brought out for company, but the duchess loved the attention. He imagined that marrying into exile had been a bit of a letdown for the vivacious American divorcée. His family had never forgiven them, and his countrymen had all but forgotten them. Nobody ever asked for his advice anymore about anything; the only noteworthy thing left for him to do was die.

"Anything interesting, Pookie?" the duchess asked.

"Just the usual. The Duff Coopers are having a cocktail party Saturday for some American film star. Princess Grace will soon be in town with her new yacht. There's a cocktail party at the Argentinean Embassy Friday next. And Foxie sent you a postal card from Paris; she says that next season's hemlines are disgracefully short. She writes, 'If one did not have a dressmaker of one's own, one would be forced to get one.' "

The duchess laughed. "That Foxie!"

"Here's a letter from Lord Reginald Wooley-Booley," the duke said with some surprise. They weren't in the habit of corresponding. Lord Reginald was on their Christmas card list, but so were three thousand others, give or take a hundred.

"Who?" the duchess asked. She took a sip of her oolong tea.

"He's the son of my old pal Lord Chumley. Surely you remember Chumpers. He came to our aquatic party in Fifty-five dressed as a female channel swimmer."

"Oh, *him!* He got petroleum jelly on my mermaid costume. I suppose his son wants an invitation to our villa. Well, the answer is no. If

I am forced to run this place with a reduced staff, I cannot possibly take on the burden of a guest. Pass the sugar."

"Wally," the duke said excitedly, having read further, "listen to this! The Sons of Britain Society, a venerable group much respected by those in high places, has decided to restore England to its glorious imperialist past. And they want me to rule! They intend to put me back on the throne, with you as my queen!"

Tears filled the duchess's eyes; it had been years since they had played this charade. In the beginning of their marriage, she had indulged the duke in his fantasies of returning to power. She had even gone so far as to disguise her hand and write impassioned letters of support. But as they grew older, the possibility that they might someday return to royal life had become little more than a pleasant daydream. No one in England had expressed any real interest in them in years.

"Pookie, not tonight. I had an exhausting session with Henri today."

Her hairdresser had rolled her hair so tightly around the permanent rods that the duchess had been unable to blink for hours.

"Wally, I don't think Sir Reginald is pulling my leg. Why, the Sons of Britain Society counts amongst its ranks some of the most powerful men in Britain. *Listen.*"

What England needs most in these days of social unrest is someone with enough dignity and authority to wear the sovereign crown. In other words, a king. If we are to return to our proper place as a world power, we must have a real leader. You are our only hope to save England!

5 SEPTEMBER 1965
LONDON

The Flora Beaton Residential Hotel for Distressed Gentlewomen,
No. 7 Beesborough Place
Room 217
6:48 A.M.

O H, somebody *please* shoot me," Jane Bond groaned as she crawled off her lumpy bed and lay with her cheek pressed to the blessedly cool yellow-and-black-speckled linoleum that covered the floor of her shabby bedsit.

Last night's pub crawl had seemed like a good idea at the time, but now it was all too apparent that her plan to drink away her troubles had only multiplied them. Now she was brokenhearted *and* hungover. What's more, while she was sleeping, someone had snuck in and nailed a headache over her left eye, then made off with her shirt.

Six weeks ago, Jane had lost her lover, her best friend, and her share in a rather nice detached bungalow in the tidy London suburb of Ruislip—all in the same day. Arriving home early from work, Jane had caught the woman she loved, Astrid, in bed with her best friend, Ruth. In broad daylight. While Astrid had screamed bloody murder (as if *she* were the aggrieved spouse), Ruth had scrambled into her clothes—actually, a suit Jane had lent her for "an important date." It was all so tawdry. The revelation that Astrid was cheating on her had been shocking enough; that she was cheating on her in such an unoriginal fashion—in *their* bed with *her* best friend—had appalled her. The scenario was as stale as one of those radio weepies her mother used to follow so faithfully. Jane had always thought Astrid terribly brainy and clever, as befitting the headmistress of a girl's school, but that day she had been forced to recognize the truth. Astrid was a dull girl. The least she could have done was leave Jane with a better story to tell.

Outside the Flora Beaton

Agent Cedric Pumpernickel of Her Majesty's Secret Service crouched low in the passenger seat of his government-issue black sedan, trying to appear casual as he balanced his spy glasses on the edge of the bulletproof window. His target was a woman in a small bedsit on the second floor of a rundown brick building on the edge of Chelsea, a dreary area of London that had lately been overrun by frightening young people dressed in strange modern attire and behaving in shockingly permissive ways. The Empire was crumbling all around men like Agent Cedric Pumpernickel of Her Majesty's Secret Service and he knew it.

"Damn that blasted 007!" Agent Pumpernickel swore as he removed his trench coat and put it, neatly folded, on the seat. Their top agent had finally gone off his nut, and been shipped off to the Secret Service Spy Sanitarium in Zurich by double-0 division Chief Commander Admiral Sir Niles Needlum, known to his agents simply as "N." Agent Pumpernickel, a former double-0 man who now headed the Department of Desk Accessories, had been sent afield on a mission designed to quell the rising tide of rumors regarding Bond's breakdown. Their enemies would like nothing better than to think the world's greatest secret agent had finally been broken. Agent Pumpernickel's job was to make sure that didn't happen.

Jane hiccuped. She realized she was still a little drunk. She raked her dark wavy hair, which stank of cigarette smoke, out of her eyes and tried to calm her queasy stomach by taking deep, even breaths. As soon as the room stopped spinning she would get up and find the bromo. Or perhaps she would simply stay in that spot until the dilapidated building crumbled into a pile of dust around her. There was really no reason to get up.

Lying there with her eyes shut, she feared she would never get the sight of Astrid and Ruth out of her mind. She had known at that moment that her life with Astrid was over, yet her brain still searched for an explanation. Was Ruth ill? Was Astrid trying to comfort her with those rhythmic motions under the sheet?

Jane was never one to go gently into the night. After she had dragged Ruth unceremoniously from the bed and showed her the door, Jane made it perfectly clear, in a voice loud enough to cause a small, excited crowd to gather outside on the curb, exactly what she thought of Astrid's moral character. Astrid, in turn, recited a laundry list of Jane's shortcomings. A frightful row ensued. Dishes flew. Jane smashed Astrid's great-great-grandmother's Wellington gravy boat, which had survived three queens and two kings, but could not withstand the wrath of a lover scorned. It was then that Astrid had folded her arms over her bosom—as confidently as one can when wrapped only in a bedsheet—and smugly informed Jane that Ruth had not been her only lover. She had, in fact, been having "insignificant little flings" the entire three years they had been together. She could recite names, dates, and places.

When Jane walked away that afternoon with her clothes, a few books, mementos of her childhood, and custody of the few friends Astrid hadn't boffed, she headed to the nearest pub. She had since spent her evenings trying to break her father's drinking record. Last night, it seemed, she had finally succeeded.

A further revelation came to her this morning from her horizontal vantage point, as she realized that the black speckle pattern in the mustard-colored linoleum that covered her floor (except where it had peeled in spots) was not part of a clever texture designed to hide the dirt; it *was* dirt, trapped in layers of old wax. She sighed and closed her eyes. Good help was so hard to find.

Secret Agent Cedric Pumpernickel did not count himself among James Bond's many admirers; he thought 007 careless with his affairs and well on his way to becoming a dipsomaniac. Bond's troubles had come as no surprise to the sensible, steadfast older agent. He had always known that someday Bond would come to a ghastly end, and probably take some unfortunate girl with him. Pumpernickel had hoped he would be long gone by then. He was fifty-seven years old and had devoted his entire adult life to queen and country. This was to be his final assignment. In the last thirty years, despite his demotion from the double-0 ranks, he had gone on dozens of secret missions for his boss. He was honored to be N.'s trusted assistant, Watson to his Holmes. But he had lost his taste for this kind of work long ago.

Pumpernickel had suffered horribly during his short tenure as 001, and he had the scars to prove it.

Agent Pumpernickel tried to appear casual as he leaned against his government sedan and had a fag. He was an average-looking man, neither fat nor thin, tall nor short. His plain dark suit, now wet under the arms, was unremarkable. The only thing distinguishing him from thousands of similarly dressed middle-aged London businessmen was the miniature spy camera stitched into his right lapel, a few centimeters under a bright red carnation. That and the angry scar that snaked across his right cheek. In 1925, during a struggle with an enemy agent, Pumpernickel had been knocked unconscious. When he came to, he found he had been horribly disfigured. His career as the first double-0 agent had come to a premature and humiliating end. The Secret Service's face man had done his best, but despite his efforts, Agent Pumpernickel had been left with an S-shaped ribbon of shiny crimson flesh that stuck out on his pasty complexion like a neon badge.

"S" for spy.

8:13 A.M.

Bloody hell! The girl still hadn't left the building. Agent Pumpernickel had been there all night, and had seen her come home with another girl, a pretty redhead, shortly after midnight. They had seemed jolly and gay and rather tipsy, clinging to each other in a manner that made the prim Mr. Pumpernickel blush. Had he missed her in the crush of girls racing off to work? Hang it! He could be stuck there all day.

The life of a spy was not nearly so glamorous as the movies would have it. Agent Pumpernickel's stomach hurt from too many cups of instant coffee, his legs were cramping, his eyes bloodshot and puffy from lack of sleep. Any other day, he'd be arriving at headquarters right about now, fresh from a good night's sleep, his umbrella under one arm and the *Times* under the other. After twenty minutes with a cup of coffee and the crossword, he'd roll up his shirtsleeves and get down to the business of protecting what was left of the British Empire. Then there'd be one o'clock luncheon in the headquarters canteen with other very senior civil service staff. It was the high point of his day. Pumpernickel was a sociable man who liked nothing better than a good gossip with the boys.

He lit a cigarette and inhaled deeply. All night in that dark car he had ached for a fag, but had been afraid the glowing ember would give him away. "Thou Shalt Not Get Caught" was the spy's eleventh commandment. If he was captured, he could be interrogated in a cruel fashion, tortured out of his skull, or even executed. It was all part of the job.

Back at the Flora Beaton

"Good morning." An unfamiliar voice came from somewhere above Jane's head. Jane's eyes blinked open. Only weeks ago she would have woken to the sweet sound of Astrid gargling.

"Oh, God," she groaned. "I've done it again." There was nothing worse than waking up with a stranger.

"Pardon?"

Jane managed to prop her back against the wall, then squinted at the girl in her bed. It was too dark to make her out properly.

"Sorry," muttered Jane. "I didn't mean to say that out loud."

"I see," the girl said uncertainly. "I wouldn't have stayed, but last night you begged so nicely."

Jane put her head in her hands. She felt sick. Since Astrid, she had become awfully good at having her own insignificant little flings. Begging strange girls to stay with her was a new low.

"The least you could do is offer me some coffee," the girl said petulantly.

"I'd make you a cup, but I think something's living in the jar," Jane explained. The previous tenant had graciously left behind a hot plate, a kettle, and a jar of Nescafé whose contents had hardened into coal.

"Would you like an aspirin?" the girl asked.

The thought of putting even that in her stomach made Jane want to retch.

"No, thanks," she answered, unable to elaborate.

"A glass of water?"

"No."

"Isn't there anything I can get for you?"

"Got a gun?" Jane said sarcastically.

With a sigh of disgust, the girl switched on the bedside lamp.

"Turn it off." Jane cringed. In her wonky state, the beam seemed to have the intensity of a klieg light aimed straight at her eyes.

After a cruel pause, the girl adjusted the shade so it spread an even pool of light in the room.

"Thank you," Jane murmured. She found a crumpled pack of cigarettes in her trouser pocket, fished one out, and lit it. It couldn't possibly taste worse than her mouth already did.

Jane peered at the strange girl through the smoke. She had found her missing shirt—one mystery solved. She had no memory of having removed it. Or of this girl.

The girl threw back the covers and stretched her arms wide, her full breasts threatening to pop the buttons. The shirt gleamed white against her golden, sun-kissed skin. A tangled mass of wavy strawberry-blond hair flowed over her shoulders. She looked all peaches and cream, glowing and rested. And she had green eyes. Jane had a thing for green-eyed girls.

Jane realized her mouth had dropped open. She shut it quickly and gave the girl her best charmingly crooked grin, but it was too late.

"If you feel half as bad as you look, I feel sorry for you," the girl said coldly.

A memory of last night came rushing back to Jane. They had rolled around for hours in the lumpy bed, and afterward Jane had wept. She had indeed begged the girl to stay.

Jane tried to get up, but it was impossible. "I'm sorry," she said, gesturing hopelessly. "Really, I'm not at my best."

"Bully for you," the girl said snippily as she jumped out of bed, shed Jane's shirt, slipped on a light pink sleeveless shift that hugged her curves, then zipped on white, knee-high boots. She found her knickers amid the jumble of bedclothes and stuffed them in her purse.

Jane remembered that they were pink. She seemed to recall having removed them with her teeth.

"It's not too late to get coffee," Jane stammered. "There's a takeaway nearby. Just give me a minute to get on my feet."

The girl ignored her, and began painting her full lips a very vivid pink. When she was through, she stepped back and gave herself a once-over in the looking glass over the dresser. She seemed satisfied with what she saw. Jane had to agree. She was just about to say so when she saw the girl's green eyes snap with anger.

"I'd help you get up off that filthy floor," the girl told her, "but it rather suits you down there." She donned a white plastic bubble cap and dark glasses, then paused for a moment so Jane could get a good look at what she was missing. Jane wondered if it was too late to save this relationship.

"I'll make sure I don't step on you on the way out," said the girl. She slammed the door behind her.

Yes, Jane guessed, it was.

Abandoned fish finger factory
No. 12 Beesborough Place
9:02 A.M.

Agent Pumpernickel strolled casually toward the back door of an abandoned fish finger factory that offered a bird's-eye view of the Flora Beaton. After a furtive glance around to make sure he wasn't being watched, he bent down and pretended to tighten the laces on his plain black, antisqueak, rubber-soled shoes. With his thumb, he slid the tongue of his right shoe forward and removed a wafer-thin leather case. Inside was a complete set of miniature lock picks, favored by the top spies of the Western world and all the best jewel thieves. He selected a double-sided tension wrench and a feeler pick, and, using his body to block the view from the street, went to work.

Pumpernickel was out of practice; the last lock he had prised open had been on his own desk. He had locked his tea biscuits in his bottom drawer and forgotten the key at home. For that, he had used his letter opener. A simple pin tumbler lock like this should be child's play for an experienced secret agent, but the hands of his Poljot antimagnetic wristwatch ticked off three excruciating minutes before he managed to crack it and slip inside.

He leaned against the banister and caught his breath.

"Nothing to it," he told himself. He wiped his clammy hands on his trouser legs, then puffed his way up the four flights of stairs to the roof, with only his pen-torch for illumination. It was clear from the thick layer of dust on the stairs that he was the first person to have entered this place in a very long time. He reached a hand out to turn the knob of the door leading to the roof, then recoiled in horror. The doorway was covered with cobwebs as thick as spun sugar. Hundreds of insects were trapped in the webs in varying stages of decay, glittering like jewels suspended in midair. It was like something out of his worst nightmares.

Sickened, Pumpernickel backed down the stairs to the landing below, sank to the bottom step, and put his head between his knees. It took great effort to keep down the three cold sausage biscuits he had eaten in the car a few hours ago. He could barely get his hands to stop shaking long enough to light a cigarette.

Cedric Pumpernickel was a man of extreme habits and tastes. He always cracked his morning egg with his sterling silver baby spoon; if the spoon had been misplaced in the evening wash-up he ate dry toast instead. He had a strong prejudice against men who wore woolly socks, and made no attempt to hide it. He refused to turn his back on the queen's image, and since each senior official at headquarters had the official coronation day portrait on the wall behind their desks, Cedric was forced to back out of these rooms. He knew the younger agents thought him dotty, but he didn't care—as long as they never found out about his One Great Fear. Any bit of damaging information was grist for those sadists, especially the new recruit, 008. When 008 wasn't snooping in other agents' files or flirting with the secretaries, he seemed to spend his time thinking up elaborate pranks to pull on Pumpernickel. The younger agent would tease him mercilessly if he found out about this little weakness. He wouldn't be happy until Pumpernickel had been driven mad and had gone the way of Agent Basil Tingly, who had leapt from the roof one day and splattered bits of himself clear to the other side of the street.

During his first assignment as 001, Pumpernickel had been dropped onto a remote South Pacific island with orders to assassinate a mad biologist planning to attack the House of Lords with an army of poisonous wolf spiders. To get to the madman's laboratory, Pumpernickel had been forced to fight his way through a web of dense cobwebs and had been bitten several times. He had blown up like a blimp. Previous to this experience, one of his favorite pastimes on balmy summer nights had been picking weevils off his roses and squishing them between his fingers; now he sprayed his roses with poison.

9:27 A.M.

Jane woke up, her back sore from sleeping against the wall. She prayed—as she always did—that when she opened her eyes, she'd be back home in her cozy bungalow in Ruislip. Astrid liked to spend Sundays in bed, so Jane would bring her breakfast, sweep the crumbs away, and have her way with Astrid. Afterward, they'd lounge in the mess of sheets, poring through Agatha Christie novels (stopping to read absurd bits aloud) and indulging in silly, disjointed conversations in the way that lovers do. She remembered in particular a long discussion about whether the squeak in the attic was a poltergeist or a squirrel.

Instead of the clean, cream-colored walls of the bungalow, her eyes opened onto hideous water-streaked, cabbage-rose wallpaper. A grim portrait of Queen Victoria glared at her. One night in a drunken state, Jane had imagined the eyes were following her with disapproval as she lured yet another nameless, intoxicated girl to the lumpy twin bed. Not that Jane didn't also disapprove.

She staggered to the shared facilities down the hall, praying she wouldn't run into Miss Tessie Twigg, the pious, ill-humored hotel proprietress who prowled the halls all day looking for criminals. There were five cardinal rules at the Flora Beaton; they were posted on the inside door of every room in Tessie Twigg's mingy handwriting:

NO LOUD CONVERSATION.
NO RUNNING IN THE HALLS.
NO SMOKING IN THE ROOMS.
NO LIQUOR ON THE PREMISES.
NO OVERNIGHT MALE VISITORS.

Jane had broken each rule but the last.

She made it to the loo safely. The office girls had put on their faces and left long ago, leaving behind a film of sweet-smelling dusting powder and a jumble of wet knickers hanging from a makeshift clothesline strung across the tub. Jane moved the damp underpants to the sink, gave the tub a good scrub, ran the water until it was almost unbearably hot, and settled in for a good, long sulk.

Her life of late reminded her of the silly puzzles her American cousins used to enclose with their letters when they were young. Her cousins were earnest and polite and ever so careful never to refer to the war, as if reminding Jane that her country was exploding all around her would be somehow impolite. They had perfect penmanship, and clipped the puzzles neatly. "For Jane" they'd write at the top. For her mother, they'd sent jokes from *Reader's Digest* and eggless cake recipes. "What's Wrong with This Picture?" the puzzles were called. They were simple line drawings of domestic scenes, with a few objects in disarray. Jane had never bothered to work them. How challenging could it be to find a lamp or a chair that had been drawn upside down? Besides, during the Blitz Jane had seen lots of households turned on end. Sometimes a dog would be wearing a hat, too, but Jane had heard that Americans made their dogs wear clothes, and so wasn't sure if that was something "wrong" or not.

During one of the first air raids, her family home had taken a direct hit. Their house had been reduced to a dent in the earth littered with bits of smashed furniture and shards of dishes. For years she had awoken in the night expecting to hear the warning sirens. After the war, all Jane thought she would ever want was a good, strong roof over her head, and cakes made with eggs. She turned on the water taps full force to mute the sound, and wept.

After thirty minutes in the tub, long after the hot water had given out, Jane finally decided not to drown herself after all; it would not be an attractive death. Tessie Twigg would find her floating in the cold water, with scum from the cheap, heavily perfumed soap clinging to her body. Besides, to do the job right, Jane would need help. She laughed bitterly. She knew plenty of girls who would be happy to hold her head under water.

Since Astrid had given her the boot, Jane had been behaving like a twit. She went to the bars each night and drank until she was numb. Too lonely to return alone to her new home, she'd pick up any girl who would have her. The meanest thing she had ever done to Astrid was to break that ugly gravy boat, although it had been, in a way, a favor. Now she was suspicious and hateful to anyone who showed her the slightest bit of interest. She never went out with the same girls twice, never returned their telephone calls, and made a point of forgetting their names as soon as she had learned them. Just last week a girl had slapped Jane twice, the first time for neglecting to ring her after a night of apparently steamy sex, the second for not remembering the tryst in the first place. Jane feared she was losing her charm. The same thing had happened to her father at about her age; his had disappeared into a bottle of scotch. She released the stopper from the tub and watched the water drain away.

Secret Service headquarters, secret London location
Office of Sir Niles Needlum
Director, Double-0 Division
10:23 A.M.

The shrill ring of his private telephone shattered the silence. N. grabbed the receiver.

"What?" he barked. There was no time for superficial pleasantries in his business. He had an empire to save.

"Doctor Whitehead from the Spy Sanitarium is on the line, sir," his efficient secretary, Miss Tuppenny, announced crisply.

"Patch him through," he ordered.

Then—"What's the story on Bond?"

"Your man is a homicidal depressive paranoiac," the doctor reported.

"I know that. I want to know what's *wrong* with him! And be straight with me, man. No medical mumbo jumbo."

"He's lost his nerve."

N. had suspected as much. The booze, bullets, and birds had finally gotten to 007. He rubbed his hand across the deep worry lines etched on his forehead. 007 had put most of those lines there.

He had known for months that James Bond was slowly going to pieces. Bond had gotten sloppy, but it was nothing that couldn't be fixed. Then careless pillow talk between Bond and the wife of a high-ranking Russian official had almost led to the exposure of his secret agent status. He'd let the wrong word slip while kissing persuasive lips. Many men had; they'd been assigned a desk job in another department, or farmed off to a satellite office in some godforsaken country. But Bond was the best secret agent he'd ever had. A lone wolf. A crack sharpshooter. Nerves of steel. Superb material. He'd go out the window before being chained to a desk, or stuck in Greenland. So N. had had the leak plugged. The woman had been eliminated. The usual flowers had been sent.

But there could be no more mistakes. The minute 007 lost his cloak of invisibility, he ceased to be of any use to the Secret Service. And if N. lost Bond, he lost everything. The government bean counters were just waiting for an excuse to shut down the double-0 department, by far the costliest of all the Service's operations. Assassinations had become too expensive a pursuit for a government plagued by budget problems.

"Well, fix him," N. said roughly. "Give him a pill or an electric jolt."

"I'm afraid rest is the only cure."

"How long?"

"Three days . . . three weeks . . . in cases like these it's hard to predict."

N. groaned. He had been hoping for better news. Bond was scheduled to receive the Thanks Awfully medal from the queen four days hence. (Her Majesty had begun reading spy novels lately, and was especially looking forward to conferring an award on a real live agent.) Admitting their top man was strapped to a cot in a lunatic asylum would not cast the double-0 division in a favorable light. The queen's desires were law, so an invitation to the palace was, in actuality, an order. Death was the only acceptable excuse.

"Do whatever you have to do. And Doctor—"

"Yes, sir?"

"Tick-tock. Tick-tock."

"Sir?"

"Time is running out!" He slammed the receiver onto its base. Rogue agents like 007 were going to be the death of him someday.

N. leaned back in his chair and stared out the window, his favorite position for reflection. It was too bad about the Russian official's wife, but he hadn't the luxury of regret. If he felt responsible every time he set off a chain of events that led to the destruction of human life, he'd be a piss-poor administrator. Besides, he had other fish to fry. After a long while spent staring at the jagged skyline of London, he came to a decision. He had no choice but to go through with Pumpernickel's ridiculous plan.

Fish finger factory
10:44 A.M.

Agent Pumpernickel shone his torch on the cobwebs. Hundreds of tiny flies with soulless, blank eyes stared back at him. In one corner a hairy brown spider was making a meal of a grasshopper. He shuddered. His torch fell from his sweaty hand. Although he scrambled for it, the lens shattered. He was left alone in the dark. With Them.

He swallowed hard. He had to get on the roof in order to snap surveillance photographs for his report. But what if that hairy brown spider came at him? He could return to headquarters and put in a request at the Office of Spy Supplies for a replacement torch, but it would take hours to process the paperwork. The girl could be gone by then.

This was his final assignment before retiring. Next week, there'd be a luncheon in his honor, and all the other senior civil servants would come. For privacy's sake, it would have to be in the canteen where they dined each day, but there'd be a special menu in honor of the occasion: potted shrimps and deviled kidneys followed by spotted dick or a dundee cake, and Champagne so the men could toast Agent Pumpernickel's many years of steadfast service. He'd be presented with the Jolly Good Show medal, and a letter expressing warm wishes, signed by Her Majesty herself. He had already cleared a space in his top bureau drawer for the medal and purchased an elegant silver frame for the letter. N. would present him with the standard gold-plated lock pick and, after, some lad in the motor pool would drive him home (as he'd no doubt be a little tipsy). The next morning he'd wake up in his quiet flat, crack open his morning egg, and retire to the sitting room and the soothing companionship of his radio dramas and collection of Battersea snuffboxes. He'd receive a modest monthly pension until his death; not a large sum in exchange for risking one's life for thirty years, but enough for a man of simple means to get by until the end of his days. First, though, he had to earn it.

The Flora Beaton
11:07 A.M.

Jane pried open a window and perched on the sill, searching once more for the promised view. All she saw was a string of sad-faced Victorian houses whose rooms had no doubt been chopped into tiny boxes with plasterboard walls, like hers, and the sooty, crumbly tops of abandoned warehouses. She was a long way from antiseptic Ruislip. "Ruth's Slip" was one of Jane's more polite names for the place. She hadn't wanted to live there, but she had let Astrid talk her into it. Just another dumb decision in a long line of stupid mistakes. And there was a girl behind each one of them.

Jane lit a cigarette and thought about Astrid. There were problems right from the start—things Jane had assumed would work themselves out eventually.

The day they'd moved in together, Astrid had made it a point to tell the neighbors they were sisters. Jane had been appalled. First off, they looked nothing alike—Jane being lanky and dark, and Astrid small and curvy and fair. To Jane's way of thinking, the proclamation only served to alert the neighbors to their unconventional relationship.

They had lived in a bungalow with a small neat garden in front, made possible by Jane's inheritance from her Aunt Honoria. Each weekday the wives would stand on their porches in neat housedresses, smiling and waving at their husbands departing for London. Then they'd scurry back inside to stir their quick-cook custard and start their automatic washing machines. One of their neighbors made a hobby of freezing food. Jane had gone along with the sister act for a year, until she had gotten soused at a dull neighborhood drinks party and kissed her lover in a decidedly unsisterly fashion.

"Not in front of *them*," Astrid had hissed, pushing Jane away. It was the beginning of the end.

In Ruislip, last night's rain would have made the already unnaturally vivid grass even greener. Here it just made the soot collect in little black pools on the sidewalk. The only thing remotely green in sight was the geranium dying in a rusty custard tin on Jane's windowsill, courtesy of Miss Edith Liversidge, a gentle old soul who lived in the basement flat. She appeared to subsist entirely on brown bread and kippers, which she graciously shared with her enormously stout tabby cat, King Edward, and any stray that found its way to her street-level window. Miss Liversidge was always in a grand mood. Jane suspected she took a little something in her tea.

Next to the Flora Beaton were the shops—a chemist, a pub, and a grocer. Everything a girl could need. Jane liked the sharp, slightly acrid smell of the chemist's shop, where she bought far too many tins of headache tablets, but the pub was a little too close for comfort. It wasn't even noon and the place was jumping. Pubs always reminded her of her father. His home away from home, he always said. At her age, he was already a tired old commercial traveler, permanently bowed from years of carrying his heavy sample case around. In the last years of his life he was so bent over he looked as though he were in a constant state of deference. The fabric of her life was becoming decidedly tatty around the edges; she'd be down among the dead men soon if she didn't watch it.

"H-e-l-l-o J-a-n-e—"

Edith Liversidge was standing on the kerb holding a filthy white cat.

"Hello, Miss Liversidge," Jane called down. "What's going on?"

"King Edward has finally found a bride," Miss Liversidge shouted gleefully.

Oh, dear. England hadn't had a King Edward for decades. Miss Liversidge must have drunk too much tea again.

"That's nice," Jane called down. Nothing against dear old Miss Liversidge, but here was another good reason to stop getting pissed every night.

"He gets lonely when I step out for my afternoon stroll. We're having herrings and toast fingers to celebrate. May we have the pleasure of your company?"

Oh. King Edward the *cat* was getting married. In the placid life of the building, this was an event.

"Count me in," Jane called out. She could use some food before braving the bus to work. And she had a tin of tuna in brine that would make the perfect wedding gift.

"Jane?"

"Yes, Miss Liversidge?"

"Am I crazy, or does something smell fishy?"

Jane sniffed. The air did rather stink more than usual today.

"Yes to both questions."

Miss Liversidge laughed merrily. She was Jane's only friend in the building.

Edith Liversidge was a devout Catholic, and as such, having the local priest come to her home to perform a blessing was a momentous occasion in an otherwise contented but routine existence.

"Everything was going very nicely," she said as she poured tea for Jane. She described the scene: two cats, the young priest, and a lovely box of crystallized fruits displayed on her nicest table linen. She'd had her hair done specially for the occasion, at a place that offered half-price terms for old-age pensioners between the hours of two and three P.M.

"Then, as the good father was about to bless their union, King Edward put his head in the holy water." Bright pink spots appeared on her cheeks. Miss Liversidge was clearly mortified.

King Edward snored softly in front of the electric fire. His predecessor, Prince Albert, had reached the grand old age of twenty-two before quietly expiring on a copy of the *Times* one Saturday. His ashes were in a powdered milk tin on Miss Liversidge's mantel. Much to her dismay, Miss Liversidge had had to endure snide comments from her nephew Derek about Prince Albert being in a can.

"You can never trust royalty to behave themselves," Jane said in all seriousness.

"Another cup, dear?" Miss Liversidge asked, thinking her friend looked a little sad. She buttoned her cardigan up to her neck—it was unseasonably chilly—and turned up the fire a touch. "Did you sleep poorly?"

"I had a bad night," Jane admitted.

"You sounded quite festive when you arrived home."

Jane winced. Her attempts to sneak into the Flora Beaton well past curfew were never as successful as she would have liked. She would no doubt hear about this later from Tessie Twigg. Had Tessie Twigg's parents been able to predict the future, they would have undoubtedly named their daughter something more suited to her dour nature. Brünhilda, perhaps.

"I was going to stay in, but I started to feel a bit low."

"Next time, come see me," Miss Liversidge said. "I'm always glad for the company."

"I thought about it, but decided it would be cruel to inflict myself on anyone. Well . . . anyone I know."

"Has something happened, dear?"

Jane shook her head. "I just miss Astrid. I want to go home."

"You'll get over her, Jane. Give it time."

"She's been ringing the shop. I'm afraid if I speak to her, I'll beg her to take me back."

"That would be most undignified," Miss Liversidge cautioned her.

"Why do I miss her so much? I'm not sure I even *like* her anymore. And after the way she behaved, I could never trust her again. What kind of relationship would that be?"

"Unfortunately, a rather typical one, I'm afraid." Miss Liversidge sighed. Except for Jane and some of her classmates in her self-improvement courses, she had scant use for human companionship. "Jane, have you ever thought of getting a cat?"

Secret Service headquarters
Secret agent lunchroom
12:00 P.M. sharp

Agent Cedric Pumpernickel looked positively unstrung. His face was as white as rice pudding; the scar on his right cheek stood out in vivid relief. His hair was plastered to his forehead with sweat. He reeked of smoked fish. He was, in short, a mess.

"What's up, 'nickel?" 008 asked.

Agent Pumpernickel sputtered wordlessly. The other secret agents lingering over their morning tea turned to stare. Afraid he was about to faint, Pumpernickel collapsed onto the chair across from 008.

008 stared at him with a queer expression. Pumpernickel was usually so pressed and polished.

"Care for a cuppa, old boy?" 008 offered. He could afford to be friendly to an old man whose time was almost up. Just one more week of Pumpernickel's sweaty, bug-eyed presence and infernal royal babble, and he'd be gone forever. What could it hurt to be a little chummy with the old bean?

Pumpernickel stared at the young agent across from him. He was whippet-thin, with a long, narrow face and the small, cunning eyes of a fox. Pumpernickel had never thought him particularly trustworthy, or even vaguely kind. Perhaps he had been too quick in judging the lad.

"A cup of tea would be splendid," he croaked hoarsely, discovering between his shirt cuff and wrist what felt like yet another morsel of fish finger.

Crispin's Bookshop
No. 131 King's Road
Chelsea
12:57 P.M.

"Well, look what the cat dragged in. Really, Jane, you look dreadful."

Similar compliments were always raising their pretty little heads whenever Mrs. Horace Snipe stopped in for a cackle and cake. Mrs. Snipe was the bookshop's most devoted customer; she was also the most trying.

Jane Bond, who had used up all remaining reserves on the bus ride to work, managed to resist the impulse to hurl her cup of take-away coffee at the tall, bony woman standing in front of the romance shelf. She might melt.

"Good morning, Mrs. Snipe," Jane said, taking care to keep her tone light. This was one customer who had long ago crossed the line from amusing to annoying. They had made the mistake of feeding her once, and like a stray cat she kept turning up on their doorstep. Trouble was, she actually bought books. Lots of them. So Jane had been made to promise not to physically harm her.

Mr. Snipe used to come around regularly, too, to look at bird books. He was a thin man with a pinched, goatlike face and a strange mincing walk, almost a tiptoe. He hadn't been by in months, and Mrs. Snipe hadn't mentioned him once. It was generally assumed among the local shopkeepers that Horace Snipe had finally come to his senses, packed up his bird books, and run out on the missus. But Jane was positive he was buried in the cellar.

"I came here to exchange the Muriel Spark book Mr. Crispin sold me yesterday for something interesting," Mrs. Snipe announced. She was holding a cup of tea in one hand, and balancing a piece of iced seed cake on a paper serviette in the other. Her beady brown eyes glowed the way they always did when she was getting ready to lodge a complaint.

"It's about a single woman, and Mr. Crispin knows full well that the dreary life of the single woman is of little interest to me, and, I dare say, to most people. My dearest friend, Lady Edwina Wooley-Booley, just finished a wonderful one about a lively American girl who marries a

Spaniard. They go to live on his family's ancient estate, where she introduces modern sanitation and an airstrip. Unfortunately, Edwina lent her copy to her friend, Lady Finhatten, and everyone knows what a notoriously slow reader she is."

"You don't say," Jane murmured absentmindedly, sipping the dregs of her coffee. She was busy thinking of the best way to alert the authorities to Mr. Snipe's whereabouts.

"Have I ever mentioned that Lady Edwina and I have been best friends for many, many years?"

"Maybe once or twice." When had Mrs. Snipe *not* mentioned her great dear friend, *the* Lady Edwina?

"Of course, I knew her when she was just plain old Edwina Piggott." Mrs. Snipe still hadn't gotten over the shock. Not six months ago, dull, dumpy Edwina Piggott had suddenly up and married the very eligible, very attractive Sir Reginald Wooley-Booley. Edwina had gone from being the Piggott Plumbing heiress to lady of the manor. It had all happened so fast, Edwina hadn't even had time to inform her friends. Mrs. Snipe and the other members of the Thursday Afternoon Fine Arts League had received postcards from Paris announcing the union. At first they had assumed it was a silly joke on Edwina's part, but when the *Times* announced the marriage, they realized the unthinkable had happened. It was like a movie, remarked one overly imaginative member of their little group—not a very good one, Mrs. Snipe had wanted to add.

"Now she and Princess Margaret get their hair done at the same salon, and all of Edwina's clothes are handmade. Even her underwear. I knew her when she was so stingy she used to set her own hair at home, in one of her old ratty slips. She looked like she'd been pulled through a hedge backward."

Mrs. Snipe looked as if it pained her to reveal this information.

"Edwina is so frightfully insecure she's forever calling on me for help. She asks me to all their most important social functions. Last month I went up to their estate in the Cotswolds to hold her hand while Sir Reginald hosted his annual grouse shoot. Every time they entertain, Edwina is worried she'll make a dog's dinner of it. Don't you agree that hunting is such a healthy hobby for a man?"

Perhaps an anonymous letter to Scotland Yard would do the trick, Jane thought.

Mrs. Snipe paused to catch her breath, took a big bite of her cake, swallowed with heroic effort, licked her lips, and continued with the latest in a series of discourses on the subject of "Dear Edwina and Her Impetuous Marriage." "Edwina married rather later in life, but better late than never, don't you agree, Jane? She is a dear soul, but she does have, shall we say, a quantity of whimsy that might drive a person crazy. I imagine marriage will iron out the lumps in her personality, though I do think she's letting her new status go to her head. She's started dyeing her hair—at her age!"

Or, Jane reflected, perhaps a call to the gas people to complain about a nasty odor coming from the Snipe house, in the vicinity of the cellar.

"I believe she fancies herself another Duchess of Windsor. Did I mention that Edwina and the duchess have struck up a friendship through the mail? What those two have to correspond about, short of marrying late in life, heaven only knows. The way Edwina goes on about the duchess, one would think those two were the best of friends when in truth, I am the best friend Edwina could ever hope to have." She paused for a breath. A big one.

"Did I mention I'm having the very latest in central heating installed at my house?"

Only a dozen times, Jane thought. "Will they have to knock around in the basement?" she asked innocently.

"Don't be daft. How would I know? What is keeping Mr. Crispin? Would you inform him that I'm a busy woman?"

Jane backed slowly away from Mrs. Snipe, having made it a policy never to turn her back on the woman. She smacked right into Simon Crispin, her best friend and the proprietor of the bookshop. He placed a stack of books on the counter.

"Do any of these interest you, Mrs. Snipe?"

Mrs. Snipe frowned even before she could read the titles. A reflex action, Jane supposed.

"I shan't want the Virginia Woolf," she decided right away. "She's awfully anti-male, don't you think?"

"I like her." Jane shrugged.

Mrs. Snipe gave her a mean look. "Of course you do, dear."

"This biography of Lady Churchill is very popular," Simon jumped in.

"Fine. I'll take that and a mystery. Wrap them up, and hurry. I'm going to be late for my migraine sufferers meeting."

"Do you think they give them or get them?" Jane commented the minute Mrs. Snipe was out the door.

"Give them, I imagine."

"What an irritating blister that woman can be," Jane groused. "Me, anti-male? What could be more anti-male than killing your husband and burying him in the cellar? I half wanted to slap her."

"You showed admirable restraint," Simon said with relief.

"Thank you."

"She drives me bloody crazy, too, Jane, but we need the business." Ever since the Council to Extirpate Moral Turpitude had fined Simon five hundred pounds for distributing pornographic materials to a minor (he had sold a copy of *Ahoy, Sailor* to a seventeen-year-old boy), the shop had been teetering on the verge of financial ruin.

"Would you please reconsider my offer to go on the dole?" Jane pleaded. "I could still work here; it wouldn't be illegal if you stopped paying me, would it?" Not that she cared too much about that. "Then when business is better, you can officially rehire me."

"Business may never get better. As of late, the English economy seems to rely almost entirely on the sale of paper dresses and plastic boots. I'm thinking of selling the store to a boutique."

"Simon, you've been here for years! You can't just give up like that."

"People just aren't buying books like they used to," he sighed. It was, to the detriment of people like Simon Crispin, a mod, mod, mod, mod world.

"Something will happen. It always does."

"Yes, but this time it has to be something good. We're so far in arrears our distributor is threatening to cut us off. And just when the newest Agatha Christie is due out."

"And I thought I had rotten luck," said Jane.

"You do, Jane."

"Thank you."

"Don't mention it."

"Is there any cake, or did Snippity-Snipe eat it all?"

"I hid a few pieces."

Jane made tea while Simon got the cake. They sat in silence in the deserted bookshop, perched on wooden stools, and ate with newspaper on their laps to catch the crumbs. Jane and Simon had been friends forever and she thought of him as the brother God had *meant* to give her. Although only a few years older, he was considerably more sensible than Jane, who ricocheted between elation and despair.

It started to rain. Simon turned on the little electric heater, and pulled the sleeves of his sweater down over his hands. His elbows stuck out through the large holes in the sleeves.

"The first thing I'm going to do when I win the sweepstakes is get you new clothes," said Jane. Simon hadn't added to his wardrobe in the seven years Jane had known him. He owned three pairs of worn brown corduroy trousers, and half a dozen ratty, hole-riddled sweaters of some indeterminate dark color.

"There's no reason to replace anything unless it's properly worn out," insisted Simon.

"Simon, that sweater is unknitting itself."

Astrid, fearful of what the neighbors might think, had always insisted Jane wear a skirt. One of the first things Jane did after the breakup was buy three pairs of trousers, an expensive navy wool peacoat, and a pricey pair of Beatle boots from a men's shop on Carnaby Street. Although she missed Astrid horribly, Jane didn't miss the constant harping about Jane's less-than-feminine appearance. Apparently the good people of Ruislip had never seen a woman in trousers, and would die if forced to view such an unnatural sight. For three years, Jane had left the house wearing an ugly, itchy skirt, and changed into trousers once she arrived at the bookshop. The charade, thankfully, was over. Her new clothes made her feel at home for the first time in her tall, rangy body. Last Christmas, Astrid had presented her with a single beautifully wrapped box that contained yet another ugly knee-length woolen skirt and a lacy dickie to go under her best sweater. Why she hadn't left Astrid at that moment was a mystery.

They finished the cake and moved on to crisps. Simon opened the bag, popped a crisp in his mouth, then rested the bag on his belly.

"I gain a half-stone every time you go through a breakup," he complained. "Byron says you've simply got to settle down before I break my side of the bed."

Jane shut her eyes and leaned against the romantic poets.

"Need an aspirin?"

"Yes, please." Jane always thought that in another life Simon must have been a Girl Guide. He was always prepared.

"Two or three?"

"Four."

Simon tossed her the tin of headache tablets he had started keeping in his pocket just for Jane.

"I hope you had a good time."

"So do I," Jane said wistfully.

Simon paused with a crisp halfway to his mouth. "Jane!"

"Don't say it, Simon. I know I'm drinking too much. And I've been a royal pain to work with."

"As a matter of fact, you have, but that's not what I was going to say."

Jane got up, opened the door for some fresh air, leaned in the frame, and lit a cigarette. The rain was letting up. She could hear Mrs. Snipe talking in the bakery next door to some fresh victims.

"You're going to kill yourself if you keep going like this. Just like your father."

"He was hit by a runaway double-decker. It was an accident."

"He was drunk and didn't see it coming. You told me so yourself."

An awkward pause followed. Jane hated to talk about her father.

"I'm sorry, Simon," she said finally. "I've been dreadful lately. I just haven't been myself since the breakup."

"Since before then, actually. Crisp?"

Simon took a deep breath. He had been rehearsing this conversation in his head for a while now. In six weeks he'd seen his best friend go from a social drinker to a decidedly antisocial one. Jane wasn't cut out to be a drunk; at least, he was hoping she wasn't.

"It seems to me that you've divided your life into two parts: before and after Astrid, as if your life together was perfect. I'm telling you, Jane, you and Astrid were not that happy."

Simon was so wrong. A vision of their happy life came to her, a memory of their first night in the bungalow before the furniture arrived. Jane had made a candlelight supper of baked beans on toast, and splurged for a bottle of Chianti. Afterward, they had made love in front of the electric heater in the sitting room. For weeks after, even walking into that room would make them blush and laugh.

Jane's eyes stung. "This morning I was thinking about how we would spend every Sunday in bed together and I would bring her all her meals."

"Yes, while she pouted and complained about the cold tea," Simon snapped. "Remember that time you had the grippe and Astrid refused to run to the store for a tin of soup?"

"But that was the night of her Cordon Bleu cookery class!" Jane still remembered the congealed bit of white sauce with which Astrid had guiltily returned home, offering to serve it over some day-old rice. Simon was right; her relationship with Astrid hadn't been so idyllic. Sometimes, being with Astrid hadn't ended Jane's loneliness, it had added to it.

"Simon, you're like the bossy older sister I never wanted," she said, tears streaking her face.

Simon handed Jane his handkerchief, and clumsily patted her arm. "Well, listen to your big sis before anything happens you can't charm your way out of."

Jane wiped her eyes. Good old Simon always had a handkerchief when she needed one. "I can't get over how Astrid treated me. People are not tissues to be used and then discarded."

"Speaking of which, someone named Bunny was by here earlier looking for you."

"You're very subtle, Simon." Jane sniffled.

Who on earth was Bunny? Jane threw her fag end into the street and closed the door. Mrs. Snipe's voice dropped in volume, but still came through.

"I hesitate to tell you this," Simon added, "but she said she'd like to buy you a drink tonight at the bar."

"No more drinking for me. I dragged some poor girl home last night and this morning treated her like she had the plague. She was nice, too; she kept asking me if I needed anything."

"Oh, I hate that. Whenever Byron tries to do something nice for me, I make him sleep on the couch."

"Shut up and pass the crisps."

Secret Service headquarters
Employee lunchroom
1:00 P.M. on the dot

008 frowned. The lunch lady had filled his bowl of toad in the hole to the brim, and he had dragged the right cuff of his new shirt through the gravy. He was anxious enough as it was. A call from Miss Tuppenny requesting his presence in N.'s office that afternoon had put him on edge. He had an ardent hope that the meeting would result in his first real Secret Service assignment. His long apprenticeship would finally be over. The British Empire was, once again, under attack. Luckily he always kept a spare shirt in his bottom desk drawer.

008 scrubbed his cuff with his handkerchief, all the while thinking about tall, gorgeous Miss Tuppenny, whose reserved beauty and cool air of authority intimidated every man who passed her desk on the way to N.'s office. She was every secret agent's dream of a girl Friday: she had thick brunette hair confined to a prim bun that begged to be set free. Her dark tailored suits were the perfect fit; just snug enough to give one a maddening hint of the dangerous curves underneath. Like many brave men before him, 008 had made multiple campaigns against her virtue. And, like the others, he had been firmly rebuffed.

Even the great Jack-the-lad James Bond had failed to ignite a spark in the aloof Miss Tuppenny. She was clearly frigid; it made the idea of seducing her even more exciting. She was a nut he'd love to crack—and soon. By 008's reckoning, Miss Tuppenny was fast approaching thirty. Unless she married soon, or took a lover, she'd be doomed to the life of a lonely spinster, with only other lonely single girls and perhaps a tatty cat or two to keep her company. It would be a bloody shame if Miss Tuppenny died an old maid, he thought. Her death notice would be sad and short:

> Miss Tuppenny, dedicated civil servant and lover of cats, returned to her Maker unopened.

Back at the bookshop

"Do you think it's too late for me to go to girls' boarding school?" Jane wondered aloud. "They're giving out scholarships to worthy girls everywhere. I believe I qualify. I wonder if I could get my own room?" When they were bored, she and Simon made a game of reading the classifieds. They had started with the "Lonely Hearts" column and had worked their way to "Jobs for Ladies."

"Here's something for you, Jane: 'Miss Prunella N. Valentine, of the Middlesex Higher Secretarial College, is accepting applications for instructors in Typing One, Two, and Three. Send sample.' I forget—can you type?"

"No, but I have awfully nice handwriting."

"Then you can learn speedwriting in the privacy of your own home."

"There is no privacy in my own home. My landlady is probably going through my drawers at this very moment."

"You wish. What else?"

" 'TV writing earns you top money!' They put an exclamation mark at the end. That means it's a really fabulous job. Now, what could we write about?"

"We could write about a nice little bookshop—"

"—run by a lovely bugger—"

"—and his charming lesbian friend—"

"—who is polite to all the customers."

Jane snorted. "It'll be a mystery. We'll call it *Whatever Happened to Horace Snipe?* Based on a true story. Brought to you by Bird's Instant Custard: 'It's not as lumpy as the rest.' In the final installment, Mrs. Snipe will confess that she did indeed kill her husband and bury his body in the cellar. He's under the preserve cabinet."

"In his pajamas and slippers?"

Jane nodded. "With a look of surprise on his face."

"How'd she do it?"

"Dug a hole with a shovel, I imagine."

"No—how'd she kill him?"

"Arsenic in the custard."

"We'll lose our sponsors."

"Maybe she bored him to death."

"Is that possible?"

Jane laughed bitterly. "According to Astrid it is."

A funny look crossed Simon's face. "I forget to tell you—she rang again."

So far Jane had refused to take her former lover's calls. What more could Astrid possibly have to say?

"I bet the honeymoon with Ruth is over and she's beginning to miss you," Simon suggested.

"Astrid always did have a short attention span," said Jane bitterly.

"You wouldn't go back to her, would you?"

"Of course not! Maybe. I don't know!" Jane cried. "Each morning when I wake my first thought is: God, I hate Astrid. But as the day goes on, I start missing her. By night I'm wishing we could work things out."

"Loneliness can make you temporarily insane, especially at night. Jane, Astrid was *horrid* to you."

"What if Astrid is the best I get?"

"Once a cheater, always a cheater."

"People can change."

"Not that much. Just promise you'll talk to me first before making any decision."

"I swear I'll discuss the whole sordid thing with you in excruciating detail before making a move. Happy?"

"You know nothing makes me happier than hearing all about Astrid."

"Don't be such a wanker—she wasn't that bad."

"Jane—and I'm saying this as a friend—you're a bloody idiot when it comes to girls."

"All that's changed," Jane promised. "I swear I am *never* going to let some girl lead me around by the bra straps again—even if I have to be alone the rest of my life."

The sound of a book hitting the floor with a resounding thwack, followed by a shy "So sorry," startled them both. It had come from the royalty corner.

"I didn't know we had a customer," said Simon under his breath. "He must have wandered in while I was putting the history section to rights. Jane, when I come back I want to hear all about this epiphany. Right now I've got to run off to the Bank of England and try to talk them into lending me money."

"Didn't they already turn you down?"

"Yes, but this time I've got an appointment with Byron's ex-boyfriend's boyfriend. I figure that practically makes us related. Try to sell that fellow something pricey, like that full-color book on the chamberpots of Balmoral Castle. Ta." He grabbed his worn mac and went out the door.

Poor Simon, Jane thought. His "ta" sounded so sad. She walked toward the man who had dropped the book, determined to make a sale.

"Need any help?" Jane asked politely.

He had his face buried in a rather dry history of the Queen Mum's hats. He looked to her like a typical civil servant—dark suit, dark shoes, perfect posture. Thinning light brown hair. Pasty, freckled forehead.

Then he looked up.

Jane tried not to stare at the scar on the man's cheek.

"Hello," he said, almost in a whisper. He seemed terribly ill at ease. He was no doubt looking for the mature-reading section. Jane rolled her eyes. Why hadn't he just asked Simon?

"It's through the curtain," Jane said helpfully.

The man blinked at her stupidly, then handed her a small leather-bound volume, *The Complete History of English Snuffboxes*, with thirteen exquisite color plates.

"I would like to purchase this, please. Would you wrap it?" His hand trembled.

He followed Jane to the front counter, where she wrapped the book in brown paper and wrote out a slip. He had a funny way of looking at her, almost in profile. His way, no doubt, of trying to hide the scar.

"I'm a collector," he blurted out.

"Professional?"

"Oh, no, no, no. I'm strictly an amateur. It's just that I find it a very satisfactory way to pass the time."

"Been collecting for a long time, have you?" Jane asked.

He nodded. "The first one was a gift from a . . . a . . . friend, when I was but a lad." His face became scarlet, whereupon the scar stuck out in vivid relief. "After that, I became quite enamored of them. They're exquisite little objects."

"My father collected matchbooks," Jane said. "I still have boxes full of them. I don't know why I keep them."

"Sentiment, I suppose. I have my mother's glove collection, wrapped in the original tissue. She had very tiny hands, even for a woman."

Jane smiled. He was a pleasant enough old bean. "If there's anything else you need, stop around when Simon is here. Antiques and collectibles are his department."

"Thank you, Miss Bond." The moment the words were out of his mouth, he jumped back and gasped, as if they might turn around and bite him.

"Do I know you?" Jane asked. He did seem familiar, but she couldn't place him. He was about the same age her father would have been had he been living. He could be one of her father's old war chums, which would explain the scar. Funny she couldn't place him; he had the kind of disfigurement a child would remember.

"You've never seen me before today!" the man cried defensively. He dropped a handful of bills on the counter—far too much for the dusty little book—grabbed his parcel, and fled. The world was full of nuts, Jane thought, as she busied herself picking cat hair off her coat. And most of them, sooner or later, made their way to the shop.

Secret Service headquarters
Office of Miss Tuppenny
2:30 P.M.

"Sir, Agent Pumpernickel is here."

"Send him in straightaway."

Miss Tuppenny gave Agent Cedric Pumpernickel an encouraging smile as he walked slowly, reluctantly—like a boy who had been called to the headmaster's for a caning—into N.'s office. As soon as the lead-lined door to N.'s inner sanctum clicked shut, the green light on the wall above it flicked on.

Miss Tuppenny had heard about that morning's fire at the fish finger factory. Poor Agent Pumpernickel; he was the least objectionable of N.'s minions. True, his incessant nattering about his snuffbox collection had, on more than one occasion, left Miss Tuppenny verging on sleep, but in contrast to the homicidal paranoiacs who usually passed through her office on their way into the den of the Great White Hunter, Pumpernickel was a gem. He was also the biggest closet case she'd run into in her seven years at the Service. Only once had a whisper of scandal (involving a holiday to Greece and a rent boy) gotten as far as her office. She had stopped it cold with an elaborate tale of a top secret operation involving orders that had come from high above. Miss Tuppenny hoped that once Pumpernickel retired from the watchful eyes of the Service, he'd find a nice gent to share his snuffboxes with.

N. was standing by the window staring at the throng of early-afternoon traffic when Agent Pumpernickel walked in.

"Sit down," he ordered in his typically curt tone. He did not turn around. Pumpernickel could barely hear the buzz of traffic above the hammering of his heart. Using one of the button-size bombs on his coat to clear away the cobwebs at the fish finger factory had been a serious miscalculation on his part. How was he to know they were so powerful?

Pumpernickel had spent the morning in his office typing up his report while waiting for the police to show up and take him to the gaol, making him an object of ridicule and scorn to his colleagues. But they hadn't come. If he hadn't presented such a distraught figure in the lunchroom, blurting out his misdeed to 008, no one at headquarters would know he was the firebug. It was too late now; he had overheard two stenographers talking about it in the lift.

Pumpernickel feared he was about to be given a dishonorable discharge from the Service. A pension would be out of the question. Restitution would be impossible. He might even go to jail; someplace horrid like Wormwood Scrubs where they would make him wear paper slippers instead of his warm leather mocs.

He waited for N. to turn around and tell him: "You're of no use to us anymore. Sorry. It's been nice knowing you, but there it is."

Pumpernickel ground his nails into his palms. A reading lamp with a green glass shade made a pool of light across the blue paper blotter on top of the broad desk. A brown file with a red star sat on the blue blotter. He would never forget this scene, not as long as he lived.

There was a knock at the door. When N. turned around, his expression was impossible to read.

"Come in." Short and sharp.

Miss Tuppenny set a tray with coffee, buttered buns, a small pitcher of milk, and a bowl of sugar on the corner of N.'s desk. N. sent her away with a curt wave of his pipe.

"You play mother," he ordered Agent Pumpernickel.

"Black or white?" Pumpernickel could barely get his mouth around the words.

"White. Two lumps."

With sweaty hands, he poured two cups of coffee, then placed a buttered bun on each plate.

"Let's get down to the business at hand, shall we?" N. perched on the edge of his desk, tapped tobacco into the bowl of his pipe, and lit it. He put the pipe in his mouth and pulled at it. It flared, then went out. He reached for another match, and wasted some time getting his pipe going again. Then he leaned close, his face just inches from Pumpernickel's own. Pumpernickel could smell the tobacco on N.'s breath. A bubble of spit clung to N.'s thin lower lip. Pumpernickel thought N., with his small mean eyes and open-mouthed expression, looked awfully like a fish. Pumpernickel didn't like fish; they seemed so cold and slimy. A friendly little cat would suit him much better.

N. tapped the file on his desk with the stem of his pipe.

"Explain your actions, Pumpernickel," he finally hissed.

"There were spiders, sir, covering the door. My torch broke, and I couldn't see my way through. I tried to eliminate the obstacle with a small explosive device." Pumpernickel realized how idiotic his explanation seemed in light of the damage he had caused. The fish finger factory was nothing more than charred ruins.

"It was a somewhat ill-advised decision," he added lamely.

"Spiders?"

Pumpernickel shifted uncomfortably in his chair. "I have a terrible fear of them, sir, and of all things creepy-crawly."

"Oh, yes. That mission in the South Pacific where you nearly went nutters."

"You remembered, sir," said Agent Pumpernickel with a sense of relief. So N. did understand.

"Awfully long ago, wasn't it?"

"Phobias can last a lifetime, sir."

"Indeed."

"Please don't discharge me, sir. I've only three days to go before retirement."

"You made a mess of it, man." He had no intention of discharging Pumpernickel, but the man didn't have to know that yet. It would be good for him to get a little moist about the collar. Keep him in line.

Tears began to course down Agent Pumpernickel's face.

"I'll go to the police and turn myself in. I'll make complete restitution. Only please don't discharge me!" Meeting the queen had been his dream for as long as he could remember. Having the opportunity taken away would be a far greater punishment than a stint in paper slippers.

"That won't be necessary," N. said, realizing he had gone too far. He needed Pumpernickel to be at the top of his game right now. The building meant nothing.

"Anyone can make a mistake. Why, I even made one once."

N. bared his teeth, like a dog about to bite. Pumpernickel was alarmed until he realized that N. was smiling. He hadn't noticed before how really bad his teeth were. Poor bugger; no wonder he always looked so stern.

Pumpernickel felt a flood of affection for this man, a man who for years had sent other men into perilous situations without showing a twitch of emotion. Behind those cold blue eyes was a real flesh-and-blood person. He relaxed in his chair, took a big gulp of coffee, and almost choked on a sugar cube. He swallowed it whole, praying N. hadn't noticed his sputtering. He hadn't. N. was absorbed in the file on his desk.

"Let's see what you've found out about Miss Jane Bond," said N.

Name: Jane Honoria Bond, 35, unmarried
Place of Residence: The Flora Beaton Residential Hotel for Distressed Gentlewomen, No. 7 Beesborough Place, Chelsea SW1, Rm. 217
Eyes: Black
Hair: Dark brown, slightly wavy, medium length
Complexion: fair with olive undertones
Distinguishing features: Favors mannish dress
Born Liverpool, 2 May 1930. Only daughter of Sylvia Bond, deceased, and James Bond, Sr., deceased. One brother, James Bond, aka 007, age 35, Secret Service Agent attached to the elite double-0 group.

Subject has held a variety of jobs, including a six-month stint as a London bus conductor from which she was dismissed for impersonating a man in order to avoid wearing the blue serge dress required for female conductors. She is currently employed as a clerk in a bookshop.

Between approximately 10:00 A.M. and 6 P.M., Tuesday through Saturday, subject is at Crispin's Books, 131 King's Road, Chelsea SW1. During the week Subject spends her evenings at "The Gateways," also known as "The Gates," a members-only club that caters to a largely homosexual clientele. She has been observed in the company of a number of different females. Subject has been detained by police on nine occasions in the last six weeks for public drunkenness and behavior unbecoming to a lady. Subject has £7.3.5 on account at the Bank of England and is two weeks past due on her rent.

Known associates:

• Simon Crispin, 42, bachelor. Proprietor, Crispin's Bookshop.
Police record:
1949 conviction for cottaging. Sentenced to nine months Wormwood Scrubs.
1956 arrest for impersonating a police officer. Fined and released.
1961 conviction for selling indecent books. Fined and released.
Member: The Homosexual Law Reform Society, Greater London Zinnia Association.

• Miss Edith Liversidge, 72, spinster. The Flora Beaton Residential Hotel for Distressed Gentlewomen. Retired BBC stenographer.
Police record:
1918 arrest with Miss Emmeline Pankhurst for suffrage protest at Buckingham Palace. Fined and released.
1921 removal from the gallery of the House of Commons for shouting pro-vote slogans. Fined and released.
1925 arrest for pelting Lord Mortimer Finhatten, a member of the House of Lords, with rotten eggs. Sentenced to three months Wormwood Scrubs.
1955 arrest for willfully disrupting a Yorkshire foxhunt. Fined and released. Banned from all further foxhunts for life.
Member: The Cat Reform League, The Society for the Prevention of Cruelty to Cats, The London Association for Kitten Foundlings.

"Some pretty rough trade," N. murmured. He sorted through a stack of materials: photographs of Jane engaged in various activities, fingerprints lifted from a bottle of stout, a terse letter regarding the sale of a house, and three torrid love letters from someone named Bunny. N. curled his lip in disgust when he came across a picture of Jane locked in a clinch with a willowy brunette. Pumpernickel had snapped it inside a bar with his hidden carnation camera.

"This paints a pretty picture of English womanhood, eh, Pumpernickel?" N. grimaced as he held up the photograph.

"Yes, sir," Agent Pumpernickel squirmed. He developed a deep and sudden interest in his shoes.

"England's not a man's world anymore," N. lamented. "It's this permissive society. We're all supposed to be so bloody broad-minded—well, never mind. Now, this girl entering Bond's residence—"

"Last night's paramour, sir. I was rather surprised when I ran her through the records." Pumpernickel handed N. another folder. This one was purple. It meant that the person described within was a member of the nobility, and, as such, must be treated with kid gloves.

N. whistled when he opened the folder.

"Lady Bridget Genevieve Norbert-Nilbert St. Claire, daughter of Emerald Norbert-Nilbert Smythe-Pargeter St. Claire, the Duchess of Malmesbury and England's best-known hostess?"

"Yes, sir," Pumpernickel admitted unhappily. Taking telephoto snaps of a lady was, to his mind, a disgraceful pursuit. He had thought he recognized the girl at the bar, but when he had developed the pictures, he was certain of it—she was the daughter of one of England's favorite hostesses, a woman whose career he had followed for years.

N. looked delighted. If there was an attachment between the two, he could use it to his advantage. The girl could come in handy if Miss Bond needed a little shove in the right direction. Surely her noble girlfriend wouldn't want the shameful details of her lesbian love affair to be splashed all over the *Mirror*. And with photos, he thought wickedly.

Name: Lady Bridget Genevieve Norbert-Nilbert St. Claire, single career girl. Sales representative for Powder Puff Cosmetics, 1973 Kingsland Rd. E2

Place of Residence: The Royal Arms Flats.

Eyes: Green

Hair: Reddish-blond

Complexion: Peaches and cream

Police Record: None

Member: Royal Ascot Advisory Board, Orphan's Aid Society, Hospital Visiting Association, The Opera Club

Subject is the only child of society hostess Emerald Norbert-Nilbert Smythe-Pargeter St. Claire, the Duchess of Malmesbury, great-grandniece to Lady Sophia Montacute of Spain, and a cousin 27 times removed from the House of Windsor.

N. shook his head in disgust. "It's a sad commentary on English society when the queen's cousin has to ply cosmetics door-to-door."

"Yes, sir."

"Good job, Pumpernickel. I think this little plan of mine will work brilliantly. It's quite ingenious, don't you agree?"

"It's a fine plan, sir." Actually, it had been Pumpernickel's, and when he had proposed it, N. had laughed. But that was neither here nor there.

"Pick up Miss Bond. Bring her in. I'd like to have a little chat with her."

"Right away, sir. Thank you, sir, for, um, understanding about the explosion."

N. didn't say another word. His head was bent over a stack of reports. In deference to the queen's portrait hanging behind N.'s desk, Agent Pumpernickel bowed, then backed slowly out of the room.

Crispin's Bookshop
2:47 P.M.

Simon came back looking even more discouraged than when he had left.

"No loan?"

"No, but I was asked to lunch."

"What happened?"

"Our eyes met. His knee brushed mine—"

"About the money."

"Costs are up, sales are down. He recommends I stock up on plastic jewelry and paper dresses. And my three arrests didn't exactly impress his superiors."

"I thought you've only been arrested twice. You've been holding out on me, Simon."

"I like to keep a little mystery in our relationship."

"Do you realize I've been arrested more in the last fortnight than you have in your entire life?"

"It's not a competition, Jane." He sighed. "I can't pay you this week."

"Don't worry about me."

"How many tins of spaghetti have you eaten this month?"

"Oh, it's an old family recipe. Besides, Astrid's buying my half of the house—the first payment should be here any day. We'll split it."

"Absolutely not."

"Simon, listen to me. How many times have you rescued me? How many nights have I slept on that ugly couch of yours because of a dustup with Astrid?"

"You don't like our furniture?"

"Something good will come along; it always does. Cheer up—maybe the Council to Extirpate Moral Turpitude will ban another book."

Every time the minister of morality got fired up about a "dirty" book, business flourished. Hundreds of copies of *Dikes of Holland* had flown out of the shop a few years back before the police arrived to shut them down.

"Maybe we can even start the ball rolling ourselves. I'll drop a few well-placed hints with my landlady, and before you know it, indignant clubwomen and their vicars will be picketing us. We won't even need an actual book; all we need to do is spread a rumor that we're getting in a torrid tale of perverse desires. It will be full of heaving bosoms. It'll jump right off the shelves."

"Why don't you just write it?"

"That would take too long. We need money now."

Lunch was a sad affair; potted-meat sandwiches and tea.

"So, what are you doing tonight?"

"I thought I'd get soused and see if there's anyone at the bar I haven't slept with," said Jane. She went back to studying an old geological map of England she had found in a dusty textbook. She was comparing it to a recent London street map. "Look, Simon—Mrs. Snipe's house is built in an area that was once marshland. Do you know what that means?"

"That our little chat this morning about you mending your ways has already been forgotten?"

"It means that the soil under her foundation is all damp and squishy." She looked triumphantly at Simon. He looked puzzled.

"Which means that if she did want to dig a hole big enough to hold a body, it would be entirely possible."

Simon was just about to suggest Jane get another hobby when the phone rang.

"Bet you it's a creditor." He groaned.

"I'd advise you not to throw around the few bob you have left," Jane said tartly as she snatched up the receiver.

"Crispin's Free Unasked-for Advice Service. How may he help you?" she asked in a pleasant, singsong voice. Then, "Excuse me? Did you say you have gas?"

Jane put her hand over the mouthpiece.

"What do you recommend for gas, Simon?" she asked. A muffled voice came through the receiver.

"What's that?" Jane asked. "Oh—I see. You're from the gas company. Well, of course you have gas; we would expect no less of you. Thank you for calling. Good day."

She hung up. "How much do we owe them, Simon?"

"Not nearly as much as we owe for the electric," he fretted.

"Stop worrying. It causes wrinkles. Astrid's check will be here by month's end. We'll pay the bills and all will be forgiven."

"And in the meantime? We haven't had a customer in more than an hour."

The phone rang again. Jane picked up the receiver, barked, "Wrong number," and slammed it down.

"In the meantime," she said, "we'll go to the cinema."

"You're in a better mood. You didn't do anything you shouldn't have, did you? Like agree to get back with Astrid?"

"I haven't thought of her for minutes," Jane assured him. "Come on, let's go. Your choice."

"Even?—"

"Even that." Jane sighed.

Secret Service headquarters
Office of Miss Tuppenny
4:26 P.M.

008 lit a cigarette, drew the smoke deep into his lungs, and exhaled with a prolonged, annoying hiss. He had arrived forty minutes early for his appointment, and had spent the time since making a general nuisance of himself. First he had eaten all the toffees from the bowl on Miss Tuppenny's desk, leaving the pink cellophane wrappers on the floor in a ring around his chair. Then he had made several lame passes in her direction, all of which she ignored; borrowed numerous ciga-

rettes, which he needed help lighting; and was now engaged in biting his fingernails to the quick. He reminded Miss Tuppeny of a rabbit caught in the crosshairs of a shotgun. He was all twitch and shudder. She had the urge to shoot him, but instead smiled thinly at his latest witticism, put in her earplugs, and turned on her Dictaphone.

"What happened to the other double-0 agents?" he wondered aloud. His thumbnail was bleeding a little. He had three spots of crimson blood on the front of his shirt. He had been a nervous wreck since talking to Agent Pumpernickel in the lunchroom, where 008 had heard some very interesting information. Why had Pumpernickel been sent out on a top secret assignment, and not 008? And what did Bond's sister have to do with any of it? It didn't make any sense. Pumpernickel must have exaggerated the importance of his so-called mission.

"Excuse me?" Miss Tuppeny turned down the volume on the weapons report she had been transcribing.

"There are only two of us—007 and me. Where are the first six?"

"Scattered about," Miss Tuppeny replied. She got back to work. Really, these tapes had to be typed up before day's end.

"They've retired to the country on their pensions, eh? Growing roses and all that."

"Not quite." The very patient Miss Tuppeny looked at the nervous young man awaiting his first private interview with the boss and turned off her Dictaphone. She'd just have to stay a little late to finish her work.

"Agent Pumpernickel was 001. It's obvious why he was called back from the field."

008 was surprised to learn that the doddering old fool who wore white socks with dark suits and kept a collection of rubber band balls on his desk had once been part of the elite double-0 team.

"002 was found during the war floating down the Rhine. Well, what was left of him."

008 blanched.

"004 fell prey to a lethal injection of Philopon, a Japanese mind-control drug that induces an acute persecution complex. He jumped out of a hotel window in Tokyo in Fifty-seven when a maid entered the room unannounced with a stack of clean linens," Miss Tuppeny said crisply, adding, "005 ejected from his aircraft over the Russian Sea. Apparently he neglected to pack his shark repellent."

008 loosened his narrow brown tie, as if to get more air. Miss Tuppenny poured him a cup of water from the pitcher on her desk.

"What about 006?"

"Death by lead poisoning."

"At least he didn't die on the job."

"It means having been shot," Miss Tuppenny said dryly. Really, if he insisted on being a secret agent, he was going to have to learn the lingo.

"Double-0 must be an unlucky title." 008 was worried. "Aren't any of them alive?"

"003 is." She paused. "Well, he's presumed to be alive."

"Presumed?"

"003 vanished into the Dirty Half Mile in Singapore ten years back, and hasn't been heard from since."

"Good God." 008 blinked stupidly.

"Until the body is located, he's considered an active agent. He's accruing holiday time as we speak." A red light on the white telephone on Miss Tuppenny's gunmetal-gray desk started to flash. Miss Tuppenny picked up the receiver.

"Yes, sir. Right away, sir." She then pushed a button on the underside of her desk. The lead-lined door to N.'s office swung open.

"It's time," Miss Tuppenny told him.

008 pulled himself together as best he could, and strode into N.'s office.

As the door shut behind him, a pretty brunette entered Miss Tuppenny's office wheeling a handcart containing the weekly diplomatic bags from Istanbul, Washington, and Tokyo, and a stack of brown folders with top secret red stars. For N.'s eyes only. Miss Tuppenny briskly signed a chit acknowledging the delivery, and the girl left. Not a word had passed between them, but Miss Tuppenny had caught the hint of a smile playing at the corner of the girl's mouth. She had news.

It was time for Miss Tuppenny to powder her patrician nose.

The second-floor powder room was large and airy, equipped with three commodes, two fainting cots, and a coffeepot. Secretaries from all three floors congregated there several times a day to comb their hair, refresh their makeup, and share interesting tidbits picked up around their particular sector. The "powder vine," the men called it.

Security considered the powder vine a potential security risk, but N. thought gossip was just one of the by-products that came with hiring females, and no more disruptive than the occasional hysterical outburst at one's desk. Better they gossip among friends, he reasoned. Surely it was little more than the typical feminine babble regarding romantic liaisons and pretty new dresses. If, on occasion, a girl did accidentally repeat important information, it wouldn't come to much.

"For God's sake, they're not highly skilled agents, they're young, public-spirited girls who answer phones and file papers and type up encoded transmissions that they couldn't possibly understand."

What harm was some idle chitchat if it kept them happy, and made them feel part of the drama and romance of the world of important men making important decisions? Besides, they recruited only the best girls to fill the lesser posts at Secret Service headquarters. Who could be more loyal than the daughters of the aristocracy—patriotic debutantes, sisters of agents, even wives, although Secret Service Agents were encouraged to stay single. This sometimes made it hard to weed out those with homosexual tendencies, but N. prided himself on his ability to sniff out a nelly boy right off the bat.

There were really only two principal secretaries who had access to the innermost secrets of the Service: the trustworthy-beyond-a-doubt marvelous Miss Tuppenny, and the peculiar Miss Bettina Loomis, who oversaw the girls in the Department of Records. Miss Loomis was a sourball with sallow skin who had sat behind a big desk in the sublevel basement registry room for years, wearing the same apple-green button-up sweater and irked expression each and every day. Every year at Christmas the boys sent her a bag of lemons as a joke. Miss Tuppenny could be trusted with the most intimate state secret, and Miss Loomis, well, no one spoke to her unless they were trying to get her to drop the drawbridge and let them pass. She'd die with her secrets intact.

Miss Pinkerton from the first-floor steno pool was powdering her pert, kittenish nose when Miss Tuppenny walked in. Miss Tinkham from Supplies was lying on the couch with a cold cloth over her eyes.

"Tink, are you sick?"

"Yes I am, Tupps. Sick of immature Secret Service boys and their temper tantrums," she replied with a sigh.

Miss Pinkerton explained. "That new rat-faced boy in your division made a scene in the cafeteria and tossed tea all over Tink's new suit."

"Two pounds four shillings on sale at Harrods. I waited six weeks for it to get that low!"

"How rude." Miss Tuppenny frowned slightly as she dug in her purse for her lipstick. It was a new color for her—Rubyfruit Red. The name was a trifle wild, but the color suited her fair complexion quite nicely.

"I overheard Agent Pumpernickel say he accidentally set a fish finger factory on fire while on a secret mission," Pink confided.

"Pumpernickel on a secret mission?" Tink said in surprise. She sat up and the cloth fell to her lap. The tea stains on her skirt would probably never come out. She sighed. She'd have to dye the suit.

"The fellow from Desk Accessories who's always locking himself out of his office?"

"The same."

"Did N. say anything to you, Tupps?" Tink asked.

"Not a word. I have no idea what's going on."

"I'll bet he was bragging to impress the boy," Tink suggested.

"Perhaps," Pink said. "But he did smell rather fishy."

Secret Service headquarters
Office of Sir Niles Needlum
4:33 P.M.

"But sir, don't you think it's a waste of my training?" 008 pleaded. He had just been informed that he was to be Agent Pumpernickel's replacement as head of Office of Desk Accessories.

N. glared at the boy. "008, you have shown an alarming propensity for whining about your assignments. I have no position on my team to offer you at this moment. I advise you to return to your office and do the job that's been given you. Your turn will come."

"When, sir?"

"Patience is a virtue, 008. Or haven't you heard?"

"But I've been patient for a whole year now."

"Good gracious, lad, a whole year! Why, we've had agents imprisoned behind enemy lines for a whole year who never uttered one word of complaint. Men who were chained to walls and never allowed to sleep and who existed on a diet of gruel and mealworms."

At that moment, 008 thought it a better fate than following in the footsteps of Agent Pumpernickel. "Dear God," he had thought when first setting foot inside Pumpernickel's office and laying eyes on Pumpernickel's shrine to the royal family. It was understandable that very senior officers should display the queen's portrait; she was, after all, their boss. But candles and a kneeler? Pumpernickel was clearly demented; how he had lasted this long in the service was a great mystery to 008. And why N. had chosen Agent Pumpernickel over him for a special assignment was an even greater mystery.

"I know Agent Pumpernickel is on assignment," he said defiantly. "I think you owe me an explanation as to why I wasn't chosen instead."

N. raised an eyebrow at the lad's effrontery. This meeting would definitely go in his permanent record. "What makes you think Agent Pumpernickel is on a mission?"

"There's a field surveillance kit in the boot of his car."

"Were you authorized to examine his boot?"

"No, sir. I took it upon myself to investigate his recent peculiar behavior."

"I'm touched by your concern, 008." The sneaky little bastard would make an excellent secret agent some day. "However, your assumptions are off the mark. Agent Pumpernickel is not on a secret mission. He's using government equipment to spy on women; snapping them in their intimate apparel."

"That poofter?"

N. nodded sadly. He unlocked his middle desk drawer and pulled out a purple file. He showed 008 a photograph of Bridget in her knickers, bra, and go-go boots.

008 whistled. "That dog! And we all thought he was a flaming queer." He felt a spark of respect for the old 'Nickel.

"He is nothing of the sort. Poofters wear silk shirts and walk in a mincing manner. Have you ever seen Agent Pumpernickel mince?"

"He does creep a little, sir."

"Creep, yes. Mince, no."

"But he wears slippers at the office, sir." That alone made Pumpernickel suspect. There were just some things men did not do.

"They're not ballet slippers, are they?"

"No, sir. Good brown leather."

"There you go. Everyone knows poofters don't like leather." N. buzzed his secretary.

"Miss Tuppenny, get a "How to Spot a Homo" pamphlet from the files for 008 and bring it in here." He leaned back in his chair.

"Sir, I don't think I need—"

A rap at the door interrupted 008. The very attractive, very efficient Miss Tuppenny poked her head into N.'s lead-lined inner sanctum and N. waved her in. To Miss Tuppenny, the distance between the bullet-proof door and N.'s desk seemed to stretch for miles. She could feel two sets of X-ray eyes taking in every curve beneath her tailored cocoa-brown suit.

"Your pamphlet, 008." She wore her customary serene expression.

"That will be all, Miss Tuppenny," N. said. Then, to 008: "You're dismissed."

"Thank you, sir. I'm sorry I assumed Pumpernickel had taken an assignment intended for me."

008 knew immediately from the expression on N.'s face that he had spoken out of turn. After all, Miss Tuppenny was still in the room.

"Do you know what happens when secret agents assume?" N. snarled.

008 colored. He looked to Miss Tuppenny for help. She just smiled and quietly left the room. Word of his humiliation would be all over the building by tomorrow.

"Yes, sir," he said meekly.

"Well?"

" 'When we assume,' " he recited, " 'we make an ass of u and me.' " Blimey, this was worse than being called into the prefect's office for a whipping. 008 could almost hear the sound of his career being flushed down the loo.

"Now go, before I lose my temper and assign you the position of lunch lady!"

"Yes, sir," 008 concurred.

"Congratulations on your appointment to Desk Accessories," Miss Tuppenny called out warmly as 008 passed through her office. He ignored her.

Really, the boy ought to be taught some manners, Miss Tuppenny *tsk-tsk*ed as she turned on her Dictaphone and started to type.

Secret Service headquarters
Department of Records
6:22 P.M.

Once a week Miss Tuppenny, the most dedicated principal secretary the Secret Service had ever known, spent an evening putting disorderly files to rights in the room officially designated as the records depository, but nicknamed the "ant farm" by some long-ago employee who had gone mad after only a few months below ground. The name had stuck.

The girls who spent their days in the subbasement room (the so-called file queens) spent long days sorting, checking, filing, and distributing thousands of pieces of minutiae. Government-gray file cabinets were stacked to the ceiling. Cooled air was pumped in twenty-four hours a day so as to maintain the physical integrity of the files; it made for a somewhat chilly environment. Fluorescent lights gave the girls' skin—already ashen from long days spent underground—an unhealthy-looking green glow. The girls wore black smocks over their clothing to protect their outfits from dust, and those who handled delicate documents wore white gloves. Their constant motion was dizzying. They suffered from migraines, eyestrain, and paper cuts.

From 7 A.M. to 5 P.M., five days a week, dozens of girls were hunched over huge library tables reading the thousands of new documents collected each week. Their job was to categorize each tidbit and decide how it would be filed in the vast tomb. Other girls were kept busy scrambling up ladders, filing, and retrieving the folders. Outside the room was a track with a dozen trolleys that led to a special lift, so files could be quickly moved from dungeon to office and back again. For modesty's sake, the girls who operated the trolleys were permitted to wear trousers, as their job required an inordinate amount of bending over.

The boys upstairs believed that the enormous volume of information precluded any threat of leaks. It was assumed that as soon as a reader was finished with a document, she immediately forgot the contents and went on to the next one. So often the information was vague, or peculiar, or nonsensical: a scrap of paper with one word on it, in a hasty scrawl; the fingerprint of a Russian agent lifted from a cocktail glass; a spot of blood on a handkerchief.

Miss Tuppeny's head ached, as she hadn't had a break since afternoon tea. She had spent more than an hour climbing up and down ladders looking for missing documents. Agents were forever putting things back in the wrong folder. It was not uncommon for them to check out a number of files on disparate topics at the same time and mix up their papers, and it took quite a bit of work to correct the mess. Miss Tuppenny really was the best girl for the job; she had an amazingly keen mind for detail and a near-perfect photographic memory. N. often said that if she were a man she'd make a top-notch secret agent.

She located the first dozen errant documents on her list right off the bat; they had all been misfiled by 008, and Miss Tuppenny felt like wringing his scrawny little neck. She gave a little start when she heard the hand-operated lift start up, then realized it had to be the sweepers moving between floors. They were a team of retired principal secretaries who came in after hours to hoover the place and empty the rubbish bins. She was the only one on the lower level tonight. Sometimes X., the elderly but brilliant scientist who ran the Department of Spy Gimcracks and Gizmos, would tinker in his basement workshop after hours, but tonight she was all alone.

Secret Service headquarters
Office of Agent Cedric Pumpernickel
Director, Department of Desk Accessories
6:50 P.M.

The decline of a once-powerful and influential empire was a serious matter. Soon, though, it would be a matter with which the younger men would have to contend.

Agent Pumpernickel knew he would miss this place; miss the cacophony of the typewriters and the incessant ringing of the telephones. He munched on a chocolate-covered peppermint crisp; it was a favorite of the queen's and his. Mercifully, his final assignment was almost over. All he wanted now was to get home and have a good scrub. He had already decided to burn his suit, one of three that constituted his work uniform. The arm was scorched beyond repair, and he feared he would never get the smell out. He was retiring soon anyway—what would he need with three suits? A man only needed one to be buried in.

Burning down the fish finger factory had been a bit of a blunder on his part. He had panicked in the face of fear. Then, he had been in such a state, he had foolishly confided in 008. The boy had taken the news of Pumpernickel's mission rather badly. His reaction was understandable; the lad was champing at the bit to get out into the spy world. Still and all, his slip was a minor one. They were on the same side, after all.

It was time to start the chore of cleaning out his desk. He had brought a shoebox from home for his personal things. His tenure wasn't officially up for nearly another week, but there was no sense leaving it to the last minute. The Wedgwood cup and saucer in which he always took tea would need to be carefully wrapped for the bus ride home. His rubber band ball collection wasn't nearly as fragile, but he wanted to make sure he had all of it. The other agents sometimes borrowed one when they were low on rubber bands, not realizing that each ball represented months of hard work on his part.

He had been with the Secret Service his entire adult life, although he had originally wanted to go onstage, like his mother. Until she married Mr. Pumpernickel, his mother had been a regional actress who toured the countryside acting out biblical tableaux. Such was their love of acting, they had gone to the cinema two or three times a week, even on Christmas day. He had only signed up with the department to please his father, Ethelbert, who had been a code breaker during the war but had become too nearsighted to be a proper secret agent. After Pumpernickel's accident, it had been impossible for him to change careers; who would pay to see an actor with such a hideous scar? He probably couldn't act, anyway.

He had spent the years since in the Department of Desk Accessories performing routine office tasks. It was not the kind of job for which young, adventure-seeking men yearned; they all wanted to be assassins these days. They had no idea how important his work really was. They hadn't been around during the war years when pencils were almost impossible to get; now the young lads took their pencils a box at a time. Back then, once or twice a year, N. would call him to his office to ask if Agent Pumpernickel, the most trusted man there, would be willing to make one more small sacrifice for his king.

The answer was always yes.

8:00 P.M.

Miss Tuppenny took the lift to her third-floor office. The files were in order, except for two that had been checked out by 007 months ago and never returned. It wouldn't be the first time.

It was late, but Miss Tuppenny was determined to finish the job. Her tenacity was just one of the qualities that made her such a valuable principal secretary. What if an agent needed those files tomorrow, and they weren't available because they were stuck in Bond's desk drawer under his Turkish cigarettes and girlie magazines? Miss Tuppenny knew only too well that the success of a case could hinge on one small detail. So she removed a hairpin from her tidy bun and broke into his office.

It was just as she had suspected—the missing files were in his desk drawer, shoved under a pornographic magazine. Miss Tuppenny wrinkled her nose with distaste as she pushed aside the March 1963 issue of *Girlie Whirl*—there were aspects to 007's personality she'd rather not know about—and retrieved the files. She put everything back in place, and locked the drawer. No one would ever know she had been there.

The Coronet Cinema
Notting Hill Gate
8:17 P.M.

"That's the last time I'm seeing that movie," Jane vowed. "I'm starting to have a reaction to Julie Andrews. Look at my arm—it's all red."

"That's where I grabbed you when I thought they were going to be captured by the Nazis," Simon said apologetically.

"Simon."

"Yes?"

"How many times have you seen this movie?"

"Three. Four at most."

"More like twelve. Do they ever get captured by the Nazis?"

"They haven't yet."

"You need a new hobby. See you tomorrow." Jane laughed and headed for the Tube.

The Flora Beaton
A short time later

When Tessie Twigg had something unpleasant to report, she had all the fervor of a street corner missionary.

"Oh, Miss Bond! Miss Bond!" She leapt up from her place at the card table and raced through the lobby after Jane. Although the nightly whist game was in full swing, whatever Miss Twigg had to report obviously couldn't wait. Jane was tempted to run up the stairs and lock herself in her room, but her rent was a few days past due. Being nice was her only option.

"Yes, Miss Twigg?"

"There's a peeper in the neighborhood." She sounded almost gleeful. "Miss Perkins in one-A got a good look at him, and I called the police. They came out straightaway and took a report. Miss Perkins said he had the ugliest face she had ever seen, but he was nicely dressed; like a real gent. Mind you, I think he's the one who set fire to the fish finger factory this morning. They say sexual perversion and arson often go hand in hand."

Jane was sure that last part had been added for her benefit.

"Thank you for that bit of news," Jane said. She had to get out of this mausoleum soon, before she became one of the depressed zombies who shuffled through the halls in their carpet slippers and dressing gowns, with bottles of cheap sherry in their pockets. Jane decided she'd just have to break down and call Astrid. Not tonight, but soon. Maybe Simon was right; maybe Astrid did want her back. Jane realized, to her horror, that the longer they were apart, the better life with Astrid was looking. Maybe Astrid had changed. Maybe she finally understood what she had done to Jane. Maybe she was calling to beg her forgiveness. And maybe the queen would sprout wings and fly.

By nine o'clock, Jane had tidied her bedsit, eaten a packet of stale biscuits, smoked a half-pack of cigarettes, and been down to Miss Liversidge's room three times looking for company. On her last trip, after Tessie Twigg had scolded her for running through the halls, Jane remembered that tonight was Miss Liversidge's astral-projection class at the British Psychic Society. There was no telling when she'd return.

Jane considered, then rejected, ringing Simon; she had forced her misery on him and his lover, Byron, far too often lately. Besides, they could be so annoyingly happy at times.

She spent the next hour composing a letter to Astrid. She was chatty and pleasant, making it perfectly clear that she was doing splendidly, thank you. A short reminder, not too sentimental, of their happy times together followed. (Jane was a little depressed when she realized that most of them had taken place in the first two years of their three-year union, but never mind that.) Simon was probably right when he had said she and Astrid hadn't been all that happy. They hadn't been all that miserable, either. Five drafts later, she decided to just ring up Astrid and get it over with. A few quick jabs with her penknife and she was in Tessie Twigg's dumpy little office, which contained the only telephone in the building. She sat for a moment and got her wits about her, then dialed the telephone number she had been trying so very hard to forget.

For the last six weeks, Jane had been having the same fantasy. It began with Astrid begging Jane to forgive her. Their time apart had made Astrid realize that Jane was the love of her life. Jane, being the soul of generosity that she was, would indeed forgive her. They would make passionate love in positions they had not practiced for years. Jane would buy Astrid a new gravy boat. In years to come, they would speak of this time carefully, each understanding what they had almost lost.

"Hello?"

"Astrid?"

"No, it's Ruth."

Jane froze. In her imaginary conversations with Astrid, Ruth had never come up.

"Astrid's not home yet, but I expect her shortly."

Ruth's familiar tone made Jane's blood boil. She wanted to reach through the phone line and smack her former best friend.

"Care to leave a message?"

"Please tell Astrid that Nurse, er, Tessie Twigg from the County Health Board called and that her test was positive," Jane said in her best Twigg imitation.

"What test?"

Ruth sounded worried. She should be, Jane thought nastily.

Astrid's extensive extramarital activities were public knowledge; Jane had seen to that. It was some small consolation.

"I'm sorry, dear, but I'm not at liberty to say. Cheerio."

"Jane, is that you?"

Jane hung up, and burst into tears. She was daft. Astrid was probably calling her to talk about nothing more romantic than new plumbing for the house. She wiped her face on her shirtsleeve. Of course Ruth was living with Astrid; Astrid was incapable of blowing her nose without an audience.

Jane had a smoke while waiting for her face to return to normal. She stared at the flocked green water-stained wallpaper (circa 1918 or thereabouts) peeling in wide strips from the top of the wall. They looked like palm fronds. A hot ember from Jane's cigarette fell on the dirty white linoleum floor. Jane rubbed it with the toe of her boot, but it left a smudge. Tessie Twigg would spot it the moment she came in. Another black mark on Jane Bond's soul. Jane went upstairs and wrote a second letter. In it, she accused Astrid of every crime, aside from the two World Wars, known to mankind, and mustered all her civility to sign it "Sod off—Jane. P.S. And Ruth, too."

She posted it on her way to the bar.

The Gates
9:45 P.M.

Jane knocked on the metal door. A girl on the other side slid open the peephole cover and peered out. Jane flashed her pass. The girl let her in. Jane headed for the bar. There wasn't enough alcohol in this room to drink away her mood, but she'd give it a try anyway.

A bit later, standing at the bar

"I think you owe me a drink," a girl murmured in Jane's ear. Jane jerked around, almost spilling her pint of black and tan.

The gorgeous girl who had been in her bed that morning slid into the space next to Jane and leaned against the bar. She was wearing a sleeveless lime-green minidress whose only ornament was a long gold zipper that ran from neck to hem. It was not an especially long journey, as the dress ended well above her lime-green knee-high boots. She flipped her strawberry-blond hair behind one shoulder, and gave Jane a seductive but wary smile.

It was a typical Friday night; the place was jammed with people talking, laughing, flirting, and, in Jane's case, trying to forget. Jane was grateful for the company; the room was full of couples and she was beginning to feel like she stuck out. She put her hand lightly on the girl's smooth, tanned arm and leaned close to her. She had just enough liquor in her to make her bold.

"I think I owe you a lot more than that," Jane admitted bashfully. The girl's body gave off a perfumed heat. Bugger Astrid, Jane thought. She should aim higher.

"We'll start with the drink." Bridget laughed, clearly pleased. "Martini, please. With an olive. Stirred, not shaken."

Jane paid for the drink with the last bit of change in her pocket, and led the girl to a table in a dark corner of the large basement room. She was back in familiar territory.

When Jane pulled out a chair for her, Bridget realized that it was impossible to sit down in a micromini dress and remain dignified. This was the last time she would wear an outfit of Bibi's without test-driving it first. Thank goodness the outfit came with matching knickers.

Bridget realized Jane was staring at her. "This dress is awfully short," she said, blushing.

"You look smashing," Jane assured her.

Bridget gave Jane a bold once-over, and liked what she saw. Jane had a wide, slightly crooked smile and large, liquid dark eyes that—when they weren't glazed over from excessive drink—seemed warm and inviting.

"When you're not hungover, you're a very handsome girl," Bridget teased. Jane laughed, revealing a little dimple in her right cheek. They stared at each other. Bridget realized she was going to have to buy Bibi a new pair of lime-green knickers.

"I'm sorry I was such bloody idiot to you this morning," Jane started. She bent her head a little, shyly. An errant lock of dark hair fell over her forehead. Bridget had the urge to brush it aside. "I've never treated a girl that way."

"I'm flattered." Bridget sipped her martini.

Jane looked stricken. "Everything I say around you comes out all wrong."

"Why do you think that is?"

"You do own a looking glass, don't you?"

Bridget leaned over the table, fully aware that as she did so her zipper migrated south. When she saw the expression on Jane's face, she knew Bibi had been right when she said this was an outfit that paid for itself in just one date. She covered Jane's hand with her own small, cool hand, and stroked her palm with her frosty-white nails. She'd kiss her soon enough, but first Jane would have to squirm a bit more.

Bridget realized they were being watched. A tough-looking blond and a mousy brunette seemed riveted to the scene playing out at the table.

"Who are your friends?" Bridget asked Jane, gesturing toward the bar.

Jane looked over her shoulder. Astrid was standing with her arm around Ruth. She looked a little worse for the wear.

"My ex-girlfriend and her new lover," Jane said in a tight voice. She jerked her hand away.

Bridget took her compact from her purse and positioned herself so she could get a clear view of the infamous Astrid.

"Which one? The mean-looking blond or the dumpy brunette?" Bridget wondered. She gave her lips an unnecessary second coat of vivid pink lipstick.

Jane gave a sharp laugh. "The mean-looking blond. I caught her—"

"—in bed with your best friend Ruth. You broke her great-grandmother's gravy boat. You'll love her until the day you die."

Jane had the good grace to cringe. "I said all that?"

"Right before your bra came off."

Jane winced. "God, I'm sorry."

"Yes, I'd recommend dropping that line," Bridget suggested. She snapped her compact shut and dropped it in her purse. "Look out, she's on her way over here."

"Astrid? Oh, Jesus." Jane looked pained.

"Quick—kiss me."

"What?"

Bridget grasped Jane by the front of her shirt, and planted a big wet kiss on her lips. When she let go, Jane put one finger through the circular gold zipper pull and pulled her back for another.

"Hello, Jane," Astrid interrupted them.

Not only did Astrid have a dreadful name, she was rude, Bridget thought.

"Hello," Jane said, her eyes still on Bridget.

"Hello, you," Bridget murmured back.

Astrid tapped her short, blunt nails on the tabletop nervously.

Bridget looked amused. She leaned across Jane, making sure she got the full view revealed by the migrating zipper.

"Hi. I'm Bridget." She stuck out her hand.

"Astrid." She gave Bridget a weak shake with a moist hand.

If her hand were ever that clammy, she'd wear gloves, Bridget thought nastily.

"Did you say *Aspic*?" she asked innocently, batting her eyelashes.

Jane laughed.

"As-*trid*. Could I talk to you, Jane?" she asked in a pitiful little-girl-lost voice. Bridget wanted to strangle her with that tacky chiffon scarf she had tied around her neck. It was *so* 1964.

Bridget excused herself. "I think my nose is shiny."

"No—" Jane held her back.

"I'll be at the bar." Bridget gave Jane another kiss—for luck—and brushed past Astrid. She could feel Jane watch her walk away. She made sure she had something to watch.

"What do you want, Astrid?" Jane asked coldly.

In the last six weeks, they had exchanged a few letters about the sale of their home, but this was the first time they had actually seen each other. Jane had nothing to say to her ex-girlfriend; her letter said it all.

Astrid plopped down into Bridget's chair and looked at Jane with those big blue eyes that used to drive Jane wild.

"I'm busy, Astrid. Can't this wait?"

"I miss you, Jane," she said in a low, throaty voice—another thing that used to drive Jane wild.

Jane had been waiting weeks to hear that; funny, it didn't affect her one bit.

"You should. I was a great girlfriend."

"I know that—now." Astrid sighed prettily.

Jane realized Astrid was flirting with her. How nauseating.

"What about Ruth?"

"It's not working out."

"Does she know this?"

Astrid shrugged. Jane suddenly felt sorry for Ruth, realizing that even if she lived the rest of her life at the Flora Beaton, she was still better off than Ruth. She decided to stop hating her. She knew first-hand how very persuasive Astrid could be.

"Jane, I miss you so much." Astrid put her hand on Jane's. She was wearing the ring Jane had given her on their first anniversary. "You were the best lover I ever had."

"That's high praise coming from someone who's had so very many," Jane said.

"I deserve that." Tears welled in those big blue eyes. Six weeks ago, those tears would have broken Jane's heart; now they just infuriated her. Ignoring Jane's stony expression, Astrid leaned forward until her face was within kissing distance of her ex-lover.

"We were so good together," she murmured. "You know, in bed. I really miss that, and I was wondering, well, for old times' sake, if you'd come back to the bungalow and have a friendly shag with me and Ruth."

Astrid put her hand on Jane's thigh and slid it upward in a familiar manner.

Out of the corner of her eye, Jane saw Ruth. She was watching them with the same horrified expression that had most likely been on Jane's face all those weeks ago.

Jane put her hand on Astrid's and gave it a light squeeze. Then she gave it a harder one.

"Ow!" Astrid shrieked. "Jane!"

"Get your poxy hands off me."

Astrid rubbed her wrist. "But I love you, Jane."

"Right. That's why you tupped all our friends and tossed me out onto the street."

"You were always so angry, Jane," Astrid spat back.

"I'm finished, Astrid," Jane said calmly. "I don't like you enough to fight with you. Besides, I've got a date with that gorgeous redhead. Oh, and don't forget the money you owe me. Maybe you can get it from Ruth." Jane waved at Ruth. Ruth waved back weakly, then turned away.

"At least Ruth has the good grace to be embarrassed by that little scene you treated me to," Jane said caustically.

Astrid sat back for a moment, stunned, then cruelly slapped Jane, scratching her cheek with her long nails. Jane laughed. Simon always said that someday some girl would slap some sense into her. Who would have thought it would be Astrid?

Jane got up, slung her jacket over her shoulder, and tossed down Bridget's martini. There was no sense letting good liquor go to waste. Except for the part where she choked on the olive, Jane thought it was a rather smooth exit.

Three blocks west of Charing Cross Station
The Royal Arms Flats
11:39 P.M.

Bridget caressed the back of Jane's neck and gave her one last kiss.

"I'd ask you up, but I live with three stewardesses and frankly, I'm not in the mood for the competition."

"I don't think you have to worry about that," Jane murmured. She pulled Bridget back for another kiss. She was a tiny girl; a good four inches shorter than Jane. "Let's go to my place. The bugs will all be asleep."

"Maybe next time," Bridget demurred. She untangled herself from Jane and started up the stairs to a large concrete apartment complex; an ugly box of small flats squeezed between two old grand private homes. It was a step up from Jane's current home. When Bridget reached the top step, she turned around and said, very ladylike,

"Thank you, Jane, for a lovely evening. It was so nice meeting Astrid. I must say, I think your taste in girls has improved."

"Without a doubt," Jane agreed. She was rewarded with a sweet smile.

"Good night, then—"

"Wait—I don't have your number."

"I'll call you," Bridget said before turning around and going inside, leaving Jane standing on the street wondering if she'd ever see her again.

Back at the Flora Beaton
12:00 A.M.

Jane sat in her only chair—a threadbare pink horsehair monstrosity—staring out the window and smoking. Her room was dark. Each time she took a drag on the cigarette, her reflection was illuminated in the window glass. The image startled her. All she needed was a drink in her hand, and she'd be her father. The nights when he was home had all been spent in the sitting room, alone, quietly smoking and drinking.

There was a knock at her door. Jane frowned. What rule of Tessie Twigg's had she broken this time? She flung open the door, annoyed at having her bad mood disturbed, only to find Bridget St. Claire standing on the other side, looking a little apprehensive. And completely adorable. She was clutching a pink Powder Puff cosmetics case.

"I was wondering if you wouldn't mind helping me test our new line of lipsticks," she said shyly.

Ten minutes later

Bridget St. Claire slid one arm around Jane's neck, brushed away the comma of black hair that habitually fell over her forehead, and kissed her long and hard.

"And that," she murmured, a few minutes later, "is what Pussycat Pink tastes like."

"I think I need to try that one again." Jane said lazily as she slowly unzipped Bridget's dress. She put one hand on Bridget's right breast and slipped the other down the length of her spine. She held Bridget hard against her body and kissed her again.

"Okay, next," she said finally.

Bridget flipped open her compact, wiped the remains of Pussycat Pink from her lips, and applied a coat of Watusi White.

Jane pulled her closer. After Jane felt she had kissed her sufficiently, she let her mouth wander down the lovely girl, from her neck to the sweet cleft of her luscious breasts.

"I think we should move to the bed," said Jane. She took one last lick. "I can't get my neck to bend much farther."

Bridget pulled Jane up for air. "Pay attention. Now which is your favorite? Very Very Cherry, Go-Go Girl Green, Pussycat Pink, or Watusi White?"

Jane licked her lips. "Pussycat Pink," she said.

"You sure?"

"Absolutely."

"You're not just saying that so you can carry me off to bed and take advantage of me, are you?"

"No and yes, in that order."

"Then that's all I'll wear from now on," Bridget promised. "Unless it clashes with my outfit, of course."

Jane laughed. "I would expect nothing less from you."

Bridget purred happily. "We at Powder Puff Cosmetics thank you for your interest in our new line."

6 <u>SEPTEMBER</u> 1965

The Flora Beaton
Bedsit of Jane Bond
5:23 A.M.

BRIDGET was naked under the thin white sheet that hugged her body. She studied Jane in the pearly, predawn light creeping into the room.

"You have the funniest expression on that gorgeous face of yours," she said in a sleepy voice. Jane pushed back the sheet and fumbled for a cigarette. Damn. She had given her last pack to Miss Liversidge.

"Bridget, I want to ask you a question and I want you to tell me the truth—no matter what it is."

Bridget sat up. She tucked her knees under her, leaned back, and stared at Jane. Her eyes widened. "Okay," she said in a low voice.

"Is there anything I should know about you before, you know, before we go any further?"

A flash of emotion—was it guilt?—crossed Bridget's face. "As in— am I a duchess or a spy or something?"

"No." Jane rolled her eyes. "Be serious."

"You want to know if insanity runs in my family, don't you?"

"Does it?"

Bridget laughed. "Sure. All the best people have it."

"I was just wondering if, well, if you already have a girlfriend." Jane could feel a flush creeping over her ears. That was not at all how she meant to put it. She had meant to sound interested, but in a casual sort of way; the "already" part had just slipped out. She hoped it didn't make her sound too besotted.

Bridget laughed lightly. She looked at Jane, her wide green eyes narrowing to sultry slits. The sheet dropped to her lap.

"I think that's up to you."

9:34 A.M.

"Hide your eyes. Don't you dare peek until I've got my face on." Bridget wrapped the sheet around her body and picked up her purse. She took out her compact and examined her face in the small round mirror.

"I have you to thank for the shadows under my eyes," she told Jane happily. "Tonight we've got to get some sleep."

"I promise I'll have you in bed by half-past seven."

Bridget arched one shapely eyebrow at Jane, who was lying crossways on the bed, then opened a jar of cold cream. She paused, a dollop of it on her finger.

"I don't think I know you well enough to do this in front of you," she said.

"That's not what you said last night," Jane protested as she rolled onto her side and slipped her hand under the sheet.

"Save it for later," Bridget said gently, removing Jane's hand from between her legs. She needed a clear head this morning. She kissed Jane's palm before handing it back.

"Now, out! I've got work to do." Bridget pulled Jane off the bed, gave her a lingering kiss, and pushed her toward the door. Jane found her surprisingly strong.

"Go down the hall and do whatever it is your type does in the morning. Come back in twenty minutes. I'll give you a ride to work on my scooter, and along the way, you can think about what you're planning on doing with me tonight."

Jane sat on the edge of the tub, already dressed, trying to gather her wits. She didn't even know where to begin figuring out what was wrong with this picture. This was happening far too fast. Jane should get out now, before she lost the little bit of her heart Astrid had left intact. Trouble was, once you got a taste of Pussycat Pink, there seemed to be no turning back.

Bridget was creamed, cleaned, powdered, and painted in less than five minutes. She was a professional, after all. She put her hair in a simple chignon, tucked her knickers into her purse, and slipped on the wrinkle-resistant, drip-dry daisy dress she always carried in her cosmetics case in case of emergency.

Then she locked Jane's door.

Jane had a stack of unopened mail on her mantel that looked promising. Bill, bill, advert—ah, a letter. Bridget turned up her nose when she got a whiff of the cheap floral perfume on the envelope. Some girls had no taste.

She took a long, thin hairpin from her bun and inserted it into a tiny gap on the side of the envelope where the flap glue hadn't taken (a trick she had picked up from her mother). Expertly, she rolled the paper into a thin scroll, and drew it out of the envelope. She was immediately sorry she had. It was a rather cloying letter from a love-struck girl who couldn't understand why Jane hadn't called after they had shagged. It was all there, down to the most lubricious detail, and it was signed, "XOXOXO, Bunny."

"How very juvenile." Bridget sniffed. She had half a mind to destroy the vulgar squib. Instead she put it back inside its stinky envelope and returned it to the mantel. Jane must never suspect she had interfered with her things.

A check of Jane's coat pockets revealed nothing more than bits of tobacco and a matchbook from the Gates, the scene of their first encounter. Some pushy girl had scribbled her number on the back. Bridget was relieved to see it was hers.

Next came the small bureau. The two bottom drawers held only clothes. The top drawer was more enticing. It was stuffed with a jumble of objects: pencils, a half-empty pack of chewing gum, a Violet Crumble, pay packet slips, an overdue rent notice, and a bundle of letters tied with a blue ribbon. Bridget was prepared to be nauseated— they were most certainly from Astrid. She was charmed (and relieved) to see they were from an elderly aunt. Bridget opened a Thorne's Toffee tin decorated with three gray-and-white kittens on a bright red background. (She had had that very same tin as a child; when the toffee was gone, she'd stored her diary in it.) Inside Jane's tin was a snapshot of a pretty woman in a flowered dress holding the hand of dark-haired twins—a girl and a boy. They were standing on a seaside promenade. TORQUAY, 1938, someone had written in pencil. Under the picture was a faded death notice, dated 11, May 1943.

Mrs. Sylvia Bond, 42, in hospital Monday last. Survived by husband, James Bond, and children, James Jr. and Jane.

"Her name is Bond," Bridget said to herself. "Jane Bond." She stared at the boy in the photograph. Even at age eight, James had a cruel glint in his eyes. Had he dreamt, even then, of the life of a killer? Bridget put the snapshot back in the tin, but kept the yellowed clipping.

Jane called to her from outside. Bridget put the drawer in order, took a deep breath, and stuck her head out the window. Jane was just as attractive from this view.

"Are you gorgeous yet?" asked Jane. She was with a rail-thin, elderly woman holding the fattest cat Bridget had ever seen. They were both puffing away like chimneys.

"Just about. Look here, that's an awfully nasty habit you've got going," Bridget scolded Jane.

"I've got a lot of nasty habits," Jane assured her.

"I'll be right down. Do you have your key?"

Jane shook her head. "Don't bother—I don't have anything worth stealing."

Bridget shut the window and made a quick scan of the room to make sure everything was in place. Perfect. Jane would never suspect a thing. Then she opened her pink marbleized Lucite compact, with its gold double-P emblem, and spoke quickly, but distinctly, into the transmitter concealed there.

"Agent St. Claire calling Agent Gallini. I repeat, Agent St. Claire calling Agent Gallini."

"Agent Gallini here," came a girl's sleepy voice.

"Fancy a coffee before work?"

"If you're buying I'm your girl."

Before snapping the compact shut, Bridget redid her lipstick. Jane was right. Pussycat Pink *was* her color.

In northeast London, in a plain, two-story warehouse, are the offices and laboratories of Powder Puff Cosmetics, a small company that produces quality cosmetics sold directly to the customer. Each day, a small army of girls in mod pink minis hop on their equally pink scooters and travel door-to-door, offering free beauty consultations. An unobtrusive brass sign to the right of the front door reads POWDER PUFF COSMETICS, LTD. PLEASE RING.

This modest enterprise is, in reality, the London headquarters of the Greater European Organization of Radical Girls Interdicting Evil (G.E.O.R.G.I.E.), a group of brave girl spies whose sworn mission is to stop people like N. and his chauvinistic, bumbling cronies from destroying the world.

A cosmetics company had proven to be a brilliant cover. Its agents could travel as far as their scooters could take them without raising suspicion. What housewife would dream that the friendly girl knocking at her door with a cosmetics case in hand and a clutch of free samples in the other was really a dedicated spy? Not once in G.E.O.R.G.I.E.'s sixteen-year history had a Powder Puff Girl been questioned. Their potions and lotions were authentic. Well, at least the ones in the pink-and-gold containers were. A second, deadlier set was packaged in cobalt-blue glass for easy identification. It would never do for a G.E.O.R.G.I.E. Girl to use the wrong Femme Fatale lipstick—say, Kiss Me Deadly or Farewell My Sweet—on an innocent customer. The sales of the real cosmetics not only provided them with an ingenious cover, it kept their operation afloat. Espionage was an expensive pursuit.

Loon's Teashop
Off King's Road
11:20 A.M.

"Oh, I'm having such trouble!" Agent Bibi Gallini collapsed onto the chair across from Bridget and folded her arms across her chest. She looked thoroughly exasperated.

"Love trouble?" Bridget said sympathetically. She was in such a good mood.

"If only I had the time. It's my hair! I'm testing the new batch of bulletproof hair spray, and it's impossible to get out. It makes me mourn the passing of the beehive, which was practically bulletproof all by itself. Now we've got to empty a bottle of this spray on our heads just to get the same resistance factor."

"I had a similar problem with the new invisible-ink top secret cipher panties," Bridget told her. "The ink was far too strong and a rise in my body temperature set it off. When I got out of bed this morning, I had a map of East Berlin printed on my arse."

Because of budget constraints, G.E.O.R.G.I.E. agents personally tested all the products invented in the Powder Puff laboratories by

Miss Bluma Trell, a retired public school chemistry teacher. Everything from Nite-Nite Skin Cream (made of milk and honey and a gentle sleeping potion) to the new Femme Fatale lipstick line, made of six vibrant colors that covered a spy girl's every need, was put through a rigorous trial before earning the pink-and-gold Powder Puff label. Everyone especially loved the single-shot lipstick-tube gun; Bluma Trell's girls couldn't make them fast enough.

"And my feet are killing me!" Bibi moaned as kicked off her ankle-high white plastic boots. She was exhausted from a morning spent demonstrating eyeliner application to a group of young, bored Royal Navy wives whose husbands were at sea. Lonely women talked, and it was Agent Bibi Gallini's duty to listen.

"Any sales?"

"Six, and a very pretty captain's wife slipped me her number," Bibi grinned. "Her husband's in Borneo for the rest of the year." Bibi was forever falling in love with married women.

"Bibi," Bridget scolded, "remember what the boss said at the last staff meeting about dating the customers? Remember the sticky situation with the Sloane Square matron?" Bibi was a charmer; all she needed to do was get one boot in the door, and soon the lady of the house was pouring out her troubles while being mud-masked.

"But she looked like Audrey Hepburn. And she was very lonely. She said so when she pressed her card into my palm." She batted her eyes at her friend. " 'I'm *so-o-o* lonely.' "

Bridget rolled her eyes. She adored Bibi—everyone at G.E.O.R.G.I.E. did—but when it came to love, Agent Bibi Gallini had the attention span of a fruit fly.

Bibi flagged down the sweets trolley passing their table. She selected the chocolate pudding and ordered an orangeade over ice.

"I love Audrey Hepburn," Bibi said dreamily as she licked the creamy pudding off her spoon. "Her dressmaker really knows how to show off those gamine features of hers."

"She's scrawny." Bridget sniffed. "She does have beautiful clothes, though. I wish we could get Givenchy to do our uniforms."

Bibi laughed. Everyone knew that Bridget positively loathed the pink vinyl minidress G.E.O.R.G.I.E. agents were required to wear as part of their Powder Puff Girls disguise. Bibi thought they were sexy in a kittenish sort of way, and surprisingly comfortable in warm weather.

The white mesh peek-a-boo strip around the waist kept the plastic dress from being too hot. Bridget thought the outfit made them look like they belonged in cages at some downtown club, doing the Frug.

"Nobody takes us seriously in these getups. We're just silly birds on scooters."

"*Pink* scooters," Bibi rubbed it in. She merrily slurped her drink, then crunched a piece of ice. She didn't care what people thought of her. "Poor Bridget," she added. "It must be hell having such high standards."

"That's *Lady* Bridget to you." Bridget stuck out her tongue. She was the only member of the sales staff who knew firsthand how dry the queen's skin really was. Each year for Her Majesty's birthday Lady St. Claire sent the queen a large jar of Miracle Moisturizing Cream. Each year she received a gracious note thanking her for the splendid product.

Bibi changed the subject. Bridget was awfully touchy when it came to the topic of her social standing.

"Anything interesting happen last night after I left the bar?"

"I hooked up with Jane again."

"Miss Tragic Romantic? Yesterday you loathed her." Typically, it was Bibi who was dotty over about some girl. She had flung herself on her desk in tears so many times, she had all but put a dent in it.

"Did I?"

Bibi looked at her suspiciously. Bridget seemed awfully cavalier today.

"I thought she drank too much and was in love with her ex."

"I took care of that," Bridget said. "After last night, I think Astrid is just a bad memory."

"I've never liked the name Astrid." Bibi wrinkled her nose. "It sounds too much like 'aspic.' "

Bridget concurred. "Or 'asterisk.' And what would you call an Astrid for short? Ass?"

Bibi snorted. A dollop of pudding flew across the table in a decidedly unladylike fashion. After she stopped laughing, she said, "I had an aunt whose husband hated her name so much he refused to call her by it."

"It wasn't Astrid, was it?"

"No. Shirley."

"What did he call her instead?"

"Gertrude."

"You'll never believe what I found in Jane's flat."

"You're such a snoop," said Bibi.

"It's an occupational hazard," Bridget said somewhat defensively. (In truth, she was a born snoop.) "It's fine with me if you don't want to know—"

"What did you find?"

Bridget reached into her purse and took out the death notice. Bibi whistled when she read it.

"Will you tell the chief, or shall I?" said Bibi as she slid it back across the table to Bridget.

"Let's keep it our little secret, shall we? I see no reason to mix business with pleasure."

"Bibi, do you ever wish you were in another line of work? One with regular hours so we could have a real home life, without all this awful secrecy, where we could talk about our day?"

"Only every time I wake up alone," Bibi said.

Bridget gave her a sharp look. Bibi meant it. There was a lot more under Bibi's bubble hat than she let on.

"It's too bad our romance fizzled, hey, Bridget? Everything was going so well, and then it just fell apart for no reason."

"Bibi, we broke up because you borrowed my favorite 'Chanel' cocktail dress for a date with that girl from Product Packaging, and got clam sauce all over it."

"Which bothered you more?"

"I don't know."

Bibi laughed. She picked up her pink vinyl Powder Puff Cosmetics sample case—she had an appointment for a bubble bath demonstration—and sashayed out of the cafe.

"Don't forget to pay the bill, Duchess," she cried over her shoulder.

Secret Service headquarters
Office of Agent Cedric Pumpernickel
12:07 P.M.

"In this first cabinet are files A through M, beginning with 'automatic pencil' and ending with 'manila envelopes.' Now, you may be asking yourself, "Why this particular system? Why not file this information under 'pencil, automatic,' and 'Envelopes, Manila?' Well, I'll tell you—"

"That won't be necessary," 008 sneered, looking at Agent Pumpernickel with something akin to murder in his eyes.

"Oh." Agent Pumpernickel seemed disappointed. "Well, we'll move on, then. This next cabinet contains N through Y: 'naugahyde chairs' through 'yellow legal pads.' As you can see, there is no Z. I have never been able to locate an office supply beginning with Z. I so wish I had; it was a little goal of mine to complete the alphabet before I retired. Alas, it was never meant to be.

"I hate leaving with a sense of incompleteness," he continued. "These files really should read from A to Z. The file dividers came labeled that way, but I finally gave up in 1957, and discarded the Z. I hate waste, don't you? After all, paper doesn't grow on trees." He paused. 008 realized Agent Pumpernickel was waiting for him to laugh. He had probably waited years for the opportunity to use that line.

"Ha, ha," 008 said weakly.

Pumpernickel smiled. "At the end of each week," he continued, "I stay late to take inventory of the supply closet. I like to know what I'm missing. 'Always be prepared'—that's the motto of the man behind the Desk Accessories desk."

008 felt like jumping out the window.

Crispin's Bookshop
12:20 P.M.

Mrs. Snipe had a bee in her bonnet. She huffed into the bookshop, her back ramrod straight and her face contorted with indignation. She then slammed a copy of *Lady Chatterly's Lover* on the counter.

"I'm here to return this book. Last night I read the whole thing from cover to cover, and I found it most obscene!"

"I'm so sorry, Mrs. Snipe," Jane said. "I realized after you had left that I had given you the wrong book. I do hope your delicate sensitivities weren't too offended."

"You needn't worry about me; I'm quite a woman of the world. But I do not wish to have this kind of reading material in my home where others might see it. Especially the charwoman," she added, lowering her voice.

"Would you like to look around, or shall I just credit your account?" Jane asked politely.

Simon was in the back restocking the mature-reading shelf, listening to the exchange in amazement.

"I'll look around."

"Very well. Let me know if you need any help. By the way, that's a lovely outfit you have on, Mrs. Snipe."

"It's a Harris Tweed," Mrs. Snipe informed her, sounding pleased. "I picked it up at Martha Manning for a song. I could take you there if you like."

What was Jane up to? Simon wondered. He poked his head out from behind the curtain.

"Jane, may I see you for a moment?"

"Excuse me, Mrs. Snipe. I'll be right back and then we can continue our discussion."

Mrs. Snipe preened. There was nothing like a good tweed to reinforce social distinctions.

"Jane, did you have whiskey for breakfast again?" Simon's voice was low and strained.

"I'm just chatting up the customers like you said."

"Why are you being so nice to her? You're scaring me. *'That's a lovely outfit you have on, Mrs. Snipe.'* Jane! You hate tweed!"

"Tweed's not so bad." Jane shrugged. "It's certainly nothing to get worked up about."

"You haven't been snooping around her cellar again, have you?"

"No! And I haven't been drinking."

"Or—?"

"Not that, either. Can't I just be nice to Mrs. Snipe without causing suspicion?"

"No. It's unnatural." Simon stared at Jane. If she wasn't drunk or high, there was only one explanation for her behavior.

"You're in love!" Simon hissed.

"I am not!"

"Yes, you are! You met someone, didn't you? You have a new girl-friend!"

"I had a date last night, that's all."

"You've already fallen for her. I can see it in your eyes. You look so strange, so *happy.*"

"Aren't you tired of me being a miserable sod?"

"Of course I am. I just don't want you to get hurt again."

"How could I feel any worse than I did? Besides, she's crazy about me. You should have heard her last night when Astrid came over to our table at the bar. Her claws came out. It was an inspiring performance. No one's ever defended me like that before."

Simon looked hurt.

"I mean, no one I've slept with."

"What's her name?" He sighed.

"Bridget."

"Bridget what?"

"Let me think a minute."

"*Jane!*"

"Have you ever thought of having children, Simon? You're such a mother hen."

"I've considered it. But they say you never really do get your figure back."

The bell over the shop door chimed.

"Jane, there's someone here to see you," Mrs. Snipe trilled. "It's important."

"I bet it's Astrid with my money," whispered Jane. "After last night she probably wants nothing to do with me."

Jane pasted a smug smile on her face and parted the curtain. Her knees went all wobbly when she saw it was Bridget. From the top of her pink vinyl cap to the tips of her square-toed, midcalf shiny white go-go boots, she was a vision. Her strawberry-blond hair was styled in a saucy flip that framed a determined-looking jaw, and her lips were full and rather sulky in appearance. It was the kind of mouth people used to call sinful, a mouth just begging to be kissed. The overall impression of a pet waiting to be stroked was leveled by wide green eyes that shone with intelligence and strength. She looked expensive, and a bit headstrong, and very kissable. Loving her would be very agreeable, Jane thought.

Simon dug his elbow into her rib. "Is that *her*?"

Jane nodded.

Simon had never seen Jane so thoroughly undone. "Go out there and say hello," he said, giving her a shove.

"Jane, this girl is a Powder Puff Cosmetics Girl," Mrs. Snipe announced. She had an intense look of concentration on her face, like a falcon homing in on its prey.

Bridget was clearly embarrassed. "I was getting you sticky buns," she stammered, holding out a paper sack.

Simon took them gratefully. "I'm Simon. Jane's older sister."

"I'm Bridget St. Claire," replied Bridget, not missing a beat. "Jane has said so many lovely things about you."

Simon looked pleased. She was cute and polite and employed.

Mrs. Snipe cried, gesturing at Jane, "Just look at her, why, sometimes I don't know if I'm seeing a Martha or an Arthur!" Mrs. Snipe sighed dramatically. "Now, Jane, I know we've had this discussion before, but a little window dressing couldn't hurt anything, now could it? Just because a girl isn't pretty doesn't mean she can't make something of herself. Why, the Duchess of Windsor is homely too, but she dresses with such style and flair, nobody notices."

"Thank you, Mrs. Snipe," Jane said coldly.

Bridget coughed, hiding a laugh. With a flourish, she put her pink vinyl cosmetics case on the counter and began rummaging through it.

"I'd start with a good moisturizer," Mrs. Snipe advised. "And something for those dark circles under her eyes."

"I don't need to slather myself with goo to get people to pay attention to me," Jane protested.

"True, it is hard to ignore someone when she's standing on a barstool, waving her glass and singing 'It's Not Unusual,'" Bridget teased.

Jane reddened. She had hoped Bridget wouldn't remember much from the night they had met.

"And a little something for that ruddiness," Mrs. Snipe thought aloud. "Jane, this could be your lucky day! This girl could be just what you need. You shouldn't keep your light hidden under a bushel."

"My bushel gets me into no end of trouble," Jane said, sighing.

Simon started to choke on a bun. Bridget buried her face in her cosmetics case and shook with suppressed laughter.

Mrs. Snipe took no notice. "So, will you take her on?" she demanded of Bridget. "I haven't all day. I have my tabletop topiary class to go to."

"My schedule's full, but I'll see if I can squeeze her in," promised Bridget.

A short time later, she left the shop with an order for two jars of Cucumber Peel-off Mask Frappé (Jane bought one for herself and one for Simon, as there was no sense in only one of them being fresh and new) and a date for that evening.

"Jane! How marvelous! I bet that girl can do wonders for you!" cried Mrs. Snipe. On her way out, Bridget had slipped Mrs. Snipe a small pot of vanishing cream to thank her for the new customers.

"It's not a makeover she's going to get," Simon said archly.

True, Jane seemed unmoved by the potential for beauty that the Powder Puff Girl's pink sample case so amply contained. Mrs. Snipe left for her class feeling sad that she hadn't been able to reach Jane. Poor Jane. Poor *plain* Jane. The way she was going, she'd never know the bliss of matrimony.

An hour later

"She seems awfully smitten with you," Simon noticed. "Be careful, Jane."

"Too late. I've already picked out the china pattern. Want to go to Harrods and put a down payment on it?"

"Really, Jane, I insist you—"

The shop phone rang, ending Simon's sermon.

"That's her," said Jane, grabbing for the receiver. "She misses me already."

"Hello, beautiful," she cried.

"Jane?" said a dull voice on the line. "It's Astrid. I want you to stop telling people I have a disease."

"I want you to give me back my house!"

"Bitch."

"Slag."

"Ignorant shop girl."

"Slag."

"Oh, Jane, you're such an original thinker."

"Oh, Astrid, you're such an enormous slag. And the funny thing is, for someone who's had so much practice, you're really a terrible roll."

That shut her up. For a minute.

"I'm calling to tell you not to expect any money from me. I've consulted a solicitor and I'm under no obligation to repay any of the down payment, as it was a gift."

"That was my inheritance!" Jane gasped. The house had been put in Astrid's name at the time of the purchase, as no bank would give Jane a loan.

"I'm not legally bound to pay you a penny," Astrid said in a haughty tone that reminded Jane of the worst of their fights.

"What about a moral obligation? Oh, I forgot. You have no morals. I should have kicked your arse down the steps along with Ruth's!"

"You have one week to get the rest of your things out of my house. Ruth and I are redecorating in the new mod colors and don't want any of your aunt's hideous Victoriana. Please ring first before coming by."

Jane slammed down the phone. It rang almost immediately. Astrid must have thought up another insult. She had quite a filthy mouth for a schoolteacher.

"What?" said Jane wearily.

"Is that you, Jane?" This time it was Bridget.

"I'm afraid so."

"Are you all right?"

"Fine now that I hear your voice."

Simon winced and held up his hands.

"You're so sweet," Bridget purred. "It makes what I have to say all the more difficult."

Jane braced herself. "Your girlfriend found out about us?" she joked weakly.

Simon looked aghast. He grabbed a piece of paper and wrote I TOLD YOU SO! in big block letters.

GO AWAY! Jane wrote back.

"Honey, you know there's no one else. I might be a little late for our date tonight."

That "honey" made something inside Jane's stomach go flip-flop.

"I'll wait," Jane promised.

"I'll make it worth your while."

"I'm sure you will."

Simon tugged on Jane's shirtsleeve.

"Hold on—I'm just been passed an urgent message. My friend Simon wants to know if you're any relation to the renowned Lady Emerald St. Claire."

"I told you there was insanity in my family." Bridget laughed.

A short time later, at the Mouldy Crown

Jane pushed aside the greasy paper piled with fish and chips. She was too angry to eat. Simon sat with his head in his hands, ignoring his bangers and mash.

"I'll burn that house to the ground before I let her have it," Jane swore.

The couple at the next table exchanged worried glances.

"Forget I said that. I'm going to kill her instead."

The couple quietly moved to another table.

"You could never kill anyone, Jane. Remember that time you borrowed my bicycle and hit that dog? You were unhinged for days. And it wasn't even really hurt."

"I think it's somewhat uncharitable of you to compare Astrid to a dog," Jane retorted. "Dogs are loyal."

"You'd better eat," Simon said, tucking into his lunch. "It could be your last meal for a while."

Jane shivered. "You make it sound as if I'm going to the gallows."

"The poorhouse is more like it. Do you have any proof of half-ownership in the house?"

"I have canceled checks somewhere."

"Good. That will help. Tomorrow you'll go see a solicitor friend of mine. Astrid's not going to get away with this. I don't understand it, anyway. Jane, are you sure you didn't cheat on her?"

"I wish I had."

"I never really liked her, but she always seemed like a decent enough person. I knew she was jealous of our friendship, and pretty rigid in her views, and not all that terribly bright, but I never before thought she was evil."

"Thank you, Simon, for that unbiased opinion."

"This new girl had better treat you well."

"I've learned my lesson," Jane swore. "At the first sign of trouble, I'm gone."

Secret Service headquarters
Office of Sir Niles Needlum
1:23 P.M.

"Of course Bond is going to be there!" N. bellowed into the phone before slamming down the receiver. In truth, that morning's progress report on 007 had been disheartening. Not only did Bond refuse to believe he was sick, he was acting as if he were on holiday. A nurse had already been fired for smuggling Champagne and caviar into his room.

N. got to his feet and flung open his door. "Where the hell is Pumpernickel?" he barked at Miss Tuppenny.

"He hasn't rung in yet today, sir."

N. scowled. He had sent Agent Pumpernickel out for Miss Bond yesterday. If they were to use her, she'd have to be brought in soon.

This was all Pumpernickel's fault. He had the idea to chat her up first before approaching her with their plan. N. thought the idiot should just drug the girl and throw her in the boot of his car. Cooperation was all well and good, but force worked wonders. He unlocked his confidential drawer and took out a folder marked BOND, JANE; MISS, and reread the dossier Pumpernickel had compiled. It would have been obvious to a child that Miss Bond was financially embarrassed. Her employer was on the verge of bankruptcy, she was living in a pigsty, and N. had more coins in his pocket than she had in the bank. If she balked at helping them, a mention of money would put everything to rights.

Thirty minutes later

"Sir, your new plastic rubber tree plant has arrived."

"Pardon?"

"I noticed the other day that your rubber tree plant was looking rather tatty around the edges, so I took the liberty of ordering you another."

"Splendid, Miss Tuppenny. Good thinking."

Miss Tuppenny wheeled the new tree in on a trolley, and traded it for the dusty old rubber tree plant that had sat in a corner of N.'s office for years. She took a cloth and a small jar of cold cream from her pocket and started to polish the leaves.

N. looked at her queerly. "What are you doing?"

"It keeps the dust off, sir," she explained. "And makes it shiny."

"Jolly good, Miss Tuppenny. You're always one step ahead of me."

"It's my job, sir."

"Will you be here much longer?"

"There are thirty-seven leaves on the average rubber tree plant, sir. I may be awhile."

"Have I ever told you how much I appreciate—how much we all appreciate—your work here?"

"Never, sir."

"Well, then—" He cleared his throat. "Good show, Miss Tuppenny. Good show."

"Thank you, sir. That's high praise coming from you."

Despite what the naysayers might think, N. thought girls made a splendid addition to the Secret Service. Girls were refreshingly simple creatures who noticed even the most inconsequential detail; it was what made them so good at filing. That and their small hands. And as for Miss Tuppenny, well, who else but Miss Tuppenny would have thought to order a fresh plastic rubber tree plant? Place couldn't run without her.

London Zoo
Regent's Park NW1
ANIMALS FED DAILY
2:50 P.M.

The man hanging around the monkey cage gave Jane the creeps. He was wearing a dark coat buttoned to the neck, and his hat was pulled low over his face. He looked like a vicar or a child molester. Or both. When he looked up she realized it was the shy snuffbox collector from that morning.

Jane had coffee while watching the fish in the indoor aquarium swim soundlessly around and around in circles. They seemed perfectly contented to do so. This soothed Jane in a way she could not explain.

She turned and started to walk away, hoping the man wouldn't pester her for his uncollected change from the day before; she wanted to mope undisturbed. But she was too late—he had spotted her.

"Miss Bond—wait up," he cried as he ran toward her.

"I don't have it with me," Jane said. "You'll have to come by the shop."

He looked puzzled.

"Your change from the book. You left yesterday without it."

"Care for a peanut?" he said. "They're for the gnus, but I don't think they'll mind."

"No, thanks," Jane said.

The man stood there, obviously uncomfortable. Jane didn't know why, but she felt a little sorry for him. He seemed lonely.

"I just ate," she explained.

"Oh. What did you have?"

"Cold fish and chips."

"I was to have a meat sandwich for lunch, but I left it on the bus," he told her. "Mashed pork with a special pickle relish my mother invented."

Lonely people were always telling Jane the small details of their days; she knew from experience that it made up for the fact that there was no one at home to listen to these things.

"I like to watch the lions being fed," said the man between nibbles from his peanut bag. "They're such majestic animals. Pity they've been hunted so."

"I like the leopards best. I can't believe people make coats of them."

"It's really we who are the wild animals, don't you think?"

"My father told me once that animals kill only for survival. People kill for all sorts of other reasons."

"We had kittens once when I was a lad. My father drowned them in the bathtub."

"That's horrid." Jane shuddered.

"My father was a military man," he said by way of explanation.

The conversation took a definite downturn.

"I'd better be getting back to work," said Jane.

He paused. "I'd like to offer you a job, Miss Bond. My card—"

Secret Agent Cedric Pumpernickel
of
Her Majesty's Secret Service
London Office

She handed it back. "And I'm the queen." She laughed derisively and a bit uncomfortably. This chap was no more a secret agent than she was.

"I work with your brother," he explained patiently.

"My brother works at Amalgamated Widget."

"That's what he'd like you to think, Miss Bond."

"And that's good enough for me. Good-bye, secret agent man."

"Your brother—"

"Haven't heard from him, and what's more, I have no interest in his affairs." Dear old James had probably gotten some poor stenographer preggers, and this nutcase was here defending her honor. Jane turned her back on him and started walking toward the Tube stop.

"Wait, Miss Bond. I have something for you," the man cried anxiously. He took a thin blue envelope from the breast pocket of his coat and held it out to her.

Jane rolled her eyes in disgust. Now for the truth. He was either a bill collector or some religious fanatic trying to sell her a place in heaven. Neither interested her. "If it's a bill, I'm strapped, and if it's a religious pamphlet, the answer is bloody hell no. Peddle it somewhere elsewhere," she said impatiently.

"Pigheadedness must run through the entire Bond family," Pumpernickel said peevishly.

"We all have short fuses, too," Jane warned him.

"You're just as difficult as your father!" Pumpernickel blurted out.

That got Jane's attention. "Who are you?"

"I'm Secret Agent—"

"Right. Pull the other one."

"You don't believe me."

"If you're a secret agent—and I doubt it—how did you know my father? He was a shoe salesman."

"Yes, he was. We were friends. Secret agents wear shoes too, you know. Rubber-soled ones, to be exact."

"How do I know you're telling me the truth?"

"I visited your home once when you were a child."

"I would have remembered you."

"It was summer. There was a swing in the back. And you had a dog. Winnie, I think. She had enormous ears, like a bat. She followed you everywhere."

"Her name was Minnie," Jane said, amazed.

"That's right. Minnie."

She stared at his face.

"I was much younger then," he explained. "I've aged."

"You do look familiar," Jane admitted.

"I'm a little difficult to miss," he said, tilting his head so his scarred right cheek was toward Jane.

Suddenly she realized where she had seen him. He had come to her father's funeral. And he had wept uncontrollably.

"I remember you," she said suddenly. "From the funeral."

He blanched at the mention. "I was greatly shocked by the suddenness of his death," he said sadly.

"So was I," said Jane.

Agent Pumpernickel held out the envelope. "Please read this, Miss Bond. If you don't want the job, you can walk away. But I must give it to you."

"If I do, will you leave me alone?"

He nodded.

Jane snatched the envelope out of his hand and tore it open. Inside was a piece of onionskin paper. Jane read the typewritten message twice, just to make sure she wasn't hallucinating.

Chief Commander Admiral Sir Niles Needlum of Her Majesty's Secret Service requests a meeting with Her Majesty's subject, Miss Jane Honoria Bond, at her convenience.

"If this is a joke, I'm not in the mood."

"I assure you, it's not."

"Did my brother put you up to this?" Jane said with some disgust. Never the best of friends, they had had a falling out years ago over their Great-Aunt Honoria's will. She had left everything to Jane: trunks of musty clothes, a box of tins filled with the ashes of her deceased pets (all small, stinky dogs), and enough money for a down payment on the house in Ruislip, the one now occupied by the evil Astrid. Astrid had happily accepted the money, but had fought Jane tooth and nail when Jane had tried to create a pet cemetery in their garden.

"James is in hospital. He had an allergic reaction to a . . . a novelty item," Pumpernickel explained hastily, "an off-brand prophylactic."

Jane laughed. This was the first bit of information she had no trouble believing.

"Everything will be explained when we get to headquarters."

"Explain it now," she said.

Pumpernickel looked around furtively. The zoo was deserted. He took off a shoe, held it up to his ear, and pulled the lace. A moment later he began murmuring into the sole.

Jesus, the loonies who were allowed to run about London unfettered, Jane thought. She started to back away slowly. If she made a dash for it, she could be at the Tube stop in a few minutes.

"Yes, sir. A little trouble, sir. Am I authorized to be truthful? One moment—" He held out his shoe. "Miss Bond, Sir Niles would like to speak with you."

"I'm not speaking into your shoe."

"Just say hello."

Jane started to back away. "Not a chance," she said.

"All right." He sighed. "Sir? No, sir. Yes, sir. I understand. Sir? No, no more fires. Over and out." The man chuckled as he slid his shoe back on and tied the laces.

"The Secret Service needs your assistance, Miss Bond. We will need only a few days of your time, and in exchange you will get the satisfaction of having served your queen. Few people ever get to come that close to Her Majesty. It's an honor, really, to be asked."

"I'm really quite satisfied with my relationship with the queen."

"May I have the letter back?"

"Why?" Jane held the sheet of paper behind her back.

"Because all communiqués are highly confidential and must be destroyed." He was becoming a tad agitated. This girl was even more vexing than her brother!

"What if I want to paste it in my scrapbook?"

"I wouldn't do that if I were you, Miss Bond."

"Why not?"

"Because it is due to self-destruct in exactly"—he checked his watch—"five seconds. Five—four—three—two—one—"

"Bloody hell!" Jane dropped the letter. The damn thing was on fire! She watched as it charred into embers, then blew away.

"You see, Miss Bond, once you open the envelope, the self-destruct mechanism is activated. I hope you didn't burn your hand." He tried to give her his soppy handkerchief. Jane pulled away.

"Miss Bond, I've been authorized to offer you a generous fee for your cooperation. We're willing to pay a portion straight away, as a good-faith agreement. This very afternoon, if you like."

He had to know about Astrid's phone call. The bookshop's line was being tapped.

"And if I say no? Will you resort to blackmail?"

Agent Pumpernickel chuckled. People saw too many ridiculous movies about the spy trade.

"Miss Bond, we are a government agency; we do not blackmail Her Majesty's subjects into working for us."

"What is this job you want me to do?"

"You'll have to come to headquarters if you want to know any more."

"Does it involve anything illegal?"

"Heavens no, it's government work!"

"Is it dangerous?"

"My superior would never ask you to do something that would put you in harm's way."

"I need to think about it."

"Think quickly, Miss Bond. Sir Niles is not a man who likes to be kept waiting."

Jane checked her pockets. She was down to three pence. "Fine. I'll listen to what he has to say."

"Splendid. We shouldn't be seen leaving the zoo together. Meet me at the tea stand catty-corner to your shop in half an hour. I'll put a red carnation in my lapel, in case you don't remember my face."

Remember his face? She wouldn't be able to forget it.

"And I'll have a rose in my teeth," said Jane.

"Jolly good, Miss Bond. Jolly good."

Jane was on the Tube when she realized what it was about Pumpernickel that made her sad. He reminded her of her father. She had a picture of him somewhere; he was only twenty at the time, but he already had the face of a man bitterly disappointed by life. With strangers he had been all fun and games, at home, secretive and quick-tempered. A few months before he was killed, he had slipped into a melancholy silence so impenetrable that by the time he died Jane was already accustomed to mourning him. He had loved her mother a great deal, of that she was certain, but he'd made her miserable with his bad moods and bouts of silence. When she died, he was left with a sullen, angry son who had run off to fight as soon as he was of age, and a daughter he couldn't even begin to understand.

G.E.O.R.G.I.E. headquarters
3:10 P.M.

Agent Bibi Gallini parked herself on the edge of Bridget's desk, and read aloud from the magazine in her hands.

" 'Reporter Abby Lancock interviews the Duchess of Windsor from her palatial French chateau regarding the state of world affairs, life in exile, and recent fashion trends.' Shall I continue?"

"Must you?"

"Did you know the duke has his shoelaces ironed every day?"

"Don't we all."

"And when they dine out, they consider it patronizing to tip."

"It figures."

"And the duchess refuses to discuss her exile in the Bahamas during the war. And I quote: 'Across such hideous scenes I draw a veil.' "

"She should be our next poet laureate," Bridget said dryly. "Now, will you go away so I can get some work done?"

"With the amount of sex you're getting, I should think you'd be in a better mood," Bibi said snippily.

"Go away."

"Before I do, I have one thing to say. I think Pussycat Pink is definitely your color, too." She giggled.

"Where did you hear—oh, no, I must have had my transmitter on!"

"You used to tell me everything, Bridget. Lately you're so secretive. Now I have to spy on you if I want any information."

"I'm sorry, Bibi. I have a lot on my mind these days."

"And her name is Jane," Bibi retorted. She dipped into her purse and handed Bridget a reel of audiotape.

"Here, I made you a copy for those long, lonely nights when we're on assignment."

"Bibi, sometimes you go too far!" said Bridget, blushing angrily.

"I was just joking. I would never tape someone else having sex. It's a studio copy of a Dusty Springfield session."

"Sorry."

"Sure you are." Bibi pouted.

"Bibi, are you really upset with me?"

"I'm just bored."

"Then go cause trouble somewhere else."

Secret Service headquarters
Office of Miss Tuppenny
3:20 P.M.

N. strolled into Miss Tuppenny's office and leaned against her desk the way the other fellows did when they were trying to cozy up to her. She put aside the stack of confidential memos she was secretly memorizing, and gave him one of her "I'm busy but never too busy to talk to you" smiles.

"Miss Tuppenny, I've decided to close the office a little early today. I want you to put on your coat, grab your handbag, and go out and have some fun."

"But, sir, I have so much work to see to."

"Nonsense. I think the empire will still be standing come morning. You must stop working so hard. I insist. Go have your hair done. Or buy a hat."

"Thank you, sir."

"See you bright and early, then."

"Good night, sir."

"Good night, Miss Tuppenny."

What was the old bugger up to? Miss Tuppenny wondered as she tidied her desk and put the dustcloth over her government-issue manual typewriter. Before she left, she pressed a button under her desk that switched on a wire that crept under the carpet that went through the wall that attached to the miniature microphone hidden in the rubber tree plant in N.'s office. Then she got her handbag and went to the powder room.

Miss Tuppenny was touching up her brows when Miss Loomis from Records walked in.

"Hello, Miss Loomis."

"Hello, Miss Tuppenny."

Miss Loomis walked to the sink. She had carbon smudges on her blouse sleeve.

"How are you?" she asked as she dried her hands, then scrubbed at the sleeve with a wet towel.

"Fine. And you?"

"Not bad, Miss Tuppenny. Are you doing anything exciting tonight?"

"Nothing really. I need to take up some hems. Dust my flat. You know—the usual." Save the queen's life, she thought inwardly. Bring down a fascist brotherhood.

"A woman's work is never done." Miss Loomis sighed as she ran a comb through her frizzy red curls.

"I couldn't agree more, Miss Loomis."

Miss Tuppenny took down her long, thick auburn hair, brushed it until it shone, then pinned it back into a neat bun. In this disorderly world, some days her hair was the only thing Miss Tuppenny could control.

En route to Secret Service headquarters
3:33 P.M.

They made their way down Gower Street toward Trafalgar Square. Jane slumped against the car door, suddenly exhausted by the events of the day. She wanted nothing more than to go home, crawl into bed, and pull the covers over her head.

"We'll be there shortly," Agent Pumpernickel burbled like the mother of a difficult child. He was greatly relieved that Jane had agreed to this. It appeared he was going to complete this assignment satisfactorily for all parties concerned.

"I'm retiring Monday," he confided to Jane. "And the very next day I'm departing on an autobus tour of the great estates of northern England. I've been meaning to go for years. We were to start in the Cotswolds with the magnificent Wooley-Booley estate, Grouse Manor, but that's been taken off the tour route due to renovation. Have you ever toured our great estates? I only ask because often schoolchildren are taken by bus to see them. I do think the tax levied on the estate holders should be removed. Someone's got to keep up these magnificent reminders of our past. What do you think, Miss Bond?"

Jane thought Agent Pumpernickel drove like her great-aunt Honoria, but even slower; only, he was tall enough to see over the dash. Aunt Honoria had had to sit on an orange rubber pillow that looked like a giant donut. Jane had wanted to bury it with her, but the vicar, who had never met Aunt Honoria and so didn't realize how very attached she had been to the pillow, had refused.

"Miss Bond. Are you feeling a little under the weather?"

"It's been a very strange day," she explained.

"Do tell me about it. I'd be happy to listen."

"I wouldn't know where to begin," Jane admitted. She cranked down the window and opened a pack of cigarettes.

"Fag?"

"Yes, thanks."

If this bloke is a secret agent, he should drive a little faster, Jane thought. Everyone was honking at them; it made them awfully conspicuous. He should change out of that moth-eaten trench coat and bowler hat, too. It made him look like an extra in a bad spy movie. If this was a prank, she was going to kill James.

Jane wished she had called Simon to tell him what she was up to. What if this Pumpernickel chap was crazy, and she ended up floating in the Thames? Who would tell Bridget? Why was she thinking of a girl she hardly knew at a time like this? Damn Astrid. This was all her fault. Simon was so, *so* right.

"I say, are you feeling all right, Miss Bond?" Agent Pumpernickel asked.

"Not really," Jane admitted. "I'm a little nervous." And insane, she neglected to add.

"Shall we stop for a cup of tea? We've time."

"I don't think that will help my particular problem," Jane answered. "But thank you."

A few minutes later, Agent Pumpernickel turned into the unmarked entrance of a short block of anonymous-looking buildings. Sandwiched between the Tip-Tap-Toe Dance Studio and an Indian takeaway was an austere-looking granite building with a discreet brass plaque to the right of the door: AMALGAMATED WIDGET, INC. He parked his black sedan in front.

"This, Miss Bond, is the nerve center of the Secret Service; a place few civilians have been," he informed her in a reverential tone. "I shall tell you the procedure so that nothing comes as a surprise. The girl at the reception desk in the lobby will buzz us in. Then, although she sees me every day and knows who I am, she will ask for my credentials. That's how things are done here; top secret all the way. Only members of the Secret Service, who are sworn to protect Her Royal Highness, even know of the existence of this building."

"I know where it is," Jane pointed out.

Agent Pumpernickel gasped. "I forgot to blindfold you! Now you know where we are!"

"I won't tell anyone. Who would I tell? Who would even know to ask?"

"What if a foreign agent offered you a great sum of money to divulge the location?"

"Then I'd tell."

Agent Pumpernickel looked stricken.

"I'm joking," Jane assured him. "I've already forgotten where we are. Honestly, I wasn't paying all that much attention. I was thinking about—well, never mind. Let's just say my mind was elsewhere."

"Would you mind terribly slipping on this blindfold, then? Just until we get inside."

Secret Service headquarters
Office of Secret-Agent-in-Training 008
3:47 P.M.

By now 008 knew more than he had ever wanted to know—more than he had ever thought possible to know—about rubber bands. There existed, in Britain alone, seventeen rubber band factories. Agent Pumpernickel had given each company a try before settling on one supplier. Paperwork existed for each of the seventeen factories. In triplicate.

The mountain of files spread across 008's desk represented years of hard work on Agent Pumpernickel's part. Having failed as an assassin, Agent Pumpernickel had set out to do his very best in his new job. He had come to love it; not so much for the desk accessories themselves, but for the conversations he had with the salesmen. Over the years he had listened attentively while men told him about their lives. Each Christmas Agent Pumpernickel would receive more cards than any other person at the London office. Rumor was he sent the cards to himself, but it wasn't true.

"Bollocks! Does the man do everything in triplicate?" 008 groused. He was in a bad humor, and wanted nothing more than to go down to the shooting range and fire off some ammo. He was done waiting for Pumpernickel to show up and give him the next batch of files; the man was doling them out like candy to a baby.

008 decided to pick the lock to Pumpernickel's office and help himself. Pumpernickel would raise a stink, but 008 would deny having breached his security. Everyone had known for years that Pumpernickel was crackers; the news that he had been peeping was the icing on the cake. The man was clearly barmy.

Office of Agent Cedric Pumpernickel
A few minutes later

As long as he was there, 008 reasoned, he might have a peek in old 'Nickel's secret drawer. It was going to be his desk, after all. The drawer was easy to locate; every desk at the secret service had one in the exact same spot. 008 never bothered to lock his; all it contained was some chewing gum. He hadn't anything secret to hide—yet.

Pumpernickel's drawer was locked up tight. He probably stashed his rubber band balls in there, as he was forever clacking about everyone stealing them. Luckily, breaking and entering was the first skill 008 had mastered.

The drawer was open in a matter of seconds. It was a clean breakin; he had left no telltale marks. Inside were two files: one manila, the other purple. 008 put his feet up on the old oak desk and began to read.

Jane followed Agent Pumpernickel down an ordinary-looking hall-way with dingy institutional-green walls to an old-fashioned, self-operated lift. It clanked and wheezed up three flights before coming to an abrupt stop.

"I'm afraid our facilities are rather out-of-date. We're hoping some-day to afford a sleek new building like the FBI headquarters in Amer-ica," he explained apologetically as Jane rubbed the elbow she had banged when the lift lurched to a stop. "They give free tours to British agents. I'm hoping to go next year. I'm rather looking forward to re-tirement. I'll be as free as a bird."

Agent Pumpernickel stopped at an unmarked door.

"This is my office," he said proudly, as he fit his key into the lock. "I can't ask you in, but you can stand out here while I take care of a lit-tle matter." Agent Pumpernickel switched on the bright overhead light and gasped in surprise. 008 was sitting in *his* chair, with his feet on *his* desk.

"I came in for more files," 008 exclaimed as he jumped up. "I didn't want to search through your things, so I decided to wait for you to return."

Pumpernickel immediately went to the desk drawer where he kept his most top secret information, and his autographed picture of Julie Andrews. It was locked.

"No harm done, lad," Pumpernickel assured the younger agent. "Here's a new stack of files. I must say, your enthusiasm for your work is infectious."

008 edged out of the room, almost knocking Jane down. He glared at her, then darted down the hall.

"No doubt he was really after my rubber band balls," murmured Pumpernickel as they continued on their way. "I have a collection that dates to the mid-Forties. The younger lads like to tease me by remov-ing bands from the balls, so I measure them each morning to see if they've shrunk. It's just a little game we play to relieve the tension."

"Anything for Queen and Country," said Jane.

"Correct."

It was just as she had always suspected. The inmates were running the asylum.

Office of Agent-in-Training 008
3:52 P.M.

008 had irrefutable proof that N. had lied to him. He was being replaced, and by a girl! What a perfect little scene it had been—he had
just finished reading Pumpernickel's top secret files when he heard him
coming down the hall. *Clip-clop, clip-clop,* like an old horse Pumpernickel had sounded. He had recognized Miss Bond right off, having
spent more time poring over the photographs of her and her lesbian
lovers than he had reading the dossier. Blimey, she got more birds than
he did! It just wasn't natural.

Office of Miss Tuppenny
3:59 P.M.

Jane followed Agent Pumpernickel into a small, windowless office
painted a ghastly civil service green. Some poor soul had tried to
brighten it with a pot of plastic violets. The gunmetal-gray desk was
bare, save for three telephones: one red, one green, and one black.
Pumpernickel picked up the receiver of the green telephone.

"Sir, we're here." Then: "Yes, sir. Of course, sir. Whatever you
say, sir."

A light over a door flashed green. "Sir Niles is ready to see you now,
Miss Bond. I'll be here to take you home after. Now, don't be put off by
his demeanor; he can sometimes seem intimidating."

"Is it too late to change my mind?" wondered Jane.

"Yes!"

Office of Sir Niles Needlum
4:00 P.M.

A middle-aged man with parchment-pale skin and thinning blond hair
was seated behind a desk covered with files of all different colors.

"Sit down," he said, waving his hand in the direction of a worn
leather club chair. He didn't bother to get up. He extracted a file from
the clutter on his desk, opened it, and spent a few minutes reading.
Jane lit a cigarette and sat quietly, watching the smoke drift idly toward
the water-stained ceiling. It was just like home, she thought.

She stared at the maps pinned to the dark wood-paneled walls. The world had changed a great deal just in her short life. Maps had been pinned directly over the older version, making the walls look like the kind of relief map schoolchildren make of flour and water. It was like being trapped in a grim and shabby geography classroom.

The man finally looked up and glared at Jane with icy, pale blue eyes. He had deep worry lines etched in his forehead, and a slight twitch about his right eyebrow that gave him the look of a celibate clergyman.

"You must be Miss Bond. Thank you for coming. You're no doubt wondering why the British Secret Service has called on an average person like yourself."

"Not really." Jane shrugged. "Things like this happen to me all the time."

"Well, yes, ha, ha." N. moved his mouth in an approximation of a smile. "Now that we've enjoyed a moment of levity, let's get down to business."

"Please," said Jane.

"Miss Bond, I'm going to tell you something very few people know. But first you must promise me that this conversation will go no further than these four walls."

"I promise," Jane lied. She couldn't wait to tell Simon everything.

"You have been led to believe all these years that your brother James is a middle-management executive with Amalgamated Widget, Incorporated. In truth, his work is of a highly specialized and secretive nature that directly affects the health and well-being of the most beloved person in England."

"Benny Hill?"

N. clenched his teeth. "Her Majesty, Queen Elizabeth."

"Oh."

"You understand now why it's so important to keep this a secret."

"My brother works for the queen?"

"For Her Majesty's Secret Service. He's one of our most important men."

"What does he do—mix her martinis?"

N. glared at her. "I'm sorry to inform you that your brother has had an unfortunate accident."

"So I've been told."

"He's expected to make a full recovery," N. said. "We wish him all the best. But enough of that. I did not ask you here to discuss your brother. Our concern is this: Your brother's accident has put the queen in a precarious position. You see, within certain foreign circles—and without naming names, for your own safety, of course—there exist people with a lunatic hatred of England, and all things English."

"It's probably that nasty habit we have of taking over their countries," Jane suggested wryly.

N. struggled to control his anger. He knew the first time he had seen her photograph that Jane Bond was going to be trouble. She had a definite criminal face; all one had to do was look at those small ears.

"The point is, there is a very important royal appearance coming up and your brother's absence will make the queen all the more vulnerable," he lied smoothly. "He maintains a highly visible presence whenever she greets her subjects. Those who wish to harm our beloved queen know that as long as James Bond is around, Her Majesty is untouchable."

Only because he doesn't fancy her, Jane thought.

He handed her file. In it were black-and-white snaps of the queen greeting her subjects at a walkabout, presiding at corgi races, and opening the May biscuit toss. In each, James was standing nearby, a scowl on his face and a beautiful woman on his arm.

"James brings his dates along?" asked Jane, looking around in vain for an ashtray.

"They're agents," N. explained hastily. Cheeky girl! Pumpernickel could have done a better job inserting those cutouts of Bond into the photographs.

"Your presence at an upcoming event would be very much appreciated."

"How will my being there affect anything?"

"You won't be there as yourself, Miss Bond. You're going to play James."

She stared at him, speechless, until the burning cigarette singed her hand. When Jane swore and shook her hand, N. produced an ashtray made of a gazelle hoof.

"You can't be serious!"

"I'm hardly given to frivolity, Miss Bond, especially when it comes to matters involving Her Royal Highness. Of course, your participation is entirely voluntary. Take a few minutes and think about it. We don't want you to do anything you'd rather not."

"You want me to pretend to be James? That's crazy."

"In 1947 you borrowed your brother's RAF uniform, picked up a girl named Margaret Browne, and corrupted her."

"The corruption was mutual!" Jane sputtered. She couldn't believe what she was hearing. "You have no right to poke into my past."

"We have every right, Miss Bond."

He tossed a plain manila envelope onto the desk. "Go on, open it. It's yours—if you agree to work with us."

Jane looked inside. One thousand pounds in crisp hundred-pound notes.

"What exactly would I be expected to do?"

"Receive a medal from the queen."

"That's quite a lot of money for getting a medal."

"When the safety of Our Majesty is at stake, no price is too high."

"Is it dangerous?"

"There's always the risk of indigestion." The palace was not known for its fine cuisine.

Jane stared at the money again. "Can I take it with me?"

"You get paid after you've completed your duties to our satisfaction. We require an immediate answer."

Still staring at the crisp, new notes, Jane nodded. Simon was going to have a good cry when she showed him the money. Bloody hell, she might, too!

"Very good. Agent Pumpernickel will be your handler; he will see to all aspects of your training and accompany you to Buckingham Palace. You will not be required to perform any of your brother's duties; we will teach you just enough to help you pass. Your lessons begin tomorrow morning at seven o'clock. I expect you to be well rested and sober. We have two days to turn you into a reasonable facsimile of your brother. You'll need to have all your wits about you, Miss Bond."

"One thing. I need a payment up front."

M. took one hundred pounds from the envelope and held it tantalizingly in front of Jane.

"Listen closely, Miss Bond. If you tell anyone about this, our deal is off and you'll forfeit the rest of the money."

Jane nodded. She could keep a secret for one thousand pounds. Even from Simon.

En route to the bookshop
4:39 P.M.

When Agent Pumpernickel gave her permission to take off her blind-fold (illusions must be maintained), Jane blinked and rubbed her eyes. The afternoon sun was brilliant compared with the dark building. She still couldn't believe what had just happened; she still half expected it to be some elaborate joke of her brother's.

"Let's get a drink, Agent Pumpernickel," she suggested. "To cele-brate my new job. Pull over here." She indicated a seedy little pub with a charming name. The Mouldy Crown.

"Absolutely not, Miss Bond. My orders are to take you home. There was no mention of stopping at a pub along the way."

When he slowed to let a woman walking a terrier cross the street, Jane hopped out of the car.

"Where are you going?" he cried after her.

"I'm thirsty. See you tomorrow."

A cab behind him beeped impatiently. Agent Pumpernickel parked the car, then chased after Jane. His orders had been to see her home safely. He had the sinking feeling she was going to be nothing but trouble.

The Mouldy Crown
4:47 P.M.

"Two stouts, please. On him."

"Miss Bond, I must protest. I tell you, N. won't like this one bit."

"So we'll have one quick drink and leave. Who's N.? Your boyfriend? Is he a teetotaler?"

Agent Pumpernickel turned beet red. He took a little sip of his stout. Relieved that the earth didn't open up and swallow him, he took another.

"N. is Sir Niles Needlum," he told her. "Head of the Secret Service."

"Oh, him. The Pukka Sahib. Mr. Personality."

Pumpernickel gasped and a bit of beer went down the wrong tube. Jane whacked him on the back.

"What do they call you?" she asked.

"My mother always called me Ceddie, but the boys at work call me Fidget. Of course, there's not an original thought amongst them. They sit around waiting for N. to tell them what to do. 'Yes, sir.' 'No, sir.' 'Of course, sir.' I tell you, in the old days, things were different. It was all for one and one for all. As a young man, I worshipped the older men. Especially this one fellow, 003. Now, he was a gentleman."

"You people have the strangest nicknames," Jane said. "Have another drink, Ceddie, and tell me all about it."

"I believe I will."

In twenty minutes, Agent Pumpernickel was asleep with his head on the bar, snoring softly into his hat. His carnation had fallen to the floor. Jane handed the barkeep a fiver and asked him to pour the inebriated agent into a taxicab. She left the bar wondering if 003 had ever returned his affections.

Crispin's Bookshop
5:21 P.M.

"Your girlfriend called."

"She's not my girlfriend," Jane replied tartly. "Not yet. Not till tomorrow, at least."

"What's in the Harrods bag?" Simon peeked inside. "Nice sheets. Egyptian cotton, no less. How'd you get these?"

"I pinched them."

"Young lady, you march right back to Harrods and steal a set for me."

"I already did." Jane handed Simon a gift-wrapped box.

"And they even wrapped them!"

"I got a job," Jane admitted. "They gave me an advance on my pay."

"You're leaving?" Simon stopped admiring the luxurious sheets and looked pained. "It's because I've been so bossy, isn't it? I promise to stop trying to run your life."

"It's only for a few days. My brother's in hospital and his boss has asked me to fill in."

"At Amalgamated Widget? What on earth will they have you do there?"

"He's made a mess of his paperwork and I'm going to straighten it out."

"How odd they came to you."

"I saw an advert in the paper this morning," said Jane. "I didn't want to say anything until I was sure I had it."

"And it's only for a few days?"

"I promise. His boss is a wanker; I couldn't bear to work for him any longer than that."

Simon was greatly relieved. He rummaged through Jane's bag, looking for sweets. He opened a small gold box that looked promising and found a sheer pink nightie. A scrap of fabric was pinned to the hem.

"What's this attached to it—a see-through handkerchief? How odd."

"They're knickers." Jane blushed furiously as she snatched them back and buried them in the bag. She handed Simon a sack of chewy sweets.

"This is what you're after," she said.

"I hope you two will be very happy," said Simon.

Poor Simon was so easily embarrassed. He had almost fainted once during a blow-by-blow description of one of Jane's dates. He was one of the few people she knew who still used the word *bosom*.

"I admit it—I like her. Is that a crime?"

"In some places, yes."

Home of Agent Cedric Pumpernickel
No. 9 Boundary Road
Camden Town
6:03 P.M.

The taxi came to an abrupt halt. Agent Pumpernickel hung his head out the taxi window, praying he wouldn't embarrass himself. Not once in his entire life had he come home intoxicated. What if the neighbors saw him? As he staggered up his walkway, he noticed his peonies looked parched. After he retired, there'd be plenty of time to tend to the garden. He went inside, loosened his tie, and lay down on the sofa, shoes and all.

When he awoke a half-hour later he felt better, and a bit hungry. He had been too nervous all day to have a proper meal. After splashing cold water on his face, he took a frozen dinner of beef-and-vegetable pie from the freezer. It was that or yesterday's cabbage, reheated. His mother hadn't approved of frozen foods, but Agent Pumpernickel found them agreeable, though a bit salty. After the washing-up, he spent some time with his snuffbox collection, giving it a light dusting. It was getting on toward nine o'clock, and he needed to get a good night's sleep. Tomorrow would begin the education of Miss Jane Bond.

He laid out his clothes for the next morning, a habit he had adopted in childhood. Look your best but be prepared for the worst, his mother always said. Solemnly, as if laying out the clothes of a dead man, he put socks, briefs, trousers, shoes, shirt, and tie (a nice maroon with a subtle white stripe) on the straightback chair next to his bed. Everything was laid out in the exact order in which he would dress. When he awoke each morning, he liked knowing what was going to happen. And in case of an emergency—if England was bombed, or someone tried to harm the queen—he could be dressed and ready in exactly forty-seven seconds.

The Flora Beaton
6:29 P.M.

Jane slipped her rent envelope under Tessie Twigg's door and crept quickly away lest her landlady catch her. Jane didn't want anything to spoil her fine mood. She hadn't felt this good in years—and she wasn't even a tiny bit drunk. She'd stopped at one beer, but not Agent Pumpernickel; two glasses of stout and he was three sheets to the wind. Jane had sat through a passionate tribute to Sir Niles, followed by an enthusiastic off-key rendition of "Hail, Britannia." The other pub patrons had been caught up in a patriotic fervor, and Agent Pumpernickel had happily led the assault. Jane's ears were still ringing.

She couldn't believe her luck. With the money she was going to make, she could pay the store's most pressing debts and still have a little left over to rent a flat; something without cockroaches would be nice. She had planned it all out on the bus ride home: A small place would do, preferably in Chelsea so she'd still be near Miss Liversidge. Then, once the job was over and she was settled into her new dwelling, Jane was going after Astrid. Even if she didn't have a legal leg to stand on, she could now afford to make Astrid's life hell. The idea pleased her, though not as much as it should have. Jane shrugged. She was in far too good a mood to hate even Astrid right now.

Everything was ready. The new sheets were on the bed. The pile of dirty clothes had been shoved into the closet. There was a bottle of good scotch on the bureau, and pink roses in what had formerly been the coffee tin. Jane had shooed away its occupants, chipped out the dried coffee, and turned the dented side toward the wall. It would do. Dating was awful, she decided. She had liked being married, even to Astrid.

She checked her watch. It was half-past eight. There was no telling when Bridget would arrive. She realized the bright spot of flowers made everything else look even tattier, and she couldn't believe Bridget felt comfortable enough to sleep in here. It was clean—Jane had seen to that—but everything in it was old and worn and depressing. From here on in, they'd simply have to go to Bridget's flat. Roommates or not, it had to be better than this.

She checked her watch again. Five minutes had passed. She was going to drive herself crazy at this rate. Maybe Simon had been right—they were jumping into things awfully quickly. This was exactly how she and Astrid had done it. They had gone to bed, gotten married, and moved to the suburbs. But Bridget wasn't anything like Astrid, who had barely finished unpacking when she began lying to the neighbors about their relationship. Jane had implored Astrid to simply keep her mouth shut—anyone with brains would eventually realize the two unmarried girls were lovers, no matter what they said. Unlike Astrid, who apparently needed everyone's approval (everyone but Jane's, that is), Jane didn't care what people thought of her. Just as long as they didn't throw rocks through that damned expensive picture window.

A knock at the door interrupted her fond reminiscing.

"Jane? It's Edith Liversidge. I need your help. King Edward is stuck in the coal chute again!"

Jane scribbled a note to Bridget, pinned it to her door, and followed Miss Liversidge to the basement. Last time he had done this, Jane had had to disassemble the chute.

A short time later

"Maybe Simon has a point," said Jane, smoothing King Edward's fur. "I may be rushing things. It was the same story with Astrid. One minute we were on a date, and the next we were buying tulip bulbs for our garden."

"It won't happen like that this time," Miss Liversidge assured her. "You're much wiser now."

"Miss Liversidge, you've only known me six weeks."

"It seems like forever, doesn't it? Care for a digestive biscuit with your sherry?"

"We're going out to dinner." Jane checked the clock on the mantel. It occurred to her that Bridget might not show up at all.

"She's coming," said Miss Liversidge, almost reaching to pat Jane's hand but only stroking King Edward's ear instead.

"I know." But Jane didn't know. "I'd better lie down. This is awfully strong sherry. The room's starting to spin."

"It looks better that way, dear."

G.E.O.R.G.I.E. headquarters
Projection room
8:00 P.M.

"What do you think of this color?" Agent Bibi Gallini extended her hand so Bridget could inspect her freshly painted fingernails.

"It's pretty," Bridget said approvingly. "In fact, this color would work perfectly with my new cocktail dress."

"It matches that truth-serum lipstick Bluma Trell's girls have been working on."

"Vérité? How's it coming?"

"I talked that new agent, Mimi Dolittle, into testing it, and I got her to admit she has a crush on me," Bibi replied happily. "The whole line should be ready tomorrow."

The sound of a pencil tapping against a file folder caused them to look up. Chief Tuppenny was standing in the doorway, a smile on her face. Bibi hastily put away her polish and looked alert.

"Good evening, Agent St. Claire, Agent Gallini. Let's get right down to it. For years, a group of men calling themselves the Sons of Britain Society has been yearning to stick the pieces of the empire back together. Their sphere of activity has, in the past, been confined to distributing pamphlets about the bygone pleasures of tiger hunting and public whippings, writing heated letters to the *Times*, and delivering diatribes in Parliament about the ruination of England by the usual culprits—homosexuals, immigrants, and emancipated women.

"In July, Scotland Yard received a letter originally sent to the Duke of Windsor. In it, a key member of this organization, Sir Reginald Wooley-Booley, announced his intention to topple the queen and place the duke and the duchess on the throne."

"I thought they were dead," Bibi whispered to Bridget.

"The letter ended up in the Department of Crackpots and Malcontents, where it was filed and summarily forgotten. Our girl at the Yard got wind of it, but before she could get to the letter, it was stolen, along with all files on the Sons of Britain Society and its members. Someone had cleaned house rather thoroughly. The same thing's happened at the Service. As far as our official intelligence-gathering institutions are concerned, the Sons of Britain Society poses no greater threat than the Boy Scouts. I believe otherwise. The members of this group have influence in every powerful institution in this country. If we can gather enough evidence of the plot, we can blackmail them into resigning their posts. If enough of them fall, we may be able to create some cracks in these institutions."

"But why would the duke expose Sir Reginald if he's going along with the plot?" Bibi wondered.

"We don't know who sent the letter on to the Yard, or even if it's genuine. For all we know, it was a bad practical joke. The rub is, since that first letter, Lady Edwina Wooley-Booley and the Duchess of Windsor have been corresponding. If there is indeed a plot, Sir Reginald and the duke may be using their wives' correspondence as a cover.

"We must get our hands on those letters. Agent Gallini, I've secured a position for you at Grunby Hall. Lady Edwina's personal maid has won a holiday sweepstakes at Bristol by the Sea, courtesy of Powder Puff Cosmetics. By all reports, she's having a splendid time."

Bibi groaned. Maid was the worst undercover job in the business. Not only did the agent have to surreptitiously plant bugs, riffle through personal papers, memorize the layout of the house, eavesdrop on conversations and telephone calls, photograph suspicious activity, and chat up the guests for tidbits of gossip, she had to actually clean.

"But those sort of people hate me. The women look down their noses at me, and the men look down my blouse."

"You're the best girl for the job, Bibi."

"I know. I'll do it," Bibi said, sighing dramatically, "but only because I look so good in uniform. I am, however, going to clout the first blueblood who pinches my bum."

It was typical of Bibi to joke about an assignment, but once she got on the job, she was sharp as a whip, and about as easy to control. She kept three cutting blades on her at all times; one in her boot, one in her hair, and one in her cigarette case. Many an adversary had learned too late never to turn his back on the sassy little brunette.

"Bibi, if there is indeed a plot against the queen, you can clout the lot of them," Agent Tuppenny promised.

"We've been handed another bit of luck. Lady Edwina is holding a charity auction. It's a very elite group—the Sons of Britain, their wives, the queen and her party guard, and England's most fabulous hostess, Emerald St. Claire. Bridget, I think it's time you joined the family business."

"This is who we're up against."

Agent Tuppenny dimmed the lights and turned on the slide projector. A middle-aged man, wearing a funny pointed party hat that looked like a child's dunce cap, was toasting the camera with a dry martini glass. His eyes were glazed over and his collar stays had come undone.

"This is Sir Reginald 'Rags' Wooley-Booley at Biddle Phelps's birthday bash last year. Sir Reginald is the last in a long line of Wooley-Booleys. He was educated at Eton, and had a brief stint as a commissioned officer during the war until his father, Lord Chumley, bought him a post in India. There he grew rich exporting elephant-leg wastebaskets and ivory toothpicks, but was expelled from the country in 1957 for behavior unbecoming a gentleman. By Fifty-eight he had lost his fortune at the crap tables at Casino Royale.

"In Fifty-nine, he opened his country estate, Grouse Manor, to the public, and for the last five years has lived off ticket proceeds and small sums of money from sales of his autobiography, 'Tigers I Have Shot.'" She paused. "I'm sure you've read it.

"Sir Reginald is a classic public school product," she continued. "He's got a stiff upper lip, is good at sport, and seems of average intelligence. Last year, he married"—she clicked on the next slide—"Edwina Piggott, sole heiress to the Piggott Plumbing fortune."

Edwina Piggott looked like an enormous, plump pigeon, strapping and box-bosomed. She was standing in front of Buckingham Palace, staring blankly at the camera. She looked like any number of women who had put on their best frock and gone to the palace hoping to catch a glimpse of the queen.

"She looks familiar," Bridget murmured.

A succession of slides flashed on the screen. Lady Edwina at Royal Ascot. Lady Edwina at the May biscuit toss in Tottingham. Lady Edwina trying on tiaras at Van Cleef and Arpels. Lady Edwina tugging at her girdle whilst browsing in the ladies' unmentionables department at Claridge's.

"Now I know where I've seen her," Bridget recalled. "In *Polite Society Quarterly*. She was in their fashion failures column, 'I'd Rather Be Dead.' She wore white shoes with black stockings to a tea. They say she looked like a spider in a milk glass."

Bibi tutted. "Would someone who paired black stockings with white shoes really have the wherewithal to engineer a transfer of the throne?"

The slide projector clicked again. "This is Lord Mortimer 'Jinx' Finhatten, an elderly peer fondly known, by friend and foe alike, as 'the old gasbag.' He's famous for his long-winded addresses to the House of Lords. In Forty-six he supported a bill to ban women from wearing trousers and tie-up shoes. In Fifty-two he led the fight to repeal the woman's vote."

Bibi hissed at the screen. She changed her tune, though, when the next slide revealed a handsome, dark-haired beauty who could have been a dead ringer for the film actress Elizabeth Taylor, save for one thing. Her eyes weren't violet—they were cold and black.

"This is Lady Lettie Apethorpe-Jones Finhatten."

"She looks young enough to be his granddaughter," Bibi whispered to Bridget.

"Lady Finhatten was born Lydia Thorne, a Sussex lighthouse-keeper's daughter. She admits to twenty-eight but is actually forty-two. During the war she was a Nazi agent; she used the lighthouse to transmit British troop movements to German warships. She was put under house arrest, but escaped before trial.

"Thorne surfaced in Argentina under the name Priscilla White, and was employed in the household of Lady and Lord Apethorpe-Jones, Nazi sympathizers who fled England after the war. Six months later, Lady Apethorpe-Jones was dead of an undetermined intestinal ailment, and Priscilla White became the next Lady Apethorpe-Jones.

"In Forty-nine, when their vast coffee plantation in Kenya was wiped out by a fire, the second Lady Apethorpe-Jones disappeared, along with the family jewels and several valuable paintings. Seven years ago, she returned to England as Lady Finhatten. Her hair's a different color, and she's had some work done on her teeth, but it's the same person. Box clever with this one—she'll stop at nothing."

The Flora Beaton
The bedsit of Miss Edith Liversidge
8:55 P.M.

A knock at the door startled Jane, who had been dozing on Miss Liversidge's daybed.

"Jane?"

"Come in." Jane yawned. "Miss Liversidge, this is Bridget St. Claire."

Miss Liversidge patted the daybed. "Have a seat, Miss St. Claire."

"Call me Bridget, please."

"Tell me, Bridget, you're not related to that woman who has parties, are you?"

"Vaguely."

"I remember reading that she puts goldfish in her fingerbowls. Is that true? What happens to them after? She sets them free, doesn't she?" Miss Liversidge asked worriedly. "Unless it's a just a tale. Sometimes I wonder if the newspapers don't make these things up."

"It's hard to know what to believe," Bridget agreed.

"Sherry, dear?"

"Please."

While Miss Liversidge fetched another jam jar from the bureau, Jane gave Bridget a kiss. Bridget took a handkerchief from her purse and wiped a smear of coal dust from Jane's forehead.

"What on earth have you two been doing?" she asked.

"We were in the cellar," Miss Liversidge explained.

"Burying the evidence," Jane added.

"Jane rescued King Edward from certain death," Miss Liversidge explained. "Here's your sherry, dear."

"He was stuck in the coal chute," Jane said. "He wasn't in any real danger."

"He goes in there occasionally to be alone. I don't think married life suits him," Miss Liversidge confided.

Jane gestured toward a lump of white fur snoring in a little bed in front of the electric heater.

"Meet the wife," she said.

The wall above the heater was covered with paper certificates attesting to Miss Liversidge's achievements in levitation, palmistry, and the reading of tea leaves.

"Miss Liversidge leads a highly stimulating life," Jane told Bridget.

"Since my retirement I have devoted myself to the pursuit of higher learning," Miss Liversidge explained. "And call me Edith, dear."

"Where do you study?"

"I am currently completing a series of courses at the British Psychic College."

"That little place in Camden Road? I've always been curious about it."

"You should come to a lecture sometime. They're free. At the moment I've been studying astral projection. I think the professors at the college are on the verge of making a real breakthrough. It's a perfectly respectable institution. The college was established during the war. A group of leading psychics came together in order to pool their brain energy, trying to help with the war effort."

"I've heard about that," Bridget remembered. "It's a fascinating story."

"Everyone did their part in those days. Did you know Jane helped put out fires during the Blitz? And she was only nine at the time."

"I carried sand around in buckets for the firefighters," Jane amended the story. "All my friends did."

"Where were you, dear?" Miss Liversidge asked Bridget. "During the war, I mean. You must have been awfully young."

Bridget flushed. Her parents had sent her to live in New York with a wealthy aunt. They'd dined on lobster and ice cream sundaes at the Ritz while Jane was dodging bombs in London.

"I was sent away," Bridget said truthfully. "I lived with an elderly aunt."

"That's hard on a child." Miss Liversidge shook her head. "More sherry?"

While they drank their second glass, Miss Liversidge provided a potted history of the Flora Beaton Hotel. "This used to be a very tony place," she asserted. "Flora Beaton and I were great friends back in the old days. We chained ourselves to the gates of the House of Commons in 1946 in support of the woman's vote. She bought this building so suffragettes who had been disowned by their families could have a place to go. Unfortunately, after she bought it, her family disowned her. That's why the place is in its original condition."

"So that's why Queen Victoria is still hanging in my room," Jane realized. "I tried to take her down, but she's covering a hole in the wallboard."

"We had an electrical fire in 1952." Miss Liversidge nodded. "The wiring here is very old. The gas lamps were changed over to electric, but whoever did it knew nothing about electricity."

"This place just looks better and better, don't you think?" Jane said to Bridget.

"I think it's charming."

Jane gave Bridget a peck on the cheek. "You're very cute," she said. "May I take you to dinner?"

"You want to go out?" Bridget knew how strapped Jane was. She felt content to stay in.

"Jane got a new job today," Miss Liversidge said happily. "Although I'm a little confused about what exactly it is she'll be doing."

"Let's not talk about work on an empty stomach," Jane pleaded.

Bridget whispered something in Jane's ear.

"Are you sure?"

Bridget nodded.

"Look here, Miss Liversidge, when's the last time I took you out for dinner?" Jane asked.

"Never, dear. Although you did have me up for tinned spaghetti and powdered anchovy paste, which was very filling."

"Put on your best frock, then. You're going out with us."

"But you don't want me along," Miss Liversidge protested.

"Yes we do," Bridget assured her. "I seldom meet people who are so well versed in the study of psychic phenomena."

"But I've nothing suitable to wear."

"We'll go somewhere dark," Jane said. "And the cinema, too if you like."

"There is one picture I've been longing to see."

"It's settled, then," Jane said. "Tidy up, and we'll meet you downstairs in ten minutes."

Miss Liversidge realized she did have a brown artificial-silk dress that had seen little wear in the last decade. There was a stain on the collar, but her cameo pin would conceal it quite nicely.

"I'll inform King Edward," she said excitedly. Miss Liversidge had never had supper out *and* a trip to the cinema in the same night. It was the sort of treat she could ill afford. She only hoped Jane and her friend liked musicals about nuns.

Some hours, and many drinks, later

Jane, Bridget, and Miss Liversidge crept through the lobby of the Flora Beaton well after curfew. Because of her close association with Miss Beaton, no one could touch Miss Liversidge. Her rent papers clearly stated that Miss Edith Liversidge (along with her cats) was to remain in the building, without a rent raise, until the end of her days. Tessie Twigg couldn't harass Miss Liversidge, but she could make Jane's life unpleasant.

They were doing their best to walk the straight and narrow. It wasn't easy. They hadn't meant to stop off at the pub, but after the movie Jane had desperately needed a drink. They tried a new café on Kings Road; Miss Liversidge had declared it too fancy for her taste, so they had moved to a corner table at the Mouldy Crown. After three beers, Miss Liversidge had become involved in a heated discussion regarding London's stray cat problem with a man at the next table. He was advocating—rather rudely and rather loudly, Jane thought—that the cats be rounded up and shipped to Australia.

"I forgot my paper crown!" Miss Liversidge suddenly shrieked.

"I have it," Bridget whispered. They had gotten a silver-paper child-size crown at a penny arcade; with alterations, it would fit King Edward nicely.

"We don't want to wake the Twigg," Jane added, in a low voice.

"Tessie is the eyes and ears of this building," Miss Liversidge whispered to Bridget. "She knows everything."

"That's because she snoops—and she has spies," Jane added.

"Spies?" Miss Liversidge looked alarmed. "Here?"

"The McGuire sisters. They're twins who sit in the lobby all day, drinking tea," Jane explained to Bridget.

"Oh, no—they hate Tessie," Miss Liversidge assured her. "They wouldn't tell her if her bloomers were on fire. The one with the thick spectacles—what's her name?"

"Louise. Bessie is the one who keeps birds."

"She thinks you're very polite. She also thinks Jane is a funny name for a boy."

Bridget found this exceedingly funny. She pressed into Jane, trying to muffle her laughs.

"No wonder Louise knocks on my door every time she wants furniture moved," Jane said.

Bridget giggled some more.

"Good night, Miss Liversidge," said Jane as she pushed Bridget up the stairs. They laughed as they clung to each other.

Miss Liversidge stood on the landing, in her best dress, long after the girls were gone. It was nice to see Jane so happy.

7 SEPTEMBER 1965

The Flora Beaton
Bedsit of Jane Bond
6:12 A.M.

CIGARETTE in hand, Jane sat, dressed, on the edge of the bed and watched Bridget sleep. She hated to wake her—it seemed they had just fallen asleep—but she had to go. Agent Pumpernickel was due any minute. Jane leaned over and gave Bridget a kiss on the forehead. Bridget opened one sleepy eye and smiled. She pulled Jane onto the bed and curled herself around her.

"I was having the most marvelous dream," Bridget murmured as she began unbuttoning Jane's shirt. She slipped her hand under the rough cotton and cupped one breast. Jane took a sharp inward breath, her nipple sore from last night's lovemaking. When Bridget replaced her hand with her mouth, Jane ceased to protest.

Bridget used her tongue to trace a path down Jane's belly while her hand steadied Jane's hip. She managed to undo the top button of Jane's trousers before Jane grabbed her wrist. Bridget twisted out of her grasp, and, none too gently, pushed Jane back onto the bed, pinning her wrists with one hand while unzipping her trousers with the other.

"You're pretty strong for such a small girl," Jane said, laughing, as she halfheartedly struggled to break free.

"Just do what I say and no one will get hurt," Bridget whispered as she slipped her hand inside Jane's trousers.

"God, you're bossy."

"You don't know the half of it," Bridget replied. Jane had a feeling she was about to find out.

She was half out of her trousers when a sudden shout from the landing almost finished the job.

"Miss Bond—visitor!" Tessie Twigg bellowed up the stairs in her usual charming manner. Then, in a stage whisper that could be heard all the way to Albert Hall, she added, "I think it's the police!"

Jane groaned. Bloody hell. Pumpernickel was early!

"I'm going to kill her," she promised Bridget, as she yanked on her trousers and buttoned her shirt. She was knackered. Knackered but happy.

"Miss Bond!" Tessie Twigg was bellowing like a sick water buffalo.

Jane gave Bridget a final kiss. "I have to go to work," she explained, shrugging on her jacket and fumbling through her pockets for a cigarette. She wanted to get out of there before Bridget asked any questions about her new job.

"Honey, why don't you stay and sleep?" she said to Bridget. "You're safe here during daylight hours. The creepy-crawlies only come out at night."

Bridget spied a fresh pack of fags on the nightstand and snatched it.

"Come and get them," she said, hiding the pack in the bedcovers.

"If I get back in that bed I'm not getting out again," Jane warned. "I'll lose this job, and will no longer be able to afford to keep you in the lap of luxury."

Bridget laughed as she looked around the shabby room.

"I'm going to quit soon," Jane promised. "Really I am. Just not today."

"I don't want anything to happen to you," Bridget said.

"And I appreciate it. But it's too soon for me to admit I'm wrapped around your finger. Give me a few more weeks of pretending."

Bridget smiled, kissed her, and slid the pack into Jane's coat pocket.

"You're a good girl," Jane murmured. "See you tonight? Same place?"

"Don't forget where we left off. Now go to work so you can afford to keep me in style."

"Yes, dear," said Jane.

"Hurry, Miss Bond!" Tessie Twigg insisted, loud enough to wake the dead (by Jane's estimation, a good half of the Flora Beaton residents).

Jane flung open her door.

"I will not have my building getting a reputation as a haven for criminals!" Tessie Twigg cried.

"If you'd shut your cake hole, no one would know," muttered Jane.

"What's that?"

"I said, Thank you Miss Twigg." Jane headed for the frigid loo, lit a cigarette, and tried to wake up. She had promised to be sober and alert for today's job; she was neither. She wasn't all that worried, though; she was, after all, replacing her brother—a man who had once broken both legs trying to drink a martini while skiing. Jane did wish she had something to conceal the shadows under her eyes. For once Mrs. Snipe was right—Jane could use some makeup. She waved the smoke out the small window, then opened the door and headed down the stairs.

"Were you smoking up there?" Tessie wanted to know when Jane got to the lobby.

"No, Miss Twigg. I know it's against the rules." Now that Jane could afford to move, she took a perverse pleasure in being polite to her landlady.

Agent Pumpernickel was sitting on the red horsehair sofa in the lobby, hat in hand. "Good morning, Miss Bond. I must apologize for arriving early, but I'm rather anxious to get started." The task of turning Jane into her brother was a bit daunting. Pumpernickel had stayed awake most of the night reading his manual, and so this morning had drunk several cups of coffee to compensate for lack of sleep. He realized it would be impossible to cram the entire spy school curriculum into forty-eight hours, but he had to teach Jane enough to make her a credible substitute.

"I'm a little anxious myself," Jane told him. A little hungover, too, but she thought she'd better keep that to herself.

As soon as they left, Tessie Twigg went running to the room shared by the McGuire sisters to inform them that Jane Bond had been taken away by an official-looking man, most probably a police detective. She couldn't be certain (she hadn't asked, as she didn't like to pry), but the man looked straight out of Scotland Yard.

En route to Secret Service headquarters

"Your landlady certainly is a colorful character." Agent Pumpernickel was tooling along in his usual turtlelike fashion. Slow and steady stays the course, thought Jane, as they sped down the street neck and neck with a woman pushing a pram.

"She's a royal pain in the arse," Jane said bluntly.

"You shouldn't use the world *royal* when describing something unpleasant," Agent Pumpernickel admonished her. "People might over-hear and get the wrong impression."

"Such as?"

"They might think you're one of those radical antimonarchists."

Pumpernickel knew there existed in his country an eccentric minority, for the most part shallow people of poor character and bad breeding, who bore ill feelings against the monarchy. He hoped Jane wasn't among them. He knew she was anti–nuclear war, but no one had said anything about her not liking the queen.

"Heavens, no. I think it's worth the millions of pounds it costs to keep the royals in horses and dowdy hats."

Pumpernickel bristled at her contemptuous tone. As a child, he had drunk his cocoa each morning from a tin King George V coronation cup. In 1953 he had even taken a day off work to watch the queen's coronation on the telly. His neighbor Mrs. Figgis had come over and they had eaten cream buns while Elizabeth was crowned. It had been one of the most moving experiences in his life. When the bejeweled crown had been placed on the young queen's head, Pumpernickel could feel the clamp and glory of it upon his own.

"You're too young to remember the old days when those in power kept themselves far removed from their people. You're accustomed to the queen's Christmas Day address to her people, but it wasn't until her father began giving his radio addresses in Thirty-seven that people outside court even heard a royal voice. Surely you remember their bravery during the Blitz, which gave us all the courage to carry on." The royal family stayed in London during the war and were subjected to the same dangers as their people.

"I do recall sharing a stale biscuit or two with Princess Margaret down in the Tube during the worst of the shellings," Jane remarked.

Pumpernickel sighed. Miss Bond was the perfect illustration of all that was wrong with the younger generation. They had no respect for tradition.

"They needn't literally be among us to show their compassion. As they travel through the land, they cast a mist with thousands of motes of gold dust that settle on each and every one of us. That's what Mother always told me. Miss Bond, I have witnessed a queen's walk-about in which her subjects were reduced to tears by the mere sight of her."

"Because they're thinking, 'All that money and still she dresses like a greengrocer's wife?' "

"What quarrel have you with the royal family?"

"For one, they're bloody expensive to keep. And what is it they do, really? Go to the races and the opera, support the hat and feather industry, hand out medals to their friends. Face it—they're on the dole, but at the end of the month they're not eating tinned beans on stale bread."

Pumpernickel gripped the steering wheel and tried to keep his eyes on the road.

"Off with their heads—is that how you'd have it?" he asked angrily.

"Maybe they could just earn their keep like the rest of us. Or get their jobs based on some criterion other than birth. When you think about it, the notion of inherited rule is absurd. I can understand picking out a dog according to bloodlines, but a king or a queen?"

"Royalty cannot be taught; it must be in one's blood. And they do work as hard as you and I. All day long they have to be gracious and smiling, and keep changing their outfits. The superficiality their jobs require takes a lifetime to learn."

"So you admit they actually do very little."

"I admit to nothing of the sort. You are twisting my words."

"You have a real queen fixation, don't you?"

"And you have an attitude I find most disrespectful," he grumbled, snapping on the turn signal with unnecessary vigor. "You'd best keep those opinions to yourself, Miss Bond, or I'm afraid your employment with Her Majesty's Secret Service will be over before it begins."

They rode in silence for a few awkward minutes.

"I didn't mean to be brusque with you, Miss Bond. It's just that I was raised to think of the royal family as an extension of my own, and now that Mother is gone, well—" Pumpernickel's voice thickened.

"I'm sorry," Jane said. "Really, I am." She needed to learn when to keep her big mouth shut. She hadn't meant to hurt his feelings, and she had no intention of losing this job. She was not only desperate for the money, the source of it amused her. It was high time the queen started supporting *her*.

"The Queen Mum seems like a lovely person," she said, trying to appease him.

"Oh, she is," he assured her.

"I like the dogs, too. I find short dogs to be very sincere-looking."

"I find all dogs to be quite messy. Their hair sticks to the carpet and is impossible to sweep up."

"Yes, but they're such good company. And they're always happy to see you." And you never find them in bed with someone else, she wanted to add.

"My neighbor's dog barks quite a lot. She's more an irritant than anything. I wish they would get rid of her."

"You know the way you feel about the royal family?"

"Yes."

"That's how I feel about dogs," Jane warned.

"Birdie's really not such a bad dog," Pumpernickel said meekly. "I give her table scraps on occasion."

Jane laughed. One more fight and they'd be married.

Pumpernickel gave a little chuckle. He wasn't exactly sure why, but it seemed like a good idea.

"So, Agent Pumpernickel, do you think this plan is going to work? My impersonating James, I mean?"

"Our experts could transform you into anyone," he assured her. "Plus you have the added advantage of looking like your brother."

"Actually, he looks like me."

"You're a much friendlier person," said Agent Pumpernickel, eager to put their quarrel behind them.

"Except when I'm being a royal—I mean, bloody—pain." Jane grinned.

"I wasn't going to say that."

"You were thinking it."

"Just a little."

Jane smiled again.

"My brother's not the warmest fellow, is he?"

"Despite that, he seems to do very well with the ladies."

"That runs in the family, too."

"Here we are!" Agent Pumpernickel announced with obvious relief as he spied the Tip-Tap-Toe Dance Studio.

Bridget, though she felt a little guilty to be snooping on Jane again, found herself smiling as she listened to the exchange. She had donned a dark wig and sunglasses and was following a safe distance behind the plain black sedan carrying Jane and Agent Pumpernickel to Secret Service headquarters. Jane was turning out to be a very different person than Bridget had first imagined. She was really very sweet, and seemed sincere in her affections. Perhaps she could work for G.E.O.R.G.I.E. Miss Tuppenny could dispose of Jane's file in one of her regular cleanup sessions in the records room; there would be nothing on paper connecting Jane to the Secret Service. She would be a free agent.

Secret Service headquarters
Lobby
7:00 A.M.

A cool blonde seated at a reception desk in the lobby was painting her nails dark coral when they walked in. She examined Jane's pass while Agent Pumpernickel used her telephone to call Sir Niles. Then she examined Jane.

"We've arrived, sir," Pumpernickel announced triumphantly, as if their trip through the streets of London had been fraught with danger. He was relieved to have gotten Miss Bond this far.

"Fine. Take Miss Bond to Disguise and Deception. I'll meet you there."

"Yes, sir. One question—"

"What is it, Pumpernickel?" N. was in a bad humor. Just moments ago he had received an upsetting communiqué from Zurich. Bond had escaped from the sanitarium, and taken a nurse with him. They had last been seen skiing down the mountain to the main village. All N. wanted right now was for 007 to stay out of sight until his sister made her appearance. Then N. would personally see to it that 007 was brought back to London, nervous breakdown be damned. If the man was steady enough to go skiing, he was steady enough to hold a gun.

"Did *it* arrive?"

"Did what—? Oh—that. It's on her desk."

"Splendid. She's going to be so excited when—" But he was talking to thin air, for N. had slammed down the receiver and was rummaging through his desk for his antiindigestion tablets. He was in no mood to listen to Pumpernickel blather on. And he wasn't looking forward to another meeting with Miss Bond. When he had discovered there existed a Miss Bond, an unmarried woman of a certain age who worked in a small bookshop, he had expected a modest, bookish woman who would jump at the opportunity to serve Her Majesty. She was nothing like he had imagined. What was happening to English womanhood these days?

Agent Pumpernickel made a cup of instant coffee in the agents' lounge and meandered around the third floor. He was to retrieve Miss Bond in an hour, after she had been measured for her James Bond suit. He had a few things to finish up in his office, but first he wanted to take advantage of the peace and quiet and have one last good look around. He would miss this place. He would even miss these repellent green walls and horrid brown carpet.

The light was on in 008's office. He was a good lad, Pumpernickel thought; hardworking and devoted. He had certainly misjudged him. He had thought 008 would be disappointed at being given his old slot, but the lad had gone right to work. Pumpernickel no longer had to worry about retiring; the Department of Desk Accessories was in good hands.

He wanted to remember every bit of these last few days. After this assignment, his life as a secret agent would cease to exist; it couldn't even be a memory. Memories had a way of popping up unexpectedly. Liquor was usually to blame for the loosening of the tongue; he had seen too many agents climb inside a bottle and not come out. Yesterday was a mistake he did not care to repeat.

As far as his neighbors were concerned, Mr. Cedric Pumpernickel worked for Amalgamated Widget, Inc. No one had ever asked what it was he did, which was just as well. The profession of intelligence was a solitary one; since the largest part of yourself could not be shared, contacts with the outside world were, by nature, superficial. In the end, an agent was left alone with his secrets.

"This," he said aloud solemnly, "is the last time I will walk the halls like this." It felt good to speak the truth, even to an empty corridor.

"This is the last time I will sip a cup of coffee while walking these halls," he added for good measure.

He hoped it was the last time he would spill coffee on his coat, but he doubted it.

7:27 A.M.

"Hold still, Miss Bond!"

Jane was being measured, poked, and prodded by a tiny, sharp-beaked, sour-faced woman. While she pinned Jane into her James Bond suit, Sir Niles Needlum sat slumped in a nearby chair, looking cross. He hadn't been able to find his stomach tablets.

"Do something about those bumps," he ordered the woman.

"You mean my hips?" Jane was beginning to miss Agent Pumpernickel. Sir Niles was nothing but a grouchy old stick.

The woman fitting Jane shot N. a sharp look. "I know how to disguise them," she assured him.

"I really don't appreciate your talking about me as if I'm not here," Jane groused. According to N., her breasts were too big, her lips were too full, and her bum was too round. He did know she was a woman; what did he expect?

"Quiet!" the seamstress demanded. Then, to N., "Sit up straight, Needy."

"I told you not to call me that at work, Mother," he said, hissing.

Jane bit the inside of her cheek to keep from laughing. She had thought the two might be related. They had the same blunt manner and sour expression.

"Do you slouch like that all day? No wonder your posture is so poor. Your spine must be all out of alignment."

"Mother—" Sir Niles said in a warning tone.

"Don't you 'Mother' me. And you," she scolded Jane, "stop wriggling about, or I'll poke you so you can't sit down."

Jane froze. Mrs. Needlum sounded like she meant it. Now Jane knew where N. had gotten his winning manners.

7:46 A.M.

When Miss Tuppenny stepped off the lift and turned down the hall, she was startled to see that the door to her office was open. She reached into her purse for a single-shot lipstick gun, and tiptoed down the hall. The night cleaning crew had never forgotten to lock up before, and it was too early for N. to be in.

She cautiously peeked inside. Agent Pumpernickel was sitting at her desk, looking like the cat that had eaten the canary. Had she been found out? Would they let her resign quietly, or would the pristine Miss Tuppenny and her famously flawless bun land in the lockup? She decided to take the offensive.

"Agent Pumpernickel, whatever are you doing here?" she cried.

"I'm working."

"I mean, what are you doing in my office?"

"Do you always come in on Saturdays? Really, Miss Tuppenny, I'm going to speak to N. about your long hours. He's overworking you."

"That won't be necessary, Agent Pumpernickel. I came in to get a novel I left in my desk. If you'll excuse me—"

Pumpernickel stood up, but seemed reluctant to let her approach her desk. She tightened her grip on her deadly lipstick, and pushed past him.

"Where's my typewriter?" cried Miss Tuppenny when she saw her desk. In the spot where her black manual typewriter usually sat was a brand new, turquoise-and-tan Corona electric typewriter.

"Surprise!" Agent Pumpernickel exclaimed.

"What?"

"It's your surprise. Sir Niles and I got it for you. It's the only one in the building, and it cost a pretty penny. You'll be the envy of all the other girls."

"I'm shocked," Miss Tuppenny said honestly.

"I told him you would be."

"Was this his idea?" Had she been found out?

"I can't take all the credit; N. did approve the expense. In all the years I've been here, I've never seen a principal secretary work as hard as you do, Miss Tuppenny. Without fail you're the first to arrive and the last to go home."

"Where is the old one?"

"On the way to the trash heap."

Miss Tuppenny had to sit down.

"Isn't it just the most modern thing? Sir Niles liked the all-tan one, but I thought you'd appreciate a little color in here. And with the automatic touch-type keys, your fingers won't get nearly so tired. And it comes with a plastic dustcover. See?"

"It's very nice. Thank you."

Pumpernickel beamed. "My pleasure, Miss Tuppenny. I just hope that when you're sitting here typing, you'll occasionally think of me."

"You can be certain of that, Agent Pumpernickel."

He left her office feeling quite pleased with himself. Surprises were always so nice.

Miss Tuppenny followed him into the hallway. "Oh—Agent Pumpernickel. There's something on your coat. A black speck."

He whirled around in terror. "What? A bug. Oh, get it off me!"

Miss Tuppenny brushed at a speck on the back of his collar. "It was only soot," she said soothingly.

Office of Agent Pumpernickel
8:34 A.M.

"Read this, then sign here—and here—and here."

It was a simple contract guaranteeing Jane one thousand pounds for the assignment, with one important codicil—Jane was never to talk or write about her experience with the Secret Service. She shrugged and signed the paper. She wasn't planning a tell-all book anytime soon.

"From this point on in you will be known as 007 and a half," Agent Pumpernickel informed her.

"Why?"

"All agents are given a numerical classification."

"Why the half?"

"Your brother is 007; as his substitute, you are 007 and a half. Or 007.5—whichever you prefer."

"I think I'm insulted. Can't I be 008?"

"There's already a 008; that young man you met in my office yesterday."

"That nasty ferret-face is a secret agent?" Jane thought he looked more like a bank clerk, the kind who took pleasure in informing you your account has been closed due to lack of funds.

"He's really quite a nice fellow once you get to know him. And it's hardly his fault that his eyes are small and set so close together."

Jane snorted. "You could do better."

Agent Pumpernickel pretended not to hear her.

"Take a seat, Miss Bond, and let's begin."

Jane sat on the metal chair facing the screen. Agent Pumpernickel switched on an 8mm film projector, then dimmed the lights.

"This isn't one of those hygiene movies, is it?" she wondered. "Because I already know to scrub behind my ears each day."

"*Sssh*, Miss Bond. The filmstrip is about to begin."

A man sitting at a plain wooden desk came on screen. He was pretending to read a file. He looked up and smiled, closed the file, took off his black thick-rimmed glasses, polished them on a handkerchief, and put them back on.

"Hello," he said. "I am Agent Basil Herringbone, a member of Her Majesty's Secret Service. I am not an actor, but an actual secret agent."

"Could have fooled me," Jane said to the screen.

"Until you were approached by one of our men, no doubt you had never even heard of us. You're here today because sometimes we are forced to call upon you—the decent, public-spirited men and women of this country—for help."

"That leaves me out," Jane murmured.

Pumpernickel glared at her.

"You're probably thinking, Who, me?" Agent Basil Herringbone added, an exaggerated expression of surprise on his face. "What could *I* possibly do to help my queen and country?"

"That's *exactly* what I was thinking," Jane said back to the screen.

"I'll answer that question, and many more, in this short and informative filmstrip. So sit back, relax, and enjoy *The Secret Service and You.*"

"No popcorn?"

Pumpernickel took a deep breath and counted backward from ten to one, slowly. He could feel his blood pressure rising. Miss Bond had so far exhibited a disturbingly blasé attitude toward authority, and her chattiness was getting on his nerves. People who talked during movies should be publicly reprimanded. He got up and switched off the filmstrip projector.

"Now I'll never know how it ends," Jane protested weakly.

"Miss Bond, this is a very serious mission we are undertaking. It is also the last one of my career. I would like to leave knowing I had done my duty."

"I won't make any more disparaging remarks," Jane promised. "I won't even think them."

"That's better. Now pay attention," he said, switching the projector back on. "We don't have time to watch this twice."

Twenty minutes later

Pumpernickel blew his nose (rather noisily, Jane thought. Why did men have to honk so?) and wiped tears from his eyes.

"I never get tired of viewing this," he admitted.

"I had no idea the hearts and minds of the British people were so vulnerable to the lure of godless communism," Jane said. She had nodded off for most of the film, but had woken up in time for the climactic dramatization of London under communist rule, in which the queen and her family were forced to don overalls and work in a tractor factory.

"Now you know, Miss Bond. Now you know."

"What's next?"

"The rest of the day will be spent perfecting your disguise. You'll learn to walk, talk, and contort your face into expressions commonly employed by your brother."

"Can we get something to eat first?" All she'd had for breakfast was a cigarette and Bridget's kisses.

Agent Pumpernickel checked his watch.

"It is about nine; why don't we head to the cafeteria for tea."

"There's a cafeteria here?"

"We put on our trousers one leg at a time around here, Miss Bond." Pumpernickel chuckled. "We're all quite normal. Now, let's go get a cuppa and a bikky before turning you into a man."

Secret Service headquarters
Employee lunchroom
9:07 A.M.

Pumpernickel nodded at a few familiar faces, then steered Jane toward an isolated table in the far corner of the room. He took his tea with milk and two lumps of sugar. Jane took her coffee black.

"It's like being in school again," she commented as she looked around the room. The walls were a dingy yellow, the day's special had been scribbled on a small blackboard, and the lunch lady was wearing a stained white uniform and a hairnet.

"What did you expect?"

"I don't know. Nothing this ordinary. My job is going to be boring, isn't it?"

"On the contrary! You're going to meet the queen!" And so was Agent Pumpernickel. As Jane's handler, he would go everywhere she went.

Jane noticed that whenever Pumpernickel mentioned the queen, he lapsed into a hypnotic state. She sipped her coffee and waited for him to resurface.

Pumpernickel touched the S-shaped scar on his right cheek. When Jane had her photograph taken with the queen at the ceremony, he would be there beside her. There was no reason he couldn't appear in the photo too if he played it just right. And if he positioned himself on Jane's right (the queen's left) Her Majesty wouldn't have to gaze upon his deformity.

"Wake up, Pumpernickel," Jane whispered urgently. "Your boyfriend just walked in."

Pumpernickel gasped. He had never before uttered the word—never even *thought* it—within these walls.

"Let's ask him to sit with us," she said. "Over here, 008," she called.

"Miss Bond," Pumpernickel said through his teeth, "I would thank you to stop meddling in my affairs." He reddened. That wasn't at all how he had meant to put it. Now everyone was staring at him as if they could read his mind.

"Let's get back to work," he muttered.

The Sons of Britain Society Club
No. 23 Oxwells Place
Westminster
9:34 A.M.

Sir Reginald "Rags" Wooley-Booley had the looks of a fading matinee idol and the mien of an aristocrat. He had thick white hair, which he oiled with pomade imported from Paris and brushed to a sheen with a handmade boar-bristle brush from Nairobi. He had inherited his mother's imperious aquiline nose and feminine mouth, and his father's chiseled jaw and membership in the Sons of Britain, but little else. As the second son, Sir Reginald had been denied the right to sit in the House of Lords. That honor had gone to his brother, Lord Montague Wooley-Booley, a miscreant who had sold his title to an American land developer a decade ago, then run off to Australia with his stable boy.

For years Sir Reginald had traded on his charms and courted recklessly, going about with married women with no income of their own, or young, unsuitable shop girls with soft white hands but accents that grated on his nerves. The only women worthy of the Wooley-Booley name were, like him, members of the impoverished landed gentry, saddled with crumbling country houses, the remnants of once-glorious estates whose fortunes had been squandered foolishly by some idiot ancestor. In Sir Reginald's case, it had been his father.

Sir Reginald had tried to make his way in the new world. It wasn't that he was poorly educated; he was, after all, a well-recognized authority on fox hunting and lunch. It's just that these particular skills were no longer seen as valuable in this godless modern society. The pillars of society were crumbling—the church, the Tory party, the law— all had been shaken by an evil force washing over this green and pleasant land. All sorts of ill-mannered people were demanding to have a voice in a new England. Sir Reginald's circle had been hit hard. And now they were hitting back.

He raised his glass to the coronation portrait of King Edward VIII that hung over the mantel of the library.

"To the past and future king. This time around, long may he reign," Sir Reginald said solemnly.

"Here, here!" cried Lord Finhatten. His voice reverberated through the large mahogany-paneled library. Brandy ran down his chins. He hiccuped softly.

"What has happened to England?" he bemoaned. It was the usual diatribe that came on after three brandies. "Everything good and fine is disappearing before our eyes while the young dance in the streets. We were once the most gracious people God had ever put on this earth. Now we're becoming a nation of communists, and shrill women who run around noisily demanding their 'rights' as if this were a democracy."

Lord Finhatten had a face like a cream puff, pasty and overstuffed, with alabaster jowls that spilled over his shirt collar like inner tubes.

Earlier that day he had wrenched his neck watching a cricket match, and as a result was feeling rather sorry for himself.

"We should ship the lot of them to America," Sir Reginald agreed. He signaled for another snifter of two-hundred-year-old Napoleon brandy.

"I remember that last bleak day in Calcutta." Lord Finhatten sighed. A glazed look came over his beady brown eyes, part longing, part drink.

"The British Army Band played 'Auld Lang Syne' as the first Lady Finhatten and I left the government house. After we got to England, we received dispatches reporting that the natives had overrun the house and slashed the queen's portrait. Savages!"

Sir Reginald had heard this story many times before, but he humored his friend. Poor Jinx hadn't been his peppy self since they lost India in '47.

"Cheer up, old man," he said. "Think of Fifty-two. We reached Everest *and* won the Cup final. And don't forget the atomic bomb we detonated in Australia."

"But that was more than a decade ago. Since then we've done nothing but sit and watch while England hemorrhages. There'll be nothing left of her unless we stop talking and actually *do* something."

"I was saving this for the meeting, but I suppose I can tell you now. The queen is coming to Grunby Hall."

Lord Finhatten became overheated at the news. He loosened his collar and fanned himself with the latest issue of *Guns & Hounds.*

"Rags, do you really think our plan will work?"

A look of steely determination turned Sir Reginald's handsome face into something tight and mean, like a clenched fist. "Just you wait, old boy. We'll show them the Englishman is a mad dog still."

Secret Service headquarters
Office of Agent Cedric Pumpernickel
10:02 A.M.

"I've spent some time studying photographs of your brother. He seems to have three essential facial expressions: leering, smirking, and sneering. He also uses his eyebrows to indicate emotion. Can you raise and lower yours at will?"

"It's another family trait. Whenever we were naughty, all my mother had to do was raise one brow and we knew we were in for it."

"Excellent. Now, I want you to practice curling your lip."

Jane tried.

"Not so extreme."

She tried again.

"Better. Now—raise a brow *and* curl your lip."

Jane couldn't do it without some degree of difficulty. Pumpernickel made a tick on his list.

"You'll have to work on that one at home. Now, let's practice leering at the ladies."

"I know how I do it—how does he?"

"He rolls his eyes over their curves. I believe there is a bit of winking involved. That's what I've been led to understand, based on information from the other agents. They've been studying his moves for years."

"Could we get a girl in here?" Jane wondered. "How about that blond at the front desk. She has more curves than a roller coaster."

"I'll have to do, Miss Bond."

Jane gave Agent Pumpernickel the once-over.

"That's too subtle."

"I generally try to be discreet," Jane said. "I don't like to make a girl feel ogled."

"No need for discretion. Remember, you're a man. You're expected to look the ladies over as if you were choosing chops for that night's supper."

Jane tried again. Pumpernickel didn't have any curves to speak of, but she did her best.

"Much better. Practice that one tonight too."

The Sons of Britain Society Club
10:31 A.M.

Sir Reginald tapped his pipe on the rosewood regency sideboard.

"This meeting of the Sons of Britain Society is now in session. We will begin, as always, with the secret pledge."

Men from the most influential institutions in England got to their feet and solemnly intoned:

*The ship of state is sinking, but the Sons of Britain will wrest
    the helm;*
*We, the best men in the world, shall restore our exiled king to
    his proper place, and restore the proper order;*
*No more queens! No longer will they undermine the manly
    glory of empire!*
Rule Britannia, Britannia ruled by S.O.B.S.!

A moment of silence, then the sound of Lord Finhatten sniffing. Sir
Reginald cringed. Finhatten was rather a crybaby when it came to the
subject of the empire. It was most embarrassing for a man of his standing to be so public with his emotions.

"Gentlemen, good news. The queen is coming to Grunby Hall."

"Jolly good show!" someone cried—it sounded like Lord Tytten-
hanger, their man in the House of Commons—and discreet cheering
followed. For more than a hundred years the Sons of Britain Society
had been little more than a comfortable men's club; a refuge from
wives in particular, and women in general. Until a few months ago, that
is, when Sir Reginald had come up with a brilliant plan to engineer a
transfer of power. They would seize the throne for their exiled king.

They had nothing, really, against Queen Elizabeth. She seemed a
perfectly sensible woman and an adequate monarch. Her head fit the
crown and she carried herself with dignity. She was, however, through
no fault of her own, a female. And the Sons of Britain firmly believed
that what England needed most, in these days of social unrest, was
someone with authority, power, and strength.

In other words, a king.

Once the Duke of Windsor was crowned, the landed gentry would
once again become a protected species, and men like Sir Reginald, who
had been forced to open their grand country estates to the vulgar
masses in order to make a living, could return to their former occupa-
tion—that of gentleman.

"The chair recognizes Baron Owlpen from the planning committee."

"Harrumph!" Baron Owlpen cleared his throat before reading the
planning committee's report. "The kidnapping will take place during
the auction for the Daughters of the Dispossessed Aristocracy, the
queen's favorite charity.

"Halfway through the cocktail hour, Lord Blickling, our man in the palace"—Lord Blickling acknowledged his name with a modest nod of his head—"will escort Her Majesty to the drawing room under the pretext of showing her a rare collection of corgi aquatints. Once there, the queen will be chloroformed, taken to a waiting van disguised as a bakery truck, and driven to Grouse Manor, where she will be escorted to her new quarters."

Lord Bolderbrooke objected. "I still think the choice of Grouse Manor is awfully risky. What if tourists come across the queen?"

"The grounds have been closed to autobus tours for months," Sir Reginald snapped. "And I have spent weeks personally selecting the furnishings for the new royal quarters."

Baron Owlpen continued. "As I said, the queen will be chloroformed and then a substitute will take her place at the party, thus affording us the necessary time to get her out of London. Once the real queen is safely ensconced in the dungeon, the impostor queen will excuse herself to go powder her nose. She will take off her disguise, and plant a letter in the ladies' telling the world she has fallen in love with the keeper of the silver stick and run off with him to raise corgis on a ranch in deepest Australia."

The room was abuzz with questions.

"What about the queen's bodyguard?"

"I've already assigned a rather sympathetic man to guard the queen that evening," explained Lord Blickling, their man in the Palace. He had procured Her Majesty's authentic signature on a piece of palace stationery. The letter announcing her abdication would be composed on the same typewriter employed by the queen's social secretary.

"I've had to promise him membership to the club."

"Are you suggesting we allow working men into our society?" The Right Honorable John Thimblebee thundered. "That's strictly against our charter. Haven't you any sense of propriety, man?"

"Gentlemen, we'll have to make a few concessions here," Sir Reginald insisted. "I have, after all, spent a tremendous sum expanding the wine cellar to accommodate our royal guest."

"And the keeper of the silver stick?" Lord Tuttlewaddle wanted to know. "Do we pay him to disappear, or is he to be sent to the wine cellar too?"

Lord Finhatten gasped at the suggestion. The queen sharing her quarters with a man who was not her husband? Impossible!

"He'll be pushing up daisies in Hyde Park long before anyone realizes either one of them is gone," Sir Reginald assured them.

Lord Finhatten was greatly relieved to hear it.

"We swore not to tell our wives about our plan," Viscount Littlecote reminded Sir Reginald. "Have you reversed your feelings on the matter?"

"Good Lord, man, what do you take me for?"

"Then who's to be queen?"

"I propose our very own Lord Sissyhurst for the part of Her Majesty. With the addition of a wig, some stage makeup, and a boxy hat, he'll be a dead ringer."

"Me!" cried Lord Sissyhurst.

"As I remember, you were a rather convincing Ophelia at Eton. And you have a strikingly similar profile."

"But a nicer nose," Lord Finhatten assured him.

"I'm afraid I've grown rather thick through the middle since those days," Lord Sissyhurst demurred. "I haven't the proper shape for the job anymore."

"We'll get you a girdle."

"How long can we keep the queen captive?" Lord Tuttlewaddle worried. "If it comes out we took her there against her will, it could be a sticky wicket."

"We have a spot reserved for her in a very private American sanitarium called Happy Acres. They specialize in superiority complexes. A few minor surgical alterations and daily doses of hallucinogenic drugs, and Her Majesty will be just one more hysterical housewife who imagines herself a queen."

Thanks to Edwina's vast fortune, Sir Reginald had been able to afford a small army of private detectives to compile extensive dossiers on every member of Parliament, and a few key men on Fleet Street. Any man of consequence who opposed the duke's return would find his foibles and fetishes the talk of the town.

"When the rabble start yapping about the queen's betrayal of her oath, we will step forward and wax romantic about a sovereign with a heart. They will be reminded of another royal figure who gave up everything for love. Our compassion for the queen will win over her subjects, and the duke's rush to save the monarchy will be seen as a grand gesture. We will be the saviors of England."

"Our names will be read in Westminster Abbey at Christmastime, when the bishop prays for the souls of England's important people," Lord Finhatten gushed. "It will be the royal family, the PM, pop stars, fashion designers, and the Sons of Britain."

"It will be the Sons of Britain, the royal family, the PM, fashion designers, *then* pop stars," Sir Reginald corrected him.

"Then, guided by our new king, we and other like-minded men will return England to its glorious imperial past," Lord Owlpen added.

"It will take time," cautioned Sir Reginald.

"We can wait," Viscount Littlecote said, nodding sagely. "Just as long as England is moving in the right direction—away from the tide of socialism that is lapping at our shores, ruining our prized institutions, and undermining the most gracious way of life the world has ever known."

"The map will soon be pink again." Lord Finhatten sighed happily. "And schoolchildren will celebrate Empire Day as in my youth."

"All in favor say 'Aye'!"

"Aye!"

It was unanimous.

Office of Agent Pumpernickel
10:50 A.M.

Jane lifted the cocktail glass from the tray Pumpernickel had extended toward her, sniffed the contents, and curled her lip in disgust.

"No, you save sneers for enemies, not alcohol."

"I wasn't practicing. I can't drink this. It's far too strong."

"James Bond without his martini is like the queen without her crown. You must learn to love them."

"Can't we fake it and just use water?"

"No. It's always the smallest slip that queers the deal."

Jane held her nose and took a sip. She shuddered as it trickled down her throat.

"That's not quite the expression we're looking for." Agent Pumpernickel sighed unhappily.

Jane popped the olive in her mouth, hoping it would kill the taste of the vodka.

Pumpernickel darted toward her. "Spit that out, Miss Bond!" he cried. "That's a radio transmitter. It's a delicate piece of equipment."

Jane spat it back into the drink. "Why is my drink bugged?"

"I'll be listening in on your conversations in case you need my assistance."

"Your boss told me I had to stay sober for the duration."

"Only when it's called for. Drinks will be served after the ceremony. You will accept three, and sip them slowly. Double martinis are your brother's favorite beverage. He's almost never seen without one."

Jane made a face. "I'm not all that fond of them. We may as well quit now." She had always known that alcohol would someday be her downfall. "But I'll do my best," Jane promised when she saw the crestfallen expression on Pumpernickel's face.

"That's the spirit! Now, when you raise the glass to take a sip, make your eyes dart back and forth, as if seeking out enemies or looking for ladies whose company you'd enjoy."

Jane tried it a couple of times, even throwing in a few eyebrow raises for effect.

"Very good." Pumpernickel applauded her. "And remember—you take them shaken, not stirred. It's all written down on this piece of vapor paper. Take it home, read over it until you're sure you've got it, then hold it near a flame."

"We wouldn't want the Russians knowing how James takes his martinis, would we?"

"Exactly, Miss Bond."

Grunby Hall
Palatial London Home of Sir and Lady Wooley-Booley
No. 7 St. James's Place
11:00 A.M.

Lady Edwina Wooley-Booley rubbed vanishing cream on her face, tissued it off, splashed on rosewater, and began lightly slapping herself, starting with her neck and working her way up, in order to increase the circulation in her face and give her cheeks the happy radiance of a newlywed. Sir Reginald had gone off to meet with his taxidermist, so

Lady Edwina was alone in her boudoir taking breakfast: warmed grapefruit wedges, a glass of orange barley water, strawberry jammers, and two cups of bitter black coffee.

As was her habit, while she ate she read—and reread—the *Times* court circular until she had worked herself into a rage. When she saw that Prince Richard of Gloucester and his wife, Princess Minnie, had taken a ride on a go-cart for charity, she wanted to weep. Not for herself, mind you, but for the rightful heirs to the English throne—the Duke and Duchess of Windsor.

"Oh, the heartaches the brave pair have borne during their long exile!" Lady Edwina cried aloud. Like Moses in the desert, the duke and duchess had endured all sorts of hardships whilst searching for a home, while the royal family blithely continued the business of monarchy. *They* should have been the ones on that go-cart!

For twenty-nine years Edwina had stewed over the terrible wrong inflicted on King Edward VIII, who had been forced to surrender his throne for the woman he loved. For Edwina, he had been the bright sun of the British Empire; young and handsome and gay like a fairy prince from a book. A prince whose bright light had been cruelly extinguished by narrow-minded court functionaries, who knew all there was to know about hoary court protocol, but nothing of the ways of true love. Every night Edwina played a recording of the king's abdication speech over and over on a little phonograph she kept by her bed, and cried herself to sleep.

She collected news accounts of the couple's indomitable courage in the face of tragedy. She had wept bitterly when she heard the news of their painful wartime exile in the Bahamas. Because of the war, the duchess had found it impossible to assemble a proper tropical wardrobe. And while the reigning royals lived like kings, the duke and duchess were forced constantly to cut corners. Edwina had read in an American magazine that, for economy's sake, the duchess had commissioned Van Cleef & Arpels to design a reversible tiara that did double duty as a necklace. The duchess was a brave and resourceful woman; just the kind of queen England needed these days.

The idea that the duke might one day return to the throne had been a long-cherished dream of hers. After a vigorous letter-writing campaign to the *Daily Mail* had failed to raise a public outcry for his reinstatement, Edwina had given up all hope.

Then she had met Sir Reginald.

He had influential friends in high places who felt as they did, that the duke and duchess were growing older and the time had come to force the issue. Sir Reginald had warned her that it would be frightfully expensive to rig a transfer of the throne, but with Edwina's vast financial reserves, and his connections and political savvy, anything was possible. All they needed was a plan. Edwina had been wracking her brains for weeks. She would spend any amount on a campaign to convince people of the very rightness of her ambitions.

"I am willing to sacrifice everything for the duchess!" she cried as she clasped the court circular to the bosom of her satin bed jacket.

A deep voice interrupted her reverie. "Excuse me, ma'am."

Edwina flushed red when she saw Sir Reginald's manservant, Nigel, peeking around her door. Nigel was forever catching Edwina at inopportune moments, like the day she had gotten her head stuck in the mouth of a stuffed bear. She had only been a lady for six months. There was still so much she had to learn.

"Yes, Nigel?"

"A letter has arrived from the queen's Office of Social Affairs."

"You read it," Edwina begged. Her hands were sticky from jam. It would never do to muss the royal missive. Her friend Mrs. Snipe would no doubt want to see it.

He broke the wax seal, carefully removed the letter, and started reading. To himself.

"No, Nigel—read it to *me*," Lady Edwina cried impatiently.

HRH Queen Elizabeth graciously accepts your invitation to the Daughters of the Dispossessed Aristocracy Charity Auction.

Jam be damned! Edwina grabbed the letter from Nigel and read it for herself. It was true! She, Edwina Piggott, the plumber's daughter, was going to entertain the queen of England! She jumped up, spilling the contents of her breakfast tray on the priceless Ausenbauss carpet, and did a triumphant jig around her bedroom. Nigel crept away to inform the others that Lady Edwina had lost her mind, and spoilt the carpet in the process.

Office of Agent Pumpernickel
11:20 A.M.

"Now walk like a man," Pumpernickel instructed her. "Women glide effortlessly; men stride as if claiming their ground."

"Where did you hear that?"

"From my father. He took me to the pictures as a youth to demonstrate."

"I've never seen a woman glide unless she was on skates."

"Not glide, per se—they just take short, even steps that give the appearance of a lovely flow. Like this."

He demonstrated.

"One—two—three—four. See how easy it is?"

"You do that very well."

"That's why my father took me to the flicks," he admitted ruefully. "You see, I was pigeon-toed as a child. Still am, a little. Corrective shoes took care of it for the most part, but I'm afraid even after seeing all those American Westerns, my gait isn't what it should be."

Jane stomped across the room like John Wayne heading into a gun battle.

"Too crude. Your brother is smooth, with just a touch of cheekiness. He's the kind of man who walks into a room knowing every man wants to be him, and every woman wants to be with him."

"You sound like a clothing advert."

Pumpernickel blushed. He had consulted many different sources for Jane's education.

"Try walking with an air of entitlement. Don't wriggle your hips."

"I don't wriggle my hips."

"Miss Bond, you do, just ever so slightly. Not that it's noticeable, but for our purposes, it won't do. I'm not finding fault with you; it's simply a matter of physiology. You're a woman. Now, shall we try it once more?"

008 had to stifle a nasty laugh. That old marnie was teaching Miss Bond to be a man? It was she who should be giving the lessons.

He was lying on the dusty floor in the vacant office next to Pumpernickel's, his ear pressed to a crack in the wall. He had first perfected this method of spying in public school; it had given him ammunition to use against his teachers. He had won an appointment to Her Majesty's

Secret Service based on those high marks, along with glowing reviews of his moral character.

Men of principle spent a great deal of time sputtering indignantly about this or that; the trick was to strike quickly and quietly. Complaining to N. had been a mongy move on his part—it did nothing but draw attention to his unhappiness. From now on, he'd act the part of a happy little desk jockey whenever anyone was around. That way, when Miss Bond met with some unfortunate accident, he'd be the last one anyone would finger. If he played it right, he could get rid of Pumpernickel and Miss Bond in one stroke, and maybe even make Pumpernickel take the blame for Miss Bond's demise.

Blimey, it had been humiliating having Pumpernickel make such a fuss over him in the cafeteria. When that girl called out, and Pumpernickel made such a to-do over it, everyone had turned to look. It was bad enough he had been given Pumpernickel's old job; now everyone would think he and the old man were friends. The word had probably gone round the whole building by now. Those hens in the powder vine would have made sure of that.

Secret Service headquarters
Shooting range
Fifteen minutes later

"Bang! Bang! You're dead!" 008 snarled. His gun was hot in his hand. It felt good. The smell of gunpowder enveloped him. His trigger finger itched to shoot again. But it wouldn't be necessary. His shot had found its mark. A clean hit right through the heart. Agent Pumpernickel was dead.

"Clean through the right ventricle. Complete and utter death. Congratulations, 008," the instructor smiled. He laid the big paper man-shaped target on the table. He pinpointed the bullet's trajectory.

"You've proven to be one of our best shots ever—almost as good as 007. You have excellent reflexes and no qualms whatsoever about blasting away. We like that in our men." Then he gave 008 the highest compliment any agent could hope to receive: "N. will be pleased."

008 glowered at the mention of N. It had always been understood that once 007 had ceased to be top action man, it would be his turn. For a year now he had honed his sharpshooter skills and read endless field

reports of long-ago missions, waiting patiently like a good lad for his turn. Two days ago, 008 had been dead certain that he was going to be the next 007. Come to find out, he was really the next Agent Pumpernickel.

N. had attempted to explain. "Until this business with 007 is resolved—blah—blah—no more missions—blah—blah—Pumpernickel retiring—blah—blah—a temporary placement—blah—blah—not to worry—blah—blah."

"Are the rumors true?" the instructor asked in a confidential tone. "Is 007 really in the nuthouse?"

"I don't know," 008 spat out. He was getting damn sick of hearing that name. "Set up another target," he ordered. Shooting always made him feel better.

"Bang! Bang!" Another bull's-eye. This time he pretended the target was James Bond.

"You're really spot-on today," the instructor said admiringly.

008 smiled smugly. The shooting range report was sure to impress Miss Tuppenny. 008 could tell she already liked him; now she'd know exactly what kind of man he was.

Office of Sir Niles Needlum
12:00 P.M.

"She does look awfully like her brother," exclaimed N. with obvious relief. He hadn't been able to bring himself to watch while Miss Bond was having her hair clipped. There was something barbarous about taking a buzzer to a woman's head. Miss Bond didn't seem to mind; it was a most unnatural attitude. He had expected more of a dustup, a few tears even, but she had gone quietly to the chair.

"Her Majesty will never know the difference," Pumpernickel assured him.

According to the palace spokesman, the queen was very much looking forward to meeting a real secret agent. She had heard rumors of a superman who had single-handedly saved England from ruination on more than one occasion. It had been her idea to present him with a medal. N. had been horrified when the request came over his desk. One does not admit to the queen that one's best secret agent is confined to a sanitarium, strapped to a bed—especially if one wishes the queen to help stop governmental budget cuts from closing one's department.

"This had better work, Pumpernickel. The future of the free world is in this girl's hands."

Jane looked startled to hear this. "You neglected to mention that yesterday. And please stop talking about me as if I'm not in the room."

Agent Pumpernickel chuckled. "I think Sir Niles is being overly dramatic in order to drive home an important point."

"Which is?"

"That this mission is a very important one."

"Then why get me to do it? Are you all out of secret agents?"

N. scowled. The girl asked far too many questions. They were using her because pulling a switch on the queen was a hanging offense. No one besides N. and Pumpernickel had any inkling of the plot. He had used the queen as a glittering carrot on many occasions to get Pumpernickel to perform odious tasks; now he could deliver the goods. And if the plan failed, the blame would fall on Pumpernickel's shoulders. It wasn't unheard of for older agents to go a little bonkers as the end ticked ever closer. Even if his plan was discovered, Pumpernickel would never mention N.'s participation. Of this N. was sure, as sure as he knew the sun would rise each day.

"Don't you usually arrest girls for dressing like this?" Jane wondered aloud.

N. held his tongue. In a few days, this would all be over. Miss Bond would be out of his hair, Pumpernickel would be retired, and—God willing—007 would be back in his rightful place.

Dottinghurst Manor
London home of Lord Mortimer and Lady Lettie Finhatten
Belgrave Square
12:30 P.M.

Lady Lettie Finhatten, known to her very best friends as Snuggs, pinned on her new yellow dove-feather hat and passed quickly in front of the full-length looking glass. Her goal was to catch a sudden glimpse of herself in her new hat to see how she looked to the casual admirer. When she was satisfied that the hat suited her from every possible angle, she checked her lipstick. Perfect. The salesgirl was right. Velvet Viper *was* her color.

Lettie was off to Grunby Hall for an afternoon of social victimization at the hands of Lady Edwina Wooley-Booley. She had befriended Edwina strictly as a favor to her husband, Lord "Jinx" Finhatten, a member of the House of Lords famous for his diatribes warning of the dangers of the insidious intrusion of foreign cuisine. Being married to a government leader was a thankless job. Unattractive people in grubby macs were constantly haranguing them on the streets of London, wanting to argue against her husband's sensible views.

On the subject of Edwina, the usually malleable Jinx had been uncharacteristically stubborn. Edwina was his best friend's wife, and so it was up to Lettie to take her under her wing. God knows Lettie had tried. Edwina's foray into high society had thus far been a disaster. Not only was Edwina lacking the most rudimentary social skills, she had the habit of blurting out unfortunate details regarding intimate matters at the most embarrassing times. Just last week, at an Yves St. Laurent fashion show, she had informed the people around them that she was wearing her first pair of handmade knickers, with Belgium lace trim. The fit was "marvelous." Apparently, her old ones had bunched.

And then there had been the Hunt Club cotillion debacle. Edwina had worn a tartan ball gown of her own design. Unfortunately, Edwina's dressmaker had also made the club's drapes—of the same fabric. And now the Comtesse de Chambrun's tea was the talk of the town. How was Lettie to know that when she suggested Edwina wear black stockings and white shoes, Edwina would take her seriously? A dog would know better. Much to her dismay, the ugly incident had only strengthened Edwina's commitment to their friendship. Edwina had misread the criticism as a critique of Lettie's taste and declared she would stand by Lettie through thick and thin. Edwina certainly was thick, Lettie smirked.

Their cozy chats, as Edwina insisted on calling their torturous meetings, always took place at Grunby Hall. Lettie disliked having Edwina at Dottinghurst Manor for fear she would drop jelly babies on the carpets Jinx's grandmother, Lady Biddle Phelps-Mumm-Paget, had had woven in Constantinople to match the coat of her favorite spaniel, Mimsy.

Grunby Hall was a fine old Edwardian mansion set back in a tree-lined London square not far from Lady Finhatten's own manse. Unfortunately, Sir Reginald had given Edwina permission to scatter a few personal effects around the house. She was certain he had meant Edwina to bring a few mementos from her flat—a family photograph nicely framed in silver, a favorite porcelain teacup, perhaps. Edwina had, unfortunately, taken his comment as a license to redecorate. Under her gilded thumb, Grunby Hall was becoming a monstrosity. It had taken hundreds of years for the home to develop the distinctively shabby look of really old money, and mere months for Edwina to undo it. The once charmingly restrained sitting room where they always took tea was now crammed with bad imitations of good furniture, dreadful paintings, mass-produced curios, and questionable objets d'art that just screamed nouveau riche. In Edwina's destructive hands, even nature wasn't safe. Instead of having servants play croquet on their off-hours so the soothing sounds of wooden balls being thwacked would reverberate throughout the house, Edwina had a reel-to-reel tape made of a single croquet game and switched it on when company called. Astute guests soon memorized the game. In the hands of the wrong people, technology could indeed be a dangerous thing.

Lettie thought Edwina embodied a native dottiness that would be all well and fine if she lived in a charming country village where she could be appreciated. Although Lettie was significantly younger than the rapidly aging Edwina, it was obvious she was by far the more sophisticated of the two. Poor Edwina was so trusting and unaffected; she reminded Lettie of the unpopular girl at boarding school who followed one around like a puppy until one was forced to be cruel and give it a little kick.

How a plumber's daughter had become intimate with the Duchess of Windsor was one of the world's great mysteries. At first Lettie thought Edwina was making up the whole thing in a pathetic attempt for attention. But they were genuine, all right; Lettie had seen them with her own eyes. The duchess seemed sincere in her affection for Edwina. Of course, the two hadn't actually met.

Lettie's assignment was to be Edwina's friend until she was able to forge her own friendship with the duchess. She had already befriended Sir Reginald—that was turning out to be an equally unpleasant experience.

Office of Agent Pumpernickel
2:00 P.M.

Looking in the mirror gave Jane the shivers. She and her brother were not, after all, the best of friends. It was amazing what a padded suit, a short haircut, and a few fake facial scars would do for a girl. There were notable drawbacks—her breasts ached from being strapped down, and the glue holding the plastic scar on her right cheek itched. Otherwise she was quite comfortable. And the suit was really very nice; made of the finest material. When this was over, she could remove the padding that broadened her shoulders and smoothed out her hipline, take in the waist, and really wear it. She'd never had anything this nice before.

In the beginning, Jane didn't think this could possibly work. Now she saw it just might. For once, she was glad to have been born a Bond. Jane had been making a mental list of what she could do with the money. The first thing she was going to do was move where Bridget wouldn't be afraid to wake up, then pay some of the bookshop's bills so Simon would stop threatening to sell. Then she'd take Miss Liversidge to one of those big cat shows at Westminster she was always talking about.

The Secret Service barber had done a good job on her hair using a photograph of James as a guide. She'd have to watch her back on the street with hair this short. Today, though, no one was going to mess with her. Nobody messed with James Bond.

"They'll expect to see a bulge," Pumpernickel added, then blushed as Jane raised an eyebrow. "Regulations, you know." He handed her a pistol filled with blanks and indicated that she should slide it into her shoulder harness. "Right, then, you practice a little in that mirror—the stance, the walk, the sneer, the ogling, all at once. I'll be back in a moment."

Shutting the door behind himself, Pumpernickel crept along the hallway a few steps and ducked into the door marked BROOM CLOSET to observe Miss Bond through the two-way mirror. She was brandishing the pistol in a most unladylike fashion. In fact, she hardly looked like a lady at all. Pumpernickel dabbed at his brow and fumbled nervously in his pockets for a fag. She was very convincing. He felt an urgent need for a rubber band run.

"Hello, Mother."

"Bridget? Is that you?"

"Yes, Mother. I have a favor to ask."

"Can't it wait, darling? I'm having the most dreadful day."

Bridget screwed up her face in annoyance and started to tap her pencil on her metal desk. Getting Emerald's attention was never easy—unless, of course, it was unwanted attention.

"Your hairdresser quit?" Bridget wondered.

"Don't be impertinent, dear. It's an unattractive quality in a single girl. As a matter of fact, he did quit. And I have two functions coming up. Who, may I ask, is going to do my hair?"

"There are hundreds of hairdressers in London, Mother."

"Bridget, I will not greet the queen with an untested hairstyle!"

Bridget rolled her eyes. Bibi, who was sitting at her desk across from Bridget, painting her nails, laughed. She found Emerald to be rather amusing in small doses.

"I'm sorry, Mother." Bridget tried to sound sympathetic. "Perhaps I can help you find a new hairstylist."

"I thought you did your own hair, dear."

Bridget chafed at the remark. It took a lot of money to keep her long hair looking casual and carefree, and her mother knew it. A long silence followed. It was always this way with Emerald.

"Bridget, you're not moping, are you?" Emerald demanded to know.

"No, Mother." She sighed.

"You were always so sensitive, even as a little girl."

"I have something to ask you."

"You've changed your mind about meeting Lord Piggertine?" Emerald asked hopefully. It would be an excellent match, as their country estates abutted one another.

"I was wondering if you would let me hostess a party?"

"I'm stunned, dear. I had no idea you were interested in following in my footsteps."

"Actually, there's a particular party I have in mind; it's the auction at Grunby Hall."

"Dear, that's a very exclusive gathering. Hadn't you better start with something small? What about throwing a little soiree here for a select few from the polo club?"

Bridget's heart sank. Emerald was always talking about getting her out of the cosmetics business and into a hostess gown. It hadn't occurred to her that Emerald might turn her down.

"I'm very interested in the Daughters of the Dispossessed Aristocracy."

"Why, dear? They're poor."

"They are not."

"They've had to sell their country estates, haven't they?"

"Mother, poor is not having enough to eat; it isn't living without a second home."

Bibi sniggered when Bridget mimed hanging herself with the strap of her handbag.

"The truth is, there's someone there I'm very interested in getting to know," added Bridget.

"It is a man?"

"Yes, Mother. It's a man." Bridget thought Sir Reginald more weasel than human.

"Dear, I'm so pleased."

"I knew you would be."

"This won't be easy, Bridget," Emerald cautioned. "Lady Edwina is rather uncouth. One never knows what ridiculous gem will fall out of her mouth. At Sibyl Colefax's last dinner party, she let us all in on the unsavory news that Lord Wooley-Booley slips into angora on the sly. Could you honestly handle a situation like that?"

Bridget thought about it. In the four years since becoming a G.E.O.R.G.I.E. Girl, she had broken into the Bank of England, scaled the back wall of Liberty's in pursuit of a master poisoner, and dipped her entire body in quality chocolate to entice a Swiss diplomat.

"I'm certain I could," she said, with all confidence.

They talked for more than an hour, ironing out auction details and going over the menu. If it had been a sit-down dinner, Emerald would never have agreed to hand it over to her daughter. However, Lady Edwina and her husband insisted the refreshments be served buffet-style. It was an American custom Emerald found vulgar and common, but Sir Reginald intended the event to be small and exclusive, with as few servants as possible fluttering about.

"The things I do for England," Bridget said, sighing, when she finally hung up the phone.

Grunby Hall sitting room
3:40 P.M.

"I have wonderful news," Edwina cried, her cheeks pink with excitement. She squeezed Lettie's hand with her own moist, plump little hand.

"Just this morning I received a reply from the queen. She's coming to our charity auction!" She paused so Lettie could savor the moment.

"Of course she is," Lettie said blandly. "Everyone knows the Daughters of the Dispossessed Aristocracy is one of her pet charities."

"Oh. Well then, I have other news that's equally exciting. In her last letter, the duchess informed me that she and the duke are ready to come home at a moment's notice."

"That is good news," said Lettie. The sooner the duchess dropped Edwina, the sooner Lettie could too.

"I've come up with an idea to fix it so the duke can take over the throne," Edwina ventured. "It's probably not any good, but it's all I could think of."

Lettie thought Edwina looked as solemn as one could look while wearing a lumpy heather-tweed wool jumper and girlish cotton blouse with a Peter Pan collar. When the Duchess of Windsor was finally crowned queen, Lettie was going to ask her to please, please outlaw Peter Pan collars for anyone over the age of eight.

"I propose we appeal to the basic decency of the queen and ask her to let the Duke of Windsor live out his remaining years on the throne with the understanding that when he dies, she can have it back."

Lettie smiled thinly.

Edwina perked up. "The first thing we would do is create a petition asking Her Majesty to graciously step down," she explained excitedly. "We can take the petition to church fetes and jumble sales and ask people to sign it. Then Jinx can use his influence in the House of Lords to put our idea across. What do you think? Be honest." Edwina turned large, wet cow eyes on her friend.

"I think the queen won't be able to help but be impressed by your rational thinking and clear logic." Lettie smirked.

"Just think—we can be ladies-in-waiting together!"

"It will be nice to have someone with taste in charge," Lettie conceded. "If I were queen, the first thing I'd do is open the windows. I was there last year when Lord Finhatten's nephew was knighted, and it positively stinks of dog."

"The duchess keeps a number of pug dogs," Edwina reminded her. "She might not notice the odor."

Lettie shook her head. "Well, I'm not going to be a lady-in-waiting until the place is aired out."

Office of Miss Tuppenny
4:00 P.M.

Sir Niles rushed into Miss Tuppenny's office and threw a stack of messy files on her desk. "Hold the fort, Miss Tuppenny. I'm in budget meetings the rest of the afternoon."

Miss Tuppenny, who was engaged in the distasteful task of reading Sir Reginald Wooley-Booley's medical records, searching for evidence of any weakness that G.E.O.R.G.I.E. might exploit, smiled at her boss and, when he had left, swept the pile into a drawer she kept empty for this purpose. She locked Sir Wooley-Booley's file in a secret compartment of her desk, and put the dustcover on her typewriter—her sign that she had stepped out. Pinned to the underside of her bra strap was her copy of the key to N.'s office. It was clear he needed extra help with his paperwork.

Having penetrated the inner sanctum, Miss Tuppenny closed the door gently behind herself and deactivated the floor alarm with the tap-dance signal that N. had devised. She moved to his desk and ran her hands along the bottom of the middle desk drawer. The false panel had to be there. She had ordered the extra-large, walnut-finish executive desk herself, specifying brass pulls and a built-in secret compartment.

Her nail hit a tiny groove. She tapped on the wood. Hollow. The bottom of the drawer slid completely out, revealing a cozy hiding place. Inside was a brown file with a red star, labeled BOND, JANE, and a plain manila envelope. She adjusted the desk lamp so it would cast an even light over the documents. With the camera concealed in her steno pad, she coolly and quickly photographed the contents, inwardly marveling at the physical resemblance between Jane and her brother. She stopped and stared at a small snapshot of Jane with her arm around a sumptuous-looking redhead. It was Bridget St. Claire, her very own G.E.O.R.G.I.E. agent.

Tuppenny had just finished when she heard the unmistakable squeak of Cedric Pumpernickel's office mocs outside N.'s door. Everyone knew Fidget was a bit of a snooper, but since he never took anything but rubber bands for his collection, no one really cared. Hastily, she put everything back in order. The doorknob turned slowly. There was a pause. Aware that it was highly irregular for a secretary to enter an executive office without explicit permission, Tuppenny frantically scanned for a hiding place. Pumpernickel would talk; she couldn't risk any hint of unseemly behavior.

Thank goodness the Secret Service insisted its secretaries wear sensible, low-heeled shoes; it made the climb out N.'s third-story window that much easier.

"Good Lord, Miss Tuppenny, whatever are you doing on that ledge? Come in at once! It's that blasted Bond, isn't it? The news of his accident has left you despondent. I wish he'd leave you girls alone! Don't jump, Miss Tuppenny, he's not worth it. He's not a very nice chap. Take my hand, please—that's it, easy peasy—and I'll drop you at home. You'll feel better after some tea and a good night's sleep. It's always darkest before the dawn."

"I do feel a bit under the weather," Miss Tuppenny admitted, stepping back daintily onto the worn carpet of N.'s office. "But there's no need to put yourself out. I'll treat myself to a taxi."

Pleased with himself for having saved such a young and vital government employee from early retirement, Pumpernickel put his hand in his pocket where he kept his sweets and handed Miss Tuppenny a humbug. "Sweets for the sweet." He smiled.

Grunby Hall
4:14 P.M.

"So then I said to my friend Mildred Snipe . . ."

Lettie leaned back into the hideously overstuffed chair and breathed in deeply, practically feeling the dreadful synthetic fabric through her clothing. She was trying to stem the headache she had felt coming on since viewing Edwina's auction donation: twin gilded centaur lamps with crystal-drop shades. Lettie thought that when Edwina was finished making Grunby Hall "modern and gay," it should reopen to the public as the Edwina Piggott Museum of Bad Taste. (Lettie almost laughed out loud at her own cleverness. She must remember to repeat it.)

Like a magpie, Edwina had to have every shiny thing that caught her eye. Her interests were as vast as her pocketbook was deep; she'd complete one collection only to start another. She was currently collecting elephant figurines. In Lettie's purse was a gift for Edwina from Jinx's India collection—a small ivory carving of a baby elephant. It had been Jinx's idea; an apology of sorts for the latest fashion debacle. What's more, her husband had made her promise never to interfere with Edwina's wardrobe again. From here on in, when Edwina asked for advice, Lettie was to say, "Whatever you select will certainly do."

". . . and then Mildred tried to talk me into going shopping at Martha Manning, but I told her I had to come home and oversee the raking of the gravel driveway. Well, you should have heard her reply! My old friends simply do not understand how many obligations I have now as lady of the house."

"It looks very nice." Lettie yawned.

"Thank you. Crumpet?"

"I must be going," Lettie said. "I'll leave you to work on your ingenious proposal."

"But we haven't even begun to discuss what we're going to wear at the auction," Edwina protested.

"You must learn to rely on your own good sense, Edwina."

"Do you think I'm ready?"

"You're as ready as you'll ever be," Lettie said truthfully. She had no intention of being dragged through the ready-wear shops for a dress that would make the dull and dumpy Edwina fit to meet the queen. Besides, she had other fish to fry. Before she left, she took the ivory elephant out of her purse and slipped it under the cushion of her chair. She'd telephone Edwina later and tell her she'd left a surprise for her in the sitting room.

G.E.O.R.G.I.E. headquarters
Office of Chief Tuppenny
5:30 P.M.

It was a drizzly evening, but Miss Tuppenny didn't mind. She loved this kind of night; the city was winding down, the evening rain washing away all memory of the frenzied day. She found the patter of soft rain against her office window soothing after a long day performing tedious tasks: typing, filing, dodging sexual advances, and being forced to listen to the ridiculous dreams of self-absorbed men. Miss Tuppenny had to be patient and competent and efficient and calm and never drop one hint that she was engaged in espionage work of her own. It was easy, really, as long as she didn't get caught with her nose in a top secret file. N. had never once, in seven years, asked Miss Tuppenny what she did in the evenings.

There was a knock at the door. It was Agent Gallini.

"Chief, here are the photos from that roll of film you gave me, and these are the latest blotter-paper transcriptions." Each night, a sweeper put a fresh piece of blotter paper on N.'s desk, and brought the old one to G.E.O.R.G.I.E. headquarters for analysis. The thick cotton rag paper would then be soaked in a phosphorous solution and examined under a special light, thus revealing every mark N. made with his pen. The man doodled excessively; his blotters were covered with battle scenes between strange little stick men with daggers for eyes and bubble-headed, three-eyed martians.

"What are you doing here so late?" Miss Tuppenny asked.

"Trying on my maid's uniform. And Bridget has a date."

"Thank you, Agent Gallini."

She lingered in the doorway looking back at Tuppenny. "I'm your devoted slave," Bibi murmured.

Tuppenny blushed despite herself. She wished Bibi would settle down. Although she preferred that her girls not date one another—a policy they patently ignored—she did sometimes wish that Bibi's affair with Bridget had turned into something more permanent. Bridget was a levelheaded girl; she would have kept Bibi on a short leash.

Bibi had the makings of a great secret agent, but she was too easily distracted by a pretty face and shapely pair of legs. Bridget would never let a girl distract her from the duty at hand, whereas Bibi always managed to muddy the waters with some kind of romantic drama. She averaged one affair per assignment.

It was hard to be alone with your secrets—no one had to tell Miss Tuppenny that. She knew all too well how difficult it was to sustain a relationship with an outsider unless she, too, became an agent. Girlfriends who weren't spy material had to be kept in the dark. The atmosphere of secrecy, the weight of unspoken words, the sudden business trips, the occasional unexplainable bruise—all inevitably led to the accusation of infidelity. It was a lonely business sometimes.

She gazed again at that photo of Jane with her arms around Bridget and decided that Bridget was in over her head. She would have to have a little chat with her. On the other hand, if Sir Niles actually carried off this deception, and Jane was willing to be drawn into G.E.O.R.G.I.E., it could mean everything to their operations.

Think of how far inside they could get with their own James Bond.

The Sons of Britain Society Club
6:10 P.M.

Lord Finhatten sank into the leather club chair, and disconsolately sipped his WWI-vintage Armagnac. It was his third that evening. With a solemn air, he intoned solemnly:

> *The tumult and the shouting dies,*
> *The Captains and the Kings depart—*
> *Still stands Thine ancient sacrifice,*
> *An humble and contrite heart.*
> *Lord God of Hosts, be with us yet,*
> *Lest we forget, Lest we forget.*

He raised his snifter to the portrait of King Edward VIII over the Indian rosewood mantelpiece, and drank deeply. A bit of it dribbled down his chins.

"You're down tonight, old chap. Your horse lose again?"

"There's something troubling me, Rags. It's of a highly personal nature and I hesitate to mention it, but you are my closest friend."

Sir Reginald sighed and closed his eyes. Armagnac and Kipling were always a lethal combination for the old boy.

Jinx unfolded his handkerchief and—rather noisily—blew his nose. He took a deep, melodramatic breath. "I have reason to believe my wife has taken a lover!"

"Nonsense!" Sir Reginald cried.

"I've always known that Lettie was an adventuress at heart," Jinx continued miserably. "Lately she seems a trifle bored by our sedate life. Perhaps it was capricious of me to marry a girl young enough to be my granddaughter." He stared into his glass as if hoping to find an answer in the amber-colored liquid. "Do you ever worry about Edwina straying?"

"I *wish* Edwina would have an affair; it would keep her out of my hair."

Jinx was a little shocked at his friend's insouciant manner. Only a cad would speak of his wife in such terms. Still, he pressed on with his confidences, his voice reduced to a whisper.

"Lettie doesn't love me anymore." There, he had said it.

Sir Reginald thought Jinx might very well become hysterical. The man was becoming weak as water in old age.

"Poppycock! I'm certain Lettie's feelings for you haven't changed one whit!"

"They have, I'm telling you. The servants are beginning to talk. I'm thinking of consulting my solicitor." If he couldn't save his marriage, he could at least secure the family silver.

"Servants lie," Sir Reginald said bluntly. "You mustn't believe a word they say."

"The proof is irrefutable. Lettie's been coming and going at all hours of the day. And when she's home, she taken to locking herself in her wing. And she's had a private telephone line installed."

"She doesn't want to bore you with her frivolous female chatter. You know how she and Edwina prattle on for hours about scandals and hairstyles and what everyone's wearing."

"I hadn't considered that," Jinx admitted.

"Have another drink, old man, and pull yourself together. Have you forgotten you're a Finhatten? Think of your Uncle Sedgewick—why, he stood up to Hitler! Surely you can stomach a few false rumors."

During the Blitz, Lord Sedgewick Finhatten, in the tradition of Finhattens, had bravely carried on. Each afternoon, as he had done for years, he sat under the glass roof of the Langham Hotel and did his daily crossword puzzle, in ink, in defiance of the German bombers fly-ing overhead.

"He was blown to bits!" Jinx cried.

"Tut-tut!" replied Sir Reginald, waving away that irrelevant detail. "This is no time to be worrying about domestic troubles. You'll have to stand in the House and plead our case; if you're involved in a scandal, no one will be listening. They'll be too busy imagining Lettie in com-promising positions. Put your suspicions aside. We must get on with the business of running this country."

Jinx wiped his eyes. "That's exactly what I'm going to do—" he de-clared.

"That's the way, old man."

"—just as soon as I find out who the cad is. Tomorrow I'm going to a detective agency and hire a fellow to follow her. If I find out she's got a lover—why, right after the coronation, I'll kill them both!"

G.E.O.R.G.I.E. headquarters
Office of Chief Tuppenny
6:32 P.M.

Bridget sank deeper into the squeaky inflatable chair across from Chief Tuppenny's desk. In her hand was a photograph of her in Jane's bedsit. Bridget was clad in nothing more than knickers, a bra, go-go boots, and a big smile. How could she have not noticed that she was under sur-veillance? She placed the picture back on Agent Tuppenny's desk and let her head drop into her hands.

"Nice knickers . . ." Chief Tuppenny remarked dryly.

"This has never happened to me before!" cried Bridget. "Well, not in front of a camera," she amended. "I mean, not without my permis-sion! I'm a disgrace!"

Bridget's obvious discomfort touched the chief. "The negatives will be destroyed, you needn't worry. But you can't see Jane at the moment. It's too dangerous. We can't afford to have you in the Secret Service files. And besides, you'll be needed at Grunby Hall. I'm putting Agent Mimi Dolittle on Jane."

Bridget looked alarmed. Agent Dolittle was a very attractive blond who bore more than a slight resemblance to Astrid, Jane's former lover.

"It's just for a few days," the chief said soothingly. "And strictly business."

"The next time I become involved with the relative of an enemy agent, I'll let you know," Bridget promised.

Chief Tuppenny didn't skip a beat. "I hear the head of the KGB has a very attractive daughter."

Bridget smiled. Tuppenny was a dream. Bridget slipped on her white vinyl trench coat and paused long enough to brush her long hair away from her face.

"One more thing—" The chief's tone had turned serious. Hidden in her top desk drawer were explicit photographs of Jane with other women, photographs she'd rather Bridget didn't see.

"I know what you're going to say," said Bridget. "But she's nothing like her brother."

Chief Tuppenny opened her mouth to speak, then thought better of it. Nothing she would say would change Bridget's feelings for the girl.

Crispin's Bookshop
7:12 P.M.

Pumpernickel dropped Jane at Simon's shop. She had left her suit and scars at headquarters for the night, for tomorrow the lessons would continue. The day would be devoted to court etiquette. Jane would be in the presence of the queen for less than a minute, and, according to Pumpernickel, the earth would fall off its axis if, in the course of that time, she blundered in the slightest, or let slip an improper remark along the lines of "Love your hat." (That had been Pumpernickel's example.)

Mrs. Snipe greeted her at the door with a horrified stare.

"Jane Bond—what on earth did you do to your hair? It's so short, people will think you're a man!"

Jane smiled wanly. And to think she had missed this place today. "Is Simon here?"

"Downstairs."

Jane went to the cellar, where Simon was unpacking a new shipment of books.

"The Christie came in?"

"Yes, thanks to you." As Jane had paid their distributor, Simon could now afford to restock the shelves. He tossed her a copy.

"Thanks. I need a new read."

"Your hair is quite shocking. It suits you, though."

"Mrs. Snipe says it makes me look like a man."

Simon squinted at her. "Maybe a little. But you do nothing at all for me, I must say. How's life at Amalgamated Widget?"

"Smashing."

"How do they feel about the haircut?"

"Too long in front." Jane plopped down on a box and stretched her legs.

"Are you working tomorrow?" Simon asked.

"Amalgamated can't do without me for the next two days. Why— do you need me?"

"I miss you."

"That's sweet of you."

"Not really. Mrs. Snipe is driving me up a wall."

"Poor Simon. I'll do what I can to wear her out," Jane promised.

"Bridget called. You're to meet her at the bar around nine. She seems very nice." Her manners were miles and away above Astrid's, who had barely acknowledged his existence when calling the shop to badger Jane. "She invited me to stop around for a drink. I won't if you don't want me to, but it's a good sign."

Jane thought so too. When a girl wanted to get to know your friends, it could mean only one thing: she was getting serious.

The Empire Hotel
ROOMS BY THE HOUR OR THE DAY
Picketts Locks Lane W3
7:12 P.M.

"You told him I was *what*?"

Lady Lettie Finhatten was sitting at the dressing table in Room 313 of the Empire Hotel, in pearls and pumps and nothing more, plucking her brows into two perfect crescents. She frowned ever so slightly, although not too much, as it caused wrinkles.

"It was the only thing I could think of," Sir Reginald explained. He was sprawled on the bed, clad in Y-fronts and argyle socks. "He was going to put a detective on you in the morning. The last thing we need is someone snooping around. I thought it was rather a clever explanation for all your mysterious absences."

"It sounds suspiciously like Daphne du Maurier's main character in *Rebecca*. Good thing my husband is practically illiterate."

Sir Reginald looked puzzled.

Lettie rolled her eyes. "Rebecca is a beautiful unhappily married woman who secretly seeks medical attention. When she finds out she's dying, she provokes her husband into killing her. In the film version, Lawrence Olivier played the husband and Joan Fontaine was the little mouse he marries after doing away with the stunning Rebecca." Lettie suddenly looked very gay. "Can you imagine Lawrence Olivier playing Jinx?"

"So you'll go along with the story?"

"Do I have any choice? What did you tell him I was suffering from?"

"An unspecified female disorder. He wouldn't let me go into detail."

"And how, pray tell, did you explain how you came by this bit of information, while my darling husband had no idea?"

"From my darling wife, of course."

"And what if he tries to discuss it with Edwina, and she says she doesn't know a thing about my so-called condition?" Honestly, sometimes she thought her lover was as dim as her husband.

"I told him you begged Edwina to pretend to be totally dumb on the subject, so as not to worry him."

"At last, a role Edwina can handle." Lettie smiled smugly.

"Snuggs—"

"Yes, Rags?"

"You must start being more discreet."

Lettie's frown was genuine this time. Sir Reginald was the one acting like a simpering schoolboy. Lettie didn't dare let Edwina see the two of them together; it was pathetically obvious Rags was mad about her.

"So what if he's suspicious?" Lettie started to outline her lips in a cool red that contrasted nicely with her blue-black hair. She plucked a gray strand that had popped up at her hairline suddenly. Twenty-eight was far too early for one's hair to turn; she wouldn't want to let her secret slip.

"Lettie, your husband threatened to kill us both."

She laughed merrily, ruining her lip line.

"You know all those tiger skins and lion heads and God know what else he brought back from India?" She paused to blot. "Jinx had his servants shoot them. All he did was pose with the carcasses."

Sir Reginald was aghast.

"So you see, Rags, we have absolutely nothing to worry about. Jinx is not a man of violence."

"Well, there is one more thing, darling."

"What is it?"

"We need you to play Queen Elizabeth."

Lettie laughed. "That's rich, Rags. Me, play a frumpy queen?"

"The success of our plan hinges on getting her out of London before anyone realizes she's gone. Lord Sissyhurst won't do it, though he's a dead ringer for her. So it's either you or Edwina, and you can imagine how she'll muck it up."

Lettie powdered her nose, and considered the proposal.

"Absolutely not," she decided. "I wouldn't be caught dead in one of those ghastly frocks."

Sir Reginald sat up and arranged his corrupt and weathered facial features into a winsome smile. This expression had served him well in his dealings with the ladies. It had landed him the Piggott Plumbing fortune, after all.

"You'll be amply rewarded."

Lettie narrowed her eyes, like a cat about to pounce. Her features were distorted by greed.

"How?" she asked.

Sir Reginald put out his arms for a hug. "You'll have my undying gratitude, darling."

Lettie wasn't impressed. She went back to admiring herself in the mirror.

"And?" she asked.

His arms dropped. He should have known what a clever minx Lettie would be.

"And that leopard coat you've been wanting." He sighed. He'd been saving the money for a new heraldic crest, but it would have to be postponed.

"I do look rather nice in spots." Lettie smiled.

The Gates
9:25 P.M.

Bridget was just late enough for Jane to suspect she wasn't coming at all.

"Do you think she forgot?" Jane checked her watch.

"Give me that!" Simon said, tearing the shredded pack of cigarettes from her hands. She had been toying with them relentlessly since they had arrived at the bar.

"I never thought I would say this, but Jane—relax and have a drink!" Simon ordered as he brushed away the heap of loose tobacco that had gathered on the table in front of them.

"Oh, bother," said Jane, running her hand through her shorn locks nervously and realizing that Bridget hadn't yet seen her new cut. "What if she hates my hair?"

"You look fine," he told her, glancing over her shoulder at a handsome sporting type.

Jane suddenly perked up at the scent of Chanel No. 5.

"She's here!"

They both looked around in vain for a moment. Bridget must have passed by the open window near them. She should have been here by now. Jane felt a stab of anxiety.

"Give me those cigarettes!" she ordered Simon.

"I'll take those," said Bridget quietly, her manicured hand reaching over Jane's shoulder, snatching the pack away and dropping it into the pocket of her trench coat.

"Whatever you say, dear," said Jane, moving aside on the bench.

"I love your hair," Bridget said, when she had gotten settled. She caressed the nape of Jane's neck.

"You don't think it's too short?" Jane fished.

Bridget pressed her lips to Jane's neck. "Just one more place to kiss you."

Simon's mouth dropped open. Not since the early days with Astrid had he seen Jane melt like this.

"I'll let you two get to know each other," Jane said, getting up to go for another round. She gave Bridget a kiss on the top of her head. "Don't believe a word he says about me."

Bridget looped her finger around Jane's belt and pulled her in for a swift kiss. "Honey, I don't believe a word anyone says about you," she smiled.

Jane gulped. Simon laughed. This girl was exactly what Jane needed.

Bedsit of Jane Bond
Later that night

There was something Bridget needed to say, but she couldn't remember it. Or she couldn't find the words for it. Or something.

"Mmm."

"Yes?" Jane stopped moving.

"Don't stop!"

"Everything fine?"

"Mm-hmmm."

"Hmm?"

"Huh . . ." What had she wanted to say? It clearly didn't matter.

"Would you roll over, honey?"

"Pardon? Oh, right, anything you want." Dreamily, Bridget began to roll onto her stomach, taking a large section of the bed covers with her. With a horrible thud, she and Jane landed on the linoleum.

"Fuck!" she cried.

"That's awfully unladylike!" said Jane, bursting into laughter. They lay in a heap on the floor, naked and giggling, until a scurrying noise outside the door made Bridget clap her hand over Jane's mouth. Her lipstick gun was within reach, but she suspected it was only Tessie Twigg, Jane's nosy landlady.

"You mustn't make a sound," Bridget whispered. "One more infraction and you're out, remember?"

Jane squirmed under Bridget and nodded her head slowly.

Bridget nudged Jane's legs apart. She was planning on taking advantage of this compromising position.

8 SEPTEMBER 1965

The Flora Beaton
8:18 A.M.

WHEN Jane awoke, Bridget was already gone, leaving the lingering scent of Chanel No. 5, and a note on the pillow beginning with the word "Darling." Jane had reread the opening several times.

> *Darling—didn't want to wake you after such a rough night. Off to Dover to visit a sick aunt. Back in a few days.*
> *B.*

It was signed with a Pussycat Pink kiss.

Jane burrowed into the bedclothes, contented to stay in that warm, sweet-smelling place all day thinking about Bridget. She was almost asleep when the alarm rang, ruining what would have been a perfectly delightful dream. She opened one eye. It was twenty past eight. She was supposed to meet Agent Pumpernickel in ten minutes. She grudgingly rolled out of bed, threw on some clothes, and dashed to the loo for a quick splash. Her hair startled her for a moment. She squinted at herself in the mirror, and supposed she did look like her brother. She scrubbed her teeth and washed her face, and was soon ready for another day of training at Secret Service headquarters.

Loon's Café
8:53 A.M.

"Black—right?" Pumpernickel handed Jane a cup of coffee in a take-away cup. The café was all but deserted; the only customer besides them was a middle-aged man reading a newspaper. He glanced up now and then to stare at the street.

"He's waiting for the bus," Pumpernickel said under his breath. "He's recently divorced and comes here for breakfast every morning."

"How can you tell all that?"

"See his ring finger? That white band of flesh means he recently took off his ring."

"Maybe he's a widower."

Pumpernickel shook his head. "If he was, he'd be better dressed. Widowers are ten times more likely to remarry than are widows. They've had their wives taking care of them all these years and they're anxious to get a replacement. See how tattered his shirt cuffs are? No self-respecting wife would let her husband go off to work like that. I looked over his shoulder earlier to see what he was reading. It's a nervous habit of mine. He's looking for a bedsit to rent, not a flat. He plans on eating all his meals out."

Jane was impressed. "What else?"

"See how he's still got some summer sun? He and his wife went on holiday before they split up. Maybe to Spain on one of those package deals. And he's been sleeping on a friend's couch for a week or so. He's probably even slept on a few park benches. See how rumpled his overcoat is? He's used it as a blanket."

"Why'd they break up?"

"He flirted with some bottle blond in Spain and his wife found out, I imagine." Pumpernickel was warming to the game. "I wouldn't say he's any Romeo. He's the type of fellow who is basically faithful. He slips now and then, at office parties or when he's out of town, but these liaisons are meaningless. He can't imagine living with anyone but his wife. He's miserable without her. Look at the coffee stains on his tie. It's no doubt the very same one he was wearing when she threw him out. He's not buying another because he still hopes she'll take him back. And he's a bit of a tightwad."

"Is she going to give him another chance?"

"That information is well beyond my powers of perception, Miss Bond. The ways of the human heart are a mystery to me. We'd better run along."

G.E.O.R.G.I.E. headquarters
9:37 A.M.

Dear Jane,
The weather here is splendid. Aunt Lillian is doing nicely.
I hope to be back in London soon.

Love, Bridget.
P.S. I miss you.

"What do you think of that?"

"I think the postscript is pathetic," Bibi said. She was idly flipping through the latest issue of *Spy Girl Monthly*, waiting for Bridget to finish fussing over a simple postcard.

"Do you think I should send two postcards? One to the bookshop and one to her home? What if one gets lost in the post?"

"That's a bit much."

"I'll wait a day before sending another. I don't want her to think I'm too pushy."

"Pushy doesn't seem to be a problem with this girl," Bibi pointed out. "Drop the P.S. It makes you sound insecure." She peered over the magazine at Bridget. "What are you going to do if Jane takes a tumble for Agent Dolittle while you're gone?"

"It's not as if we're married," Bridget said, trying to sound nonchalant but failing miserably.

"So you wouldn't mind?"

"I'd mind terribly. I just think it's too early to be staking my claim."

"It's never too early," Bibi told her. "You don't have anything to worry about. She's really stuck on you."

"Have you been bugging me again?"

Bibi looked a little sheepish.

"Hadn't you better get back to Grunby Hall before Lady Edwina finds out you've gone?"

Bibi put down her magazine. "I've been sent on a top-secret mission to pick up a case of Cadbury bars while she's at a ladies' gymnasium over on Bleekner Street. She won't be finished being steam-shrunk for at least another hour. Edwina already adores me," Bibi said confidently. "Think I can get her to leave me her fortune?"

"Not after you have her husband arrested for treason."

"She's sick of him, but she doesn't know it yet."

"I'm already sick of him and we haven't even met." A few days before, they had sent Lady Edwina a transmitter brooch, with a typewritten note reading, "Wear this always to remind you of your dear friend the duchess." Edwina had taken the command to heart; what they had originally thought was static turned out to be light snoring. Lady Edwina had worn the brooch to bed.

"If Jane talked to me the way Sir Reginald does to Edwina," Bridget sniffed, "I'd be out the door before she could drop to her knees to beg for forgiveness."

"He's a rotter," agreed Bibi, adding, "last night Edwina asked me to rinse her knickers."

"Did you?"

"Of course not. I'm a terrible ladies' maid," she confessed. "I can't remember how to get chocolate out of fine linen, or how to give milady a soothing facial rub."

"Just flatter her endlessly. It works with Mother."

As she read, Bridget's feelings toward Lady Edwina seesawed between annoyance and pity. Spineless women made her blood boil.

Yet she felt sorry for her, too. It must have seemed the height of romance to marry Sir Reginald. The society columns had been agog over the match; speculation as to why a notorious gadabout had settled on Miss Edwina Piggott had become a parlor game among high society. It was quite obvious why he had chosen her; obvious to everyone but Lady Edwina. She should divorce him, Bridget decided. It was much easier than one would think, especially when one had money. Her own mother had been divorced four times so far. Or was it five?

Bridget was always jumbling up husbands number two and three. They had both been dukes, and had looked sufficiently alike to meld in her mind. She had been away at boarding school when Emerald had divorced the one duke and married the other, so Bridget had come home for holiday and realized that the man sitting at the breakfast table across from her mother was a stranger. Emerald, who recorded every detail of every party she attended in long, tiresome letters to her daughter, had neglected to mention she had changed dukes. Husband number four—a baron this time—had had a little black mustache that gave him a sinister appearance not unlike that of a villain in a silent movie.

He had once even twirled one end of his mustache between his fingers. Bridget would have laughed had he not also been propositioning her at the time.

Secret Service headquarters
10:17 A.M.

"On the second of June, nineteen hundred and fifty-three, Queen Elizabeth was crowned."

Jane felt her eyes start to close. She jerked awake.

"She had studied her entire life for this moment, for she had always known one day she would be queen. It was her destiny."

Jane knew better than to interrupt when Agent Pumpernickel was on a royal roll. She pasted an expression of interest on her face, and tried to stay awake. She'd really have to get some sleep tonight; it was the only good thing about Bridget leaving town.

"In her veins runs the blood of a thousand kings."

"I can't believe a mere mortal like myself is going to stand in her presence." Jane yawned.

"Exactly, Miss Bond. That is why today is devoted to courtly etiquette."

"The whole day? You said I was only going to spend ten seconds with her."

"And those will be the most important ten seconds of your life. Nothing can go wrong. Now, let's begin with a few critical rules.

"Number one—never look directly at the queen. Look just above her left shoulder."

"If I do look directly at her, will my eyes be smote from my head?"

"Yes. Number two—never turn your back on the queen."

"How do I leave?"

"You walk out backward."

"You're having me on."

"Indeed I am not. The last rule is—and I believe this one is entirely self-explanatory—never, ever, sneeze on the queen."

"It would never have occurred to me. But now that you've mentioned it, it's all I'm going to be thinking of when I meet her. You know how sometimes, when you think of something too much, you make it happen?"

Agent Pumpernickel looked aghast. Gathering himself, he again consulted the list in his hand.

"Now what is the most important thing to remember when we're out on assignment?" he asked her.

"Um . . . to use the men's loo?"

"Besides that."

"To follow your orders."

"Right."

"And keep my mouth shut unless you indicate otherwise."

"Yes."

"What if the queen asks me a question? What do I do?"

"Mumble something incoherent. The queen never listens unless it's written into her schedule. You're not down for a speaking part; there's no need to worry. She'll hand you your medal in a small velveteen box, you will bow, and by the time you see the tips of your shoes, she will have moved on.

"Just before the queen hands you the box, however, I am going to take your picture with a hidden camera. For our records. When I tip my hat, you give me your best James Bond look."

"A smirk or a sneer?"

"Neither, really. It can't seem as if you're making faces at Her Majesty. Look very somber and proper, and perhaps lift an eyebrow in an expression of controlled happiness."

"Would you write that down, please?"

"Certainly. Just promise me you'll eat the paper after memorizing your instructions."

"Naturally. Where are you hiding this camera?"

"In my carnation. Why?"

"It's too bad I can't wear one, too, and get a picture of you with the queen."

"The queen does not pose for snapshots like some tourist attraction."

"Maybe not, but she's got to pass by you to get to the next medal recipient, right?"

"I do see the logic."

"What's the harm in taking a snap for your scrapbook?"

"It *would* be rather disappointing to come away without a souvenir." He did have a picture of himself with the queen hanging at home; well, it was actually a picture of his hand waving as the queen walked by. His neighbor Mrs. Figgis had snapped it during the queen's walkabout a few years back. It would be nice to have one in which his face appeared as well. Now that was something he could show people:

And this is from the time I visited Buckingham Palace for a little awards cere-mony. Me? Goodness, no. I wasn't receiving an award that day. I'd already been put up for a Jolly Good Show medal. Would you like to see it? Oh, it's no trouble at all—it's right over here in this little velvet box.

"Hello . . ." Jane waved her hand in front of Pumpernickel's face. He had that misty look in his eyes again.

"You could always wear a tie-clip camera," he decided. "But you mustn't tell anyone of our plan. Every move we make is supposed to be authorized by Sir Niles."

Jane patted his arm. "Your secret is safe with me."

G.E.O.R.G.I.E. headquarters
10:21 A.M.

"Coffee, tea, or me?"

Bibi was dressed in a blue-and-white nylon air hostess uniform, low-heeled white pumps, and a perky little cap. She twirled around so Bridget could get the full effect.

"It's charming." Stewardess was Bridget's least favorite disguise. The uniforms were an open invitation to every wolf in London. Bibi didn't mind—she kept a long, sharp hatpin on hand and simply poked anyone who tried to molest her—but Bridget was weary of the battle. Someday she was just going to take out her one-shot lipstick gun and give some groper his comeuppance.

Bibi pouted; she thought she looked dashing in the new stew-ardess costume.

"Aren't you supposed to be a maid?" Bridget asked, realizing she had ruffled Bibi's feathers. "I bet you look adorable in that uniform."

"It's being altered." Bibi sighed. "The dress is fine but it comes with a frilly hat that makes me look like a shepherdess."

"You suffer so," Bridget teased.

"Don't I know it."

A knock at their office door interrupted their chat.

"Agent St. Claire?" A tall blond with a cap of soft hair peered hesitantly into the room. "I'm Agent Mimi Dolittle. I'll be handling the surveillance on Jane Bond from here on in."

Bridget was struck by how closely Agent Dolittle resembled Jane's former lover Astrid.

"I've read over your report," Agent Dolittle added. "It seems a straightforward assignment. Is there anything you'd like to add?"

"Everything you need to know is there," Bridget said curtly.

Agent Dolittle looked to Bibi for guidance, but Bibi only shrugged. She wouldn't get involved.

"Then I'll get to work," replied Agent Dolittle. "What fun it looks, too. At the bar, night after night . . ."

Bridget busied herself sorting through her desk drawer. The conversation was clearly over. Agent Dolittle smiled and left.

"What's got up your nose?" asked Bibi.

"She looks just like Astrid."

"Want me to talk to her?"

"*No!*" The last thing Bridget wanted was to become the object of gossip.

Bibi unzipped her shiny blue patent leather flight bag and took out two tiny bottles of Dewar's scotch. "I insisted on all the amenities this time."

Bridget shook her head. "We've got a meeting with Bluma Trell in five minutes. We can't go in with scotch on our breath."

Out came breath mints. "We're a full-service airline," Bibi said, smiling.

Laboratory of scientist Bluma Trell
10:32 A.M.

"These, girls, are a breakthrough in lipstick technology." Bluma Trell waved her hands over an array of gold tubes on the table in front of her. "As you can see, they're packaged in this charming titanium tube to distinguish them from your everyday line. Don't mix them up, especially the reds!" She passed the first tube to Bridget, who examined the color, nodded approvingly, and passed it on to the next agent.

"Kiss Me Deadly," Bluma said. "Kills on contact. Farewell My

Sweet—same fatal results, but takes a little longer. Flight to Fantasy—leaves the kissee in a narcotic daze. This one can last for the life of a marriage! Seventh Heaven—contains a knockout drug. Vérité—a truth serum. Charmer, a hypnotic.

"Always wear the protective balm underneath the Deadly Shades. As an added safety measure, the girls in Action Accessories cooked up these—" Bluma Trell gave each girl a set of clear plastic bubble rings with liquid centers. "These contain fast-acting antidotes. Always coordinate your lipstick with the correct antidote ring before walking out the door."

Bridget was frankly dismayed to see their latest accessory. It wasn't just the modern material that put her off. A chunky Lucite ring with a bright-colored center would surely call attention to itself when paired with formal eveningwear. It was the small details that often gave a spy away. Smoking an American cigarette behind the Iron Curtain, say, or having the wrong currency in one's purse.

"Could these be fashioned into brooches?" she asked. "Perhaps a starburst shape with the antidote in the center jewel? Gold plate would do."

"My girls will have them to you tomorrow," Bluma Trell assured her. "One more thing—we do not recommend you wear these lipsticks at home. They're for fighting evil, not your girlfriends."

The laughter cut the tension in the room. Sometimes, when an agent was packing her cosmetics case with dusting powder and foaming bath beads, it was easy to forget that under the sweet-smelling samples was a secret compartment with all the tools of the spy trade. A lock-picking kit. Gas grenades. Steel-tip tranquilizer darts. A subminiature camera concealed in a cigarette pack. Invisible-ink top secret cipher panties. And a Beretta 7.65mm pistol with silencer.

The Sons of Britain Society Club
11:00 A.M.

"Sir Reginald—telephone."

"Over here, boy."

"Rags, dear, it's Edwina. I missed you at breakfast this morning."

"Sorry, old girl. You know how hard it is to find a good taxidermist these days."

Edwina frowned. "Old girl" hardly sounded romantic.

"It seems like days since I've seen you, Rags."

"Edwina, you sound as if you have a mouthful of marbles."

"I do. I'm practicing for the queen."

There was an awkward silence.

"Are you calling about anything in particular, Edwina?"

"Would you be a dear and stop by Wimpole Buttery Bakery on your way home and get one of those delicious creamy walnut cakes? I'd go myself, but I've an appointment in another part of town and you're so close."

"I'm afraid that will be impossible."

"Why?"

"Because you eat so many sweets you're beginning to look like a Cadbury egg. My dear, if you're going to entertain the queen, you'll simply have to slim down."

Edwina gasped, almost swallowing a marble.

"You must take this in the manner in which it is intended, as helpful criticism from your loving husband."

"Yes, Rags."

Sir Reginald closed his eyes, and, with his long elegant fingers, rubbed the temples of his throbbing head. Edwina always had this effect on him; his head would begin to pound and soon his stomach would chime in. He rang for a bromo.

Sir Reginald thought there could be no two people more like cheese and chalk. He was a sensitive, sentimental man. In 1959 he had actually wept (in private, of course) when he had been forced, due to financial embarrassment, to open the doors of Grouse Manor to any ill-bred fellow with ten shillings in his grubby paw. Edwina, on the other hand, was a woman who talked to shopkeepers with a gushing enthusiasm that ill fitted her new station in life.

He was the product of a good, sound public school education, and as such, believed in simple food, hard chairs, abrasive towels, and carbolic soap. She ate raspberry bonbons by the box, and insisted on carrying, at all times, a small satin pillow upon which to sit.

As her husband, he had endeavored to teach his wife a few simple social skills, such as how to yawn with her mouth closed, and the correct way to ride a bicycle, should the need ever arise. (One propels the pedals with the ball of the foot and not the instep, which causes the front of the foot to protrude and is most unattractive.) He believed that women were, by nature, scatterbrained and undisciplined, and so he forgave Edwina when she dripped treacle pudding on the Saxony carpet that had come from the Tuttlewaddle side of his family. Each Sunday he quietly had his man scrape the melted toffees, sherbet dabs, and jelly babies off the rosewood Indian tabletops. He was a good husband. He wasn't addicted to whiskey or dyed blonds like so many of his peers.

They had met six months ago when Edwina came to Grouse Manor on an autobus tour with her Thursday afternoon Fine Arts League. Not five minutes into the tour she had stumbled, sending a priceless Staffordshire spaniel crashing to the Italian marble floor. She had apologized profusely, then offered to pay for the antique from the thick roll of bills in her dowdy patent-leather purse. The sight of cash went a long way to restoring his esteem for this flower of good, modest, middle-class English womanhood.

By the time the second pot had been drunk, Sir Reginald had decided he would seduce this rather plain and dumpy, but endearingly rich, commoner. Edwina's mind had begun wandering in the same direction. She was tired of being known as the Piggott Plumbing heiress. Sir Reginald was sick to death of having strangers gawk at his heirlooms. They shared a passionate, almost obsessive interest in the exiled Duke and Duchess of Windsor. And so they had married.

"Wake up, Jinx," he said, nudging his old chum, who was sprawled on a worn leather club chair in a brandy-induced stupor. "We've got a monarchy to overthrow."

Crispin's Bookshop
11:13 A.M.

Simon stared past Mrs. Snipe's shoulder at the crack in the wall just over the archaeology section. He'd have to replaster and paint if he was going to sell the shop. He and Jane could do the job in a day's time and still wait on customers; there were so few these days.

"At first I thought Edwina was ringing me about the two-for-one sale at Martha Manning. Then I remembered that *I* had told *her* about it the other day. Then I thought, What could have possibly gotten Edwina out of bed before noon? Since her marriage she's picked up some bad habits, like having her maid separate her jujubes by color and staying up to all hours. Early to bed and early to rise, I always say. Don't you agree, Mr. Crispin?"

"What? Oh, yes, Mrs. Snipe. Whatever you say."

He missed Jane. He hadn't realized until now how very much Mrs. Snipe talked. Jane made listening look so easy. She could even do a crossword puzzle and still look as if she were paying attention.

"I'm afraid I must toddle off now." Mrs. Snipe thrust her empty teacup into Simon's hand. "I've dozens of errands to run before meeting Edwina. If you ask me, I think there's trouble brewing in paradise. I told her not to marry that man."

"I thought you found out about the wedding after the fact." Despite valiant attempts to in one ear and out the other with her, he had still absorbed dozens of bits of minutiae about Lady Edwina. He knew she had a bunion on her left foot, wore wrinkle tape on her face to bed, and had saggy elastic on her knickers.

"It's what I *would* have told her had I had the chance. Tell me, Mr. Crispin—what is a friend for if not to tell you when you're being made a fool of?"

G.E.O.R.G.I.E. headquarters
11:29 A.M.

"Very ladylike," said Chief Tuppenny.

Bridget had on a cream-colored shantung silk blouse with a deep V neck and a slim charcoal skirt. The neutral colors showed off her suntan; her red hair was up in a sophisticated twist. A small square Cartier watch with a delicate black strap was her only piece of jewelry.

"Thanks. I've never been a hostess before," Bridget confessed. "I'm hoping Lady Edwina doesn't pick up on that."

"I hear Lady Edwina is terrified of your mother. I'd use that if I were you."

"Everyone is terrified of her—she has a sadistic streak as wide as the Thames; you never know when she's having you on. At her last dinner party, Mother put live goldfish in her finger bowls and Lady Edwina thought it was some exotic soup only the upper class ate, and drank it straight down."

Tuppenny laughed. "Good luck."

"I'll need it. Mother's dragging me to some dull social event as payback. Have to keep on her good side, you know."

"We appreciate it, Agent St. Claire. Your mother has opened a lot of doors for us. I know she can be a trial at times."

"That's a lovely way to put it." Bridget paused and lowered her voice in confidence. "Chief Tuppenny—about Jane." The mention of her name in front of her commanding officer made Bridget blush. She still hadn't forgotten yesterday's scolding. "She can't possibly know what she's getting into. What if someone really thinks she's 007 and takes a shot at her?"

"She's only in costume a few hours, and Agent Dolittle is on her tail."

Bridget flinched. It was not an image she relished.

"Don't worry," Tuppenny added. "She's in good hands." Sensing Bridget's need for reassurance, Chief Tuppenny reached across her desk and gave Bridget's hand a little pat.

What a difference a day could make, Bridget thought as she put her silver Zapata Spyder in drive, and headed for Grunby Hall. Empires could crumble, hemlines could change, and a girl could fall in love.

Grunby Hall
12:25 P.M.

"Bibi!" Lady Edwina bellowed. When her call wasn't answered immediately, she took the little brass bell she kept in the pocket of her worn corduroy housecoat and rang it frantically.

Agent Bibi Gallini, clad in a form-fitting black taffeta maid's uniform, starched apron, and stocking feet, came scampering down the magnificent mahogany staircase. She had a fashion magazine in one hand and a Coca-Cola in the other.

"Yes, madam?"

"What time is it, Bibi?"

"Almost half past twelve, madam."

Lady Edwina's stomach growled. She had been too anxious to sit down and have her elevenses, and now it was too late. Lady Bridget St.

Claire was expected at one o'clock, and she still had to bathe and dress. Everything had to be perfect today. Edwina's previous encounter with a St. Claire had ended in humiliation; she vowed that today she would triumph. To greet the daughter of her most vocal critic, she was going to wear the elegant blue crepe dress in which she had been married, with a string of pearls her husband had given her on their honeymoon. She would look refined and reserved; very much the lady of the manor. She took a butterscotch candy from the pocket of her worn housecoat, unwrapped it, and popped it in her mouth. Yes, everything was going to be just perfect.

"Madam?"

"Yes, Bibi?"

"Lady Bridget is here."

"Welcome to Grunby Hall, Lady Bridget," Edwina stammered. She wished she had given in to her impulse to run up the back stairs and change her clothes. Which was worse, she wondered—appearing in her housecoat in front of a lady, or making her wait? There were simply too many things to remember these days. No matter how often Reginald coached her, she still couldn't remember the ducal order. Lord, earl, baron, count, marquis—they all scared her. Life had been so much simpler as a plumber's daughter.

"It's nice to finally meet you, Lady Wooley-Booley. I've heard so much about you." As she spoke, Bridget pressed the decorative gold clasp on her purse, activating the miniaturized reel-to-reel recorder concealed within.

"I thought it was soup," Lady Edwina blurted out.

For a moment, Bridget was puzzled. Then Bibi, standing behind Edwina, pantomimed the act of drinking from a bowl, and Bridget remembered the live fish fiasco.

"I've done the same thing myself," Bridget told her. She had arrived early to throw Lady Edwina off balance, but she could see it wasn't necessary. Edwina was spinning like a top.

Lady Edwina stood stone still, with a smile frozen on her face. Bridget just knew her hands were clammy.

"This is a very interesting foyer," Bridget said, trying to break the awkward silence.

The double-height great hall had all the charm of a morgue. It was enormous—the entry alone would have housed the entire G.E.O.R.G.I.E. operation with space left over for a conga room. The chilly black marble floor was dotted with zebra skins, heads intact. The red moiré walls provided a bloody background for the mounted, stuffed, glassy-eyed animal heads that lined the hall from wainscot to ceiling. Bridget decided at that very moment to become a vegetarian.

"I was thinking we'd display the auction items in here, on long tables from the library," Edwina said. "Unless you think that's a bad idea."

"I think this is the perfect place."

"My friend the Duchess of Windsor says that the great hall of a manor is the path to the soul of the house. It's how you show the world you have a deep, inner spiritual self and a richness of heart."

"And what do you think this room says about you, Lady Edwina?"

"That I love animals?" she said hopefully.

Bridget frowned, but said nothing. All those staring blank eyes gave her the willies, but they would be the perfect place to plant surveillance equipment. She'd get a photograph of every S.O.B. who walked through the door, suitable for framing. And blackmail.

Bibi cleared her throat. If they didn't need her, she would get back to work exploring the contents of Sir Reginald's desk.

"Lady Bridget, this is my maid, Bibi."

Bibi curtsied. "Pleased to meet you, I'm sure."

"Charmed," Bridget said dryly.

Edwina blanched when she realized her maid wasn't wearing any shoes. She had made the same mistake a number of times, before Sir Reginald had informed her that one does not receive visitors in one's bare feet. Edwina looked down. She hoped bunny slippers counted.

"Would you care for some tea, Lady Bridget?"

"That would be lovely."

"We'd like tea, dear. Anything else, Lady Bridget?"

"I'd like my trunk brought in from the car."

"Bibi, please get Lady Bridget's trunk from her car."

"Be very careful with it; it's got the queen's personal cocktail service inside," Bridget warned.

"I can't lift heavy things," Bibi reminded Lady Edwina.

"I'm sorry, dear; you did tell me that. Poor Bibi has terrible trouble with her back. And she's allergic to all sorts of things: dish soap, dust, furniture wax, and silver polish. I'll get Sir Reginald's manservant to do it. No, I'll get the trunk myself," Lady Edwina decided.

"You have no idea what I'm going through," Bibi moaned as soon as Edwina left the room. "Sir Reginald popped in to take a peek at the new help. I had to accidentally-on-purpose spill coffee in his lap to get him to leave me alone. I'm going to put an electrical charge in my skirt and blow out his false teeth the next time he comes near me. And they're going to make me sleep in the drafty, dusty, spidery attic. Edwina said I could use any room I wanted, but Sir Roaming Hands said I had to stay in the servants' quarters."

"What are you two girls talking about?" Edwina meant to sound breezy and gay, but her voice came out shrill and nervous. She hoped Bibi wasn't telling Lady Bridget about the terrible row she and Sir Reginald had had that morning over the 22-karat gold bathtub. It was their first real fight. Could it be that after only six months the bloom was already off the rose?

"We were talking about how closely your marriage parallels that of the Duke and Duchess of Windsor," Bridget said smoothly, adding, "except you're not in exile."

Edwina brightened considerably. "I've always thought so, too. While it's true Sir Reginald and I may not have been run out of England, we have had our share of adversity. What I mean is, it took a while for his friends to accept me."

"Every new couple has its adjustments," Bridget assured her. "Look at the in-law problems the duke and duchess have even after all these years of marriage."

Lady Edwina smiled. Lady Bridget was so much more sympathetic than her mother. She felt as if she could tell her anything.

Grouse Manor
1:30 P.M.

Sir Reginald and Lady Lettie were in the gazebo, discussing their future.

"If Edwina doesn't stop spending her money beautifying Grunby Hall, there's going to be nothing left for us," he was complaining. "She actually proposed we have water piped in from Lourdes!"

"Dear God, why? Is she planning to open a church?"

He mimicked Edwina. " 'Because the duchess bathes in it every day.' I'm beginning to think her attachment to that woman is a bit unnatural. Edwina tells her everything; the last letter was full of so many complaints about me, I had to burn it."

"I think I'll write Edwina a letter," Lettie said.

"You have been neglecting her terribly."

"I mean, a letter from the duchess, telling her to put her inheritance into your hands. I'll tell her that only then can she achieve true marital bliss. You cannot do your husbandly duties until she gives over total control to you."

"Do you think she'll do it?"

"If the duchess jumped off London Bridge, would Edwina?"

Back at Grunby Hall
Lady Edwina's rococo-revival sitting room
A short time later

"I thought we'd have the refreshments in here before the bidding begins," announced Lady Edwina, as a petulant Bibi served tea.

"It's dazzling," Bridget said truthfully. The garish red-and-gold-striped wallpaper was giving Bridget a headache. Practically every surface and object had been gilded; she was certain the room would glow in the dark.

"It is, isn't it? I plan to redo the entire house in the very same manner."

Edwina caught Bridget staring at the large, shockingly lifelike portrait of Edwina that hung at one end of the room. She had been painted perched on a Queen Anne wing chair, wearing a tweed suit and a tiara. She looked keenly alert, like a deer in crosshairs. On the opposite wall was a painting of Mary, Queen of Scots, losing her head at the chopping block; she looked more relaxed. Both were disquieting.

"This portrait was my wedding gift to Sir Reginald. I intended it for his bedchamber, but he'd rather it stayed out here so everyone can enjoy it. In order to look my best, I dieted for two weeks before, eating only hard-boiled eggs and cubes of ice. That's what the duchess did before her wedding."

"It's completely like you," Bridget said.

Edwina beamed. "I think it looks rather well with the other portrait, don't you think? Sir Reginald loves Queen Mary so much he always takes tea facing her. Except when he's trying to slim; then he faces my portrait. I think he finds it bracing."

"Where did you get these unique gilded centaur lamps?"

"From Le Maison de Gaudy," Edwina said proudly.

"This room just screams your name."

"Thank you, Lady Bridget." Edwina blushed and looked away. This was more than she had dared hope for.

After they'd had their fill of thin crustless watercress white bread sandwiches and sugary, milky oolong tea, Edwina had Bibi wheel in a cart loaded with cakes and puddings.

"You go first," Edwina said.

"I'll have the custard tart, and some fresh raspberries," Bridget decided.

"And I'll have the flummery, and a piece of tipsy cake, dear. Cook makes the most delicious tipsy cake I've ever tasted. When Grouse Manor was open to the public, people who ordered it during the light refreshment portion of the tour would simply beg for the recipe. I keep telling Sir Reginald that we should market it, but he says being in trade is vulgar."

Bibi put a dish of slippery egg-white almond-flavored jelly on the tea table in front of Edwina.

"No tipsy cake?" Edwina asked Bibi with obvious disappointment.

"No tipsy cake."

Edwina scrutinized the dessert cart. "I was sure there was a piece left over from yesterday."

"Haven't seen it." Bibi shrugged. It *was* the best tipsy cake she had ever eaten.

"Sometimes having thirty-two rooms can be a trial." Edwina sighed. "It's awfully easy to misplace things around here."

Back at Grouse Manor
3:17 P.M.

"Happy, darling?"

"Very."

"I love you, Lettie."

"I love you too, Rags," Lettie lied. "I can't wait until we're married."

"What?" Sir Reginald cried.

"I said, I can't wait until we're married. Once our engagement is announced, I'm going to restore Grunby Hall, starting with that god-awful sitting room of Edwina's. I've already had my decorator start the sketches."

"But we're already married to other people."

"Which is why they invented this thing called divorce, silly."

"I can't divorce Edwina so soon!" Sir Reginald protested. "Everyone will think I married her for her money."

"Everyone already knows you married her for her money. Why else would you have taken the plumber's daughter as your"—she shuddered—"bride?"

"It would be bad form to dump the old girl so soon after we seize the throne," he pointed out. "I do owe her something, after all."

"You gave her the Wooley-Booley name and introduced her to handmade knickers—isn't that enough?"

"What about Jinx?"

"Jinx is ancient," she pointed out. "He could go at any time."

Lettie had naturally assumed Jinx would be dead by now. She did everything possible to tax his wonky heart, raise his blood pressure, and give him indigestion. Still, the old goat hung on.

"And the duchess? Edwina's going to cry on her shoulder about the divorce. What if we go to all this trouble to put them on the throne, and then they refuse to have anything to do with us?"

"*Ssh*, darling," Lettie said. "You're getting yourself all worked up. Once the duchess meets Edwina, she'll realize how common she is. By then I will have ingratiated myself to her. I've been studying up interests dear to her heart—fashion, small ugly dogs, and menu planning."

"Don't overwhelm her with your intelligence, darling. Just be your charming self."

"Aren't I always?"

Lettie got up and put her dress back on before Sir Reginald could get any ideas about an encore. He grabbed her by the ankle. She kicked him in the face. She loathed being pawed.

"Sorry, darling. Reflex. You'd better run along and put a bottle of chilled Champagne on that."

Once they were married, she wouldn't have to put up with his feeble advances. He'd never dare divorce her; she knew where all the bodies were buried.

Grunby Hall
3:25 P.M.

"And is it true that one can't acquire good taste, no matter how much one spends?" Lady Edwina's round, wet eyes and sincere expression made her look like a sad little dog.

"Biscuit?" Bridget offered kindly.

"Thank you."

"Who said that?"

"Your mother, Lady Emerald St. Claire. I overheard her say it at a dinner party after my unfortunate incident with a finger bowl. I can't help but think she was referring, in a roundabout way, to me."

The minute Bridget had laid eyes on the very anxious Lady Edwina, in rumpled housecoat and bunny slippers, she had decided to befriend her. She'd learn so much more that way.

"If my mother said it, then it must be wrong," Bridget assured her. Lady Edwina chortled, sending a sip of tea down the wrong pipe. She began to hiccup, and it took several minutes before she could calm herself. Bridget wished she had brought a Valium to slip in Edwina's tea. She made a mental note to bring medication to the charity auction; it might be a good idea to keep Edwina under sedation.

"I firmly believe that in this day and age, good taste is very much up to the individual," Bridget went on.

"Please tell that to my husband," begged Edwina. "He insists we remove my lamps from the auction."

"Perhaps he's afraid someone will steal them," Bridget suggested.

Edwina looked puzzled. "But we're not inviting thieves! Only people from the upper *upper* crust are coming to the charity auction. And the queen."

"Kleptomania runs in the best of families," said Bridget with a confidential air. "Even the Windsors have been known to have sticky fingers." It was no secret that all the Queen Mother had to do was admire an object, and it was as good as gone.

"There's so much I have to learn, Lady Bridget."

"Just put yourself in my hands, Lady Edwina, and everything will go just as planned."

"I've been practicing my curtsey for days. Want to see it?" Edwina jumped up, inadvertently spilling her flummery on the gold brocade love seat, and curtsied deeply.

"Perfect," Bridget told her.

"I had my husband tutor me."

"Where *is* Sir Reginald?"

"He's at his club, working on his memoirs. I'm afraid he won't be back until late this evening. You may not get a chance to meet him until the auction," Edwina apologized.

"I can wait," Bridget assured her.

"He's quite charming. Right, Bibi?"

"A real prince," Bibi said as she rubbed the bruise on her right hip. She was going to make sure that Sir Roaming Hands got exactly what he deserved. Now it was personal.

"I brought you a little something to study, Lady Edwina. It's a booklet my mother put together for my thirteenth birthday."

The book was bound in soft white calfskin leather, with gold embossed lettering: BRIDGET'S BOOK OF MANNERS, BY HER MOTHER.

"It's so elegant," Edwina exclaimed. "And it's just what I need—practical advice right from the horse's mouth." She instantly clapped her hand over her mouth. "I didn't mean to call your mother a horse."

"She's been called worse." Bridget smiled.

Edwina giggled. "Oh, thank you, Lady Bridget."

"Now, you go and study while I discuss the auction with your maid."

Lady Edwina's bedchamber
3:37 P.M.

Lady Edwina grabbed a box of chocolates she kept hidden under the skirts of a delft shepardess and retrieved the latest *Pigeon Racing News* from under the cushion of a Louis XIV chair in which no one was allowed to sit. She kicked off her shoes, ripped the cellophane off the box, and flopped onto a Flemish tapestry armchair with wide arms perfect for holding a box of candy or a cup of tea. She wasn't supposed to sit in this chair, either. What was the point of having chairs you couldn't sit in?

Lady Bridget was darling, but Edwina was beginning to realize she was in over her head. And she was beginning to regret her hasty marriage; of course she could never admit it to anyone, especially Mildred Snipe, who saw Edwina's nuptials as a beacon of hope. She would be crushed.

Edwina sighed heavily. She had been perfectly happy in her old life, free to do as she pleased with no one but Mildred to criticize her. "You made your bed, Edwina, now you must lie in it." That's what Mildred would say. Mildred was a great believer in loyalty. Even now, months after her husband had disappeared without so much as a note, she refused to speak ill of him. Perhaps after the duke and duchess had been crowned Edwina would consider a divorce. Plenty of people were getting them in this day and age. Why, the duchess herself had been divorced twice already. Unlike the duchess, Edwina had no intention of remarrying. Sir Reginald had not turned out to be her knight in shining armor. One husband was enough for her, thank you very much.

She popped a chocolate in her mouth. It had a raspberry crème center. She much preferred the coconut crèmes. She was beginning to wish she had never let Sir Reginald talk her into having the charity auction at Grunby Hall. Thank goodness Lady Bridget was there to hold her hand. And Bibi was turning out to be such a dear girl. What would she do without them?

Back in the sitting room
3:49 P.M.

Bibi glared at the flummery stain on the sofa, flipped the cushion, plopped down, and poured herself a cup of tea.

"Poor Edwina. I'm beginning to feel sorry for her. She may have more money than the Bank of England, but she's not at all stuck up. She's nice."

"If she's so nice, why is she planning to kidnap the queen?" Bridget wondered.

"I don't think she has any idea what Sir Reginald's up to. She's not the brightest bulb in the chandelier."

"True. She does believe your allergy act."

"Which, by the way, is backfiring. Sure I'll leave here with soft hands and flawless nails, but I can't do any snooping with her following me around the house, chatting."

"You might find out something."

"I already have; all there is to know about church fetes, jumble sales, and pigeon racing. It's hard to believe someone as cheerful and, well, messy as Edwina could be party to this. I've just never before met an anarchist who had jelly smeared on her clothes."

"I'll admit she doesn't seem much like a Mata Hari," Bridget agreed. "But I wouldn't feel too sorry for Edwina. She may be in the dark, but she's still one of them. Leaving all the decisions to her husband is no excuse; women have got to stop being so naive. She's not a child, after all."

"She seems to know about as much as one."

"Don't let her lull you into complacency."

Bridget picked at a loose thread in Edwina's gold brocade love seat. "This is the ugliest sofa I've ever seen," she groused.

"You're in a good mood."

"Sorry. I've been feeling cross all day." The thread she had been worrying broke, leaving an obvious run in the fabric.

"Oops," said Bridget. Bibi simply threw a pillow over the spot.

"You're worried about Jane, aren't you?"

"What if someone takes a shot at her?"

"Relax—she's in good hands."

"I wish everyone would stop saying that!" Bridget snapped.

Secret Service headquarters
Third-floor ladies' loo
4:00 P.M.

Jane looked in the mirror. Her brother looked back.

Agent Pumpernickel stood outside the third-floor ladies' and guarded the door. Jane had insisted on using the ladies' facilities while they were still in the safety of the Secret Service headquarters. She wrinkled up her nose at the suggestion that she begin her charade immediately, protesting, "The men's loo is always filthy."

Just as he was hoping no one had seen them creep down the hall, 008 suddenly appeared as if out of nowhere—and in his stocking feet!

"You'll catch a cold," Pumpernickel scolded him.

"What are you doing hovering about the ladies', you old perv?" 008 elbowed him and winked.

Pumpernickel mopped his forehead with his handkerchief. This would be a most inopportune moment for Miss Bond to make her debut.

"So, 008, how's it going with my files?" he boomed heartily.

"I'm not deaf," 008 shouted back.

"Sorry, lad."

Jane shook her head. What Pumpernickel saw in that boy, she'd never know. When this was over, she was going to have to get Simon to introduce Agent Pumpernickel to a few nice gents. She lit a cigarette, and plopped onto the cot in the corner. She was stuck in here until 008 left. Pumpernickel had made it clear that no one was to see her in costume until tomorrow. If she screwed up, it'd be the men's loo for her.

008 knew very well that Pumpernickel had Miss Bond in there. Yesterday he had hidden a tracking device in a cheap plastic pen purchased from the Buckingham Palace gift shop and left outside Pumpernickel's door with a little note congratulating him on his retirement. Being pally with the old marnie sickened him, but it was necessary to his plan.

"Join me for a spot of tea, old man?" 008 knew very well Pumpernickel couldn't leave his post, not with Miss Bond in man-drag hiding in the loo. But he couldn't help tormenting the man. It was as easy—and satisfying—as tearing the wings off a fly. Pumpernickel was such an insect.

"Thank you, no. I appreciate the offer, though. Really, I do."

"All right. But you'll miss me when you're gone," 008 taunted him.

Pumpernickel knew that was true. This friendship had taken him by surprise; he would have never guessed that the ill-mannered young agent harbored friendly feelings toward him. The gift, a fine souvenir pen from his favorite place on earth, had convinced him of the boy's warm feelings. Only a true friend would have done something so thoughtful.

Office of Sir Niles Needlum
4:07 P.M.

N.'s direct line to the palace lit up. He jumped for the phone.

"Sir Niles here."

"Is everything set for tomorrow's ceremony?"

"Bond will be there."

N. had just been reviewing photographs of Miss Bond in costume. Pumpernickel had done a good job with her. Unless the palace guards strip-searched her, their ruse would go undetected. For the first time since 007's breakdown, N. felt a sense of calm. Tomorrow at this time, the whole thing would be over. Her Majesty would get her wish to meet her top secret agent. News of Bond's appearance at the Palace would spread throughout the spy community. And the double-0 division would be spared. Their palace liaison had all but guaranteed a kind word from the queen on behalf of the department—*if* they could produce Bond. It wasn't the right Bond, but she would do.

"Her Majesty has expressed much excitement about meeting her top agent. He's in good shape, is he?"

"Fit as a fiddle. You've met him, of course."

"Never. Just heard rumors of his spectacular exploits."

"He's everything you've heard," N. assured him. "And more."

Back in Agent Pumpernickel's office

Jane daubed the prosthetic scars on her face with turpentine, and peeled them off. The glue took the top layer of skin with it.

"Ouch! Why do they have to be glued on?" she complained. "Can't we just use that gummy stuff actors use to stick on false beards?"

"They must not come off. Your brother's scars are like a general's medals."

"No one's going to tug at them to see if they're real," she pointed out. "It's not as if I'm wearing a bad toupee, like your boss."

Pumpernickel sighed. "Miss Bond—"

"I know—just do as I'm told. There are reasons for every decision, and I'm not to question why."

"Exactly. There's some ointment in the first aid kit on the shelf."

"Well, that's attractive," Jane said, daubing the white bacterial cream on her raw skin. "Good thing my girlfriend's out of town."

She looked at Agent Pumpernickel, slumped in his chair.

"You look tired."

"I am. These last few days have been long ones."

"Bet you're looking forward to retirement."

"I am," he admitted. "I'm getting too old for these kinds of things."

"What kind of things? Cross-dressing?"

Pumpernickel chose to ignore that remark. He took his new ball-point pen from his shirt pocket and admired it.

Jane spread cold cream on her face and wiped off the five o'clock shadow Pumpernickel insisted she sport all day.

"Can I wear the suit home?" she asked.

"Certainly not."

"Then leave so I can change," she said, wiping off the cream.

Pumpernickel put his pen back in his pocket and made haste for the door.

The man had made it abundantly clear that she was not to make a move without him. Jane was already tired of being here. Mrs. Snipe notwithstanding, she missed the bookshop. This place gave her the heebie-jeebies; she felt as if she was always being watched.

Jane changed clothes and opened the door.

"I'm ready. Let's go get a drink."

"Not tonight, Miss Bond. Once I drop you home, you're not to leave your room until morning. You're to go to bed and get a good night's sleep. Tomorrow I'll be by bright and early to get you. We're going to have one more trial run before the ceremony."

"But it's not even five. I told Simon I'd stop by the shop."

"You'll see him soon enough, Miss Bond."

The Flora Beaton
5:12 P.M.

"Jane?"

Edith Liversidge was standing in worn carpet slippers on the equally worn lobby carpet. She had a thin cotton robe wrapped around her bony frame.

"Some candy arrived for you. I took the liberty of signing for it."

Jane smiled when she saw an enormous box of Vera Lynn salt-water taffy.

"From Bridget?" asked Miss Liversidge.

Jane read the card, and nodded.

"Tessie Twigg was eyeing the box, so I stayed out here to protect it."

"Thanks, Miss Liversidge," Jane said, opening the box and offering her some.

Miss Liversidge selected a piece of orange taffy, then said, "Care for a sherry?"

"Not tonight. I've got to get to bed. I have a big day ahead of me tomorrow at work."

"What is it you do at your new job, dear?"

"It's hard to explain, Miss Liversidge."

Outside the Flora Beaton
5:37 P.M.

Agent Pumpernickel sat in his car, waiting for the light to go on in Jane's bedsit. She didn't understand how important her appearance tomorrow was to the future of the department; she didn't understand because it hadn't been fully explained to her. There was no need to fill her mind with too many specifics, N. had said. If Miss Bond knew how vital she was to this operation, she might hold out for more money. They were scraping the bottom of the budget as it was. Any more would have to come out of pocket.

Miss Bond was in absolutely no danger; that Pumpernickel was certain of. Her appearance tomorrow as 007 would be brief. It would have been a mistake to tell the girl the truth about her brother, that he was a government assassin. Even the queen wasn't aware of the true nature of Bond's work. But Miss Bond had every right to be a little nervous.

Something caught Pumpernickel's eye in the rearview mirror. He turned in time to see a man darting from between parked cars into the thick bushes ringing the small courtyard of the Flora Beaton. He seemed to be up to no good. Probably a peeping tom or a cat burglar. Pumpernickel looked up. Jane's light had flicked on.

He got out of his car and strolled casually toward the courtyard. When he reached the thatch of bushes, he made a great show of lighting a cigarette. He lit match after match. He put his hands in his pockets and rocked on his heels. He hummed.

The man got the message. He leapt from his hiding place and ran away, eyes to the ground. Pumpernickel got a glimpse of a dog collar. A vicar in the bushes? What was the world coming to?

Pleased with himself, he got in his car, started the engine, and beetled off toward home. Miss Bond wasn't the only one who needed a good night's sleep.

Grunby Hall
Lady Edwina's bedchamber
7:54 P.M.

"I'll never forget the day I heard the official news crackling over the little radio set we had in the parlor. King Edward VIII had decided to give up his throne for the woman he loved. Of course, I was but a child when it happened," Lady Edwina hastened to add. "Me mum and me— I mean, Mumsy and I—were absolutely heartbroken. He was the best and brightest of all our kings. I passed him on a London street once, long before the scandal. It was raining and he was wearing a mac. He looked lonely, so I smiled as I passed. He gave me a little smile back. I'll never forget it, not as long as I live. His eyes had a tragic sadness in them and his smile was kind."

Lady Edwina and Bibi were sitting on the carpet, wading through a great ocean of newsclips about the abdication and the subsequent travels of the Duke and Duchess of Windsor. The earlier clippings were yellowed with age, and crumbling. Bibi was struggling to glue these fragile relics into a scrapbook.

"Sometimes I think—" Edwina started wistfully, then shook her head.

"Madam?"

"You'll think me awfully silly."

"Oh, no, madam."

"Sometimes, Bibi, I think I must understand the duchess just about more than anyone. Our lives have turned out so similarly. We both married later in life, and both our marriages caused considerable consternation amongst our friends. Of course, Sir Reginald didn't have to give up a throne for me."

"But he did move out of Grouse Manor to be with you in London," Bibi pointed out. She could tell Lady Edwina was dying to talk.

"It's really because the manor is in such dreadful shape that we live in London," Edwina admitted. "It could be years and years before that old place is fit to live in. Once the heating and plumbing and electrical are finished, there's still the decorating to consider. Sir Reginald says I can't even begin thinking about that until our plan to—"

Bibi waited patiently. Lady Edwina kept alluding to some big secret.

"You can tell me anything, Lady Edwina," Bibi said soothingly, secretly switching on the micromini recorder hidden in her frilly maid's cap. "My friends all say I'm as loyal as a dog."

"—our plan to ask Her Majesty to give her uncle back the throne. The duchess has expressed interest in our plan, and Sir Reginald and his friends have been trying to figure a way to gracefully bring up the subject to Her Majesty. Would you please pass the chocolates, Bibi?"

Edwina popped one in her mouth and chewed thoughtfully.

"This one is raspberry crème," she reported. "Do you want to see the letters from the duchess?" she asked with bright eyes. "I keep them in my hosiery drawer. I'm saving them for posterity."

"It would be an honor," Bibi replied. "Why don't you close your eyes and I'll read them to you?"

"That sounds quite soothing," Edwina cried as she got the packet of letters, tied with a Wallis-blue ribbon, and a pair of white gloves from her bureau.

"Put these gloves on first, Bibi. Someday these letters will be on display at the Victoria and Albert, and we'd be in a right nice pickle if they got damaged!"

3 June 1965

Dear Lady Wooley-Booley,
I cried tears of joy when I read of your sincere desire to put the duke back on the throne, with his humble wife (me) as his queen consort. How happy we are after all these years to find we are still wanted!
We accept!
It will be a relief to finally settle in one place. The duke es-

pecially feels the strain of our nomadic existence. Did you know it takes seven servants three hours to load our Louis Vuitton luggage each time we move? One does get so tired of living in exile!

I must go and immediately have my decorator begin sketches for redecorating the palace. The first thing I'm going to do is paper those cold stone walls.

> *Sincerely,*
> *The Duchess of Windsor*

17 July 1965

Dear Lady Wooley-Booley,
The news of the white shoes incident has just hit the French newspapers. As I am well acquainted with the unpleasantness of having people turn and stare as if one were an animal in a zoo, I felt compelled to pen this little note of support. I think your critics are being awfully provincial. If one cannot be chic, why not be different?

I must bid you a hasty adieu, as my friend Foxie and I are jetting to Milan for a quick peek at the winter lines. The duke must stay at home, as he is bilious. Boo-hoo!

> *Sincerely,*
> *The Duchess of Windsor*

8 August 1965

Dear Lady Wooley-Booley,
I am afraid I will not be able to visit you in London until after the overthrow, as I simply have too much to do! A coup d'état is trying under the best of circumstances, and all the more so when one is not prepared. Women understand, as the men do not, the time it takes to arrange these things.

We must be ready. When the Queen runs off, the court will of course go into mourning. I shall have to have the proper clothes already in hand, as will my ladies-in-waiting. To do otherwise would be rude. Black with gray and lavender touches

will do; a month later we'll be able to add white cuffs and
collars. Do instruct your dressmaker accordingly.

Sincerely,
The Duchess of Windsor

Dottinghurst Manor
Lettie Finhatten's bedchamber
Sometime after nine

Lettie's hands shook as she inserted the needle through the bottom of the bonbon and into its lemon crème center. She was never one of those girls who was good at working with her hands. And why should she be? In Lettie's experience, girls who learned to cook and sew and clean usually ended up cooking and sewing and cleaning. Lettie had a pretty face and a clever mind; she could make other people, particularly men, do just about anything she wanted.

"Bloody hell!" She had applied too much pressure, and the needle had come through the other end, cracking the chocolate shell. She tossed the bonbon in the rubbish bin and grabbed another. She was no doubt being too picky; Edwina gobbled sweets so quickly chances were she'd never notice any imperfections. Still, Lettie couldn't take any chances. She refilled the plunger with the milky fluid, picked up another candy, and injected the center.

"Perfect," she said, admiring her handiwork. She put the candy back in the box and, buoyed by her success, worked steadily until she had twelve perfect poison bonbons. Lettie thought they looked awfully pretty lined up two-by-two in their little gold box. Good enough to eat, she thought wickedly. Now for the crowning touch.

The problem with Lettie was that she was a perfectionist. For hours she sat hunched over her dressing table, practicing her handwriting until it was flawless. She checked it against the letter she had stolen from Edwina. Perfect. She wrapped the box of chocolates in gold foil paper, tied it with a Wallis-blue ribbon—a nice touch, she thought—and taped a card to the top of the box.

To Edwina, from her loving friend the Duchess of Windsor.

9 SEPTEMBER 1965

The Flora Beaton lobby
8:00 A.M.

"HELLO, Miss Bond."

Agent Pumpernickel was sitting on the red horsehair settee in the lobby, drinking tea with Miss Liversidge. Jane thought he looked awfully jolly for that hour of the morning. Grumbling something unintelligible to them both, Jane poured herself a cup and slumped onto the seat.

"Dear, you didn't tell me you were going to see the queen," Miss Liversidge scolded her. She turned to Agent Pumpernickel, a plate in her hand.

"They're charcoal health biscuits. Care for one?"

Jane shot him a warning glance. Agent Pumpernickel politely declined.

"And you never told me you had an Uncle Cedric," Miss Liversidge continued.

"It's news to me." Jane yawned.

"We haven't seen each other in years," Agent Pumpernickel hastily explained. "Not since Jane was a girl."

"Are you her father's brother or her mother's?"

"Neither, actually. More a distant family relation."

"What's your line of work, Mr. Pumpernickel?"

"I own a rubber band factory."

Jane almost dropped her teacup. This fellow lied with remarkable ease.

"How fascinating!" said Miss Liversidge as she refilled Pumpernickel's cup. "Is it very big?"

"Oh, no," he demurred. "I have only seven employees. Well, eight."

"The compulsive chap who lies all the time is retiring—remember?" Jane corrected him.

Agent Pumpernickel cleared his throat.

Sensing some tension between the two, Miss Liversidge jumped in with a cheerful "Tell me, do you know how to make those rubber band balls?"

"I certainly do. It's been a hobby of mine for years. My biggest is the size of the royal orb."

"Why, that's remarkable! Do tell me how it's done."

"It's a fine art. You start with a cork, cut so it's as long as it is wide. Otherwise your ball will end up looking more like an egg. Mind you, there's nothing wrong with that, but if it's a world record you're after, you must hue to the traditional rounded shape. And only use the very best elastics. Bad ones break easily, and if one snaps—well, then the whole thing will go bouncing out of control. Let me draw you a step-by-step diagram—"

Jane's eyelids grew heavy. This seemed like a good time for a catnap.

En route to headquarters
8:23 A.M.

"I thought no one was supposed to know about this, Uncle Pumpernickel," Jane said as they crept toward headquarters. "I've been lying to my friends and you go ahead and give it away over a cup of tea."

"It slipped out," he explained sheepishly. He was having a little trouble containing himself. The idea of being in such close proximity to the queen was making him feel positively giddy.

"I didn't tell her you were going as a secret agent," he pointed out. The minute the words were out, Pumpernickel knew he had slipped up.

"I thought my brother was a bodyguard."

"He is. He's a secret agent bodyguard. It's merely a matter of semantics."

"Oh." Jane opened the window a crack and lit a cigarette.

"Must you?" Agent Pumpernickel asked.

"You smoke."

"Not in a government vehicle."

Jane flipped the cigarette out the window. "You're as bad as my girlfriend," she said, sighing. Thinking of Bridget gave her the most delicious feeling. She put her coat over her head and leaned back in her seat.

"Wake me when we get there," she said. "And not a minute sooner."

Meanwhile, at Grunby Hall

The most important event of Edwina's life—besides her wedding day, of course—was just around the corner, and her husband, who had stood up before a magistrate and pledged to care for her through good times and bad, simply refused to come home. Ever since receiving the queen's R.S.V.P., Edwina had been plagued by doubts and insecurities. Each night she had the same dream; a nightmare, really. The members of the Sons of Britain Society and their wives were standing in the magnificent great hall, cocktails in hand, waiting for Edwina to make her entrance. The queen was there, dressed in an elegant (yet sensible) gown, wearing her coronation crown. As Edwina gracefully descended the stairs, exactly as she had been taught at Miss Lermer's School of Charm all those years ago, everyone turned to stare—*at Edwina in her slip!* Not one of her lovely, handmade lace-trimmed ones, mind you, but an old shapeless one with grayish straps from her premarital days.

It was at this point that she awoke screaming.

Her party was going to be a disaster. No one would bid on her lamps. Overwhelmed by a sense of doom, Edwina pulled the covers over head and wept. A knock on her door interrupted her pitiful sobs.

"Lady Edwina?"

She sat up in bed, wiping her eyes with the corner of her cashmere coverlet.

"Yes, Bibi?" she sniffled.

"Breakfast, madam."

"Come in."

Bibi noticed Edwina's red eyes at once, but said nothing. Edwina would tell her soon enough.

"Eggs, madam, nice and runny just the way you like. And crumpets."

"Thank you, Bibi," Edwina said gratefully. Tears filled her eyes when she saw that Bibi had remembered to cut her crumpet in little triangles. When they were first married—oh, months ago!—her husband had taken great pleasure in cutting her food into bite-size morsels with a sharp, silver-handled knife.

"Please inform Sir Reginald that I am awake and receiving visitors."

"He's already left, madam."

"Without saying good-bye?" Edwina whimpered fretfully.

"I offered to wake you, madam, but he said you needed your beauty sleep." He had said this while making a grab for Bibi's thigh.

Edwina bit her lower lip to keep from crying. Was Sir Reginald avoiding her?

"Bibi—" she started, tentatively.

"Yes, madam?"

Edwina remembered her husband's warning about her familiarity with the servants.

"Oh, nothing." She sighed pitifully.

"Is there anything else, madam?"

"No thank you, Bibi."

As she gnawed on a crumpet triangle, Edwina contemplated her marriage. They had been wed less than a year, and already it seemed that the magic was gone. Before becoming Lady Edwina, she had spent most of her time with her dear friend Mildred. They had enjoyed an intimacy that seemed a true union of souls. Edwina had naturally assumed that she would develop the same kind of kinship with her husband.

Perhaps she was just being a jealous little wife. Sir Reginald was hard at work every day on *Zebras I Have Shot*, the sequel to his first well-received tome, *Tigers I Have Shot*. Edwina thought the titles quite clever, although why he had picked this week to finish his manuscript was beyond her comprehension. She was trying her best to be understanding, but she was beginning to feel a tiny bit resentful of all those dead animals. Did her husband really find them better company than his dear wife? She'd had no idea Reginald was such a prodigious talent when she married him. Now she knew how Shakespeare's wife must have felt.

It seemed Lettie had deserted her as well. She had promised to help Edwina select a dress for the charity auction, but every time Edwina called, Lettie was indisposed. The other day, Jinx had made a reference to "Lettie's brave struggle," and at the time, Edwina had thought he was referring to the ever-increasing gray strands in her friend's black hair. Was Lettie ill?

Dottinghurst Manor
9:00 A.M.

The mousy brown curls bobbled when she moved her head. The ridiculous flowered hat did little to disguise the drab hairdo. Lettie Finhatten ripped off the wig in disgust and threw it across the room. She hated that wig. It was ugly and hot and unflattering. Leave it to England to have a queen with absolutely no style sense.

What a relief it would be when the duchess was crowned queen. The people would, at long last, have a queen who understood how fashion and beauty could heal a troubled country. Lettie firmly believed that if people dressed better, they'd behave better. Criminals would think twice before committing crimes that would muss their outfits.

A knock at the door interrupted her musings.

"Telephone, madam."

"I said no interruptions!" Lettie snapped.

"It's Lady Edwina, and she's most anxious to speak to you."

"I don't care if it's the godforsaken pope! Leave me alone!"

Why the hell had she agreed to this masquerade? It meant she'd have to spend half the party hideously costumed. Lettie peeled off the padded girdle and kicked it under her bed. Unattractive things always made her cross.

Secret Service headquarters
Office of Agent Cedric Pumpernickel
9:14 A.M.

Jane turned up her nose at the weak coffee and plain biscuits.

"This isn't going to do it," she told Pumpernickel. "I need some real food."

"There are leftovers from the Indian take-away in the secret agents' lounge. We could sniff the bag and see if it's still edible."

Jane turned up her nose at the suggestion.

"How can you even think of food at a time like this?" he pressed her.

"I eat when I'm nervous."

"We shouldn't leave the building."

"Why not? I'm not in costume."

"Sir Niles might come looking for us."

"He's not due until half-past nine. If you could manage to drive closer to the posted speed, we could make it to that bakery we went to the other day and back in fifteen minutes."

"I could use a good strong cup of coffee," he admitted. "But it's not in our schedule. We should really stay here. We've so much to get through today."

"We could be eating right now if you'd stop talking."

"You are a bad influence on me, Miss Bond," Pumpernickel said as he shrugged on his trench coat.

Secret Service headquarters
11:00 A.M.

Agent Pumpernickel knocked on the door of the ladies' loo. It was taking Jane a frightfully long time to apply her makeup. He had always heard that women took longer to get ready than men.

"Miss Bond, you must make haste. Sir Niles will be down in a minute to inspect you." The ceremony was not for another two hours, but he wanted to allow for traffic.

Jane flung open the door, a martini in one hand and an expensive Turkish cigarette in the other. She had applied the makeup and prosthetic scars precisely as she'd been taught. She swirled the contents of her glass, narrowed her dark eyes into sinister slits, and sneered, "That's *Mr.* Bond to you."

If Agent Pumpernickel hadn't known she was an imposter, he would have thought Agent 007 was standing in the doorway of the ladies' room.

Office of Sir Niles Needlum
11:34 A.M.

N. wanted to make certain Agent Pumpernickel knew exactly what he was to do. To that effect, he had purchased a set of small plastic figures representing the characters of *The Avengers*, the popular television show about secret agents. Green army men would fill in for the rest. He positioned the miniature Emma Peel and John Steed on an aerial photograph of Buckingham Palace and its surrounding acres.

"The ceremony will take place in the queen's rose garden, where all public ceremonies are held, weather permitting," he began.

"The sky this morning was blue and clear," Agent Pumpernickel reported. "It looks like it's going to hold, sir."

"Thank you for that weather report," N. said testily. "Please don't interrupt."

"Yes, sir."

"You two pick at each other like an old married couple," Jane said. She scratched the skin around the fake scar on her forehead. It itched terribly.

"Pay attention, Miss Bond," N. snapped. He picked up John Steed and showed Jane her route. "After you pass through the palace gate, you will be directed to the garden entrance. Once there you will find your table and sit."

Agent Pumpernickel was confused. "Excuse me, sir. Aren't I to accompany Miss Bond?"

"We've been over this a million times, Pumpernickel." N. sighed. "You are never to leave her side."

"Then where am I, sir? Am I Mrs. Peel?"

"The queen is Mrs. Peel, Agent Pumpernickel."

"Am I one of the green army men, then? It's hard to tell—they all look so much alike."

N. grabbed an inkwell from his desk and slammed it down next to John Steed. The army men shook; a few toppled over.

"Those must be the people who fainted from the sheer delight of meeting the queen," Jane surmised.

N. glared at them. They were acting like children. Particularly daft ones.

"Miss Bond, do not speak to anyone unless absolutely necessary. If you're recognized, pretend you have a cold. I've already informed the palace that you've got a case of laryngitis picked up on assignment in Antarctica, and the queen understands." Miss Bond looked the part, but her voice was several octaves too high. Surgery on her vocal cords would have remedied that, but they hadn't the time. The girl would just have to keep her mouth shut.

"She'll pretend to have a coughing fit and I'll hand her my hand-kerchief," Agent Pumpernickel offered.

N. paused. "That will be fine," he said. "Now, at two o'clock you will be asked to take your place in the receiving line." He put John Steed in a receiving line of green army men. Pumpernickel followed with the inkwell.

N. continued. "The queen is a very busy woman. She has allotted fifteen minutes for the presentation of the medals. Accompanied by the keeper of the velvet boxes, the queen will greet each one of you—except you, Pumpernickel, as you're not receiving a medal—and hand you a box. There are forty-two people being honored today. Miss Bond, you will have perhaps seven or eight seconds with the queen, but they're the most important seconds of your life. The queen will be whisked away, and you will be free to go. On rare occasions, the queen will invite a few honorees—a Nobel Prize winner or an actor—to the public sitting room for a drink. If you are not selected—but I predict, given Her Majesty's interest in spy novels, that you will be—return directly to headquarters, where you will resume your true identity."

"That's it? That's the extent of my top secret job?"

"It may not seem important to you, Miss Bond, but much is riding on your shoulders."

"She knows exactly what to do, sir," Agent Pumpernickel assured him. "We've been over it a dozen times."

"Any last questions?"

"What if someone tries something?" asked Jane.

"The queen has a strategically placed panic button on the underside of her pocketbook."

"I meant *me*. Tries to hurt *me*."

"There is absolutely no danger in this assignment, Miss Bond. Remember—you're there to make an appearance, not to actually *do* anything. Just stand around and look manly. Think you can handle that?"

"I think I can," Jane said coolly, her hands deep in her trouser pockets.

"If there's nothing more, I have work to do."

"May I have my action figure?"

"Certainly not," N. snapped. "It's government property."

When he turned to pick up a ringing telephone, Jane pocketed it.

Someday she'd tell Bridget all about these peculiar men and their preposterous little games, and this would be her proof.

008 switched on the tracking device. It began to beep immediately. The radio transmitter hidden in Agent Pumpernickel's pen was coming in loud and clear. 008 had decided on a collapsible slingshot as his weapon of choice. He strapped it to his calf, using an elastic filched from Pumpernickel's favorite ball to secure it. He already knew they were headed for Buck House, having found the invitations in Agent Pumpernickel's drawer. 008 had been able to create a decent enough facsimile. And he had the perfect disguise, one that would deflect suspicion as surely as a bulletproof shield deflects a bullet.

En route to Buckingham Palace
12:00 P.M. EXACTLY

"Am I getting the rest of my money today?"

"As soon as Sir Niles determines the mission has been successful you will receive the balance."

"When will that be?"

"Most likely tomorrow, Miss Bond. Perhaps the day after. Soon."

"Good, because we've already rung up our creditors and promised payment. Simon will have to shutter the shop if I don't come through."

"You worry too much, Miss Bond. Look out the window—it's a beautiful day, and we're on our way to see the queen."

Pumpernickel began to hum "Hail, Britannia" off-key.

"A little excited, are we?"

"Quite, Miss Bond. I've been waiting for this day my entire life."

"I promise not to muck it up."

"I don't mind admitting that at times I've been doubtful of your sincerity regarding this mission. But you've been an exemplary student. You've done very well."

"Scared you, did I?"

"I am not accustomed to women who speak their mind so freely," he admitted. "You're a trifle independent."

"It runs in the family."

Agent Pumpernickel smiled. "Your father would be very proud of you today, Miss Bond."

Jane slid her hand through her cropped hair (a mistake given the amount of pomade in it) and looked out the window.

Buckingham Palace
London home of Her Majesty, Queen Elizabeth II
12:30 P.M.

Jane Bond and Agent Pumpernickel got to the palace just as people were milling up to the rails to see the changing of the guard.

"Take my picture standing by a member of the palace guard," Agent Pumpernickel urged. He was thinking of putting together a scrapbook devoted entirely to this day.

"Say cheese!"

"Cheddar!" He smiled widely.

Jane tugged on her tie, which set off the shutter in the miniaturized camera hidden in her tie-tack.

"Let's go to the gift shop and get some picture postcards," Jane suggested. She had promised Miss Liversidge a bonny Prince Charles to round out her collection.

"We should find our table, lest we fall behind schedule," said Agent Pumpernickel.

"I hear there are new Queen Mum mugs."

He reconsidered. "Maybe we could pop in and have a quick look."

"Have a lovely tea, Father," the palace guard said, smiling at 008 as he waved him through the gates. Just as 008 had suspected, his clerical collar and a quick flash of the invitation was sufficient to get him in. He made a mental note of the guard's face. The queen's head of security would surely want to know that the man had been derelict in his duty. What if the rock in 008's pocket had had the queen's name on it?

Bunches of scarlet and lemon dahlias had been placed just so on the snowy-white tablecloths. A man was measuring the distance between each silver teaspoon and saucer, while another followed close behind, counting the number of spoons at each table and ticking them off in a little book.

"What are they doing?"

"The keeper of the silver spoons measures the spoon and saucer at each place setting to make sure they are separated by a measure equal to the exact length of the reigning monarch's pinkie finger. Later, the counter of the silver spoons will collect and count them. At each tea, a few unsavory subjects make off with the spoons, even though there are perfectly nice silver-plate ones available at a reasonable price in the gift shop."

"Do they frisk you on the way out?"

"Goodness, no," he answered. A look of horror crept across his face. "You wouldn't!"

"I promise the last thing I want is a silver spoon," Jane assured him. Miss Liversidge, however, would simply adore one.

The medal recipients, embalmed in their Sunday best, were beginning to arrive. Jane and Agent Pumpernickel found their name cards and sat down, Agent Pumpernickel slipping his into his pocket as a souvenir. He switched his two-way wristwatch receiver to the whisper setting.

"Agent Pumpernickel to Agent Bond. I repeat. Agent Pumpernickel to Agent Bond. Come in, Agent Bond."

Jane felt a vibration on her wrist. She had a call. "I'm sitting right next to you," she said to him.

"This is a test. Agent Pumpernickel to Agent Bond. I repeat. Agent Pumpernickel to Agent Bond. Come in, Agent Bond."

Jane put her watch up to her face and pretended to check the time, as she had been taught. "Hello?" she said.

"You're supposed to say, 'Agent Bond here.'"

"You were expecting someone else?" Jane shot back, a trifle to loud. A woman seated at the table next to them turned to stare. She was a pretty brunette with porcelain skin and a ridiculous hat. Her lavender chiffon dress hugged an hourglass figure.

Jane gave her a lascivious wink. It worked. The woman gasped, stiffened her spine, and made a great show of turning her back on Jane.

"Agent Bond, do you read me? Come in, Agent Bond."

"Agent Bond here," Jane said in a low tone. "What is it?"

"This has been a test. Keep your line open for further instructions. Agent Pumpernickel, over and out." A moment of silence followed.

He reached across the table and nudged her. "And you say?"

Pumpernickel was beginning to try her nerves. He needed a hobby. Or a husband.

Jane kept her voice low and her tone dead serious. "Agent Bond, over and out."

Emerald Norbert-Nilbert Smythe-Pargater St. Claire, Duchess of Malmesbury and one of England's most important hostesses, surveyed the queen's tea tables with a sharp eye. Once again, the master of the royal flower arrangements had chosen unimaginative arrangements of garden-variety flowers. He should be flogged.

"Look at those homely bunches of weeds," she said to her daughter, who had agreed to accompany her as her current husband was that day competing in a yacht race. The duchess was to receive a medal for her many good works.

"Aren't they just the most earnest little things you've ever seen? The only thing more deadly would be bunches of violets in paper cones bought from a rag woman."

"Mother, must you be such a harsh critic?" Lady Bridget St. Claire chided her. "The flowers are very sweet."

Emerald St. Claire shook her head. Sometimes her daughter could be so exasperatingly charitable. She didn't know where she had picked it up; certainly not at the exclusive, horsey boarding school to which she had been sent.

"Bridget, if we don't have any standards, people will come to believe that they can rely on their own judgment in matters of taste."

Bridget flagged down a waiter. "May I have a martini?"

"If we are all right, then who is left to be wrong?"

"Make it a double," she pleaded.

There was danger about; the smell of it was insistent. What had activated Pumpernickel's secret agent sixth sense, he didn't know.

"What's the matter?" Jane asked.

"Something's not on the up and up," he said.

Jane made an unpleasant face. "It's these seaweed sandwiches," she said.

"They're watercress, Miss Bond."

Agent Pumpernickel looked around, but everything seemed fine. He had been right about the weather—there wasn't a cloud in the sky. It was a good omen. But still he felt anxious. He rolled his spoon between his fingers until he lost his grip and dropped it on the manicured lawn. He bent to pick it up, and hit his head on the table on the trip back up.

"You're just nervous about meeting the queen," Jane said. "Relax— I promise not to muck this up. Smile—the prime minister is right behind you." She took another snap with the miniature camera hidden in her tie.

"You might not want to keep that one," she said. "You look a little green."

"I'm certain something's wrong—I can feel it. But I can't put my finger on it."

"Go over your morning step by step. Did you forget to turn off the kettle?"

He thought back over what had been, to his mind, a typical morning. He had dressed, eaten his soft-boiled egg, then done the washing-up. He had turned off the kettle, he was sure of it. But had he remembered to lock up?

"I think I left the front door unlocked," he said anxiously. "Yes, that's it. I could ring my neighbor Mrs. Figgis and ask her to pop over and check."

"Why don't you do that? We've got time."

"I'm not supposed to leave you. Besides, I realize it's too late. Mrs. Figgis takes the telephone off the hook when she watches her stories. *The Stiff Upper Lip* has already begun."

He was positive now that he had neglected to lock his door. He had been exceedingly scatterbrained all week. He kept forgetting the names of common objects, and had lost his keys twice. Then there was the matter of the fish finger factory he had set on fire. Without his daily routine, Agent Pumpernickel felt discombobulated. What was to become of him when he retired? Would he become one of those men who sat in their dressing gowns all day and wrote churlish letters to the *Times*?

"Stop worrying. As soon as I get my medal, you can go home and check your door. Let's go to the tea tent for a refill."

When they returned to the table, Pumpernickel realized his silver spoon was missing.

"Miss Bond!" he gasped.

"What?" Jane asked, feigning innocence.

"I'll just swish my tea." Pumpernickel sighed. He demonstrated and in the process, splashed the queen's special blend of oolong tea on his trousers.

"Oh, no!" he wailed, jumping up and shaking his trouser leg. Could this day get any worse?

"Run to the loo and get some cold water on that," said Jane. "Quick, before it sets."

"Don't go anywhere or talk to anyone while I'm gone," he ordered.

Meanwhile, at the Duchess of Malmesbury's table

"You look awfully worn out, dear." Lady Emerald St. Claire was concerned about the dark shadows under her daughter's eyes. "It's that dreadful job on that scooter, isn't it? Sending you all over London at a moment's notice. You'd think they'd give you a day off now and then so you could see your family."

"I'm here with you now, Mother," said Bridget as she plucked an olive from her martini and popped it in her mouth.

"Yes, but you haven't listened to a thing I've said."

"I've heard every word," Bridget insisted as she opened her compact and discreetly studied the other guests. People were sipping tea and eating biscuits; they appeared to be having a perfectly nice time. It made her miss Jane.

"Bridget dear, don't use your compact in public; it's simply not done."

Bridget snapped her compact shut and dropped it in her handbag. She was the only G.E.O.R.G.I.E. agent with an inside to the palace; otherwise she'd never take this rubbish from her mother.

"Oh, look, there's Lady Lettie Finhatten wearing a ridiculously youthful frock. How brave of her to sit there smiling, all the while knowing that the color clashes horribly with the table linens. I wonder why *she's* receiving a medal. All she's done is bring crusts on tea sandwiches back in vogue."

"Do you know her well?" asked Bridget.

"Only socially," her mother answered as she took a pair of pearl-encrusted opera glasses from her clutch. She wanted to see exactly how low Lettie's neckline was today.

"She's making eyes at a handsome, dark-haired man at the next table. How very common. Now she's getting up to speak to him—right in front of her husband!"

"Mother, don't stare."

"Hush," said her mother, steadying the opera glasses. "I'm trying to read their lips."

Her daughter had a habit of being forthcoming with her opinion, a trait sure to scare off suitable suitors. But for all of Bridget's faults, she had never once embarrassed Emerald by flirting in public with a man.

"So you do remember me, James. I'm sorry I had to act so aloof; Jinx was watching."

Lady Lettie Finhatten had snuck up behind Jane at her table and was now pressed against her chair. She bent down, as if murmuring in her ear, and began nibbling on Jane's neck. When Jane failed to respond, Lettie slipped her hand under the flap of her suit coat, pinched her bum lightly, and snaked her fingers over her thigh toward her crotch, where they met a pincer grip.

"James, you're hurting me," Lettie breathed in Jane's ear.

"Go away," Jane whispered fiercely in the deepest voice she could muster.

"You must meet me later," Lettie whispered in Jane's ear.

Jane grunted.

"Be at Swan Lake in one hour. I'm not going until you say yes."

"All right," Jane hissed. "Now go away!" She could see Pumpernickel wending his way through the tables. This would surely overtax his already frazzled nerves.

Emerald St. Claire had seen the entire exchange. From the frantic whispering and groping going on, she had little doubt what had occurred.

"Lettie has just arranged a tryst with that man—I'm almost certain of it. Imagine—adultery at the palace!"

"Unthinkable," Bridget said sarcastically.

"Poor Jinx. I've always thought Lettie was a bit of a vixen, and now here's the proof."

Bridget had to admit she was a little curious. It wouldn't hurt to get a look at Lady Lettie in the flesh.

"May I, Mother?"

Emerald thrust the opera glasses at her daughter.

"Look and learn, Bridget. Look and learn. This is not how one conducts oneself at a queen's tea."

"It certainly is not!" cried Bridget when she spied Lady Lettie Finhatten mauling Jane. She jumped to her feet, infuriated. There was nothing she could do—she was supposed to be in Dover on a mission of mercy.

"Sit down, Bridget—people are staring. You needn't be so prudish, dear." Emerald found her daughter's prim attitude toward sex rather unsettling. All her friends' daughters had lost their virginity years ago.

Bridget continued to examine Lettie through the opera glasses.

"She's awfully taut," Bridget sniffed. "And she's forty if she's a day."

"Word is they pulled her face so tight she can't close her eyes," her mother informed her. It was nice to see Bridget taking an interest in society.

Five minutes later

Emerald stood and adjusted her hat. It was time to receive yet another accolade.

"Do I look divine, dear?"

"Oh, yes. Divine."

"Come watch mother get her little tin badge," said Emerald.

"Start without me. I'll catch up." Bridget realized she should have informed Chief Tuppenny of her trip to the palace. What if Jane had already spotted her? She moved her chair so it was obscured by a potted palm and stared at Jane. From a distance of eight tea tables, she did indeed resemble 007. The question was, did Jane share her brother's cavalier attitude toward love?

A nearby thicket of Queen Alexandra rosebushes

008 had almost let the rock fly a minute ago, but a woman in a lavender dress had suddenly popped up behind Bond. He wanted this to be a clean shot. There was no need for innocent bystanders to become involved.

Good. The woman had gone. 008 steadied his firing arm and fixed on his target. If he didn't scare off Miss Bond, chances were he'd be a Pumpernickel the rest of his life.

"One—two—three—" The rock went flying. A second later, one of the queen's speckled-tailed songbirds screeched in surprise and fell lifeless to the ground. A waiter rushed over, wrapped the bird in a napkin, and carried it away. A few people looked to the sky, but other than that, his first hit went unnoticed.

"It's a bad sign," Pumpernickel said to Jane.

"What is?" Jane was busy reading the historical facts on her paper place mat. She had had no idea that the queen possessed one thousand, four hundred and thirty-seven clocks.

"A bird just fell dead from a tree."

As soon as her mother had gone, Bridget ducked inside a thatch of rosebushes, nearly colliding with a vicar concealed within.

"Excuse me," Bridget said frostily. He was no doubt intending to use the queen's rosebush as a lavatory.

"Pardon me, miss," he stammered as he backed out of the bushes, ripping his suit on the prickly thorns.

"Next time, try the gents'!" Bridget shouted after him.

She took her compact from her purse, raised the antenna, and spoke into the microphone hidden underneath the powder insert.

"Agent St. Claire calling Agent Dolittle. Come in, Agent Dolittle."

"Agent Dolittle here."

"I'm in the queen's rose garden. Bond is here. State your location, agent," Bridget said tersely.

"I'm outside the palace at the west gate," Mimi admitted. "I didn't realize this event was closed to the public. Next time I'll—"

"There may not be a next time," Bridget cut her off. She was thoroughly annoyed. Mimi should have come to her for a palace pass. "I've got to get out of here before Bond spots me. Meet me at the Albert memorial and I'll give you my credentials.

"And Dolittle—"

"Yes, Agent St. Claire?"

"Don't lose Bond again!"

1:53 P.M.

"Bond, James. Agent, secret." A man with a clipboard was going round to all the tables, collecting the medal recipients.

Jane produced her Secret Service credentials.

"Very good. Come this way, Agent Bond."

"I'm to come too, aren't I?" Agent Pumpernickel asked anxiously.

"Pumpernickel, Cedric. Agent, secret." He showed the man with the clipboard his identification. "I'm not scheduled to receive a medal today, but I'm to accompany Agent Bond."

The man studied his list while Pumpernickel sweated. Was nothing to go right today?

Jane patted his arm. "Breathe," she whispered.

"Here you are," the man apologized. "Pumpernickel, Cedric. Agent, secret. The list's alphabetical. It didn't pop out right off."

"See?" Jane said. "Everything is going to be fine." The poor chap was going to have a breakdown by the time the queen got to him. Good thing she was there to keep him standing.

"Do I look alright?" Agent Pumpernickel whispered as they followed the palace official to the receiving line.

"Mop your forehead," Jane whispered. "And straighten your tie."

He frantically tried to make himself presentable. "Better?"

"You look very nice," Jane told him. "Your mother would be proud."

The Jolly Good Show receiving line
2:10 P.M.

Jane waved discreetly to Agent Pumpernickel. He waved forlornly back. She was second in line, and he was almost at the end. They had been arranged alphabetically. On Jane's left was the Right Honorable Reverend John Abernathy. (He had already introduced himself with a hearty handshake.) On her right was a handsome older woman who was chatting with the woman on her right.

"Chin up, old man," she whispered into her transmitter. She pointed to her tie and nodded. Agent Pumpernickel looked somewhat relieved. He would still have his photo taken with the queen. Granted, it wouldn't be an intimate portrait, but they'd be in the same frame.

"Any questions, Agent Bond?" Agent Pumpernickel whispered frantically into her ear.

"No," Jane whispered tersely. Pumpernickel was making her nervous. All of a sudden, she couldn't remember how to bow. First off, she didn't believe in it, but that was another matter. They had gone over the simple maneuver ad nauseam, and now it had flown from her head.

The chatty redhead next to her wasn't helping matters any. The topic of conversation had moved on to the burden of unmarried daughters.

"She turns up her nose at every young man I introduce her to. She seems to prefer the company of her roommate, a girl with the ridiculous name of Bibi. Mind you, it's a perfectly adorable name if one happens to be a poodle. And this girl is no one. Her people are not even listed in Debrett's. Now, I ask you, what kind of man is my daughter going to meet through her? And what is the point of living with another unmarried woman if not to meet potential beaux?"

Apparently, the Mrs. Snipes of the world were everywhere.

"I tell her all the time: Dear, fruit that sits on the shelf too long is wont to get a soggy bottom."

Jane stifled a laugh and leaned closer so as not to miss one gem.

"And she's such a pretty girl; looks nothing like her father. You'll see in a moment. Where has she got off to? She's probably still at the table, painting her face. Young girls are always pulling out their compacts in public these days."

The band struck up "God Save the Queen," and Jane cursed her sentimentality as a little chill went down her spine.

A long, narrow red carpet had been laid on the manicured lawn for the queen's feet. Not so for the forty-two lucky souls waiting for their sovereign. The wet grass was squishy under the soles of her black government-issue shoes. They had been made especially for her, and were probably the only pair of handmade shoes she'd ever own. The

Secret Service was not getting these back. Or Miss Liversidge's silver spoon.

The queen was being escorted from her outdoor throne toward the receiving line. The people in line grew still.

"Agent Bond!" crackled the transmitter in her ear. "Here comes the queen!"

Jane sent a glare down the forty-one medal honorees between them.

"Eyes straight ahead," he screeched in her ear.

Crimey! It was like having a little Pumpernickel in her head. As the queen grew nearer, Pumpernickel continued to buzz like a gnat. He was making Jane nervous. She had been taught not to make any sudden movement in the vicinity of the queen, and so slowly, imperceptibly, she reached over and turned off her transmitter watch. She nodded a few times, as if she were still listening to Pumpernickel, then stopped. The queen had arrived at the receiving line, preceded by a man holding a stack of small velvet boxes.

"Your Majesty, may I present the Right Honorable Reverend John Abernathy," the man said.

"Your Majesty," the reverend said respectfully, then bowed.

"Thanks awfully," the queen said as she handed him a velvet box. The whole thing was over in an instant.

This isn't so hard, Jane thought with relief. Then, suddenly, she was staring right into the face of the queen of England. Christ on a cross, she thought. I'm meeting the *frickin' queen of England*! Startled by the physical sensation of awe that passed over her, still Jane could not help but notice how ordinary Her Majesty looked.

The Right Honorable Reverend John Abernathy gave her a sharp nudge with his elbow. Jane stopped staring and fixed her gaze over the queen's left shoulder.

"Your Majesty, may I present Secret Agent James Bond."

"Your Majesty," Jane said. She bowed; not quite as smoothly as she had in Agent Pumpernickel's office, but well enough, she imagined. She heard her shoes squish in the damp grass.

"Thanks awfully," the queen said as she handed her a velvet box.

Jane opened her mouth to reply, then realized none was needed. The queen had moved on. Jane was flooded with relief. She hadn't sneezed on the queen, or sneered at her, or otherwise embarrassed the Secret Service. It was almost over; all that was left was to turn in her costume and collect her pay.

"Your Majesty, may I present the Duchess of Malmesbury, Lady Emerald Norbert-Nilbert Smythe-Pargater St. Claire."

Jane froze. Had she heard correctly? The redhead was a St. Claire? Lady Emerald? *The* Lady Emerald that Bridget had admitted was "a distant relation"? She turned to look at Lady Emerald as she received her medal from the queen, noting the familiar distinctive full lips and upturned nose.

Agent Pumpernickel couldn't believe his eyes. They had been over this part several times, and Jane had scored high marks on the written quiz. She knew she was never, ever to turn her back on the queen, but there she was, clear as day, leaving her place in line and running back toward the tea area.

"Agent Bond," he hissed into his transmitter. "Halt immediately and resume your position!"

When Miss Bond acted as though she hadn't heard him, he realized he had no choice but to follow her. The queen was only up to Lady Devonshire; he had time to stop Miss Bond and rush back in time to meet the queen. He backed out of line slowly so as not to alarm anyone. When he was certain the queen could no longer see him, he turned and began to run like the dickens. Jane had a good many years on him, and the grass was slippery, but he managed to keep her in his sights until colliding with a young vicar and falling.

"I say, you startled me!" Agent Pumpernickel cried, landing on the wet grass. He blinked. For a moment he thought he recognized the mean eyes behind the thick glasses. It must be the bright sun playing tricks on his old eyes.

The vicar tipped his hat. "So sorry, sir," he said, and walked away without so much as offering a helping hand to the prostrate agent.

Pumpernickel picked himself up off the ground and resumed his chase. He lost sight of Miss Bond. Young people were so rude these days—even the clergy. The fellow must be one of those reform types. Heedless of the people around him, he began frantically shouting into his wristwatch.

"Agent Bond! Agent Bond! Come in."

He thought he must look the madman. A member of the palace

guard apparently agreed with the assessment, and asked him to please stop running in the queen's rose garden. Pumpernickel's attempts to explain his actions only caused more confusion—with his grass-stained suit and crazed expression, he looked nothing like a secret agent, especially one employed by Her Majesty. To make matters worse, in all the excitement he had lost his credentials.

Still craning his head wildly for a sight of Jane, Pumpernickel was escorted out the gate and sternly reprimanded. At last he was released. He tarried near the gate, hoping still to spot Jane, but the guards chased him off, threatening him with arrest. A crushed man, he got into his car and slowly drove off. He had lost Miss Bond. He had missed his only chance to meet Her Majesty. He didn't have the medal N. required as proof of mission accomplished. And he had left his souvenir mug behind.

LADY BRIDGET NORBERT-NILBERT ST. CLAIRE was engraved on the place card at the table. Underneath a teacup was a scribbled note. Jane's heart sank when she recognized the handwriting. It was a perfect match to the love note she had stuck in her pocket for good luck.

> *Mother, have come down with a sick headache. Will ring you later. Congratters!*
>
> *B.*

Jane sat and put her head between her knees. It was all she could do to keep those seaweed sandwiches down.

"Do you need assistance, my good man?"

The first thing she noticed was his shoes. They were government-issue plain black oxfords—just like Pumpernickel's. Jane looked up. They belonged to a young vicar with glasses so thick his almost colorless eyes looked like large misty moons. It was rare to see someone so young with such bad eyesight.

"I see you've received a medal today," the vicar chirped. "That's a reason for celebration. Why so down, then?"

"Go save someone else's soul," Jane spat out. She raced back to the receiving line, but it was already breaking up, and Agent Pumpernickel was nowhere to be seen.

"Agent Bond calling Agent Pumpernickel," she said urgently into her wristwatch transmitter. "Come in, Agent Pumpernickel!" The damn thing didn't seem to be working. She smacked it, then remembered she had switched it off. She hit the transmitter button and tried again, but there was no reply.

She raced back to the table, hoping he'd headed back there to look for her. There was no sign of him, so she grabbed the bag containing Pumpernickel's souvenir mug, Miss Liversidge's postal cards, and a miniature porcelain corgi for her collection, and headed for the gate. Plan A had been to stick together the entire ceremony. There was no plan B. She reached the west entrance just in time to see two palace guards push Agent Pumpernickel into his black sedan. She raced after him, but the crush of people leaving the palace was too great.

Le Lady Bountiful Boutique
Kensington
2:23 P.M.

They had been to the most exclusive boutiques in London, and still Edwina wasn't satisfied.

"Honestly, Edwina, I do not understand the rush. Why must you have something new? You have plenty of beautiful clothes already."

"But I don't have anything truly spectacular," Edwina explained.

"Must you have it today?"

Oh, why did her friend ask so many questions?

"My husband insists I always be well dressed. Is that a crime?"

"At these prices, yes," Mrs. Snipe sniffed. She checked the tag on a midnight-blue beaded cocktail dress. "Three hundred and fifty pounds for this! Why, I could make it for less than three pounds!"

"But the beads are crystal," Edwina cried as she touched the midnight-blue beaded dress. "Look how the light strikes them. It's so elegant."

"It's obscene," Mrs. Snipe declared. "Look how low the back dips. Why, you couldn't wear a brassiere under this."

"The bra is built in," Edwina explained.

"Honestly, how much support could that provide? Let's go to Martha Manning—she's having a two-for-one sale. We can both get something."

"I want this dress," Edwina insisted.

"It's too young for you," Mrs. Snipe declared. "And you haven't got a waist. Edwina, it will make you look like a potato. And don't forget you have that mole in the middle of your back. What about one of these roomy silk caftans? Now, they're chic."

But Edwina wasn't listening. She was imagining how she'd look as she walked down the magnificent mahogany staircase to greet her guests. The crystals on the dress would sparkle like stars in the night sky.

"I'll take it!" she decided.

Mere minutes after Edwina and Mrs. Snipe left the shop, Edwina gingerly carrying the dress in a plastic garment bag, a woman emerged from the dressing room.

"I must have that dress," she demanded, adding, "but in a much smaller size."

"Very good, Lady Finhatten." The salesgirl smiled.

3:10 P.M.

There was not a single St. Claire in the London directory. The operator searched the records for a twenty-mile radius, and then hung up when Jane asked her to check again. There was, however, a listing for Powder Puff Cosmetics.

"Powder Puff Cosmetics."

"Bridget St. Claire, please."

"Miss St. Claire is on holiday and cannot be reached. Would you care to leave a message?"

"No. No message."

3:31 P.M.

After a few false turns, Jane found the concrete apartment block where Bridget lived. There were thirty-eight flats, but no St. Claire on any of the mailboxes. Jane knocked on a door. A girl in a trim blue-and-white Lufthansa airline uniform peeked out, keeping the chain secured.

"Yes?" she asked warily.

"I'm looking for Bridget St. Claire's flat."

"Who?"

"Bridget St. Claire. She's got reddish-blond hair and rides a pink scooter."

"What's her airline?"

"Excuse me?"

"Who does she fly for? Lufthansa? British Airways?"

"She sells cosmetics door-to-door."

The girl shook her head. "She doesn't live here, then. The building's full of stewardesses. The airlines lease the whole place."

"That's impossible. I walked her here myself a few days ago."

"She lied to you."

Jane just stood there. This was not looking at all good. "Are you sure you don't know her?"

"If this is a pickup, you've come to the wrong place, mister," the girl said before slamming the door in Jane's face.

Grunby Hall
Sir Reginald's private library
4:24 P.M.

"Darling, you're home!" Edwina cried with delight when she saw Sir Reginald sitting at his desk, writing intently. "And I see you're working furiously on your novel. Aren't I the proud little wife!"

Edwina had decided to be a supportive spouse, lest her husband begin to regret their hasty union. One must not stand in the path of artistic genius.

"Let me see," Edwina cried playfully as she snatched the paper from his hands.

"No, Edwina!" he rebuked her, slapping her wrist smartly.

"You never let me read anything," she complained. "How am I ever going to be a supportive writer's wife if I don't give you any helpful suggestions? I was tops in fourth level grammar, you know."

Reginald grabbed Edwina and pried the paper from her hand.

"I don't want you to see it," he hissed, tearing the page into bits and tossing in into the fireplace.

"There's no need to be such a brute," cried Edwina. She rubbed her wrist where the diamonds on her bracelet had dented her flesh.

His voice softened. "I'm frightfully embarrassed to have anyone read my early ramblings," he explained hastily. "Especially you, my dear. What would you think of your old Rags if you knew how dreadful my first drafts were?"

Edwina understood completely. "I had no idea you thought so highly of my opinion," she beamed, blinking back tears.

"I didn't just marry you for your looks, Weenie."

He hadn't used his special nickname for her for weeks. She patted her moist eyes with the first thing she found in her pocket—a paper napkin from the Wimpole Buttery Bakery.

"Walnut cake again, darling?" Sir Reginald scolded her lightly, with the same flirty tone he used to use.

"Just the tiniest slice," she assured him. "Mildred ate twice as much as I did."

"Mildred is as thin as a crow," he reminded her. He pinched the flesh on her upper arm. "You, my dear, are more like a plump little quail."

Edwina didn't know if that was good or bad. She did know Sir Reginald was fond of quail—shooting them, that is.

He saw the look of confusion on her face. Edwina was incapable of hiding one emotion, which was why he was keeping her in the dark about the queen's kidnapping.

"They're a delicacy, Weenie," he assured her. "No one eats crow."

Edwina's petulant tone had surprised Sir Reginald. She had never been angry with him before, she had never been anything but cloying in her admiration. He didn't like this new Edwina. No doubt it was due to her socializing with that Snipe woman today.

It would behoove him to make love to her until the charity auction. If he and Edwina became estranged, the news would be all over town within hours. All eyes would be on Grunby Hall—the queen might even decide to cancel her visit. He would do whatever it took to keep his wife happy.

"Weenie," he said, using all his powers of seduction. "How about a little slap and tickle?"

Seven minutes later

"What are you doing in here?" Sir Reginald roared when he saw the new maid with her head in the fireplace.

"Cleaning, sir." Bibi palmed the charred scrap of paper Sir Reginald had tossed in there earlier, and, pretending to push the hair from her eyes, tucked it under the band of her maid's cap.

"Let's see your hands, Bibi."

Bibi got up and walked over to Sir Reginald. She put her hands out, palms up, like a child being inspected before supper. She had a razor in her shoe, and she was willing to use it. Of course, slashing Sir Reginald would no doubt have dire consequences. The auction might be called off, and they'd lose their chance to catch the S.O.B.S. with their guard down. She could kill him, she supposed, and dispose of his body in the fish pond.

"Is something wrong, sir?" she asked sweetly.

Sir Reginald looked puzzled. He could have sworn she had something in her hand.

"Carry on," he said. "But don't take all night. I still need all my shoelaces pressed."

4:39 P.M.

Jane got a bottle of brandy from the help-yourself near Victoria Station and hopped the Tube. She had been too embarrassed to ring Simon. All she wanted was to sit by the electric fire with Miss Liversidge, drink brandy-laced tea and listen to the latest developments in the life of King Edward and his bride, Peaches. And forget that she had once again been taken in by a pretty face.

The Flora Beaton
5:12 P.M.

"Miss Liversidge?"

Miss Liversidge's door was open, and the electric fire was on. Jane peered into the dimly lit room. Since Miss Liversidge's room was in the basement, the only natural light came from narrow slits of windows level with the sidewalk. It was Miss Liversidge's spy chamber, where she kept watch for hungry cats and the latest in shoe fashion. Jane switched on a lamp with a tatty coral silk shade. King Edward was sitting on his velvet pillow, licking his chops. Jane heard a whimper coming from the closet. She knew Peaches liked to sleep in there.

"Come on, Peaches," Jane called. Miss Liversidge was probably at the Park Lane Hotel in Piccadilly, one of her favorite afternoon haunts. Miss Liversidge was always trying to get Jane to go there with her to soak in the elegant atmosphere.

"Peaches?" Jane walked into the deep, narrow closet, which smelled of mothballs and the lavender water Miss Liversidge sprinkled liberally about. Peaches was probably hiding in a box in the back.

"Here, kitty, kitty—"

Peaches was, indeed, holed up in a box. Jane would have found her had she not first tripped over the body of Miss Edith Liversidge. She was alive. Her pulse was weak, but steady. Her eyes fluttered open.

"Stay right here," Jane cried. "I'll get help."

Miss Liversidge managed a small smile. "I shan't move a muscle, dear," she said weakly.

Jane had always been clearheaded in a crisis. She ran screaming through the lobby.

"Call an ambulance!" Jane yelled at Tessie Twigg, who was seated in a reproduction of a reproduction of a Queen Anne armchair, neat in a crisp housedress, wearing her lobby pearls and drinking tea.

Tessie Twigg looked right through Jane, and continued to sip her tea.

Jane rushed up to her, placed her hands on Tessie Twigg's shoulders—not on her bosoms as would later be reported—and screamed:

"Miss Liversidge is hurt! Do it or I'll rip your bloody heart out!" She ran back to be with Miss Liversidge while Tessie Twigg, for the first time in her life, did as she was told. After which she locked herself in her room and lit a candle for the lost soul of Jane Bond.

The Flora Beaton
Sitting room
An hour later

"She keeled over like a canary. The minute I heard, I jumped up and called for help. That's how I got tea all over my dress. It's probably ruined, but I don't mind. As long as I can help, in my own little way."

"You don't think she's going to die, do you?" Bessie McGuire gasped.

"She's at death's door as we speak," Tessie Twigg said importantly. "She's in a coma, and is not expected to recover."

St. Bart's Hospital
Women's charity ward
7:00 P.M.

Miss Liversidge had suffered a mild seizure brought on by a sudden shock, and would need to spend a few days recuperating in hospital. Something—or someone—had scared poor Miss Liversidge almost to death. Jane was betting it was Tessie Twigg. The bitch was always threatening to report Miss Liversidge's cat activity to "the proper authorities." Jane wished now she hadn't shaken her; what she should have done was smack her.

Miss Liversidge touched Jane's arm. "I'm sorry to have scared you, dear," she said.

"I wasn't scared," Jane scoffed. "I knew you were going to be okay. I always scream like that when I see the Twigg."

"I was writing a letter to my nephew, Derek, about the fire when I saw a vicar with a gun peering through the window. I thought perhaps the good father was still upset about the incident with the holy water. I went to the closet to get a sweater—I was going to go to the lobby to telephone the police—when suddenly I felt as weak as a rained-on bee."

Perhaps she and Miss Liversidge should both get off the sauce, Jane thought.

"The doctor says you've got to start eating more, Miss Liversidge." Jane had always suspected Miss Liversidge gave her kippers and toast to the cats, and ate the Kit-E-Kat tinned food herself. "You're much too thin."

"I'll try."

"I'll come by tomorrow and bring you something tasty."

"Some chewy sweets would be nice." Miss Liversidge yawned. "The nurse gave me a pill earlier. I think I'm getting sleepy. Jane—"

"Yes?"

"I like your hair. It suits you. I meant to mention it before."

"The Twigg thought I was a man." Jane smiled. "I gave her a fright."

Miss Liversidge giggled. "Poor Tessie. You can inherit a sour personality, you know. It gets passed down from one generation to the next, like that ugly cuckoo clock in the lobby. My mother had one, but it skipped right over me to my sister, Enid. Live and let live, I say. I've got to go feed the cats now." With that, she closed her eyes and began snoring softly.

"Sleep well, Miss Liversidge," whispered Jane as she leaned over and gave her friend a kiss on the cheek.

Back at the Flora Beaton
8:40 P.M.

Jane put two tins of sardines on the floor and watched as the cats woke up long enough to inhale them and then jump back onto Miss Liversidge's daybed.

"Thank you, Jane, for coming to feed us, even though your heart is broken," she said to herself.

The cats licked their fishy paws and yawned.

Jane helped herself to the bottle of sherry Miss Liversidge kept hidden under a knitted tea cozy on the mantel of the boarded-up fireplace. Next to it were a few dusty postal cards from Miss Liversidge's nephew, a pearl button, and a cheery pamphlet from the British Inferiority Complex Society assuring the reader that his complex could indeed be overcome for the sum of three hundred pounds. Jane put the pamphlet back. She couldn't even afford to have an inferiority complex.

"Good-bye," she said to the cats. "I'll be back. Don't be lonely."

King Edward rolled on his back and started to snore. Peaches moved to a tatty armchair, gave it a few perfunctory swipes, then curled up and fell asleep. In Jane's next life, she was going to be a cat.

Tessie Twigg was on the other side of the door, waiting to pounce. She was dressed in her funeral best, in a shapeless black dress and a black veil. Her unnaturally black hair had been freshly pin curled, and still bore the X-shaped imprints of the pins. She had even painted on eyebrows—thin, perfect crescents that made her look unduly alarmed. She was forever insisting her ink-black hair was natural: "God-given" were her exact words. Jane had always wondered why God hadn't seen fit to give her a pair of eyebrows while he was at it.

"I'm going to see poor dear Edith," she announced solemnly.

"She's not receiving visitors," Jane told her. In her drugged state, Miss Liversidge would think the angel of death had come to visit.

Tessie Twigg looked disappointed. Maybe she could find a wake to crash, Jane thought.

"A man was here to see you," Tessie Twigg mentioned. "He looked official."

"It was probably my parole officer," Jane said as she brushed past her landlady. She'd have to risk national security and go back to headquarters to find Agent Pumpernickel. Technically, she had done her bit. She wanted her money.

"We have rules against harboring criminals here," Tessie Twigg reminded her. "And dressing like a man is against the law."

"Actually, I'm not really a criminal; I'm a secret agent for the British government. Want to see my gun?"

"Miss Bond—or is it *Mr.* Bond these days?"

"Both, actually."

"I want you out of here at the end of the week."

"Shove off, Tessie."

"It's Miss Twigg, and no one speaks to me like that."

"No one speaks to you at all unless it's to complain about the roaches."

"I want you out of here right now!"

"You're going to have to pack my stuff yourself. I'm busy."

That shut her up. Tessie was a terrible snooper, but Jane had cured her early on with a couple of well-placed rubber marital aids.

"Don't forget to look under my bed!" Jane yelled as her landlady scurried off.

The Gates
9:00 P.M.

Jane ordered a stout, and sat in the dark bar thinking of Bridget. She had suspected all along this was too good to be true. So Bridget did have a girlfriend. One with a poodle's name. And she used the word "congratters." Now Jane had two reasons to despise her. She used her shirtsleeve to wipe her tears. Damn Bridget, Jane thought. She and her posh friends were probably having a good laugh about the boyish shop girl she had shagged. Fearing a waterfall, Jane made her way to the loo. A girl drawing black liner around her eyes frowned when she spotted Jane.

"The gents' is down the hall," she said.

Jane threw off her jacket, unbuttoned her shirt, and unwrapped the itchy bandages binding her breasts. The girl immediately grew more genial, offering Jane a hand.

"Not on your life." Jane scowled.

When she got back to her table, a pretty blonde dressed in a silver-lamé minidress was sitting at her table.

"Go away," Jane grumbled. She was going to get very drunk, and she didn't want company.

"I'll have what she's having," the girl told the bartender as she settled onto the stool next to Jane.

"I'm not interested," insisted Jane.

"I bet I can change your mind. My name's Bibi. What's yours?" Agent Dolittle fluttered her eyes at Jane. It was a stroke of brilliance to use Bibi's name—everyone knew she slept around.

Jane recoiled and had to reach for the bar to steady herself on the stool. So this was Bibi. She looked like a tarted-up Astrid. The false lashes ringing her big blue eyes must have been an inch long. Jane thought they looked like two spiders perched on her eyelids.

"I have a girlfriend," said Jane dismissively. "Don't you?" She marveled that both Bridget and Bibi were such cheaters.

"Oh, she won't mind. She might fancy you as well." The girl brushed the back of Jane's neck lightly with her long silver nails.

Jane stared at the girl. Was this "the first sign of trouble" that she had sworn to Simon would signal her swift departure? "You and your girlfriend can go bugger each other," said Jane as she picked up her glass and looked around for a free table.

"Wait!"

"I told you—I'm not interested."

"You took my drink by mistake."

"Sorry."

"No harm done," the girl said as they switched glasses. "See you later." She smiled.

"I hope not," Jane muttered.

Five minutes later

Jane felt a headache coming on. She couldn't possibly be blotto on one drink. Fresh air was what she needed. She staggered to the back door, made it to the alley before her legs gave out, and slumped against the brick wall. When she opened her eyes, the first thing she saw was a pair of shiny silver go-go boots; the girl in them was pacing up and down. It was the blonde from the bar, and she was talking to herself. No, she was talking to her compact. Jane closed her eyes. She had never passed out at the bar before; she'd always made it home first. Not exactly a record to be proud of, she thought. Simon was right—it was time to get off the sauce. She decided to close her eyes again—just for a minute. Then she'd get up and go home. Maybe Bridget had called. Maybe . . .

Apartment of Agent Mimi Dolittle
Clifford's Inn
9:40 P.M.

A silver apparition was leaning over her. "Are you feeling better?" a voice asked softly as a cool, damp cloth was pressed to Jane's forehead.

"What happened? Where am I?"

"We met at the bar. You passed out."

Now Jane remembered. "I only had one drink," she protested weakly. She tried to get up, but felt too woozy.

"Just rest," the girl said. "You'll be fine in an hour or two."

11:00 P.M.

Jane awoke with a clear head. She had never been here before—of that she was certain. The girl with the spider eyes was sitting at a skirted vanity table, filing her nails. Petula Clark was playing on the radio.

She tried to sit up, then realized that her arms were cuffed to the bed. She swore that first thing the next morning she was going to an Alcoholics Adrift meeting.

"I'd like to go home now," she said politely, hoping that charm would have an effect.

"I'm sorry, you'll have to stay a while longer." The girl smiled and continued working on her long nails.

The metallic taste in her mouth was making Jane sick. No Bond ever went down after one drink. She had been drugged. And here she was in the love nest that Bridget shared with this awful woman. On their bed, no less. And in handcuffs.

"Doesn't a simple 'no' mean anything to you?" Jane snapped.

The girl glowered at her.

"I think this is called kidnapping."

"A mercy mission is more like it. You drank too much and passed out. I brought you home to sober up."

"Then why am I tied up?"

Mimi paused. "I suppose I wanted you to stick around a while." She scrambled for good excuses. "And you were so wild with me, I had to restrain you."

Horribly, this made sense to Jane. It wasn't the first time in the past six weeks that she'd awakened in a strange bed with an oddly forward companion who remembered events that Jane had completely forgotten.

The girl brought her a glass of water. Jane pushed her away with her knee.

"Enough is enough. You can let me go now," she said.

"I can't do that."

"Is your name Bunny, by any chance?"

"Who's this 'Bunny'?" asked Mimi with an offended air. She put the water on the bedside table and settled herself next to Jane. "I'm Bibi, remember? We had a lovely toss, and I'm just not willing to let it end. Make yourself comfortable."

Mimi took a fresh pack of Luckies from her pocket, slit the cellophane with a long silver nail, put a cigarette between her full orange lips, and lit it. She then put the cigarette between Jane's lips, ever so slightly brushing her cheek as she did.

Jane started to choke. Mimi removed the cigarette so she could exhale.

"Thank you." Jane coughed. She might as well try to ingratiate herself with this lunatic. Poor Bridget. No wonder she'd been on the prowl.

"Are you going to be nice?" the girl wanted to know. She held the cigarette out of reach.

"Yes." Jane sighed.

The girl smiled. Jane was awfully attractive.

11:30 P.M.

"Do you like Champagne and caviar?" Mimi asked gaily. She had gone into the kitchen for a glass of water and returned with a bed tray laid out as if for a party. She had tied a flowery apron over her silver dress.

"No lobster?" Jane joked.

Mimi shook her head. "There's a tin of sardines I could open."

"This is fine," Jane said. Though she was thoroughly confused by Bibi's behavior—*what exactly did she want?*—she was feeling a bit peckish. The queen's tea was the last time she had eaten.

"Could you spread a little caviar on that toast for me?"

"I keep forgetting you're tied up."

"Me, too," Jane said. "It must be the company." The cramp in her shoulder was in its second hour. After she got even with Astrid, Mrs. Snipe, Sir Niles, Agent Pumpernickel, Tessie Twigg, and Bridget, Bibi was next.

"What's on your mind?" Mimi asked.

"Could you undo just one hand?" Jane paused, letting her eyes stray over Mimi's slender figure the way Pumpernickel had taught her to do.

"I suppose I could," said Mimi, a flush creeping up her neck. She wondered whether spy ethics permitted a quick romp with a captive enemy agent.

"I'll be a perfect gent," Jane promised.

Warily, Mimi reached into her bra for the key to the cuffs. Letting the suspense build, she leaned across Jane to the far wrist, her breast inches above Jane's mouth. True to her word, Jane behaved like a gentleman, craning up to nip at the thin fabric of Mimi's dress.

"Fresh!" Mimi slapped Jane lightly on her arm.

Jane looked up into those very blue eyes, so like her ex-lover Astrid's, and felt a mingled sense of attraction and rage. With her newly free hand, she grabbed the silver chain-link belt around Mimi's waist, and pulled her close.

"I won't tell if you won't," she said softly.

Mimi straightened up quickly and tried to think. She was Bibi. She was Bibi. Bibi would do this. In fact, she was famous for it. All Mimi had been ordered to do was keep an eye on Jane Bond. That could be arranged.

"We'll keep the lights on," she said decisively, turning so that Jane could reach the zipper on the back of her dress. It proved to be an egregious error, for as soon as the zipper came down, Mimi found herself caught between Jane Bond's well-muscled thighs, unable to wriggle free. Jane slid a hand inside the lacy cup of Mimi's bra and fetched out the key to the cuffs.

Within seconds, they had traded places.

While Mimi gasped and writhed, Jane slid off the bed and rubbed her sore wrists. She grabbed the half-empty Champagne bottle from the bedside table and drained it.

"To Bridget," she said, waving the bottle toward her would-be captor. "I think you two deserve each other."

"You can't leave me like this," Mimi cried as she struggled in vain. "I'll scream!"

Jane moved to the radio and turned the knob slowly, watching Mimi's face as the various programs tuned in and out. She settled finally on the nightly rebroadcast of an Eton cricket match, and left the room just as Mimi's angry tears spilled over onto the satin pillow.

008 knew his license to kill was useless unless he could actually hit his intended target. When Jane Bond came out of the block of flats, he would follow her and wait until they were alone in an alley or on some deserted street. It would be dark soon; it would make the hunt that much more exciting. Once he got her alone, he would use any means in his disposal to convince her to end her career with the Secret Service. And if she refused to see it his way, he couldn't be held responsible for his actions. He would stop at nothing to be the next James Bond. If he had to, he'd stab her with the collapsible bayonet tucked in his shoe, or strangle her with the wire coiled in his watch. To get that promotion, he'd squeeze the life out of her with his bare hands.

12:05 A.M.

Jane flung herself into the street, happy to be free of that silly girl. She ran until she reached a deserted footbridge spanning the Thames, then stopped to light a fag. The back of her head prickled. Jane had the queerest feeling she was being watched. There was no real evidence for it, save for a slight sensation at the back of her neck, like a whisper in the wind.

She turned. A man stepped from behind a lamppost.

"Bugger off!" she said in a menacing tone. Really, this was getting to be too much.

A garden-variety flasher in a Burberry stepped forward. "There's no need to raise your voice," he said softly as he started to fumble under his coat.

"This is really too much," Jane said with exasperation. "Go away!"

"I won't hurt you."

She drew her gun. It wasn't loaded, but he didn't know that.

The man raised his hands in surrender. His trousers fell to the ground.

"You're not a St. Claire, are you?" Jane thought anything was possible at this point.

The man shook his head.

"Step out of your trousers," Jane said as she walked toward him, holding the gun steady with both hands. "The boxers, too."

"Now, kick them over here. Now the coat. The vest, too," she said, pointing at his baggy undershirt. "You can keep the shoes and socks; it's a good look for you."

He cringed, cupping his hands over his nakedness.

"Now you're shy?"

"How will I get home?" he whimpered.

"What's your name?"

"Arthur."

"Arthur, can you swim?"

"I took two medals at Oxford," he boasted. Then he looked at the dark water. "Oh."

"Right then, Arthur, in the water."

"I'll freeze." His knobby knees were already knocking.

She cocked the trigger. "Look, Arthur, I've had a really bad day and

I don't have a lot of patience left. Get in the water or die. And if I ever catch you doing this again, first I'm going to tell your aging mum, and then I'm going to blow your willy to the south of France."

Arthur made a satisfying splash when he hit the water. Jane watched his bald bum bobbing in the dirty river, then kicked his clothes over the side. She lit a cigarette and watched as they floated away with the current. Perhaps it was time to leave London.

"Bravo, Miss Bond. You have a certain flair for this kind of work," a deep voice hissed in her ear. Something hard and unyielding jabbed into her back. "Drop your weapon and freeze."

Jane could smell cigarettes on the man's breath. She dropped her gun at her feet, then heard him kick it away.

"If you know what's good for you"—he shoved his gun so hard into Jane's ribs she thought she heard a crack—"you'll run on home and stop playing spy games."

"All right," Jane whispered, afraid to move even the muscles of her jaw.

"Give up the charade or it's curtains for you!"

His voice was strangely familiar to her, but then, so were his words, like the dialogue of a bad thriller. And his scent. Turkish tobacco. So like her brother James. A sudden blow to the back of her head sent her reeling forward. She caught the bridge railing and vomited a thin stream of soured Champagne into the water.

"Consider yourself warned. Next time you won't be so lucky."

Jane nodded dumbly.

"Now, count to thirty—slowly. And don't look back. And tell no one of our encounter. Now start counting. One—"

"One," Jane echoed as the man began to back away.

"Two—"

"Two."

"Three—" His voice was growing fainter. Jane could feel her heart start up again.

"Fo— Christ!" he screamed. A splash followed. Jane couldn't help herself; she began to laugh hysterically. Turning, she saw that Arthur had made his way up the slimy bank and was looking back in astonishment at his successor. This one had been allowed to keep his clothes. What a bad night it had been for exhibitionists.

12:45 A.M.

"Come on, Simon—answer the phone," Jane prayed. She was shaking so hard it took three tries to dial the number correctly. On the first try, she had blurted out her story to a perfect stranger, who had shrieked and hung up.

"Hello?"

Thank God it was Simon.

"Simon, help! I'm in trouble. Someone is after me."

He yawned. "Bunny again?"

"Simon—listen! I'm not working at Amalgamated Widget—I lied to you. I'm a bodyguard to the queen. I was hired by Sir Niles Needlum of the British Secret Service to pretend to be my brother. And then Bridget's girlfriend kidnapped me. And I was chased by a pervert. I got hit in the head with a gun—"

Jane took a deep gulp of the cool evening air. She had walked all the way to Charing Cross Station, her head throbbing. She felt safe with all the people about, although they were giving the girl with the bloodied head and crazed air a wide berth.

"I went to a tea at Buckingham Palace this afternoon," she went on miserably. Simon was *conspicuously* silent.

"And guess who I saw there? Bridget! Oh, Simon, she's a lady!"

"Stop it, Jane. Stop it at once. Go home immediately and sleep this off!"

"I need help!"

"Bloody hell. Come over and I'll put on the kettle."

"I'm not drunk, Simon."

"Just come over, Jane." He sighed.

Home of Mr. Simon Crispin
No. 7 Wadsworth Way
1 A.M.

Simon had set out two cups and a tin of aspirin, but when he saw Jane's bloody head, he sprinted to the cabinet for bandages and iodine.

"You're hurt!" he cried. "Sit, sit!" He grabbed a tea towel and held it to Jane's head.

"I told you someone was after me," said Jane. She repeated the events of the day, this time in detail. Simon realized that Jane was stone-cold sober.

"Do you feel dizzy?" asked Simon, staring into her eyes.

Jane shook her head. "Yes." She groaned and closed her eyes.

Simon looked concerned. He held up three fingers.

"How many fingers do you see?"

Jane sleepily opened one eye. "Six," she said. Jane started to stand, but Simon insisted she sit so he could clean the gash at the back of her head.

"That smarts!" she yelped as he poured on the iodine. "Don't get it on the suit," she ordered.

"I'll never forgive myself for thinking you were in an alcoholic daze." He fussed over her like a mother hen.

"The next time I call to tell you I almost got killed, you'll believe me."

"You're not planning on making a habit of this?"

"Of what? The secret agent business? Tea at the palace?"

"Promise me you'll never get involved with these people again. Jane, you can't trust government institutions."

"Or girls," Jane added bitterly.

"Really, Jane, you should sell this story to the papers. I especially like the bit with the handcuffs."

"And the Champagne. I quite like that myself. Very smooth, under the circumstances."

"So you've gone off Bridget?"

Jane made a face, then grimaced in pain. "And after I gave her the best seventy-two hours of my life."

"Poor Jane. It can't possibly get any worse for you."

Simon's sitting room
1:53 A.M.

"Why would this Sir Niles fellow hire you and then send someone after you? It doesn't make sense."

"They must want the suit back," Jane cracked.

Simon was camped out on a blanket in front of the door, his

mother's cast-iron frying pan in hand. Any intruder would be soundly thwacked over the head before he could get to Jane, who was curled up on the loveseat desperately tired but too upset to sleep.

"Even though my life is nothing but aggro and misery, I realized while I was being held at gunpoint that I don't want to die; not yet, at any rate. First off, who would feed Miss Liversidge's cats? For that matter, who would feed Miss Liversidge? And I have yet to find true love."

"And I would miss you."

"I would miss you too, Simon."

"Good night, Jane."

"Good night, Simon."

10 SEPTEMBER 1965

Home of Agent Cedric Pumpernickel
No. 9 Boundary Road
Camden Town
8:01 A.M.

THE telephone awoke Agent Pumpernickel from a sound sleep. He jumped from his bed, tripped over his shoes (which he had uncharacteristically left lying about), bumped his head on the corner of the bureau, swore, then ran to answer the telephone situated in the hallway between the kitchen and the pantry. His mother had liked to chat with her many theatrical friends while cooking, and so had insisted their one telephone be located in the most inconvenient spot for a secret agent. In the years since her death, he had meant to put a second telephone in his bedroom, but had never gotten around to it. A man's household obligations took a back burner when he was a secret agent.

"Pumpernickel here," he gasped out, praying the person on the other end was the missing Miss Bond. He had searched all over London for her yesterday, starting at the Flora Beaton and ending up at her favorite bar. There a fellow had insisted on buying him a sweet drink with an umbrella in it, and afterward confided that he found Pumpernickel's scar rather dashing. Pumpernickel had spun a colorful tale about a prison camp and a sadistic guard, after which the chap had insisted on buying him another drink.

"Agent Pumpernickel, you're late." N.'s stern voice came over the line. "And on your last day, no less."

Pumpernickel gasped, checking the kitchen wall clock. It was after eight!

"Sir, I'll be right in!" he cried. "I can be dressed in exactly forty-seven seconds, and the Tube should take only eleven and a half minutes."

"We do not tolerate tardiness at Her Majesty's Secret Service,

Agent Pumpernickel. I've called to tell you not to bother coming in today."

"I'm fired?" Agent Pumpernickel felt as though he had been struck in the chest. N. knew about Miss Bond disappearing. Good-bye, pension. Good-bye, snuffbox collection. He'd have to sell it off, piece by piece, to pay the taxes on the Pumpernickel family home.

N. laughed. "Of course not! Buck up, old bean. You've got the day off. Congratters! You're retiring a day early."

"What?"

"I just got off the line with our man at the palace. The queen was quite pleased with Miss Bond's performance, especially when she went into her secret agent act. Running off like that was a nice bit of theater, Pumpernickel. Made it look like she had been called off on a special mission. Her Majesty was thrilled to be in on the action."

"Yes, sir."

"Of course, you didn't run it past me first," N. scolded.

"It was a bit of an improvisational move, sir."

"Well, bravo, Agent Pumpernickel. I guess you do have a bit of sawdust in your blood."

"That's stardust, sir."

"It is? Well. Tomorrow's luncheon starts promptly at one. Look here, you won't forget to come in, will you? All the lads will be waiting to give you your due."

"Oh, no sir. I've been looking forward to this day for years," Pumpernickel assured him.

"Come by my office a little early and we'll close the case on Miss Bond. I imagine she's anxious to receive the rest of her pay."

"Sir? I have a request."

"What is it, Retired Agent Pumpernickel?"

"There's one person who deserves a day off more than I."

"I know, Pumpernickel, and I appreciate the sentiment, but the director of the most important governmental security division in the history of mankind can never rest, even when he's sleeping."

"Of course not, sir. But the woman behind the man gets tired, too."

"My mother?"

"Miss Tuppenny, sir. She's not well."

"Why, she's as healthy as a horse. She's right outside pecking happily away on her new typewriter."

"Sir, the other day I found Miss Tuppenny"—Pumpernickel paused. How to put this delicately?—"verging on hysteria over the absence of 007. I think a day away from the office would do wonders for her."

"She might be a little under the weather," N. admitted. Every time he turned around, she was off to the ladies'.

"Very well, Pumpernickel. I'll take the matter under advisement. See you tomorrow. And don't forget Miss Bond's suit and medal. We'll need them for our costume collection."

"Of course, sir."

The Flora Beaton
8:25 A.M.

"The Flora Beaton Residential Hotel for Distressed Gentlewomen. Proprietress Tessie Twigg speaking."

"Miss Bond, please."

"Is this the police?"

"Heavens, no, it's her Uncle Cedric. I'm quite anxious to find her."

"Miss Bond is not here. As happens often, she didn't come home last night. I have strict rules about that, you know. Lights out at ten P.M. and everyone in her own bed."

Pumpernickel was a bit taken aback by the news. It hadn't taken long for Miss Bond to revert to her old ways.

"Do know when I could expect her?" he asked politely.

"I'm not her mother!"

"Please tell her I'm quite desperate to get ahold of her, will you? I have some money for her—tell her that, will you?"

"Good thing, too, because she's always behind in her rent. There're plenty of girls who'd be happy for that room. It has a view, you know. What's more—"

Pumpernickel listened patiently as the queer little woman launched into a tirade concerning the morals of today's youth, and Miss Bond's in particular.

"Please relay the message to Miss Bond," he finally interrupted. The proprietress agreed to take down his telephone number and give the message to Jane the minute she arrived. And Agent Pumpernickel agreed to have a strong talk with his niece about her unseemly behavior.

Home of Simon Crispin
8:54 A.M.

"Amalgamated Widget, Inc.," said a woman with a light, pleasant voice. "How may I direct your call?"

"Cedric Pumpernickel, please."

"Hold one moment." Then: "Mr. Pumpernickel is no longer with Amalgamated Widget."

"Look here, it's imperative I find him," Jane said insistently. "Would you have his home number?"

"I'm sorry, that information is not available. Good day."

"Good day to you, too," muttered Jane as she slammed down the receiver.

Simon poured Jane a cup of coffee and handed her a bowl of Weet-Bix and milk. The breakfast room was the only modern thing about the flat; Byron had spent weeks remodeling it with all the latest conveniences. With its butter-yellow walls and shiny chrome equipment, Jane couldn't imagine a more cheerful place. It was hard to remember that just last night she had sat in that very same spot, dripping blood on the yellow Formica tabletop.

"Any luck?" asked Simon.

"I'm sorry, that information is not available," said Jane, mimicking the woman's singsong voice.

"Did you really think they would give out a secret agent's phone number?" Simon asked, his mouth full of Weet-Bix. Today, no matter what happened between Jane and Bridget (or Jane and Astrid; or Jane and Bunny; or Jane and the Secret Service), he would stick to his slimming diet.

Jane got up, went to the sitting room, and returned with the phone book.

"There are four Pumpernickels in London proper—a William, an Enid, a Charles, and an Ethelbert," she soon informed Simon.

"I propose we start with those closest to us," Simon said as he spooned up the last bit of milk in his bowl.

"I propose we crisscross London all willy-nilly, wasting time, petrol, and our patience," said Jane.

Simon looked up at her, a drop of milk clinging to his chin. Jane was back, and in fine form.

9:30 A.M.

Jane grimaced at the woman in the frowzy purple frock, frumpy hair-style, and flowery pillbox hat reflected in the looking glass. She much preferred dressing up as her brother.

"This is the best you could come up with?" complained Jane, try-ing the hat at different angles to see whether she could improve upon the picture. She couldn't.

"Simon, I look just like your mother."

Simon took umbrage at that remark. "My mother was a very hand-some woman. And stylish for her time. You simply can't go out as your brother. God knows how many secret agents are lying in wait for you."

"Your mother was a gem, Simon. But why did you keep this getup, anyway? You don't have her body in the other room, do you, Norman?"

"The outfit belongs to Byron."

"Simon, I've done some pretty outrageous things in my time, but that's just plain sick." Jane took off the hat in disgust. The little paper violets on it bobbled when she walked. It made her look ridiculous.

"My mother and Byron went to an All Hallows' Eve party once, dressed as conjoined twins."

"That explains the rip on the side."

Simon handed her a few pins, then surveyed his work.

"Your radio-transmitter watch looks terrible with that outfit," he re-alized. "I might have Mother's old Timex tucked away somewhere. You can carry that one in your handbag."

"My what?"

"Jane, surely you know a lady does not leave the house without the proper accessories."

"Simon, aren't these dowdy pumps punishment enough?"

Simon handed her a purple clutch bag, a gold broach in the shape of a Scottie, and a plastic rain scarf.

"This will teach you to get involved with the government," he scolded.

Jane simmered. "I hope Astrid burns in hell."

The Sons of Britain Society Club
10:10 A.M.

Sir Reginald reverently took the letter from Lord Finhatten and put it in the breast pocket of his coat. "You've put your fingerprints all over it," he complained to Jinx. "And you've got to stop opening the envelope—it's causing it to look dog-eared."

"A queen running away from her crown would certainly reread her abdication letter several times," Jinx pointed out. "And I'm the one who's going to find it, you know. My prints will be on it eventually."

"It's going to be in the ladies'—you can't possibly find it. Lettie will, and she'll hand it to you." They had decided Jinx was the best man to deliver the news of the queen's abdication. No one would ever believe he was bright enough to pull off a stunt like this.

"That's leaving things a bit up to chance, don't you think?"

"Lettie's going to be queen," Sir Reginald informed him. "She knows everything."

Jinx gasped. "Must I always find out intimate details of my wife's life from others?"

"We didn't tell you because we knew you'd react in this manner."

"Does Edwina know?"

"Of course not. Lettie is the only wife involved."

"What if Lettie's told her?" Jinx wrung his hands. "You know how Edwina chatters. By now every shopkeeper in London knows our plan. I'm surprised Scotland Yard's not knocking on our doors. The whole thing's no good. We'll have to abort."

"Edwina's oblivious to anything but cake and a light thrashing," said Sir Reginald sourly.

"I don't like Lettie getting involved." Jinx shook his head. "If we're caught, she could be tried for treason. Being the wife is one thing, but this makes her a party to the crime." The idea of Lettie—sweet, simple Lettie—in handcuffs brought tears to his eyes.

"But we're not going to get caught, old man. Think of what we'll have if we pull this off. The England of yore. No more Pakistani takeaways. No more Beatles. No more taxes on inherited land. Our names will be read in Parliament. And schoolchildren will learn of us in their history books."

"I have never liked my given name," Jinx admitted, sniffing quietly. "Might I ask historians to refer to me by my nickname?"

"That's the spirit, old man. Always think of the future."

Crispin's Bookshop
10:43 A.M.

Mrs. Snipe was standing in front of the shop, tapping the toe of her two-tone court shoes, when they arrived.

"Honestly, Mr. Crispin, no wonder your business is failing. I've been here almost an hour. I haven't time to stand around waiting for recalcitrant shopkeepers to wander into work. The members of my Etiquette Club need those books I ordered. If you'd rather not supply us with our reading materials, there are plenty of others who would jump at the chance."

"I have family business to attend to, Mrs. Snipe," Simon explained. "I'm not opening the shop today."

"Get her the books, Simon," said the matronly woman beside him. "A few minutes won't make any difference."

"Jane—is that you?" cried Mrs. Snipe, taking her reading glasses from her handbag for a close-up view. "I hardly recognized you in that getup. You look so . . . *different.*" Someone had given the poor girl the wrong fashion advice. However, Mrs. Snipe reflected, she was headed in the right direction.

"Next time come to me, dear." She could have lent her a smarter brooch, that was for certain.

Jane blanched. By noon everyone on the block would know that she had shown up to work in a dress. An ugly one.

"She's rehearsing for a play," Simon informed Mrs. Snipe as he unlocked the door and entered the shop. On the floor was the morning mail—all bills. He grimaced and shoved them in a box under the counter with the rest of the bunch.

Mrs. Snipe's hand fluttered to her heart. "I had no idea you went in for amateur theatrics," she trilled.

"I'd say she was practically a professional by now," Simon said dryly.

"Yes, one could say I'm quite the thespian," added Jane. She glared at Simon. "Mrs. Snipe is waiting."

"Who's putting on this little production?" Mrs. Snipe demanded to know. She pushed past Jane and seated herself on a stool, then proceeded to peel off her white gloves, her short, plump fingers emerging like uncooked sausages from their casings.

"The Flora Beaton Players. Under the direction of Tessie Twigg," Jane replied smoothly. She was becoming a damn good liar.

"Tessie Twigg? Hmmm. Yes, I believe I've heard of her."

"She's quite famous in the States."

"That's right. Broadway, isn't it? Light comedies?"

"Women's prison movies."

"Put me down for twelve tickets," said Mrs. Snipe, gesturing expansively. "I'm certain the members of my Monday Night Women's Dramatics Society will want to attend. Mind you, make sure they're good seats."

"Here are your seven copies of *Gentle Corrections for Social Infractions*," Simon said impatiently, handing Mrs. Snipe a hastily wrapped bundle.

"And not a moment too soon. Jane just talked me into purchasing a dozen tickets to her little show, and had you tarried any longer she no doubt would have talked me into trying out for a part. Jane, tell your Miss Twigg that last year I played Rosalind in a small production of *As You Like It* at a church festival and everyone said my interpretation of the role was refreshing."

Twenty minutes later, when Mrs. Snipe had finally gone, Simon began to search in the back room for the important item he had hidden there years earlier.

"That was very generous of you, giving Mrs. Snipe your role," he said.

"It's the least I could do," Jane said modestly.

"And when she shows up at the Flora Beaton at six o'clock for rehearsal and announces she's Miss Marple?"

"Tessie Twigg will try to rent her a room. Half the residents there think they're Miss Marple; the other half think they're the queen."

"Not Miss Liversidge," said Simon, his hands falling at last on the cold metallic object that he sought. He brought the gun into the light of the main room and held it awkwardly in both hands. Jane reached over easily and took it from him.

"By comparison she's perfectly sane. That reminds me—I've got to pick up some sardines for King Edward; the kind in the red can with the fish wearing glasses."

"Miss Liversidge spoils those animals," Simon opined.

Jane checked the cylinder of the revolver. There was one bullet. Smartly she snapped it shut, causing Simon to jump.

"Peaches is easy; she was a street cat and seems contented with very little, but King Edward is such a queen. It has to be the red can with the fish wearing glasses, not the blue can with the fish wearing a top hat. That he turns his nose up to."

"Royalty!" they both sniffed.

Secret Service headquarters
Third-floor powder vine
11:00 A.M.

"What's the news on 008?" Miss Tinkham wanted to know. Rumors were flying around the Department of Secret Service Supplies, so she had faked a cramp and rushed to the ladies' for Miss Tuppenny's take on the story.

"According to the brave lad, two Russian agents jumped him, tried to force the address of headquarters out of him, then tossed him in the river when he refused to sing." Miss Tuppenny took down her hair and started to run a comb through it.

"That's the official story," she added.

"What do you think really happened?" Tink lounged on the emergency cot in the corner of the stark, concrete-walled room, and popped a sweet in her mouth. Her boss, P., was terrified of even a hint of a girl's menses. She could be away from her desk for hours.

"I think he picked the wrong girl to hit on." Miss Tuppenny twisted her silky, straight hair into a bun and pinned it.

"Will he recover?"

Miss Tuppenny sighed. "Unfortunately."

Just then, Miss Loomis from Records walked in.

"Have you heard the news, Miss Loomis?" Tink asked.

"About the new mandatory shorter hemline regulations for female government employees? Yes, and I think it's disgraceful," Miss Loomis replied. "I'm drafting a rebuttal memo right away and will be circulating it to all the other girls."

"I'll be the first to sign," Tink promised solemnly. As soon as Miss Loomis left, she burst into laughter.

"You are a wicked girl," Miss Tuppenny scolded her. "Remember when you sent her the memo banning apple-green cardigans? She almost had a heart attack."

"She's such a pest. She's always poking about, listening in on my conversations."

"Maybe she's lonely," Miss Tuppenny suggested. "Thirty years is a long time to spend in the ant farm. Talk to her sometime. You'll be amazed at what you can learn.

"Wake me in an hour, will you, Tupps?" Tink asked as she closed her eyes and settled in for a nap.

Miss Tuppenny straightened her skirt and made her way out of the powder vine and back to her sleek new typewriter, inwardly cursing Agent Pumpernickel for his oafish but well-meaning replacement of one of G.E.O.R.G.I.E.'s most vital pieces of spy equipment. Where, she wondered, was Agent Dolittle? She was overdue with her surveillance report. Miss Tuppenny had a mental flash of her fledgling agent tangled in a carnal embrace with Jane Bond. She hoped, for Bridget's sake, Mimi was trodding the straight and narrow.

Home of Retired Agent Cedric Pumpernickel

By eleven o'clock on the first day of life in retirement, Retired Agent Cedric Pumpernickel had already cooked his breakfast, washed up, dusted the parlor, paid that month's bills, and carefully perused the telly digest, marking programs of interest in the coming week with a little red pencil he used for household matters. He was running low on a few things—powdered milk, eggs, shoe polish (black), and tooth powder. And he needed a new feather duster. He wrote the list on the back of a paper sack. None of these items were urgently needed.

11:17 A.M.

He saw in the advert section of the morning paper that a retired sea captain was selling a rare Battersea snuffbox that had once belonged to King Albert, documentation guaranteed. Retired Agent Cedric Pumpernickel telephoned the man, but he wasn't in.

11:24 A.M.

After laying new paper in the utensil drawer, he took the old out back for burning. He whistled for Birdie, the neighbor's collie dog, and gave her a bit of stale biscuit. He realized his kitchen windows could use a good scrubbing. There was no shortage of things for him to do now that he was retired.

11:37 A.M.

He rang the Flora Beaton again, but there had been no sign of Miss Bond. He rang up his neighbor Mrs. Figgis to invite her over for a cup of tea and to admire his fresh drawer paper, but Mrs. Figgis wasn't at home.

11:54 A.M.

Pumpernickel added the following items to his shopping list: antacid tablets, chewing gum, and stamps. When he was away next week, on his great estates of northern England tour, he would send postcards to Miss Tuppenny, Mrs. Figgis, and Miss Bond. And perhaps, as a joke, one to Birdie next door.

11:58 A.M.

Someone was knocking at his door—rather impatiently, he thought. He peered through the mail slot. A nicely dressed older woman and a youngish man were on his stoop. The man looked vaguely familiar. Pumpernickel wondered if they were from the League of Mary, which often sent mother-and-son teams door-to-door to talk about the Virgin.

"I'm not in a position to receive visitors at the moment," he bent down and said through the mail slot. "Mind leaving a pamphlet under the mat?" Pumpernickel was Church of England all the way, but there was no reason to be rude.

"Agent Pumpernickel, it's Jane Bond. I need to speak with you."

Pumpernickel jumped up, hitting his head on the old gas fixture on which he always hung his brolly. His tightened his robe sash, smoothed his hair, and opened the door a crack.

"You mustn't call me that!" he hissed. "What if the neighbors hear?"

"Let me in, Pumpernickel," said Jane, "or the neighbors will hear a lot worse." She showed him the velvet box. "I've got the medal," she said enticingly.

"Please slip it through the slot. I say, Miss Bond, you gave me quite a scare running off like that."

"You're not getting it until we have a talk," insisted Jane.

"Come in, then," he said, sighing and opening the door. "But give me forty-seven seconds to get dressed."

Pumpernickel scurried off, leaving them to make their way to a stuffy parlor, where they perched nervously on a stiff, horsehair Victorian love seat. It was in pristine condition; the plastic covering kept it dust-free, but made sitting a precarious proposition.

"This place looks like a museum," Simon said. Somehow he had imagined a secret agent's home to be a tad more modern. Every tabletop held precious bric-a-brac that would require hours of careful dusting each week. The walls were covered with framed theatrical announcements and newspaper clippings yellowed from age.

"His mother was an actress before her marriage," Jane told Simon. "She used to play the Virgin Mary in regional productions. His father used to drown kittens."

"Some marriages are just made in heaven."

"Thanks for coming along," Jane said to Simon as she slipped off the excruciating pumps and propped her feet on a small needlepoint stool.

"I needed a break from the exhaustion that comes from running a wildly successful shop," Simon said as he examined an impressive collection of snuffboxes in a locked china cabinet.

"Poor Simon—I'm certainly no help. I promise never to pretend to be a secret agent again. As soon as I get my money, I'm going back to dusting old books and entertaining Mrs. Snipe."

A guilty look washed over Simon's face.

"You sold the shop? I was gone for all of three days!"

"I'm merely entertaining an offer from a paper dress designer," Simon explained. "Byron wants to open an antique shop in South Kensington; he says it's the next up-and-coming neighborhood. Byron and I can do the buying and you can manage the shop. That way you can still dust and entertain Mrs. Snipe."

"Think she'll follow us?"

"Like a bad debt."

"Tea is served," Pumpernickel announced, pushing a tea cart nicely outfitted with fresh linens, silver teaspoons, and porcelain plates. He had put on a dark business suit, starched white shirt, and thin red tie. Over that was a crisp red-and-white checkered apron.

"Milk? Sugar? Lemon?" Agent Pumpernickel said with a smile. It was his first party since retiring. How diverting!

"How about some answers?" said Jane briskly. Her head still throbbed and stung from the blow the night before.

"Before you two start talking, I'll take a biscuit, please," Simon said meekly. He'd had only a tiny bowl of Weet-Bix that morning, and all this anxiety was making his stomach hurt.

Jane nudged him. She had business to attend to. "Agent Pumpernickel, my life was threatened last night."

Pumpernickel sat down, unperturbed, and poured tea for the three of them. "How dreadful, Miss Bond. The streets aren't safe these days. Elderly ladies are especially vulnerable. If I were you, I'd change my clothes. And by the way, I'm frightfully glad to see you."

"It was a man from your organization," Jane quickly explained. "He warned me to stay out of the spy game."

Pumpernickel jumped up, knocking his cup and saucer to the floor. The cup smashed on the threadbare carpet, the Queen Mum's head rolling under the writing desk.

"Impossible!" he blustered. "Only Sir Niles and I know of your involvement with the Secret Service, and I guarantee neither of us is out to get you."

"He knew my name!"

"He thought you were your brother. It was a disgruntled husband or such thing. It happens more often than one would like to think."

"He called me Miss Bond."

"See, that proved my point."

"What point?" Jane was the one with a head injury, but he was the one acting daft.

"Considering the kind of life you lead—" said Pumpernickel primly, recalling in particular a snapshot of Jane with her hand under a policewoman's blue serge skirt. "So you have the medal. I'm so glad. And did you bring the suit?"

"Oh, the suit," Jane said uneasily. "It came to a bad end. The medal's safe and sound, however. But you can't have it until you tell me the truth."

Pumpernickel felt his eyelid beginning to twitch. "All I have for you, Miss Bond, is your money and some timely advice. A wise secret agent keeps his own counsel."

"But I have Simon for that," said Jane rudely. She had been unpinning her hat and wig as Pumpernickel spoke, and she now turned to display the sizable bump on her head, clearly visible through her close-cropped hair.

"Heavens!" Pumpernickel cried. It was imperative that he speak to N.

"He's lying," Jane said as they made their way past Pumpernickel's puny flowerbeds to Simon's car. "Did you see his face when I showed him my head? There's something he's not telling me."

"You should have kept the medal. That was your bargaining chip."

"I did." Jane had palmed the medal and given Pumpernickel the empty velvet box. He was in such a hurry to usher them out, he hadn't taken the time to check whether the medal was inside.

"What are you going to do with it?"

Jane rubbed it against her dress until it shone and looked at it fondly. "Use it as bait, of course."

Simon didn't like the sound of that.

"Jane, give it up. You're safe now."

"What about my hair? From a distance, I still look like my brother."

"You're going to have to wear a wig."

"Or just stay home." Jane sighed.

"Good idea. You're safe there."

A few minutes later

Pumpernickel wiped his precious teacups with a warm, soapy cloth, then dried them with a fresh linen towel. They would go right back into the china cabinet before another tragedy could occur. There they would stay, dust-free, until his next tea. It was inevitable that one of the pieces should break eventually; he just wished it hadn't happened today.

The missing cup left an empty space in his carefully ordered cabinet. He placed the remaining teacups farther apart until he was satisfied that the set looked complete. Miss Bond's visit had upset him a great deal; thus he took extra care with the washing-up while contemplating just the right approach to N.

The entire mission had been nothing but a strain since its inception. He so preferred his quiet office to the unpredictable world of espionage. Although N. hadn't come right out and said so, he had obviously intended for this to be one last taste of adventure before being put out to pasture. Agent Pumpernickel was beginning to wish N. hadn't been so generous.

Outside the home of Retired Agent Pumpernickel

"Quick—hide!" Simon pushed Jane to the floor of the car.

"I don't look that bad!" she protested.

"No, it's Agent Pumpernickel. He's leaving the house. I'm going to follow him." Simon slumped in his seat until Pumpernickel got in his car and drove off.

Jane peered through the car window. "Follow that car!" she cried. "I've always wanted to say that," she added.

"I know," Simon said.

Home of Simon Crispin
1:11 P.M.

"Where did I leave my scars?" Jane was running around the flat frantically trying to change back into James Bond while Simon, equally frantic, was trying to convince her of the foolishness of her plan.

"You can't go back there! Remember last night? A fellow threatened to kill you?"

Ignoring his pleas, Jane took Simon's gun out of her handbag and placed it on the mail table next to the door.

"There's only one bullet in that!" he said to her, his voice climbing in pitch. "And do you even know how to shoot it?"

"Don't try to stop me, Simon—press these!" She thrust her rumpled suit into his hands, found some paper cement in a desk drawer, and went to the loo to make up her face.

"I'll need one of Byron's dress shirts," she called out, "and his Sandhurst tie."

Secret Service headquarters
2:00 P.M.

The cool blonde at the reception desk shrieked and threw her arms around Jane's neck.

"James! You're back!"

"Careful, baby, the suit's rented," said Jane as she pushed the girl away.

"What's happened to your voice? James, you sound so funny!"

Jane coughed, then grimaced.

"Poor baby," the girl murmured. "Switzerland's awfully cold."

Jane nodded, allowing herself the merest appraising caress of the girl's waist and hips. 007 would have done no less, and certainly considerably more.

"Pumpernickel just came in," she told Jane. "Tomorrow's the old bugger's retirement luncheon. You going?"

Jane shrugged.

"The old marnie gives me the creeps, too, but I should really go. Meet you after the party in the supply closet?"

Jane winked.

"You going up to see the old man?"

Again, Jane nodded and gave the girl a look that hovered between smirk and sneer. Blushing, the receptionist buzzed Jane through the security doors.

Office of Sir Niles Needlum
2:10 P.M.

"Thank you for seeing me, sir." Although he had been in this exact spot millions of times before, Retired Agent Pumpernickel felt as nervous as a schoolboy.

"It's been an honor serving you," he began tentatively.

"I know." N. paused, and sucked on his pipe. "Is there some reason you requested this meeting, Agent Pumpernickel?"

Pumpernickel took a deep breath. "Someone tried to kill Miss Bond last night."

"Considering the life she leads, that's no surprise."

"Oh, no, sir. You see, the attacker specifically mentioned 'the spy game.' And he knew Jane wasn't her brother."

"Impossible. No one can know of our scheme."

"Her story seems quite credible, sir, and she's got an obvious head injury."

N. sucked on his pipe and paced about his office along a counter-clockwise path. He had never hated anyone as much as he hated Pumpernickel right that minute; not even his mother. "You didn't witness this so-called assault with your own eyes?"

"No, sir." Pumpernickel reddened and looked down. It had never occurred to him that Miss Bond might be lying.

N. sensed his advantage and pressed on. "Miss Bond is obviously a loose cannon; your investigation should have uncovered her instability. But that's all water under the bridge. The question is, how much trouble is she planning on causing for us? Will she go public?"

Although N.'s argument made sense to Pumpernickel (his small experience with women had led him to expect instability and rash remarks from the fairer sex), he still had his suspicions. He remembered blurting the details of the scheme to 008 days ago.

"But, sir—" he began.

N. cut him off. "You'll pay Miss Bond a little visit, Pumpernickel, and convince her to keep her mouth shut."

"Sir!" Agent Pumpernickel started to protest. He was afraid for Jane. If anything happened to her, it would be his fault. But the look in N.'s eyes stopped him cold. They were pale, almost translucent, and void of any warmth. Pumpernickel couldn't help but shiver. He imagined that N.'s soul was as empty as his eyes. For years, he had speculated about what was under N.'s hard, frosty exterior. Now he knew. It was a hard, frosty interior. For the first time in decades, Pumpernickel thought of the man who had cut him. He had had the same look in his eyes right before he'd knocked him senseless.

Casting an angry glance at Pumpernickel, N. noted his reddening eyes. "You wouldn't be going all squishy on me, would you?"

Pumpernickel's nose started to bleed; it always did when he was frightened. He took what he thought was a paper handkerchief from N.'s desk and tried to stem the flow.

N. felt an embolism coming on. He was one of the most important men in England, and on whom did he have to rely? A drunken woman-izer currently undergoing psychological treatment, and a simpering Aunt Sally who had just wiped his nose on a top secret, highly confi-dential, impossible to replicate map of the Belgian Congo.

"I want assurance that Miss Bond is not going to cause any prob-lems for this office. Do you understand?"

"Miss Bond is so nice." Pumpernickel sniffled. "I can't imagine she'll cause us any trouble."

"The girl's a sociopath. She hates anyone with authority. She hates you, in fact. She told me so."

Pumpernickel sucked in his breath.

"Sometimes sociopaths can seem the most charming of people, Pumpernickel. You must get a grip on yourself. Go talk with her. Bring flowers. Treat her like the lovely girl she is. And don't show your face around here until you've convinced her to shut up."

Soon after

N. had put his worries aside and was perusing reports from their man in Berlin when he heard a dustup from the vicinity of Miss Tuppenny's office. Before he could activate the self-locking mechanism on his door, Miss Bond burst into the room, in full man-drag. She had the crazed look of an amazon in her eyes.

"Pray tell, Miss Bond," N. said calmly, "what can I do for you?" It was best to speak to the unhinged in cool, soothing tones.

"One of your men attacked me last night!"

"That's utter piffle, Miss Bond."

"You said there'd be no risk involved!"

He laughed patronizingly. "Miss Bond, there's risk involved every time you leave the house."

Jane was becoming angrier by the minute.

"Someone from the Secret Service followed me to the Albert bridge last night and warned me to stay away from 'the spy game.' Then he split my head with the butt of his pistol. Care to explain?"

"If I could explain the actions of every lunatic who chased after girls in the night, well—" he paused and shook his head.

"I want to know what the hell is going on!" Jane slapped her open hand on N.'s desk, causing his elephant-tusk desk accessories to move out of alignment.

N. sighed wearily. Thank God he had never married. "I'm calling security," he said evenly.

"Call them," Jane said, "and I'll go to every paper in town and tell them about how you fooled the queen."

N. froze. He could kill her right now, where she stood, but it would a messy proposition, inside his office and all that. Too many people had seen her—or, rather, seen a disheveled James Bond—walk into his office. He had a better idea, opening his secret drawer and removing a file. He tossed it toward Jane, and it flew open. Dozens of explicit photographs skittered across the executive desk.

"They can run these along with your story, Miss Bond," he said coolly, sitting back and crossing his arms.

Jane examined the pictures. They were snaps of her and a half dozen girls in various stages of undress. She winced when she saw an especially vivid snapshot of her in the alley behind the bar, her face buried between the breasts of a slinky brunette. Now she remembered Bunny. Beautiful. Bridget would kill her if she saw these.

N. rapped his knuckles on the desk. "I want you to go home, Miss Bond, and forget this ever happened. You are never to come here again, or speak to Agent Pumpernickel."

"And these photographs?"

"I'll keep them as a little insurance policy."

"Why don't you just kill me? That would keep me quiet."

N. sniffed meaningfully and glanced down at his recently buffed nails. "Because, Miss Bond, regardless of what you may think, I am not a monster."

"No, just a blackmailer," she seethed. Jane fought the urge to bludgeon him to death. The globe on the shelf beside the door would make a nice dent in his hard skull. Instead, she said, "Thanks" sarcastically. Then, "What about the person who attacked me? What if he tries again?"

"He wasn't really after you," N. said consolingly. "It's James he wants. Go back to being a girl, and I guarantee you can walk the streets unmolested."

"The women of London will be relieved to hear that," said Jane.

N. held up the envelope containing the remainder of her pay. "I shouldn't give this to you, considering how you've spoken to me. I could have you arrested, you know, for impertinence."

Jane knew to keep her mouth shut. She put her hands in her pocket and glared at him. He smiled thinly, and tossed her the envelope. She checked the contents before stuffing it in her pocket. Nine hundred pounds, and she had earned every penny of it. What she wanted most was to stuff the bills down his throat until he choked.

Turning away from Jane, N. calmly filled his pipe and lit it. He leaned back in his chair, a look of smug satisfaction on his pasty face. His hand moved to a button on a console. The door swung open.

"You are dismissed. One word of advice before you go."

Jane crossed her arms over her chest: "What?"

"Remember to look both ways before crossing heavy traffic."

"You bastard!" The globe missed his head by a mile, but it did make a nice noise when it shattered the window glass. Sir Niles's rather robotic secretary darted in, and Jane swore she saw a little smile playing at the corner of her lips as she ran to comfort N. Jane brushed past her and took the stairs three at a time to the lobby, then gave the blonde at the reception desk a good hard kiss before leaving the building, vowing never to return.

Agent Pumpernickel slumped to the side of the lift and slid to the floor. He had caught the whole show on his transmitter-radio watch. When the lift had stuck between floors, as it was wont to do, he had turned his watch on to call for help, hoping to patch into one of the radio receivers operated by the boys in transmissions. Instead, he had inadvertently connected with Miss Bond, whose transmitter was on and working splendidly. The lift started up—it always did sooner or later, although usually later—but instead of heading for the first-floor cafeteria for a cup of tea, Pumpernickel descended, with a heavy heart, into the bowels of the building. The conversation with N. had struck a long-forgotten chord in his memory.

The ant farm
2:45 P.M.

"Hello, Agent Pumpernickel," Miss Loomis said. "Fancy seeing you down here."

"I need a file, Miss Loomis," Pumpernickel said.

"Just put your request form in the box and I'll have one of the girls bring it up to you."

"No need—I'll get it myself."

Miss Loomis gasped. She had never heard an agent say that before.

Pumpernickel looked around. There were hundreds of drawers. The writing on the labels was a spidery, cramped hand of long ago—the work of the very first registry queen, a Miss Lillian Bee. Agent Pumpernickel had long frowned on the casual use of the word. Only the queen had the right to call herself a queen. The labels were almost impossible to read.

"Need help?" said Miss Loomis, putting aside a strip of dental floss used that morning by a Russian spy staying at the Savoy under an assumed name.

"I'm looking for information about a former agent."

"Alive or dead?"

"Deceased."

"Year?"

"Forty-seven."

"Name?"

"Bond. James Bond."

Without batting an eye, Miss Loomis inquired: "James Bond Senior?"

In a flash, she had located the correct drawer. Agent Pumpernickel pulled up a stool, and started to search through the musty papers. The girls in black smocks stopped to stare at the secret agent with his nose in a file cabinet. Miss Loomis shooed them back to work. There was no reason to stop and stare as if an auto accident had taken place. Still and all, it was a most peculiar sight.

The information he sought was pitifully easy to find. How careless N. had been, thought Pumpernickel. Or worse, how little he cared, how little he expected that anyone would care. Enclosed in the file was a receipt from a London costumer for a busman's uniform, size 57 long. Only one agent in the history of the Secret Service had been a 57 long; the same agent who had once bestowed on Pumpernickel a mint-condition Battersea snuffbox from 1936, featuring King Edward VIII before the abdication. N., the only man he had ever loved, had driven the bus that killed Jane's father. And again, it was Pumpernickel's fault. He had thoughtlessly confided in N. that James Bond Senior might pose a security risk, given the amount he had been drinking after the death of his wife.

Pumpernickel's heart thudded against the file stuffed under his coat. Papers were never, ever to be removed from headquarters; doing so destroyed the files' integrity. It was grounds for immediate dismissal, but he didn't care. He would no longer do the devil's work.

Grunby Hall
Lady Edwina's bedchamber
3:00 P.M.

Lady Edwina had just finished her daily Constance Spry exercise routines and was chewing on an orange sugar dab when the front doorbell rang. A minute later, there was a knock at her door.

"Madam, Lady Bridget is here," Bibi informed her.

Lady Edwina dabbed the moisture from her upper lip, tied a chiffon scarf around her pin curls, and threw on one of her nicer housecoats. It would never do to leave a lady waiting.

"Lady Bridget, how unexpected," she greeted her guest. "I mean, how nice."

"She's brought your dress back from the seamstress, madam," Bibi explained.

"Oh, you darling!" Lady Edwina clapped her hands together in delight. She had never before heard of a lady doing a favor for a mere commoner. "I'm going to tell your mother I want you for all my parties," she exclaimed.

Bridget smiled wanly. "Lady Edwina, I want you to practice your curtsey while wearing it," she said. Bluma Trell's girls had expertly wired miniature transmitters at various points throughout the dress. Edwina would serve as a giant walking radio receiver. During the auction, Chief Tuppenny would be in a greengrocer's van down the lane listening intently to the transmission and recording vital bits.

The Empire Hotel
3:15 P.M.

"And then I got the very same dress!" Lettie cried triumphantly, "but in a much smaller size."

"Why do you torment Edwina so?" Sir Reginald groaned. Every time Lettie took her down a notch, Sir Reginald had to boost her spirits with chocolate or sex.

"Because it gives me so much pleasure."

"Lettie, sometimes I believe you are a sadist."

"And marrying a dumpy commoner for her money in order to restore your family estate so it can become the prison for the queen *isn't* a touch sadistic?"

"I get scant pleasure from thinking of the queen in chains."

"Who would?" Lettie sniffed.

"Be nice to Edwina," her lover begged. "She's going to be the most notorious hostess in London after tonight. We need to stay in her good graces. Besides, the duchess seems so fond of her."

"Once she meets Edwina, the duchess will change her mind faster than she changes lovers."

"The duchess has lovers?" Somehow, the news put him off. She was, after all, going to be queen.

"Of course, darling. Everyone does; everyone but Edwina, that is." Lettie laughed. "I do think she was happier living above the plumbing shop and going to the cinema with that grubby friend of hers. What is her name? Snip? Snap? Oh, listen, darling, it sounds like a rhyme. Snip-snap. Aren't I clever?"

Sometimes Lettie scared him. He kissed her on the forehead, as if kissing a very dear, but very spoilt, child. "Yes, dear. You're frightfully clever." He was getting a tad tired of Lettie and her demands. He should really look around for a less sophisticated girl to dally with. Someone like that new maid, Bibi. It was a most beguiling name.

"What are you thinking about?" Lettie demanded to know.

"You, dear. You."

008 was relaxing on his imported fish-shaped rattan lounging chair, perusing the latest issue of *Gent* magazine, and having a stiff drink, when his direct line to headquarters rang.

"008 here!" he cried, almost tripping over the belt of his silk paisley-print lounging robe in the process.

"008—Miss Tuppenny here."

"Really? Miss Tuppenny?" She must have heard of his accident, and was calling to see how he was. That little minx! He hopped onto one of his bamboo barstools and propped his elbows on the black Lucite counter. It was embedded with little silver flakes that sparkled like stars.

"I hope I'm not disturbing you. Word is you had a rather nasty run-in with some Russian spies."

"It's all in a day's work," he said importantly. "I'm missing a few teeth, but it's all part of the job."

"That's the attitude," Miss Tuppenny cheered him. "N. will be glad to hear your spirits are high. In fact, he'd love to speak to you in person."

"An assignment?" 008 was so excited he spilled his gin and tonic, soaking the paper nudie napkins he had been saving for his next cocktail party.

Back at the Empire Hotel

"You know what you're to do."

"For God's sake, yes," Lettie said testily. They'd been over it numerous times in the last few days. "When you give the signal, I slip away to the library and wait for you to bring in the queen. Once she's there, I chloroform her and exchange frocks." Lettie paused to shiver. "Then you will pass her through the library windows to Jinx, who will hide her in the fishmonger's lorry. After a reasonable amount of time, I return to the party as the lovely Queen Elizabeth, indeed looking fresher and more radiant than usual, and dismiss my guard. I make my way to the loo, where I plant the letter of abdication, remove that monstrous frock, and return to the party as my charming self."

"One small matter. You should dismiss the guard with a wave of your hand. You're not to speak, Lettie." Sometimes—and it pained him to admit it—Lettie's high-pitched voice could make her sound coarse and of low birth.

"Of course I'm not going to *speak* to him," Lettie scoffed. "Queens don't go around chatting up the help."

"You have the letter?"

"It's in my handbag."

"Don't lose it at the party," he cautioned. "We've no more of the queen's private stationery."

"I had my girl sew a special pouch for it in my girdle," Lettie assured him.

Sir Reginald frowned. Too many strangers were involved in this. All could give evidence in court. The builders at Grouse Manor, Lettie's seamstress, Lady Bridget. God knew what Lady Bridget had picked up from that chatty new maid Bibi, who might easily have overheard bits of his telephone conversations.

Office of Sir Niles Needlum
4:00 P.M.

"Did you try to kill Miss Bond?"

"Is that what she told you?" 008 cried. "Ouch!" he added, putting a hand to his swollen face. He had knocked out his two front teeth on a river rock.

N. winced. Under the best of circumstances, 008 was not a handsome boy. N. puffed on his pipe. His special blend of Turkish tobacco sweetened the air, giving the room the atmosphere of a shabby men's club. N. hadn't time for the kind of socializing men in his position typically went in for. He had a country to run.

"Don't lie to me, 008," he warned.

"I followed her, sir," 008 confessed. He hung his head. Had he been more limber, he would have curled into a ball and kissed his arse goodbye. It was the end for Secret Agent 008.

"I thought perhaps she was trying to pull something over on us, dressing up like her brother and all. It's not natural," he added, a bit lamely. The sheets on her had been enough to make any man's confidence falter. Blimey! She got more birds in a week than he did in a year!

They both knew it was a lie, and not a very good one.

"Naturally, I prefer that my agents wait for my orders before going running around London waving their guns."

It was 008's turn to wince.

"While your actions were premature and, I must add, a bit extreme given the situation, I do applaud your initiative."

"Really, sir?" 008's mouth fell open. N. averted his eyes. The toothless mouth made his agent appear daft.

"You passed the test, 008."

"It was a test?"

"Certainly. You don't think we'd actually dress up Miss Bond like her brother and parade her in front of the queen, did you?"

"No, sir!" 008 wanted to laugh from relief, but his mouth wouldn't open that wide. "Only an imbecile would be stupid enough to think that would work," he asserted.

"She was good, though, you have to admit." N.'s voice had a steely edge to it.

"She didn't fool me," 008 bragged. "I spotted her right off."

N. turned his back to his agent and looked out the window. He sighed. His intention had been to raise 008's status to that of acting agent, but he was beginning to rethink his decision.

"How is it you let Miss Bond get the upper hand?" he asked quietly.

008 was, for once, without an easy explanation. He couldn't admit he had tripped over his own feet.

"As a gentleman, I found the idea of killing a woman repugnant," he finally replied. "She is the sister of a fellow agent. I found I could not kill her, sir. Without direct orders, that is," he added quickly.

"So you would have killed her had I told you to?"

"Yes, sir. Without hesitation."

N. smiled, pleased at this answer. Still, the boy must be taught a lesson.

"Congratulations, Agent 008," he said, extending his hand across the executive desk. "I've been holding onto a little something that I'd hoped I'd have the good fortune to pass onto you. And now, to my delight, I find that you are more than ready."

While 008 trembled in anticipation, N. felt around in his upper desk drawer, his eyes riveted paternally on 008's.

"For you, dear boy, with the gratitude of your queen and country."

008 examined the square blackened object that N. slipped into his palm and blinked uncertainly.

"It's . . . a cork, sir."

"A real corker, isn't it? Note the trimmed edges and the perfect symmetry. I've given you the beginnings of your very own rubber band ball! Use it wisely, 008, use it wisely."

Pressing the special button on his console for the second time that day, N. gave a final curt nod to 008 and dismissed him from his office.

Grunby Hall
4:27 P.M.

"Is this for me?" Edwina cried. "From Sir Reginald?"

Bibi shrugged. She had been tempted to hide the box of chocolates that had just arrived by special delivery, but common sense, and an achy tooth, had stopped her. She had been eating far too many sweets since taking this job. Besides, there was an auction item she had her eye on—a little porcelain lamp with a shepardess painted on the base. It would be adorable on her bedside table, but she couldn't in good conscience steal both.

"It's from the duchess!" exclaimed Edwina. "She's wishing me good luck for the auction. Isn't that just like her? Take this to Cook, Bibi. I'm going to display them at the party on a nice tray, with the card right in front."

Bibi coughed softly.

"Bibi?"

"Seems to me, madam, that the duchess and the queen aren't very close."

"Oh, Bibi—that's right! They refuse to speak to each other. That would have been dreadfully embarrassing! Thank you, dear."

Bibi smiled. She was developing a soft spot for Edwina. She was still going to steal that lamp, though. Once again, she settled in for her employer's excited description of that night's menu, prepared by London's finest caterer: jellied calf's brain on toast fingers, treacle pudding tarts, and vanilla ladyfingers. According to a magazine article Edwina had read at the hairdresser's, these were the queen's favorite foods. In addition, Edwina had designated her private bathroom for the queen's exclusive use, outfitting it at the last minute with 22-karat gold fittings, and stocking it with a dozen finger towels embroidered with the Windsor family crest by Carmelite nuns. An ice sculpture of Admiral Nelson at Trafalgar would grace the center of the buffet table.

Office of Sir Niles Needlum
5:12 P.M.

"I'm not looking up," said N., his gaze riveted on a street map of Cleveland in northern England that lay open on his executive desk. Somehow Pumpernickel had talked his way past Miss Tuppenny; this was a breach of discipline that N. would deal with harshly. He'd had quite enough interruptions today.

Retired Agent Cedric Pumpernickel stood trembling in front of his superior, the man he had thought of for many years as a friend. Not a very close friend, true, but an honorable man.

"You ordered the kill on Jane's father, didn't you?" he asked, his anger overcoming his fear. "Don't lie to me. I have the proof. And in exchange, I want those photos of Miss Bond, as well as those of her wellborn friend."

"Proof? Poof! Or does that strike a little close to home?" N. slowly looked up at Pumpernickel, who was turning an attractive shade of berry. "I don't know what you think you're up to, man, but you're skating on thin ice here. I haven't signed those papers for your pension yet."

Pumpernickel lost some of his bluster. Without a pension, he'd be close to penniless. He hadn't been able to save very much over the years, not with the house to keep up, and his mother's illness. It was a hard blow to take.

"Just tell me that Miss Bond is safe from—from this agency," he added quietly.

"Why, of course, dear boy," N. replied, waving away his concern. "I'll put a man right on it."

Crispin's Bookshop
5:30 P.M.

Simon had been so worried about Jane after she bolted from the Secret Service building that he had insisted she return with him to the bookshop. There was very little that couldn't be solved with a cup of tea and a bag of jelly buns.

"It challenges your faith in humanity, doesn't it," asked Simon as he poured her a cuppa.

"Oh, I never had any of that. But it's taken my mind off Astrid, I can tell you." What a week it had been. Astrid, Bridget, her father, the gash on her head. She just wanted to lie with her head on the concise edition of the Oxford English Dictionary and eat jelly buns.

Suddenly they were interrupted by the sound of the front door banging open.

"So this is how she repays me?" said Mrs. Snipe, making her way toward the curtain that separated the bookshop from the small, private space where Jane and Simon were taking tea. Her voice was especially grating today, Jane thought.

"And I'm her very best friend!" Mrs. Snipe screeched.

In alarm, Simon had spilt his tea over his lap, and now stood wearily, dabbing a towel to his crotch. The curtain flew back. Mrs. Snipe pushed her way past a pile of remaindered mystery novels and grabbed for the jelly buns.

"Don't tell me," Jane said mildly from her recumbent position. "It's Edwina again."

Her mouth satisfyingly full, Mrs. Snipe brandished a newspaper in Simon's face.

"Read!" she muttered, releasing a fine spray of crumbs onto her chin and dress front. She pointed to a paragraph in the court circular.

"Princess Beatrice of the Netherlands dined last night—"

"Lower!"

" 'Her Royal Highness will attend a charity auction tonight at Grunby Hall, the London home of Sir Reginald and Lady Edwina Wooley-Booley, in support of the Daughters of the Dispossessed Aristocracy fund.' "

"The queen!" barked Mrs. Snipe. "Did you get that part? The queen! And I'm not invited!"

With this, Mrs. Snipe burst into messy tears. "The very least she could have done was save me the humiliation of finding out in such a public manner!" she sobbed. "She knows my lifelong dream has been to meet the queen. I've been a loyal friend to Edwina, and believe me, she is not the easiest person to love. We've been through thick and thicker together, and this is how she repays me? By letting the whole world know that I am *not* invited to my best friend's house to meet the queen!"

"But you aren't mentioned here," said Simon helpfully.

Rolling her eyes, Mrs. Snipe snatched the last jelly bun, took one wet bite, and tossed it back onto the plate. She stormed out of the shop, banging the door behind her.

After a moment, Jane sat up and looked admiringly at Simon.

"Yes, I went a little far," he said, "but it felt good."

Jane reached for the paper, preparing to tear out the column to read to Miss Liversidge. "I can't believe there's such an organization as the Daughters of the Dispossessed Aristocracy. Oh, and listen to this: *'All eyes will be on Lady Edwina, as this is her first party since her nuptials six months ago. Filling her mother's shoes will be first-time hostess Lady Bridget St. Claire—'* "

"You're not serious," said Simon, grabbing the paper. "So that's what she's been up to. Not that you care."

"Oh, no, Simon," Jane said, in an entirely unconvincing manner, "I've practically forgotten her."

Simon shook his head and began to clear away the tea things. "A shame you can't go." He shot a quick glance at Jane. "I mean it, Jane, you can't. Someone may still be after you."

"Don't worry. I've got Miss Liversidge's cats to feed," said Jane, pocketing the clipping. "And I'm absolutely finished with Lady Bridget."

Grunby Hall
Maid's quarters
5:50 P.M.

"I could just kill Mother!" said Bridget St. Claire, shimmering in her sea green Chanel cocktail dress as she tossed the court circular onto Bibi's lap. "I asked her not to inform the press of the queen's appearance at the auction. Just look at this. The last thing we need is publicity. What if Jane sees it?"

"Can you picture her reading the society pages?" said Bibi smoothly. She had just pressed a new apron to go over her black satin maid's uniform, and now stood to pin her humiliating cap in place. Bridget had swept her own hair into a glamorous French twist, and looked with sympathy at her friend. Bibi was right.

Grunby Hall
Sir Reginald's study
5:52 P.M.

"I'm going to kill Edwina!" Sir Reginald swore. He threw the *Times* on the carpet and stepped all over it like a spoilt child throwing a tantrum.

"Get ahold of yourself, Rags!" cried Jinx Finhatten. Never had he seen Sir Reginald so undone.

"She's alerted the press to the queen's visit! The last thing we need are a bunch of nosy photographers snooping round while we're trying to smuggle a drugged queen out the window and into a waiting van."

Jinx smiled and shook his head. "Calm yourself, dear boy. I'll simply step outside and regale them with tales of India. Elephants and all. Empire. That's the stuff."

"Splendid idea," said Reginald through gritted teeth. It was, in a way. And it would keep Jinx away from Lettie during the crucial transformation.

The Flora Beaton
6:30 P.M.

Jane dabbed at a jelly spot on her freshly knotted tie. She wanted to look her best for Bridget. Damn Bridget, she thought. Why even speak to her again? For a moment, she regretted running out on Simon like that, and with such a miserable lie (a sick headache and exhaustion), but she couldn't miss her chance of confronting Bridget with all she had learned. After all, she and that monster Bibi might have been on the verge of breaking up. Perhaps Bridget had only needed a little more time to sever things. Perhaps she and Jane were destined for each other. The honk of the waiting taxi broke into her reverie. Jane gave a long, self-pitying sigh and rolled her eyes at her stupidity.

Secret Service headquarters
6:35 P.M.

"It's terribly simple, really," said N., creasing his face into something like a smile. "You want to become a full-fledged agent, am I right?"

Agent Horace Wattle shook his head eagerly, his upper lip flapping slightly against the gap in his front teeth. He had not dared to expect this, not after his demotion to Desk Accessories.

"And quite properly, too," N. continued. "It's the finest job for a virile young lad like yourself. But let me get down to brass tacks. That sapphic marauder, that lamb in wolf's clothing, that *Jane Bond . . .*" His voice broke away in loathing and dread. "I want her dead. She's a security risk. And Pumpernickel, too. He's a slipper-wearing fanatic. Here's your weapon."

The hand that N. extended to Wattle was closed over an item so small that the young agent feared it contained yet another cork. But it was a length of piano wire.

"You can find Miss Bond with the greatest of ease," chirped N., singing the last few words. "We sewed radioactive lint into her trouser pocket. I'd be surprised if she isn't developing a nasty red rash at this very moment. As for Pumpernickel—" N. closed his eyes for a moment in reflection, then opened them and sat upright. "Of course! He'll be after Miss Bond. Find her, and you'll find him. Finish the job cleanly—and I mean cleanly—and you'll be promoted to double-0 status. Including the pay rise, the trick shoes, and the license to kill."

Grunby Hall
7:00 P.M.

The best way to crash a party is to pretend that you belong there. Jane strode up to the open front door of the palatial Grunby Hall and simply walked in. She could hear musicians tuning up in a nearby room, and the clatter of dishes being arranged. Almost at once, a silver-haired man stepped forward to greet her. Taking in her plain black suit and lack of an evening coat, he blocked her path and directed her to the back of the building. Perhaps the suit isn't as good as I'd thought, mused Jane as she made her way to the servant's entrance.

A few minutes later, she was in the massive kitchen, tray in hand, being given orders by a small Irish woman in an apron. It wouldn't be the grand entrance she'd had in mind, but at least she was in.

7:07 P.M.

The silver-haired man glared at the chap in the dark trench coat. "Private party," he said menacingly.

Pumpernickel wished he'd had time to plan a cover story. He'd hoped to apprehend Jane outside the building, but her taxi had raced ahead of his car and he'd lost sight of her for a crucial seventy-six seconds.

"Oh, it's you!" An ebullient little woman in a flowered housecoat, her face obstructed by a thick layer of cold cream, raced down a majestic mahogany staircase and pushed the man aside. She swooped down on Agent Pumpernickel and pulled him into the house.

"I've been waiting breathlessly for your arrival," she cried, tugging her housecoat tighter around her ample waist. "I've heard all about you, although I must say you're not exactly what I'd expected."

"Is Jane here?" Pumpernickel tried to withdraw his hand from hers, but she was pulling him up the stairs with remarkable determination.

"The name's Edwina. Lady Edwina. Hurry, we haven't much time. The guests are due any minute. Is it really true you do Princess Margaret's hair?"

Pumpernickel shook off her grasp. "Madam, you are mistaken—"

"I'm sorry," Edwina cringed. "You're not really allowed to say, are you? Just like a doctor." Taking his arm again, she led him into a bedchamber, plunked herself in front of a Louis XIV dressing mirror, and announced, "You may begin."

She looked at him in utter confidence. "The queen is coming, you know," she burbled. "So I must look my very best."

"The queen? Here?"

"You'll get to meet her. Naturally, you're invited to stay." Her husband would kill her, but she couldn't very well have the most famous hairdresser in London in to do her hair, then bid him adieu before the festivities began.

Pumpernickel picked up a comb and made a tentative swipe at Edwina's hair, which hung in thin, wet hanks to her shoulders. *I am going to meet the queen*, he thought. *The queen. The queen.*

"I usually sleep in rollers," she confided, shaking him from his dream state. "And I wear it in a halo of tight curls."

"You mustn't anymore," he said authoritatively. He had to say something—anything! He hadn't even brought his own scissors.

"It's"—he paused—"unflattering."

Edwina beamed. "That's exactly what my friend Mrs. Snipe is forever saying. 'Edwina, your face is as round as a meat pie. Wear it up to give you length where there is none.' "

"Your friend is a very wise woman, Lady Edwina." He picked up a comb and ran it through Edwina's hair, making soft soothing clucks as he did. He had seen his mother's much-loved hairdresser, Mr. Edwards, do the very same thing.

Edwina thought Mr. Henri looked nothing like a famous hairdresser. With his severe suit and scarred face, he looked more like a gangster or the villain in a detective film. And for someone who styled hair, he certainly had very little of his own. He had come highly recommended, however, by Lettie, who had arranged for the visit as a little treat for Edwina on the occasion of her first real party. He was supposed to have been there an hour ago, but never mind that. With a happy sigh, Edwina closed her eyes and gave herself over to the skilled hands of Mr. Henri.

7:25 P.M.

"Pardon me," said Jane as she peered into one of the guest loos and startled a maid. "Have you seen—"

Bibi slammed the door shut indignantly. The nerve of some men. She adjusted her other stocking, then pulled out her compact and beeped Bridget.

"Agent St. Claire here."

"Where are you?"

"Here, I said." Bridget smiled, allowing herself a little joke before the difficult business of espionage and covert action got under way for the evening. Hearing no answering laugh from Bibi, she quickly added, "Actually I'm in the silver pantry, adjusting the sound levels." The stuffed heads in the main rooms had been wired for sound. The recording device was hidden in the base of a silver punch bowl.

"Everything's coming in loud and clear," she continued. "Has Lettie seen her dress?"

"Yes," Bibi snickered. "She's furious. She threw a shoe at me when I complimented her on it."

"Gather up Edwina and send her down here."

"She wants to wait until the queen is here and make a grand entrance."

"If she does, she'll be banned from polite society for the remainder of her life, plus twenty years," Bridget patiently explained. "No one upstages the queen. I'm positive Mother mentioned this in her book."

They rang off, closing their compacts simultaneously with a snappy wrist movement.

Bibi took another moment to admire herself in the mirror. She was lonely. Having spent two days fending off the clumsy advances of Sir Reginald had reminded her how few advances of the welcome sort she'd received of late.

The door flew open, hitting her squarely on her bruised right hip.

"Fuck!" she cried before catching herself.

"Well, I never!" exclaimed Lettie, as if she had never heard the term, and had no idea what it meant. Here was that damn maid again, devoting her work hours to what looked like a long session with a makeup brush and an oddly luxurious array of cosmetics.

"Sorry, madam, I was just leaving," said Bibi, hastily gathering her Powder Puff wares into her purse.

Lettie put out an arm to stop her. "What's that you've got? Is that a new line?"

Her gaze had fallen on the tube of Femme Fatale lipstick in Bibi's hand. "Oh, yes, this is Vérité." She saw Lettie's surprise that a housemaid should have such a costly collection of stylish new cosmetics. "My cousin sells Powder Puff."

"I didn't ask for your life story, dearie."

Bibi curtsied and pushed past Lettie, wishing she could unload her single-shot lipstick into the middle of her heavily powdered forehead.

The silver pantry
7:30 P.M.

The box of chocolates ostensibly sent by the Duchess of Windsor had been stowed in the little-used silver pantry until Bluma Trell's girls could analyze the contents. Bridget had spotted the deception right away, and now took a second look at the suspicious sweets. The duchess would never have sent anything as common as chocolate-covered cherries. The forger had made another mistake by penning a note in Wallis-blue ink. This season, as any truly alert member of the nobility knew, the duchess had embraced lavender as her signature color.

Lady Edwina's dressing room
7:40 P.M.

"My dress won't go over my hair!" Lady Edwina had been ruthlessly corseted and now stood in front of her full-length looking glass struggling to get her dress on without disrupting her new hairstyle.

"Try stepping into it," Lettie said wearily. She was in a foul mood. The stupid shop girl had sent her the wrong dress. Instead of a smaller version of Edwina's, Lettie had received a hideous, puffy-sleeved, pea-green chiffon affair that made her appear positively bilious.

"Hurrah!" Edwina had squeezed herself into the dress, and, like a proud four-year-old, expected to be praised. "And I didn't muss my hair," she added proudly, patting her modest bouffant.

"That hairstyle is a real improvement," Lettie admitted begrudgingly. "It gives you the appearance of a neck."

Edwina pinned her new tiara to her helmet of hair, and paused to admire herself in the looking glass. With her new dress, and a Mr. Henri hairstyle, no one would ever guess she was a Piggott.

"Mr. Henri is such a nice man." She sighed. "So gentle and modest. I think I'll start going to him every week."

"Who?" Lettie asked absentmindedly. She was beginning to wonder if Jinx, whom she had sent home an hour ago for a new gown, had gotten lost.

"Mr. Henri. He did my hair."

Lettie laughed. She had promised Edwina a session with England's most avant-garde hairdresser, but it had somehow slipped her mind. Edwina had obviously done her own hair, and was lying to make Lettie jealous. She had always suspected Edwina's cheerful act hid a vengeful heart.

"Edwina, dear." Lettie took Edwina's arm and leaned in confidentially. "Your dress does clack a wee bit. If I were you, I'd make as few movements tonight as possible." The crestfallen look on Edwina's face was Lettie's reward.

Lettie glanced at herself in the mirror, still mortified at the dress, but pleased with her hourglass figure and her high, full breasts. Her lipstick had faded slightly, and she thought with irritation of Edwina's new maid Bibi and her little handbag stuffed with the finest cosmetics London had to offer. Edwina let the girl walk all over her. Lettie had caught her taking a milk bath the day before in Edwina's new 22-karat tub. The girl had spun an improbable tale of merely following manufacturer's instructions to test the bath for leaks, something she could have done without taking off her clothes and soaking in bubbles up to her neck.

This new maid was frightfully impertinent, and far too attractive for Lettie's comfort. Not so Sir Reginald. He drooled over her like a dog over spoiled meat every time she walked into the room. It was a habit he would have to drop once he and Lettie were married.

Sir Reginald's bedchamber
8:00 P.M.

Aware that he was underdressed to meet the queen, Agent Pumpernickel had secreted himself inside the lord of the manor's voluminous dressing room and was frantically searching for something to wear. Alas, Sir Reginald had a good four stone on him, and Pumpernickel felt clownish in his suits. Finally, he settled on a simple silk ascot in a flattering shade of cocoa, the sort of thing that someone named Mr. Henri might wear. He had moved the part in his thinning hair closer to his ear, hoping to catch as many strays as possible, but the effect was not entirely pleasing. Nevertheless, it would do.

Outside Grunby Hall
8:09 P.M.

Up and over, it was really quite simple, 008 told himself as he scaled the twelve-foot-high wrought-iron gate surrounding Grunby Hall. He hadn't reckoned, however, on the spikes at the top. Thankfully he had spent a summer at a camp for wayward youth and had learned some tricks from his fellow inmates. Grunting with effort, he gripped the rails of the fence between his thighs—something in his inseam gave with a slow, sickening rip—and tore off his government-issue trenchcoat. He lay it carefully over the jagged edge and proceeded to climb over. Alas, he hadn't considered that one of the sturdy double knots of his shoelaces might catch on the spikes. The next moment, he found himself swinging upside down over a clump of shrubbery, waiting for the weight of his body to overcome the careful knot.

Grunby Hall kitchen
8:12 P.M.

Pumpernickel had never been one to push himself forward. Stroking his hair nervously, he stood near the entrance to the kitchen, hoping to blend in. Most of the guests ignored him, assuming, perhaps, that he was one of the waiters.

"Stuffed mushroom?"

"Thank you," said Pumpernickel, "They were a favorite of my mother's." He looked up at the young man holding the tray and instantly dropped his canapé. "Miss Bond," he exclaimed with relief. "I'm so glad to see you. You're in grave danger, you know." In his excitement over the queen, Pumpernickel had almost forgotten the purpose of his visit to Grunby Hall.

"It's Bridget who's in grave danger, damn it." Jane propped the tray on her hip and sampled one of the largest mushroom caps. "I've been looking all over for her."

"Never mind your girlfriend. Your life may be in jeopardy. You must leave London at once." Reluctantly, he surrendered a small folder to her. "This is my ticket for the great homes of northern England tour. All meals and lodging paid. Send me a postcard, will you?"

Jane swallowed her mushroom and weighed his proposal. "When can I come back?"

"Oh, I daresay a fortnight will do. I've just got to tidy up matters here, talk to the right people, you know."

"And when do I leave?"

"Immediately. Don't go home. Don't go the bookshop. Go directly to Victoria Station and wait for tomorrow's bus."

"I'll consider it," she said. An elegant figure with upswept red hair had caught her eye. "Take this," she added sharply, handing Pumpernickel the tray of hors d'oeuvres in exchange for the ticket.

Outside Grunby Hall
back garden
8:21 P.M.

It was not as easy to climb a drainpipe as the movies made it seem. Still smarting from his encounter with Edwina's rosebushes, 008 had scaled only a few feet of the back wall of the mansion before losing his remaining shoe. The other hung from the gate spike.

Grunby Hall
The great hall
8:30 P.M.

Guiding Edwina downstairs took far longer than Bibi had anticipated. But her steadying hand on the small of Edwina's back managed to keep the clacking of the beads to a minimum, so that the music could still be heard by the guests. When they got to the base of the stairs, Bibi found herself making eye contact with the woman known around Powder Puff as Bibi's Sloane Square matron.

"Cordelia!" Edwina clacked forward to greet the first of her guests.

"Edwina, darling!" cried the chic younger woman, flushing a little at the sight of Bibi. "You look so . . . gay."

"Aren't you a dear!" Edwina could tell already that the dress was a big hit.

"No, you! You're so . . . fresh. Speaking of which, I need to powder my nose."

"But of course. Bibi will show you to the lav."

Agent Mimi Dolittle's flat
8:33 P.M.

Chief Tuppenny reached up in a practiced gesture and removed the hairpin from her bun. Mimi's door was so thin she could probably have kicked it open, but she didn't want to alert the neighbors. With a flick of her wrist, the lock gave and the door swung open. She had put a few smoke bombs in her handbag in case she needed a quick getaway, and now held one aloft in front of her, uncertain what might await her in the dark. A radio played softly from an inner room.

"And have you accepted Jesus as your personal savior?"

Chief Tuppenny could not make out the reply, although she recognized the distinctive burr of the Hebrides. Oban, she would say. She moved stealthily through the apartment, stepping over clothes and discarded bottles of nail polish. So this is where their supply of Nude You had gone. As she got closer to what must have been the bedroom, she heard a deep sigh and soft, weary, girlish weeping.

"Ach noo," said the voice on the radio. "Ah cannee wait to tell ye. The Lord keem over the wireless an' tooched me boil."

Tuppenny rushed into the room. "Mimi!" she cried, making out the bound figure of her newest agent through the evening gloom.

"Turn it off! Turn it off!" Mimi begged, her voice raw from hours of sobbing. The pillow was so wet that it made a slurping sound as Tuppenny reached across her to tug at the handcuffs.

"You'll have to wait a moment," the chief said, thoughtfully snapping off the radio before she set to work picking the handcuff locks. Within moments, Mimi had flung her arms around Tuppenny's neck and sobbed out her tale of woe.

"She's quite resourceful, that Jane," remarked Tuppenny as she helped Mimi to the loo. Although she would never tell Mimi, Jane's actions rather pleased her. She would make an excellent Powder Puff Girl, if she could ever convince her to wear the dress.

Lady Edwina's bedchamber
8:44 P.M.

"Really, I shouldn't," Bibi protested, lolling on the bed with Cordelia. "I've a job to do."

"I've an idea," the Sloane Square matron purred. "Let's trade costumes. I'll be the maid this time."

Bibi, intrigued despite herself, started to untie her apron before her conscience got the better of her. She was more than a maid, after all. She had a queen to save.

"No," she said, pushing the matron away. "We haven't time for that. Let's keep our clothes on."

From his vantage point outside the window, 008 watched with breathless ardor as Bibi lifted her satin skirt and lay back on the bed.

"Cor," he said softly.

The great hall
8:52 P.M.

Bridget was trapped. She felt the arms of a stuffed bear behind her and the sour breath of Lord Finhatten inches from her face. His two front teeth were dead and a sickly greenish color. Surreptitiously, she kept pressing the emergency button on the base of her compact. Where was Bibi? Would no one rescue her?

"Yes, my dear, it was a bleak day in Calcutta when—"

"Hors d' oeuvres?" Jane rudely inserted her tray between the windbag and Bridget and was rewarded with a gasp from both.

"How delightful! What are those yellow things?" Lord Finhatten paused and surveyed the tray longingly.

"Cheese straws," Jane said impatiently.

"What are they made of?"

"Cheese and straw," she answered.

Lord Finhatten's face fell. Edwina and her modern ideas. "Are they American?"

"Yes, and they're delicious. Here—take them all." She grabbed Bridget by the arm and led her away.

"Jane, what are you doing here?" Bridget whispered frantically, trying to shake off her grasp.

"I've been so worried about your sick aunt that it sent me straight to the court circular. Let's go someplace private, Princess. You've got a lot of explaining to do."

Bridget pulled away. "Go home, Jane. I'll explain everything later. Please. People are beginning to stare." The moment the words were out of her mouth she knew she had said the wrong thing.

"Am I embarrassing you?" Jane asked loudly.

"Of course not, darling," said Bridget, leading Jane out of the room by the elbow.

"Save your endearments for Bibi," Jane replied, tugging her arm free.

Bridget looked at her in confusion. How did Jane know about Bibi? But before she could speak, a slightly drunk Lettie Finhatten lurched over to Jane and leaned her head on her shoulder.

"Oh, James," Lettie sighed. "You haven't forgotten me." Jane recognized Lettie as the woman who had groped her at the queen's tea.

A moment earlier, Bridget had wanted to get away from Jane. Now nothing would have torn her away from the scene.

"You naughty boy," Lettie cooed in Jane's ear. "You snuck in to see me. How clever! I do love a man who uses his brain, too. Meet me in the library in twenty minutes. Now go mingle. And keep your hands off the help."

Jane turned to Bridget with a smirk. "A bit of your own medicine, eh, Princess?"

Bridget slapped Jane soundly across the face. "That's *Lady Bridget* to you," she said, storming up the grand mahogany staircase.

Jane was left alone in the great hall in the company of a stuffed ocelot. She lit a cigarette and ran her hand through her hair. What had just happened?

"I'd like a vodka gimlet," a woman in a silver gown demanded.

"So would I," admitted Jane.

Edwina's bedchamber
9:10 P.M.

"Bibi, where are you?" Bridget had been calling into each of the darkened upstairs bedrooms, and finally burst in on Cordelia and Bibi in a pile of Edwina's bedsheets.

"Oh Bibi," she cried in disappointment. "You're supposed to be working!"

"God, has the queen arrived?" Bibi struggled to her feet and smoothed the wrinkles from her uniform. Her partner rushed from the room, touching Bridget's arm in passing.

"Not a word of this," Cordelia pleaded, one noble to another.

"Oh, who cares?" said Bridget, tumbling onto the bed and letting her tears overtake her. When Bibi had extracted the story from her, she offered to find Jane and keep her safe until after the kidnap attempt had been foiled.

"Give her this," Bridget added, scratching a quick note in Pussycat Pink on Grunby Hall stationery.

After Bibi left the room, Bridget sat up smartly and dabbed her swollen eyes. She had to pull herself together. She was a hostess, after all.

Outside Grunby Hall
9:12 P.M.

With disappointment, Agent 008 climbed into the bedroom so recently vacated by the sapphic trio. And now to work, he told himself, feeling for the piano wire in his coat pocket.

It was no longer there.

Corridor outside Lady Edwina's bedchamber
9:15 P.M.

"Not so fast, my pretty maid," said Sir Reginald, hot in pursuit of Bibi. He had only a few moments before the queen's arrival, but his preparations had been foolproof. No one would notice a brief absence on his part.

Caught, Bibi squirmed in his arms.

"What's that you've got?" he said playfully, tugging a piece of paper from the waistband of her lacy apron.

"Just a recipe for trifle," she said, looking for an avenue of escape.

"I'll trifle with *you*, darling. Now let's see . . ." He scanned the note quickly, smiled at Bibi and chucked her under the chin. "Just as I thought," he murmured, slipping away to his guests.

Bibi picked up the crumpled note from the carpet.

Meet me in the library in ten minutes.
—B.

The great hall
9:22 P.M.

Lettie checked her diamond-encrusted watch. James was waiting for her in the library. Sir Reginald was nowhere in sight. Edwina was stuffing herself on cheese straws. Jinx was chatting up a Daughter of the Dispossessed Aristocracy. She slipped up the stairs unnoticed and went to Edwina's bedchamber to prepare for her rendezvous. Once upstairs, she realized she had left her evening bag in the study where she would later transform herself into a dowdy queen. Lettie started to panic. Without lipstick, she had a decidedly weak lip line.

A quick search of Edwina's vanity table revealed unappetizing stumps of orange lipstick. With a flash, she remembered the maid's sumptuous array of new colors. Now, where would that cheeky girl keep her bag?

Lady Edwina's bedchamber
9:25 P.M.

008 cursed his luck. A quick dive under the bed had left him covered in dust and sporting a carpet burn on his right cheek. Didn't the wealthy employ maids? Before anyone else could burst into the room, he decided to make a break for it. There was no one in the corridor, either, but as he approached the great staircase he could hear the first strains of "God Save the Queen" as her entourage entered the great hall. Quickly, he darted down the back stairs to the kitchen, and, as the servants huddled around the door trying to sneak peeks at the queen, rushed into the silver pantry and locked the door behind him. He had to find a new weapon.

Servants' quarters
9:32 P.M.

Lettie couldn't believe her luck. The bag was simply bursting with colors she was dying to try. One was called Kiss Me Deadly. She opened it and checked the color. Too red. She moved on to Farewell My Sweet. Too brown. Who would wear such a shade, she sniffed. Finally, her hand closed on Vérité. She smoothed on an extra-thick coat and made her way silently to the library.

The library
9:37 P.M.

"Rags, what are you doing here?" Lettie cried. Her lips were beginning to tingle. There had to be a moisturizer in the lipstick.

"I'm looking for you, dear." Sir Reginald sounded unconvinced by his own lie. Lettie sighed. She wanted him out.

"Isn't your place by Edwina's side tonight?" she offered.

"I should think as her best friend," said Sir Reginald smoothly, "you'd want to be there to help her welcome the queen."

"We should both be there. Run along—I have to adjust my stockings. Save me a place in the receiving line."

Sir Reginald moved reluctantly toward the door. "Love me?" he asked in that pitiful little boy way of his that make Lettie's teeth hurt. She tilted her head and smiled prettily.

"Love you," she replied. Before she could stop him, he leaned in and laid his sloppy lips over her freshly painted mouth. The man was overcompensating.

Grunby Hall
Back garden
9:41 P.M.

Jane had found a quiet spot in a gazebo near a tasteless imported Italian fountain sporting a urinating cupid. On the way out through the kitchen she had snagged the bottle of Mumm and a chicken leg from the fridge. That slap from Bridget had hurt more than anything Astrid had ever done to her. She was reaching a new level of misery, one that included watching from a distance as a suspicious man climbed to the drainpipe on the back wall of the mansion and in one of the windows. Yes, she reflected, he was probably looking for her. He had probably come to kill her. In her current state, she found it mildly amusing.

Receiving line
9:46 P.M.

Not wanting to push himself in amongst his betters, Pumpernickel stood a little to one side and watched as the receiving line for the queen formed in the great hall. Lady Edwina had forgotten all about him. Still, he was part of the stirring event.

"Your Majesty, may I present Sir Reginald and Lady Edwina Wooley-Booley."

"Your Majesty," Edwina murmured as she executed a near-perfect curtsey. She found that getting back up was a far sight harder than going down, but Sir Reginald managed to grasp a bit of her dress and give her a little yank, tearing off only a few of the beads.

"Her hand was as limp as boiled pudding!" blurted out Sir Reginald, not entirely under his breath, after the queen had moved past. Edwina looked at him in astonishment. She had thought the very same thing, but would never have said so.

Sir Reginald's manservant, Nigel, sidled up to him. "Telephone, sir," he said discreetly.

Sir Reginald slid away to take the call in his study. It was Lord Owlpen, their lookout at Grouse Manor, the queen's new home.

Lord Owlpen's voice shook as he relayed the terrible news. "A busload of noisy young women all dressed in pink just pulled up to the front gate. And they're demanding a tour!"

"Codswollop!" cried Sir Reginald. "Turn them away, you bungler."

"What did you call me?"

Before he could say anything else he would regret, he rang off. Things were spinning out of his control. How could he have called Lord Owlpen, his social better, a bungler? It was time to act before things got any more complicated.

Silver pantry
9:52 P.M.

008 held another sweet up to his mouth and sucked the cherry filling through the gap where his two front teeth used to reside. Although it

stung, it was oddly comforting. There were only trays in the silver pantry. He had been over it a dozen times in his head, but there was simply no way to fashion a weapon out of one. He would have to squeeze the life out of Pumpernickel and that Bond woman with his bare hands. He hastily wiped the chocolate off of them.

The great hall
9:57 P.M.

Sir Reginald gave the sign to Lettie, who wasn't paying attention. She had backed Edwina into a corner and was energetically critiquing the décor of Grunby Hall.

"And those gold-plated centaur lamps should be a punishable offense," Lettie upbraided her. Stepping back slightly, she caught sight of Sir Reginald. He raised his glass again in a silent toast. Lettie was puzzled for a moment.

"Now?" she mouthed. She watched as Sir Reginald moved toward the queen, catching, in passing, the eye of the queen's guardsman, who was in the pay of the S.O.B.S. In fact, the fellow had ten thousand pounds of Edwina's plumbing money in his pocket. And he hadn't even had to sleep with her.

"Would Your Majesty care to see my collection of rare corgi aquatints?" said Sir Reginald.

"With pleasure," the monarch responded, glad to escape the throng.

"I'll be sure to bring her back in good health," Sir Reginald told the guard, a tad too robustly. "Unless I decide to hold her hostage," he added, winking broadly. The guard winced at the obviousness of the gesture.

The queen stiffened as Sir Reginald trotted her rudely toward the library.

"It was just a little joke," he explained. "I make bad jokes all the time. My friends laugh anyway. It's because my wife is rich. I'm sure your husband would understand, as he's also tied to your purse strings." The queen gasped.

Biting his tongue hard, Sir Reginald guided her ahead of him into the room.

The library
9:59 P.M.

Lettie was struggling to get into her queen-size girdle when she heard the door open. The woman on Sir Reginald's arm looked appalled to have come upon such a scene. She averted her gaze.

"I can see skin," she said delicately.

Sir Reginald shoved her through the doorway and bolted the door behind them.

"It's only Lettie, and I've seen her get dressed dozens of times."

The silk azaleas on the queen's hat began to bobble as she shook with indignation. "You, sir, are no gentleman. I demand you release me at once!"

"I've always heard you were a bit of a bossy boots," Lettie snapped as she felt the first beads of perspiration start to collect under the foam-padded foundation garment. Clad only in girdle, bra, and heels, Lettie advanced toward the queen.

"Off with the dress," she demanded.

The queen blanched, and hugged her ungainly pocketbook to her bosom. Frantically, she pressed the panic button on the underside of her clutch, over and over. But no one came.

"I've read about you people," she sputtered, backing up against the library door. "You're—you're swingers, aren't you?"

Lettie laughed. "We're not swingers!"

"We're adulterers!" Sir Reginald chimed in, opening a vial of chloroform and soaking his pocket handkerchief.

"And kidnappers," Lettie added helpfully. "Now hold still, Queenie, so we don't have to hurt you."

Silver pantry
10:02 P.M.

Shoeless, chilly, toothless, and covered in dust, with a fresh carpet burn on his face, 008 began to reconsider his choice of careers. He was trapped. Somehow the pantry door had been locked from the outside. And he was out of chocolates. To top it all, he could feel a tremendous stomachache coming on.

Outside the library
10:23 P.M.

Agent Pumpernickel could stand it no longer. He had stayed in the shadows like a good boy while the queen had greeted the guests, making a special point of shaking hands with each S.O.B. and his wife. So when he saw her slip off to the library with Sir Reginald, he seized this quiet moment for a tête-à-tête.

The door was locked. Normally he would never have burst in on a member of the royal family, but he was getting a wee bit anxious. And he had drunk three bracing gin and tonics. Deftly springing the lock with his belt buckle, he stood back and took a deep breath. His entrance must seem entirely natural. He could even pretend to be looking for someone else. Should he whistle? No, he concluded, no whistling. He remembered that the queen had banned her staff from whistling, even when she was away from the palace.

Pumpernickel walked in on a rather unsettling scene. The reigning monarch was in the combined embrace of Sir Reginald and a half-naked woman.

"Oh, sorry!" he said instinctively.

The queen glared at him. She looked greatly annoyed. It was the same look his mother used to give him when he was being particularly obtuse.

"We're kidnapping her," Sir Reginald confided. "Go away."

"Was there anything in particular you wanted?" asked Lettie, one hand clamped over the queen's mouth.

"I say," said Pumpernickel, his suspicions aroused. "You're not supposed to touch her! You're not even supposed to make eye contact!" He rushed to the queen's rescue, receiving the full force of Sir Reginald's swinging fist. "God save the queen!" was all he managed to gasp out before collapsing to the thick carpet.

The great hall
10:29 P.M.

They had all the evidence they needed.

"Excuse me, Lord Finhatten," Bridget murmured when she felt her compact, set to vibrate mode, go off. Three long, then three short transmissions. The S.O.B.S. had begun their operation. It was time for G.E.O.R.G.I.E. to move in.

"Good God!" Lord Finhatten cried when he glanced at his watch. He had lost track of time. He was late for his post as the lorry driver. He looked around guiltily. "Have you seen my wife?"

"I believe she's in the library with the queen and Sir Reginald," Bridget said innocently. She watched the color drain from his puffy face, giving him the appearance of an unbaked bun. He excused himself, and tottered off to take his part in history.

Bibi snuck up behind Bridget and jingled a set of keys in her ear. "He's going to have some trouble getting the truck started," she laughed.

They went to the kitchen to get their props. A terrible noise was coming from the silver pantry. Bibi looked at Bridget and said, "Did we lock anyone in there?"

"Not intentionally," Bridget answered. "Shall we open the door, Bibi?"

"Don't bother now. There'll be plenty of time later."

Jane Bond stood frozen by the door leading from the garden into the kitchen. So now the girlfriend was here. How much better could this get?

"Well, Agent St. Claire, do you think we have enough evidence on tape to indict Sir Reginald and his cronies?"

"Just about, Agent Gallini. Now let's do our duty to Queen and Country."

The library
10:31 P.M.

After the queen had been gently chloroformed and propped in a leather wingback chair, Lettie set about switching costumes. "I could use a hand here," she said to her lover. Sir Reginald took care to keep his eyes averted from the body of the queen. He was, first and foremost, a gentleman.

Lettie was dismayed to see that her ugly, pea-green frock actually suited the other woman. And it was a perfect fit. She stared at the sleeping monarch and frowned.

"Get on with it, Lettie," Sir Reginald scolded. They were running out of time. How long, really, could one admire corgi aquatints?

"And where is that damn Jinx?" Their driver was nowhere in sight.

"He's a hundred and five years old," Lettie snapped. She had donned the queen's dress and was dismayed to find that, with her padded girdle, it was a little snug at the hips. "He's a little slow."

"You're not very fond of him, are you Lettie?"

"I hate him," she said bluntly as she covered her own lovely ebony hair with a horrid brown wig. "Much as I hate you. The touch of your hand makes my skin crawl." Why was she speaking so frankly? She would never get her hands on the Piggott fortune if she kept this up. But she couldn't control herself. It was as if she was under the influence of some drug.

"Good, because I never intended to marry you. I want to be free to chase the maid. Don't you think Bibi is a charming name?"

"I don't need your money," she decided aloud. "I'll just poison Jinx and be his merry widow. It worked with all my other husbands."

"I would never kill Edwina," Sir Reginald mused. "I think about it all the time, but I would never do it."

"That's because you're weak, Rags. Rags is the perfect nickname for you. Everything about you is limp. Your spine, your morals, your—"

He had heard enough. "Jinx!" he screamed out the window. "Hurry before I kill your wife!"

"I'll kill you first," yelled Lettie, darting for an ornamental sword that hung over the mantel.

This pretty domestic scene was interrupted by Bibi, who swept into the room bearing a tray of cocktails. Behind her came Bridget, who was surprised to see Pumpernickel on the floor. Bibi dumped the tray's contents and spun the tray at Sir Reginald, hitting him squarely in the windpipe. He gasped for air and collapsed onto the carpet, its fine fibers sticking to the pomade in his matinee-idol hair.

"Anything for you, Lady Finhatten?" asked Bridget threateningly. Her single-shot lipstick in her hand, she easily overpowered Lettie, who was making a run for the window.

"I'm telling your mother you served cheese straws to the queen!" Lettie screamed.

The queen was regaining consciousness. "Mmnnn . . ." she murmured. "Cheese straws." Bibi wrapped some of the spilled ice in her apron and pressed it to the queen's forehead.

"Don't speak, Your Majesty. You may reveal a state secret."

The queen's eyes fluttered open. "I don't know any," she said softly before pushing Bibi away and sitting up. Even in just her hat and slip, she was a formidable woman. She eyed her attackers.

"We are not amused," she snapped.

Jane was waiting for Bridget in the kitchen. "Which is worse," she asked, confronting her, "having your girlfriend cheat on you or spy on you?"

Bridget gasped. "Oh, Jane, you've got it all wrong."

"How much did Sir Niles pay you to sleep with me?"

"I don't work for him."

"But you are a secret agent."

"Yes."

"And you've been lying to me all this time?"

"Yes," Bridget said miserably.

"That's all I need to know." Jane slung her suit coat over her shoulder and walked out the door.

11 SEPTEMBER 1965

The Flora Beaton
5:30 A.M.

J ANE awoke as dawn was breaking, and, before she remembered Bridget was gone, reached out to put her arm around her. It was another rude awakening.

"At least things can't get any worse," she said aloud to the empty room. It would be light soon. If she stayed in bed, she'd sink into a black morass. It would be better to get up and face the day. Last week at this time, she hadn't even known Bridget existed; it was funny how quickly some girls got under your skin.

She crawled out of bed and threw on trousers and a shirt. Her James Bond suit lay in a crumpled heap on the floor. She would never put it on again.

Miss Liversidge's cats were the only creatures that would be glad to see her at this hour, and only because they were out of food. There was an all-night grocer near the bookshop; the walk would do her good.

The semidarkness gave her pause. She smoked a cigarette on the steps of the Flora Beaton until the sky lightened a bit more. There might still be a man looking for her, she realized, but she no longer cared. She took off on foot to buy cat food in the red can for the king and his wife. She was glad she had them to fuss over. Miss Liversidge was right, Jane thought. She should get a cat.

Home of Cedric Pumpernickel
9:00 A.M.

Agent Pumpernickel's phone hadn't stopped ringing all morning. There was his face, big as life, on the front page of every London newspaper—of every newspaper in the world, for that matter—with the headline RETIRED CIVIL SERVANT SAVES QUEEN FROM KIDNAP THREAT! He would have days of clipping and pasting ahead of him. He might even have to start a new scrapbook, instead of using the back pages of his mother's theatrical memory books. "Waste not, want not," his father always said. But this was a once-in-a-lifetime event.

His neighbor Mrs. Figgis was coming by later to watch televised coverage of the story. Thus far, he had been interviewed by the BBC, the *Times*, *the Daily Mirror*, and Reuters. The rub was, he had absolutely no recollection of how he had saved the queen. The last thing he remembered was Sir Reginald's fist flying toward his face; Lady Bridget had had to fill him in on the details. Apparently, he had struggled to his feet and singlehandedly disarmed both Sir Reginald and the feisty Lady Finhatten. If only he could remember!

The telephone rang—again!

"Pumpernickel on the line." He was rather enjoying all this attention.

"N. here. Congratulations. You're quite the popular fellow."

Pumpernickel's heart sank to hear the voice of his former friend and superior. "Yes, sir," he answered dully.

"I've just had word from the palace that the queen wants you for tea at two."

"How very kind, sir."

"I wanted to let you know I've destroyed Miss Bond's file. Lady Bridget's too."

"That's good of you, sir. Very generous of you."

"Well, you are England's"—N. had to choke out the final words—"England's most popular man."

N. was actually afraid of him. The feeling was delicious, though fleeting.

"That I am, sir. That I am."

"I can't say the same for 008—I mean, Agent Horace Wattle—I'm sorry to say." With bad news to impart, N.'s spirits seemed to lift. "He's in hospital this morning with a bad case of the runs. Worst case the doctor has ever seen. Nurses won't go near the man."

"Give him my best," said Pumpernickel courteously. He felt nothing. He too would go nowhere near the man. He cleared his throat and pressed on with more important matters. "And Miss Bond?"

"Ah, yes," said N. "I thought you'd be asking. Sturdy girl. I think she'll lead a long and happy life."

Crispin's Bookshop
11:00 A.M.

Mrs. Snipe was gloating over a cup of Simon's tea. "And, of course, Edwina knew nothing whatsoever about the plot. I'm convinced that a full investigation will exonerate her. I hope she wins the London home in the divorce. I've told her to retain the best attorney money can buy. Can you imagine—they were having an affair right under her nose. And they had the gall to admit it to her face! I never liked that Lady Finhatten. She led Edwina on a very merry chase."

"Well, nice to see everything's back to normal," Jane remarked as she entered the shop.

"Jane!" Simon perked up. "Nice to see you. Did you get a good night's sleep?"

"Never mind that." Mrs. Snipe waved her hands excitedly. "Did you hear the news?"

"What news?" There was no point in telling Simon that she had gone running after Bridget. She'd save that story for another day far in the future when she'd regained her sense of humor. Seeing Mrs. Snipe inhale deeply for another rendition of Edwina's woes, Jane added more water to the kettle and put it on the hob.

"Now tell me all about it, Mrs. Snipe." She sighed.

The Château of the Duke and Duchess of Windsor
The French Riviera
1:00 P.M.

The Duke of Windsor couldn't believe it, but there it was, in black and white. And in the *Times*, no less.

"Darling, did you read about this plot to overthrow the crown? The Sons of Britain Society was actually planning to kidnap our Lilibet and put her in a dungeon!" The duke crooked his little finger at the maid standing ready at the breakfast table. It was a sign that he needed more tea.

"I say, didn't Sir Reginald Wooley-Booley write us a while back proposing something along those lines?" He folded the paper in half lengthwise so as to cover the picture of the hideously ugly fellow who had foiled the plot, and showed the article to his wife.

"Would that have been such a bad thing, dear?" the duchess asked with apparent innocence. "With the queen gone, you could sit on the throne again."

"Not bloody likely!" the duke cried. "It's so uncomfortable! Darling, I gave up that dreadful job many years ago, and I've never regretted it. You did write to the chap and refuse his offer, didn't you?"

"I sent a little bread-and-butter note to his wife. She must have misinterpreted my letters." The duchess held out her plate for another caviar-and-toast triangle. She would deny authorship of those letters until the day she died.

"What can you expect from a plumber's daughter?" she sniffed.

G.E.O.R.G.I.E. headquarters
2:00 P.M.

"What can I do to make it up to you?" Mimi had drunk enough Champagne to have the courage to approach Bridget. The agents were celebrating their victory over the Sons of Britain Society; everyone, that is, but Bridget, who stayed at her desk feeling she had little to celebrate. Jane refused to take her calls. Her flowers had been sent back, the card unopened.

"Just leave me alone," snapped Bridget. She was angry, but controlled. "You, Mimi Dolittle, are the worst agent I have ever known. How could you have let Jane find her way to Grunby Hall? Our cover could have been blown. We could have lost the queen, not to mention our chance to bring the S.O.B.S. to their knees."

Mimi sniffed pathetically. "I'll do better next time." She had been thoroughly chastised by Chief Tuppenny, and assigned to the decoding desk until further notice.

"There is no room for mistakes in this game," Bridget said tartly. She put her final report on the operation in a file and shoved it in her out box.

"I'm going home," she said.

The Flora Beaton
6:00 P.M.

Retired Agent Cedric Pumpernickel stepped out of the shadows.

"Cripes, Pumpernickel," Jane cried. "You've got to stop sneaking up on people."

"Sorry. I wanted to see you alone."

He handed her a file. "Hang on to it. You'll need it if N. should ever threaten you again."

Jane didn't need to open it to know what was inside. The name on the file told her everything. BOND, JAMES, SR.

"Is there anyone I know who's not a secret agent?" said Jane bitterly.

"Your mother."

"That's good to know."

"And Simon," he added quickly. "And Miss Liversidge. Most people, in fact. What you need to know is that your father's death had nothing to do with his drinking," Pumpernickel said. "It's all in there. He was sober when he died."

Jane felt she could carry on quite well without another urgent dispatch from the world of espionage. "Does N. know you're giving me this?"

"Bugger N." Pumpernickel nodded to her and walked away. His job was finally done.

The Flora Beaton
Bedsit of Jane Bond
7:00 P.M.

Jane put her father's file down and wiped her eyes on her shirtsleeve. She remembered everything about that day now—she even remembered Pumpernickel being there. He had screamed when her father had fallen in the path of the bus. She remembered seeing a man in the periphery of her vision double over with horror and grief. Until now, she was certain her father had stumbled drunkenly in front of the bus. They had been on their way to the library so Jane could get a book on famous sporting women. She remembered feeling pleased that he had asked to come along with her. They hadn't much in common by then.

Still, he was her father. The war was over, and he was home again. And then N. had coolly extinguished him.

The Gates
8:00 P.M.

The bar was crowded. Jane pushed through a group of girls in short skirts—one looked her over, then playfully grabbed her arm. Jane brushed her off. She had been afraid that Bridget would be there, and indeed, she was sitting at the bar, in a white minidress, her hair down, smoking the sort of Turkish cigarette that all the spies smoked.

Jane walked up to her. She had no idea what she was doing.

"You know that's a filthy habit, don't you?" she scolded, lifting the cigarette butt and taking a long hard drag. The Turkish tobacco wasn't bad. She could imagine getting used to it.

Bridget looked up at her. Despite the expert makeup job, it was clear she had been crying for hours. Jane stood there, staring, trying to think of just the right words. It was probably a mistake to stare so long into Bridget's green eyes.

"Oh, hell." Jane sighed, sitting heavily next to Bridget.

Bridget put her hand on Jane's arm, and kept it there. "Where do I start?"

"Start by sending away that tough-looking blond."

Bridget looked over her shoulder to see Astrid, sans Ruth, cruising the fresh arrivals.

"How shall I dispatch her? A knockout cocktail? A truth serum? A tranquilizing dart?"

"You've got a truth serum?" asked Jane.

"Right in my handbag."

"Take it out."

Bridget frowned slightly, but opened her bag and removed a sealed tube of Vérité.

"Put it on," said Jane. "And start talking."